ZVI SPEISER

2036

THE PROOF

2036 The Proof / Zvi Speiser

Translation from the Hebrew: Yael Schonfeld Abel
Contact: szvi@bezeqint.net

ISBN 9781546571612

2036

THE PROOF

ZVI SPEISER

TRANSLATED FROM THE HEBREW BY

YAEL SCHONFELD ABEL

The author wishes to thank Professor Zvi Mazeh, Dr. Eytan Elhanany, and engineer Moshe Weissberg for their help and advice.

CHAPTER 1

The Ark of the Covenant

Jerusalem, 586 BCE

Ahiav and Aviram heard the sounds of battle waged at the foot of the city wall. The thundering of the catapult stones as they landed was frightening, especially the sounds that the breaking, crumbling walls produced upon their collapse. The noise of the battering ram, pummeling against the entry gate again and again, was terrible. Each impact was accompanied by the rumble of wood gradually falling apart and about to collapse at any minute. But the tumult of battle was eclipsed by the screams of the many wounded, the horrific tormented shouts of those whose lives were being taken from them.

In the last meeting of the Guardians, which took place once it was discovered that Nebuchadnezzar's army had been sighted approaching the Kingdom of Judea, it was decided by majority vote that the Ark of the Covenant must vanish, to be secreted away in the hiding spot that had been designated for it back when the temple was first built. The objectors mentioned the reaction of the Holy Ark every time it was touched by a human hand, such as the incident with Uzzah, who tried to prevent the Ark from falling and was stricken dead by it. The other participants did not ignore this hazard, but made it clear that the organization's age-old duty was to prevent the Ark from falling into the hands of the Gentiles, at any cost.

Eli the High Priest was also present at the meeting, and promised to aid in concealing the Ark. His role was to make sure that the bolts on all tabernacle doors would be unlatched in time, in order to enable rapid access to the Ark and a speedy retreat. The decisions regarding the time of execution and the concealment of the Ark were assigned to the Ark Band, headed by Ahiav, son of Elisha.

The terrible sounds of battle testified that its outcome was apparent, and that Jerusalem was about to fall into the hands of the enemy very shortly. Ahiav instructed his four men to go into action. They ran into the temple, heading into the tabernacle and the Holy of Holies at its center. No man other than the high priest had ever gotten so close to the Ark of the Covenant. Ahiav froze in his place when he felt a tingling in his face, as well as in his exposed hands and feet. The other men did the same as they faced the ornamental veil shielding the Ark.

The clamor of battle outside grew stronger, indicating the infiltration of the city itself by enemy soldiers. It was obvious that the enemy's troops would stream first and foremost toward the ornate temple, which was prominent from afar. It was a location signaling the sovereignty and control of the Jewish people, as well as, and perhaps primarily, the place where many treasures could be looted.

Ahiav realized they had no more than a few moments to smuggle the Ark away. He drew one step closer to the Ark's ornamental veil and froze again. The tingling became stabs of intense pain. His men, who had also attempted to draw closer, stopped as well once the pain increased, becoming intolerable. A minute that lasted an eternity trickled by, and then, as if from a wave of an invisible magic wand, the pain disappeared. Eli the High Priest appeared in the Holy of Holies, dressed in his ceremonial garments and wearing the bejeweled priestly breastplate.

He called out urgently, "Hurry, enemy soldiers have infiltrated the city. Time is running out!"

Without stopping to think why the pain had vanished or to what extent it might come back with a vengeance, Ahiav and his band hurried inside beyond the ornamental veil and, for the first time in their lives, gazed upon the Ark of the Covenant itself.

The gold chest of the Ark rested upon the Foundation Stone, the same stone that tradition claimed was the site of the Binding of Isaac, as well as being the most elevated stone in Jerusalem and the base for the Ark of the Covenant. Most of the light in the room was emanating from the top part of the Ark, where, between two cherubs, a bluish glow spread out, accompanied by a sound resembling the buzz of bees; it was a kind of luminescence, soft and gentle yet steady and persistent, different from anything the men had ever seen before.

The awesome sight overwhelmed those entering the room and, despite the immense time pressure, they froze briefly in their spots. Eli, who had followed them in and who was accustomed to the sight of the Ark, raised his voice, urging them to keep going while he handed Ahiav the two gold-coated wooden poles intended for carrying the Ark, which had languished unused for many years.

Ahiav strode hesitantly toward the Ark. Only when he was close enough to touch it did his men dare to slowly join him. The holiness of the site and the atmosphere of mystery made them briefly forget the terrible war being waged outside the temple, as well as the fact that time was quickly running out.

Much to their surprise, the Ark was as light as a feather. In fact, it appeared to be carrying itself without requiring any investment of strength on their part. Ahiav and his men watched Eli as he removed a layer of gold from one of the temple walls, revealing a hidden door behind it. Eli urged them to hurry through the door into a secret passage beyond it.

When Ahiav noticed that Eli wasn't joining them, he stopped fleeing and asked, "Why aren't you joining our escape?"

Eli shook his head sadly, saying, "I'll return the gold coating to its place, and after I'm dead, no one can give away your location, or the place where the Ark is hidden."

The doorway revealed a wooden staircase leading down. Once the door had closed behind them, Ahiav felt as if they had been cut off from the terrible events they had left behind. What a shame that Eli hadn't joined them and saved his soul from dying, he thought. At that moment, something Eli had just said began to gnaw at him. *What exactly did Eli mean when he said that after his death, no one could give away the location of the Ark?* At the very least, Ahiav and his assistants would know the secret. *And perhaps... No, impossible*, he thought. Would he and his men not live on to reveal the location of the Ark? For a moment, he was overcome with horror. *We're heading toward certain death. None of us will survive after the Ark is hidden.* And perhaps it was better that way.

Only the death of the entire group would ensure that the location of the Ark was never discovered. Even he himself, had he been required to make such a decision, would have reached this exact same conclusion.

Once he understood what awaited them, he felt slightly more relaxed. His imminent death no longer bothered him. The goal was so much more important than the deaths of a handful of people, including his own.

The glow of the cherubs on the Ark allowed them to spot several wooden rungs leading down. They descended carefully. The wooden rungs were replaced by steps carved in stone, which stretched downward, ending in a tunnel.

The tunnel in which they walked was narrow and dark, illuminated solely by the Ark's pale blue luminescence, which occasionally cast ominous shadows on its walls. The tunnel curved, descending and ascending, sometimes revealing staircases that the Ark crossed in a near-float, almost untouched by the men carrying it.

To their surprise, even when making their way down a steep slope or climbing up, the Ark did not slide from its position on the supporting poles. It acted as if it were familiar with the route, adapting itself to the curves. The tunnel, isolated against the tumult of battle, was silent. The stillness was only interrupted by the delicate buzz emanating from the cherubs and by the soldiers' heavy breathing.

Ahiav was immensely tense. He had no idea where the tunnel led. Would they find themselves among enemy soldiers the moment they emerged? What exactly would they do with the Ark, which seemed to be cooperating with them at this stage, but might change its conduct at any moment, as it had indeed done in the past?

He emerged from these thoughts abruptly. A barrier blocking the entire width of the tunnel had materialized in front of them. A quick inspection, guided by the light of the Ark, confirmed their fear. The tunnel was entirely blocked off. There was no way to get past the barrier or go around it. The odd thing was that the barrier did not seem to signal the end of the tunnel or anything like the result of a rockslide, but was rather like a brick wall that had been intentionally built in this location. Perhaps this was the edge of the tunnel, where they should put down the Ark and return to the temple.

But no, that wasn't a logical option. The site they had left behind was surely flooded with enemy soldiers who would loot the Ark and slaughter them the moment they showed up at the temple. Eli the Priest's previous reply had also clearly conveyed that he was awaiting his death in order to ensure that the location of the Ark would not be revealed.

As he was deep in thought, he heard the voice of sharp-eyed Aviram. "There's a strange handle in the wall. I saw four loose bricks and thought I could start with them in order to gradually take apart the barrier, but I found the handle on the other side of the bricks," he explained.

In the bluish light emanating from the Ark, Ahiav examined the odd handle. It was made of metal and was large enough to be gripped by one hand. The edge of the handle was inserted into the barrier wall. Ahiav tried to twist it slowly in either direction, but the handle did not cooperate. He stared at it intently, trying to imagine which direction would enable him to exert maximum power over it. He believed pulling it outward would attain this effect.

Whoever had constructed the tunnel had expected him to pull the handle; there was no other solution. With a determined resolution, he pulled the handle as hard as he could. An immense roar of collapsing rocks echoed from every direction, and a cloud of dust obstructed any other sight from his eyes. He couldn't even see his own men. The dust made breathing difficult, and all of them began coughing violently.

"Cover your faces with fabric," Ahiav called out, as he covered his own face with his cloak. Apparently, pulling the handle had triggered the collapse of some hidden entryway in the tunnel through which they must pass, he decided. *I wonder what the tunnel exit will look like,* he thought, having an increasingly hard time breathing the dusty air.

"Everyone try to feel the walls and find out where an opening has formed in the tunnel. Anyone who finds it, let us know immediately so that we can pass through it to a less dusty area," he called out to his men.

However, the search did not reveal any opening. On the contrary. To their immense horror, they discovered a rockslide behind them, in the direction from which they had come. Apparently, the top of the tunnel had collapsed, blocking their route and flooding them with dust. They all understood that they were blocked in every direction.

It can't be, Ahiav thought. How could they conceal the Ark in a safe location if they couldn't move? Or was this the Ark's hiding place, a burial site for it and for them? Once again, he remembered what Eli had said. He was ready to sacrifice his own life in order to prevent the enemy from discovering the opening to the tunnel. And as Ahiav realized at that moment, their lives had been sacrificed as well. This was the way the tunnel had been designed many years ago, when the temple had been constructed. Anyone who knew its location had to die, taking its secret to the grave with him.

This line of thought made sense; he himself would have acted in a similar manner. But perhaps there was still an opening? Perhaps the collapse behind them had been an accident, perhaps there was an opening they hadn't discovered, perhaps it was the ceiling of the tunnel that had opened, or perhaps he hadn't pulled the handle hard enough. It was worth a try, he decided, fumbling his way back toward it. The handle was still affixed to the wall.

"I'm pulling the handle again," he called out. "Be prepared for anything."

This time, the handle moved relatively easily, as if its hidden part was moving within a viscous liquid, perhaps honey or tar, he thought. Then the handle fell loose from the wall, and he found himself holding it in its entirety. A strange, pungent smell filled the tunnel. One by one, each of them fell, suffocation and darkness engulfing them for eternity.

***

Eli only had time to take a few steps away from the hidden doorway when he was stabbed to death by a soldier from Nebuchadnezzar's army. In his last moments, he felt proud to have fulfilled his destiny on Earth, to hide the Ark of the Covenant in the place that King Solomon had designated for it when he had built the temple, and of course, to convey the knowledge of the Ark's location to his eldest son, who had left his homeland and was living in Egypt in order to preserve this immense secret, just as the high priests who had preceded him had done. At last, life in exile, far from his family, had proved to be a worthy endeavor. There would always be one among them who was far, far away from danger, who would know where the Ark was located and who had been ordered to guard the secret of the Ark and its origin, bequeathing it only to his own offspring.

The soldier who stabbed Eli didn't understand the meaning of his ecstatic smile as he lay dying.

CHAPTER 2

Kazuki

Tokyo, Thursday, August 17, 2017

Kazuki put down NASA's latest scientific report. Its main chapter dealt, naturally, with the observations of the space telescopes, whose number was gradually increasing. As of today, there were sixteen telescopes active in various ranges of the electromagnetic spectrum. Good old Hubble was still a force to be reckoned with and was providing amazing observations. There was also the Kepler telescope, which had discovered about five thousand planets whose chances of discovery had been less than 10 percent, leading to the conclusion that the universe was teeming with planets orbiting suns.

How can you stop such scientific progress? he muttered to himself. *How do you deal with an abundance of research in every area of biology, such as mapping the human genome? They're already talking about cloning a human. Who knows where all this will lead?*

The organization's work had been so easy in the 3,330 years since it had been established by Aaron the High Priest, the brother of Moses who had brought the Israelites out of Egypt. In fact, the only task the organization had dealt with since its establishment was preventing the discovery of the Ark of the Covenant, the "smoking gun," to use the legal term. The Ark had to disappear completely. Its discovery might have led to a change in the very fundamentals of existence and, in that regard, the Guardians had succeeded in their task.

Despite intensive searching throughout the years by numerous groups, the Ark was not discovered, and not even the slightest clue leading to its location was uncovered. This was aided by the spreading of quite a few rumors, the majority of them initiated by the Guardians, which had steered the search into useless venues.

From their earliest days, they had acted covertly, keeping the number of activists to a minimum. Their main occupation was accumulating property resulting from the inheritances of the organization's members and, later, from wise and extremely long-term investments.

Here and there, massive excitement broke out over the appearance of unidentified flying objects in the sky. In the pre-technological era, it was easy to attribute such phenomena to various gods, to demons and angels and other components of the believers' menagerie, including the chariots of the gods, flying dragons, vimanas, and other supposed means of transportation that they purportedly used.

During the past century, the global superpowers were also motivated to conceal the facts in order to prevent mass hysteria, and thus effectively carried out the Guardians' job. In the current era, where the media ruled the masses and every year the race for explosive journalistic scoops intensified, it required careful, constant work to blur and devalue the discoveries that they had been ordered to prevent.

Yes, it was time to call a meeting of the members. The agenda would include the latest scientific developments, allocating the tasks of monitoring pertinent research among the members, looking into the option of using external specialists, and, of course, reviewing the rules in regard to interfering with research.

CHAPTER 3

The Guardians

Tokyo, Sunday, August 20, 2017

The nice weather brought the masses to the Yumanoshima Marina in Tokyo. The fair dedicated to beach and sailing merchandise currently being held also attracted many people from the area, who were swarming every alley and dock in the marina. Everything was working in favor of the Guardians, whose members blended in with the crowd until the moment when, one by one, they boarded *The Blue Fin*, the yacht Kazuki had rented, and on which he was waiting with his right-hand man, Takumi.

First came colorful Koro, a squat Japanese man in his fifties, who was in charge of finance as well as being the liaison with various industries, some of which were fully or partially owned by the organization. Although he controlled the flow of funds, he never abused his power, always acting in accordance with the organization's decisions and never delaying payments. On the contrary, he always paid on time so as not to attract any particular attention to his activities. His colorful outfits blended in with the prevailing atmosphere in the marina, making him look like a typical visitor. No one would suspect even for a minute that Koro controlled investments worth hundreds of millions of dollars.

Next came Reo, skinny and youthful in appearance. Like most youths, he was very fond of video games, as well as being fluent in the world of computers in general. Reo was in charge of locating studies worthy of notice. Every day, he classified tremendous amounts of information that, for the most part, proved to be irrelevant. Only data that aligned with the predetermined criteria were assembled, summarized, and distributed among the members. Reo also made sure the information passed between them in roundabout ways, subsumed within articles on various general topics. An uninitiated reader could not have uncovered the connecting link between the various articles that the members received.

The third to arrive, Rokoro, was Reo's complete opposite—large and chubby, with a perpetual smile on his face. Rokoro's work was similar to the work that Reo performed; however, the two of them did not communicate. They were prohibited from sharing their work with one another. Each of them distributed the results of their studies in different ways and under different covers. Each had a different distribution list which, in various circuitous routes, ultimately made its way to the members. Generally, they were highly coordinated. Only rarely did one of them add on some important aspect that had not been detected by the other. Rokoro had only joined the crew a few years ago, when the amount of information requiring their attention had risen significantly.

The last two, who arrived together, were James, the Australian, and Uri, the Israeli. James served as a messenger and assistant to Uri, the sect's "foreign minister," responsible for the Guardians' relationship with other organizations, and particularly with the media, in all its varieties. He was the one to spread rumors, send letters, and write articles that diverted public attention in directions that suited the sect. Uri understood the human psyche and was endowed with a rare quality—people tended to listen to him attentively when he talked, and read the articles he wrote with interest, while nodding in agreement to his claims. Yes, they thought just as he did, or that, at least, was their impression. A skill of this kind could not be acquired in any academic institute; it was innate, and was further enhanced over the years.

The meetings were businesslike and focused, as usual. They did not include small talk or personal matters, and there was no socializing between the attendees before the discussion commenced. Those who were early simply sat down in their usual places, without exchanging any remarks with any of the other members. Other than Kazuki, none of them knew a thing about the others beyond their roles in the organization, and they did not interact on a social level. Kazuki, whose role included screening candidates, was well familiar with each of their backgrounds, but did not share this information with the other members.

The meeting commenced with a brief, general greeting by Kazuki, who immediately turned the stage over to Reo, who in turn proceeded to yield the floor to Rokoro once he was done. Both Reo and Rokoro briefly summed up the latest developments in the various scientific areas pertinent to the sect. Both noted the dizzying increase in the quantity and quality of studies, directly resulting from the enhancement in the quality of researchers and the exponential increase in computing power. They assessed that within twenty to thirty years, science would come close to deciphering the secrets of human existence to an extent that would require the Guardians to take action in a sphere that was dozens of times as extensive as the one in which they had acted to date. All this assuming that they maintained their current course of action.

The other attendees restricted themselves to short reports. Kazuki summed up the meeting with a general admonition that they must all be prepared for action and alert for any development. The more eyes monitoring and tracking what was going on, the earlier they'd be able to detect future threats while the reliability and the interest level these threats generated was still limited, and the better their ability to deal with them efficiently.

Prior to the meeting, Kazuki had made the decision not to share his pessimistic assessment regarding their preventive capabilities with the other members. His own evaluation matched Reo's and Rokoro's, although he had not compared notes with them before the meeting. *That's it, the end of an era is nearly upon us*, he thought. Would he get the chance to witness the exposure of the secret of the human race in his own lifetime? *And it's interesting*, he thought, *that no one has asked about the Leading Gentleman, who he is, and why he isn't meeting with us.*

Or perhaps they thought he himself was the Leading Gentleman, he reflected, his lips curving in a brief smile. There was no way he could tell them that despite the countless conversations the two of them had conducted, he had never met the Leading Gentleman face-to-face.

CHAPTER 4

The Murder

Chicago, Wednesday, July 16, 2036

"Tom, wake up... Tom, wake up..."

The voice, warm yet assertive, filled the bedroom. It was emitted by his personal assistant device, which he had affectionately nicknamed Momo, and which would not stop calling his name until he touched it. He still remembered the primitive assistant from years ago, which under similar circumstances produced a loud ring that would undoubtedly have woken Kate up. The current assistant knew that he slept next to his wife and that she should not be awakened.

The call had extracted Tom from a very deep sleep. From the corner of his eye, he saw that the clock on the nightstand was showing 3:13 a.m. He was not expecting any important messages justifying a nocturnal wake-up call. There were also no gravely ill people in his family. Kate stirred in bed beside him, almost waking up as well. He held the assistant up against his ear, saying "Hello," his voice blurry and sleepy. On the other end of the line was Steve, head of the security force at the university, who asked him to come to the lab building as soon as he could. Oleg, the night-shift security guard, had been found dead in the lab building, and the door to Tom's lab had been found wide open.

As he dressed quickly, he tried to figure out the purpose of the break-in. His lab wasn't the first one in the corridor; it was preceded by other labs on the ground floor. It also wasn't the best furnished in regard to expensive modern equipment. Quite the contrary—most of the equipment was outdated, causing numerous mishaps and requiring tests to be rerun fairly frequently. No, his lab had been broken into intentionally rather than at random, unless the burglar had had time to pass through the other labs first. If that was the case, it would have been easy to establish. Steve would have told him that other labs had been broken into, in addition to his own. No, apparently his lab was the only one to be breached.

The most unique asset of the lab was the research conducted in it. He tried to reconstruct recent events in an attempt to figure out which study might interest someone to such an extent that the intruder would be willing to commit murder to get his hands on it.

Once he was dressed, he gently woke up Kate. Her gaze wandered from her fully dressed husband to the clock on the nightstand and back. She was overcome by confusion, and barely managed to mumble, "What's going on, Tommy?"

Tom leaned in toward her, whispering in her ear, "I got a call from the university. Someone left the faucet running and the lab got flooded. I have to go see what was damaged and make sure it's not dangerous. I'll be back soon."

The cold night air outside, the roads glimmering after a rainy evening, and the calm automatic driving, with no traffic to deal with at this late hour, all allowed him to return to his contemplation. Which of the studies in which he was involved was important enough to someone to justify a murder? For the past year or so, his lab had been involved in research funded by a group of private investors, who had established the Glenhill Company. Glenhill's goal was to develop a revolutionary medical procedure to expand human longevity. All of the major pharmaceutical manufacturers had been at it for many years; in that regard, the topic wasn't unique at all. For more than ten years now, medication and self-care kits claiming to enhance longevity, which was already increasing even with no specific intervention, had been appearing on the market.

The group funding his study was made up of scientists at the forefront of biological research, who had come together in order to develop the medical procedure. The group had come up with a unique idea, and assigned the development of one of its components to Tom's lab. Other components were allocated to other labs in order to protect the group's exclusive control over the entire process. Even currently, people who took care of their health and received proper treatment had lifespans of one hundred years, and were able to maintain active lifestyles nearly until the end. Recent theoretical studies predicted a significant breakthrough on this topic. Studies on guinea pigs showed that by combining several treatments with appropriate nutrition, the lifespans of small mammals could be doubled and even tripled. There was no doubt that the right procedure would have unlimited commercial potential.

The more Tom delved into the subject, the more strongly he felt that it was this study that had interested the burglars. But perhaps it was the other study being carried out at the lab that had caught their attention? About two years ago, he had managed to get an unusual grant on the topic of conserved sequences in human DNA. He had made a massive effort to secure the grant, but encountered fierce objection from the grant committee. They presented him with other requests that had been waiting for an endowment for quite a while, and would be put off yet again because of him.

He still remembered the reasoning that had tipped the scales in his favor. Gene resilience to change might contribute significantly to the fight against cancer and various degenerative diseases. Secretly, he hoped his research would also yield a better understanding of processes of bodily aging and decay, which could lead to greater support of studies dealing with increasing longevity. Perhaps the ease with which he had won his role in the longevity-enhancement research was a result of the knowledge he had acquired in this earlier study. Understanding the mechanisms governing the resistance to change of such conserved sequences might draw many pharmaceutical companies and researchers to the lab.

Perhaps, fueled by frustration, one of those rejected researchers who had lost a grant had decided to find out what was so special about Tom's research. Or maybe the burglar was actually interested in the research he was conducting on "Ronnie," the skeleton of a two-million-year-old humanoid. This study had begun with the random discovery of an unusually well-preserved skeleton near the towering and perpetually snowy Mount Kilimanjaro in Africa. It was the most ancient humanoid skeleton found at a level of preservation that might allow significant DNA extraction. This was the reason the university demanded absolute secrecy regarding this topic, as they were hoping to win international prestige not just for discovering the skeleton, but primarily for accurate extraction of the most ancient human DNA available, and comparing it to that of contemporary humans.

During biology classes at school, Tom would gaze at length at the colorful plastic model of a DNA molecule that was hung up in the biology lab. In his imagination, the long chain of bound base pairs would dance and twist through the room, its gentle curving accompanied by celestial music.

The study was officially titled "An examination of resistance to change in the human genome," a dry definition that actually revealed very little. He didn't think such a topic would appeal to anyone other than DNA fanatics like himself, who believed that uncovering and understanding the mechanisms protecting specific genes from changing throughout thousands and millions of years of evolution might aid in preventing many illnesses resulting from exposure to factors affecting and degrading the genes, such as sun radiation and radioactivity. Resilience to radioactivity could, for example, help in significantly reducing the required load in piloted space expeditions, in which the astronauts are exposed to intense, ongoing sun radiation, as well as radiation originating in the spacecraft's engines and, of course, metabolic processes creating plenty of free radicals.

It was obvious that genes which were essential to the existence of basic life processes were carefully preserved by natural selection, as any change affecting them would have a disastrous influence on the very life of the organism. However, his study dealt with discovering conserved DNA sequences that, as far as researchers could discern, had no effect on the life of the organism, which was precisely the reason he found them fascinating.

Tom emerged from his thoughts on 59th Street, just before

the turn to South Ellis Avenue. Usually, the car's navigation system continued down 59th until it met Cottage Grove Avenue, and he would reach the western campus buildings from there. However, in view of the light traffic at this late hour, it took less time to enter from Ellis Avenue.

A quick glance at his assistant revealed the time to be 3:50 a.m. It was hard to believe that about half an hour ago, he had still been fast asleep, while now he was on his way to deal with murder and burglary. Several vehicles were clustered in the lab building's parking lot, a rare sight so late at night.

The guard stationed at the entrance of the building didn't know Tom. Luckily, his wallet was in his pocket, and contained his employee ID card, which allowed him to enter. First, however, the guard called the security center in order to authorize his entry in light of the night's events.

Steve was waiting for him at the entrance to the lab area, standing with two police officers, one man and one woman. Directly opposite the door lay what looked like a human corpse, covered with a sheet. Steve introduced Tom to the police officers. They nodded at him without saying a word, and the four immediately turned toward the lab. On the way, Steve let him know that he had delayed the police's investigative team from entering the lab until Tom arrived, so that they would not harm the equipment during their investigation. Tom nodded at Steve in gratitude for allowing him to be the first to examine the lab.

As they walked, Tom tried to imagine the lab after the break-in. About three years ago, their house had been burglarized while the entire family was celebrating their oldest daughter Lynn's eighth birthday at the venerable Ditka's, a restaurant that had retained its original name many years after the death of its original owners.

The sight of the house and the upturned drawers, their contents strewn everywhere, resurfaced from the depths of his memory as if it had all just occurred; the memory was that vivid. As he theorized once more that the longevity study had been the intruder's goal, he reached the wide-open lab door.

An expression of wonder spread across his face. The lab looked exactly as it had when he had left that evening. There was no sign of a break-in. Even following a thorough examination, conducted without touching anything while Officer Leanna and Steve trailed him, he could find no difference between the lab's current condition and the state in which he had left it when he had gone home that evening, the last to leave the premises. *It's odd*, he thought. *Maybe the murderous burglar hadn't even entered the lab? Maybe what happened scared him off, and he ran away before he could carry out his plan? Perhaps the open door was just a distraction for the true matter at hand? Too many questions and not a single answer*, he concluded.

Throughout the inspection, he heard many additional voices.

Reacting to his querying look, Leanna responded, "It's the forensics department. They'll check the entire area using sensitive technology, looking for clues regarding the perpetrators."

And indeed, when the three of them exited the lab, they saw a group of people, some wearing police uniforms while others were in civilian clothing, bustling around the body and throughout the length of the corridor.

The eldest of them, wearing civilian clothing, turned to Tom, shook his hand, and said, "Rick Heller, homicide detective. I understand that you're Dr. Lester, the head of the lab where the break-in occurred?"

"That's true, although strange as it may seem, in a cursory

inspection I just carried out in the lab, I can't see any signs of a break-in. The lab looks exactly the way it did when I left this evening. Did you find any evidence that might help with uncovering who was responsible for the murder?"

The detective ignored his question, continuing, "Once I'm done here in a few minutes, I'll ask you to accompany me to police headquarters for questioning. In the meantime, I'll ask you to stay in the building and not to talk to anyone. Also, please hand over your personal assistant."

Surprised by the lack of response to his inquiry and by the instructions he'd received, Tom immediately handed the assistant to Detective Heller. A strange sensation, almost akin to parting from an old friend, took hold of him. He had never given Momo to anyone in the two years since acquiring him, other than the one time he had to hand him over for repairs.

Tired, confused, and frustrated, Tom returned to the lab and absentmindedly sat down in his chair facing the computer, as was his custom. His thoughts wandered as he tried to organize the facts he knew into a logical narrative. A security guard had been murdered, the door to the lab had been wide open without any signs of forced entry, and there had been no signs of a break-in within the lab—all strange and extremely illogical.

As he reviewed the facts, he was overtaken by an odd feeling. A feeling that someone had made his way through the lab, apparently very cautiously, without moving a thing. Someone had hatched a plot to be carried out in the lab, in a manner that would not evoke any suspicion, until he had encountered a problem with the security guard. There must be important clues around him that had eluded Tom during his first inspection, and which would become apparent if he concentrated harder. It was impossible that a stranger had walked around his lab, touching and moving things, and that he would be unable to notice this fact. Steve, who entered the lab at that moment, distracted him briefly.

As Tom turned his chair, his ankle touched the computer tower, adjacent to the side of the desk. He leaped from his seat, calling out, "The computer's warm!"

Steve's vacant expression indicated that he had no idea what all the fuss was about.

"I power down the computer every evening. It should be completely cold. Someone turned it on during the night, and it stayed on for a while!" Tom called out, sitting down in front of the computer once more while Steve dragged over a chair and sat down beside him.

A quick inspection revealed that the burglar had been familiar with the lab's password, and had accessed current reports detailing experiments in the longevity-enhancement project, as well as the resilience-to-change project. The Ronnie study had additional unique protections, and Tom was certain the burglar hadn't managed to access it. These steps exhausted Tom's computer skills. A computer expert would be required for a more in-depth inspection and a determination of which files, if any, had been copied.

Tom got up, with Steve following, and hurried to find Rick, who was watching the male police officer photographing the body in ultraviolet light.

The detective looked up at Tom, asking, "Well?"

"The intruder turned on my computer. It was on for a while, since it was still pretty warm. I found out that the intruder used the general lab password, and therefore was able to access the latest reports on two topics the lab has been researching lately. I'm not an expert on computers, so I don't know if he copied any files."

"The computer's coming with us," the detective barked out. "It'll be a cinch for the computer experts at headquarters to hack it."

"It's absolutely prohibited to remove computers from the labs," Steve said.

Rick turned to him, his expression amused, whispering, "Don't worry."

***

Around six a.m., the police precinct was a dimly lit, bleak, ominous place. Rick sat Tom down in an interrogation room, leading Steve to an adjacent one.

The room resembled the interrogation cells he had seen in movies: it was small and its walls bare, having shed any paint ages ago. Here and there, he saw stains and dark splashes—perhaps the blood of people being interrogated, splattered during a vicious questioning? The recently washed concrete floor could have easily concealed any atrocities that had taken place within the room. It was certainly not a place in which Tom wanted to find himself. A simple wooden table and two rough chairs completed the sparse, intimidating scenery.

Tom sat down in one of the chairs, awaiting the arrival of the investigator who, for some reason, was taking his time. The minutes ticked by, his tension increasing with each one. Why were they late? What had they found in the lab that might embarrass him? Had he failed to lock the door to the lab when he had left? His fatigue got the best of him, and he laid his head down on the table and fell asleep.

***

A bang upon the table, and the resulting shock of impact, woke him into a state of panic.

Detective Heller, who looked as if hadn't slept for the last three nights, was sitting opposite him, and with no preliminaries, immediately began the interrogation.

"I'm dead on my feet. I've just questioned Steve, the head of security. I'm not a scientist, but I have to understand the details of the case sufficiently to allow me to investigate it. Please tell me exactly what you're researching in the lab. Of course, anything you say here is being recorded," he said, leaning back in his chair.

"I'll do my best," Tom began. "I'll try to keep it short and not to overdo it with complex explanations." Briefly, he debated whether to mention the Ronnie research, but immediately decided to avoid any reference to it. The intruder hadn't touched the files pertaining to this study, and there was no point sharing the information with Rick.

"Well, the lab I run is conducting two studies in the field of biology. One is a purely academic study funded by the university, and the other is applied research funded by a group of scientists who have raised a large sum of money for this purpose. Naturally, the budget for academic studies is very limited, and there are plenty of applications competing over every research grant."

"Yeah, I know what you mean," Rick interrupted him. "My cousin Larry works for IBM, at one of their non-applied, basic research departments. Although it's essentially a commercial company, it invests a lot of money in pure research. He also complains about the constant battles over acquiring research budgets that can fund expensive lab equipment and first-class researcher salaries. By the way, at what time in the evening exactly did you leave the lab on your way home?"

"It was after eight p.m.," Tom replied, startled. Up until now, he had assumed the detective was genuinely interested in the scientific aspects of his research. *Apparently, he only sees the scientific lecture as background noise for thinking about the case*, he thought, disappointed. On the other hand, Rick wasn't a scientist, and it was hard to expect him to show interest in such specialized research, especially when he was in charge of a murder investigation.

I'd better start with the human longevity-enhancement project, Tom decided. Rick was too tired to deal with a highly theoretical study such as the change-resiliency project. It would be better to direct the remaining dregs of his alertness toward a study that would certainly be of interest to any human being, and which apparently interested the murderous intruder as well.

"Many studies have been conducted for decades now in a field that people find so alluring and important. After all, everyone thinks life's too short, and we all want to live for as many years as we can. It's undoubtedly a very popular subject, and its commercial potential is boundless. Therefore, many labs and research institutes throughout the world have been looking into it for decades now. Our approach differs from the mainstream one, and only a handful of research institutes share it. Most of the labs all over the world dealing with this field focus on ways to prevent the shortening of telomeres, which are the DNA sequences at the ends of chromosomes, and which shorten with every cell division. Can I assume you know what DNA is?"

"Of course. The science shows on TV are my favorites," Rick replied.

"Excellent," Tom said. "The working hypothesis is that the shorter the telomeres are, the more the cell's ability to divide diminishes, impeding the ability of the body's tissues to rejuvenate, and therefore leading to aging and death. The assumption of a correlation between the length of the telomeres and longevity hasn't changed for several decades now, although it has ebbed every now and then. Lately, the number of scientists who believe in the essential importance of telomeres is nearly equal to the number of those who have been researching other directions.

"The group of scientists funding this project has distributed it among several different labs, each of which is carrying out a part of the whole. We don't know who the other labs are or what, exactly, they're investigating. The confidentiality is at a level that's hard to even imagine. We don't even know what the overall framework of the research is. Judging by our part of it, it's a series of means of preventing cell damage and mutations caused by factors such as free radicals and various kinds of radiation, as well as natural mutations that stem directly from the complex process of constantly replicating DNA, and so forth."

"I understand," Rick said, "that we're talking about quite a lot of money here. An effective process will generate billions for the company that successfully develops it. That's definitely significant motivation for industrial espionage. In view of that, and of your familiarity with the market, it's important that you prepare a list of institutes and people with a potential interest in this research, as soon as possible. A list like that could be an initial lead in our investigation. By the way, were you at the lab all day, or did you have any meetings or other errands anywhere else?"

"Other than leaving for lunch and one meeting in the conference room with Mike and Lise, I was in the lab all day," Tom replied.

"Great," Rick responded, scrawling a few words in his notebook.

"The other research that the lab's involved in is theoretical at this stage, although we're hoping it will yield some applicable aspects in the future. I'm sure you know that DNA is replicated from generation to generation with imperfect accuracy, meaning that occasionally, replication mistakes result in mutations. Do you have any idea how many replication errors occur in a single cell on a single day?"

"There are lots of cells in the human body." Rick started thinking out loud.

Despite his tiredness, the detective actually was listening, Tom reflected.

"If there were a lot of errors, we couldn't survive. I'd estimate that there are very few replication errors. I'd say just a few within a person's lifespan. Because any error could develop into a serious disease, right? By the way, where and with whom did you have lunch?"

Tom was stunned. He found himself beginning to alter his preconceptions regarding the intelligence level of police officers. Despite the long, sleepless night he'd experienced, Rick was managing to listen to his explanations, respond with comments that reflected his understanding, and ask pertinent questions, while at the same time, keeping in mind the investigation itself; he was, without a doubt, a talented person. Apparently, Tom thought, he had a list of questions that he'd prepared in advance and was going to sprinkle them throughout Tom's explanation. This was a unique approach to a police investigation. Perhaps he should be more detailed in his explanations. Although Rick was not a scientist and definitely wasn't a biologist, his alertness and sharp mind merited respect. And like every scientist asked about his work, Tom was enjoying the interest Rick was exhibiting in his research.

With a quick smile, Tom replied, “If every error developed into a serious disease, life wouldn’t exist in its current form. Most replication errors have no effect whatsoever. You’re going to find this hard to believe, but the actual number is about one million errors in every single body cell in one day!”

“How do we even survive?” Rick asked, perplexed. “That’s an astronomical number of mistakes, and since there are trillions of cells in the human body, you’re talking about trillions of errors in just one day. It’s unbelievable that we’re even alive.”

“You’re being optimistic, Rick,” Tom replied. “There are dozens of trillions of cells in the human body. Just to remind you, a trillion is a thousand billion, so the number of errors is indeed astronomical. But as I’ve already mentioned, most of the errors are negligible and don’t affect the organism’s life in any way.”

Rick’s obvious impatience caused Tom to pause from his lecture.

“I’m losing you,” Rick said. “You scientists tell us that DNA is the code according to which we’re constructed, meaning it is the blueprint detailing our composition. But it’s hard for me to imagine a blueprint for building a computer, for example, containing billions of errors, yet the computer constructed according to it still working pretty well for a hundred years, like the human body. Something here seems inappropriate.”

“That is indeed an excellent scientific inquiry,” Tom responded. “But let’s start with investigative matters. I ate alone at the Department of Architecture’s cafeteria. They have an excellent, appealing entrée of green peas with quinoa and red peppers—you should try it some time. That’s what I often do. I actually eat only one dish that’s not too heavy, finish pretty quickly, and go back to work, while my colleagues eat several courses, and tend to be sleepy when they go back to work. It seems like a waste of time to me, and I don't want to rush the others to finish their meals.

"Back to science. Well, the blueprint for the computer was designed by engineers who envisioned the finished computer and planned every detail so it would contribute to its ultimate performance, while keeping costs to a minimum. With that kind of approach, the absence of any detail or any less-than-optimal function would harm the entire system. That's not true for biological systems, which have developed over four billion years of evolution, starting with the first replicating molecule and the first prokaryotic cell with no nucleus, when the only force driving evolution was survival. There was no guiding hand here, unless you believe in a divine Creator who bothered to design each creature separately."

"I'm too exhausted to embark on an endless argument about the intentions of the divine Creator, if He even exists. As a cop who's encountered unbelievable amounts of evil every day of his life, I have a problem with an omnipotent Creator who's supposed to provide his flock with a good life, but lets evil run wild and often win, too."

"To get back to the research," Tom continued, "as I've explained, the force directing the evolutionary development of life is survival of the strongest or the fittest. The engine supplying the array of alternatives for evolution's selection is random replication errors and random mutations in sex cells. Most of them have no effect whatsoever, while most of the remaining ones cause changes that decrease the organism's compatibility with its environment, and therefore its survival rates, at which point evolution weeds them out and they disappear from the genome. Only a tiny portion of them enhance the organism's compatibility with its environment and increase its survival rates. That's how the amazing compatibility develops between organisms and their environment. And, through a slow and gradual process, this is also how new species evolve."

"Right, I've seen quite a few science shows on TV that explain the theory of evolution," Rick said. "Look, it's late and we're both tired. I'd prefer that you focus on the topic of your research, and less on general theory. By the way, did you run into any acquaintances when you had lunch at the cafeteria?"

"Just a minute," Tom retorted, glowering. "Am I being interrogated here? What's with all these little questions? I thought you wanted to understand my work at the lab to an extent that would help you hone in on the killer's possible motives. I didn't think my trustworthiness was under question."

"Don't get me wrong," Rick replied soothingly. "An experienced investigator learns a lot from seemingly trivial questions. Regardless of your trustworthiness, I don't know you, and it's exactly such mundane questions that help me formulate an opinion about you as a person and not just as an academic researcher. But if it bothers you, I'll avoid those kinds of questions."

"No, no, keep investigating as you see fit. I can deal with your methods. To answer your question, Mike and Lise nodded hello to me on their way to the table. I remember that seemed a bit odd to me. I didn't think there was any sort of relationship between them, you know? They're so different from one another. Anyway, I was happy to see them talking. And I spent some time on more general theories only as background for our specific research, to establish a baseline with you—no more than that. I felt it was a necessary introduction. Anyway, I'll try to focus mainly on the essential issues.

"For decades now, we've known that the great majority of the human genome, more than 95 percent, doesn't code for protein production. Over time, it was discovered that a certain portion of the genetic material that doesn't code for protein production serves to control the genes, so that the same gene will produce different proteins in the presence of various controls. All that notwithstanding, most of the genome apparently fulfills no function in our lives. Those parts of the genome are also called junk DNA."

"What did you say?" Rick cut him short. "How is that possible? You're telling me that most of the genome is junk? I really don't buy that."

"I didn't say that most of the genome was junk; I said that most of the human genome apparently doesn't fulfill a function in our lives. You've probably heard that the genome contains the code for producing the various proteins that make up our body. It turns out that most of the genome is composed of the remains of genes and their controls that have been involved in the production of proteins in the past. These leftovers don't code for proteins at all. These are the remains of genes that stopped functioning at some point in the evolution process, but the replication mechanisms—the ribosomes—continue to tirelessly replicate them and pass them on from generation to generation. Obviously, negative mutations in parts of the DNA that are crucial to our existence won't survive at all, and in contrast, any kind of mutations in the junk DNA will pile up and accumulate because they don't affect the life of the organism."

Rick responded, "I knew, probably from one of those science shows on TV, that part of human DNA is unnecessary and doesn't contribute anything to our lives, but I didn't think it was the majority of the genome. How long have we been dragging these DNA remnants with us?"

"Apparently since the beginning of life on Earth. Part of this

DNA apparently served the first life forms on the planet—replicating organic molecules and unicellular organisms with no nuclei."

Despite his fatigue, Tom felt pleased. The hard part of the explanation was behind him; it appeared that Rick, curious by nature, knew quite a bit about DNA. Apparently, the science programs on TV were watched by a broad variety of people, and were clear enough to bring scientific innovations in numerous fields into the homes of viewers who were not scientists. Now that he had explained the background of his work to Rick, all that remained was to clarify the specifics.

"In my PhD thesis, I studied DNA sequences that don't code for proteins in the human body and that haven't changed over long periods of time. Science is familiar with millions of sequences conserved to various degrees, most of them originating in fish and mammals. There are hundreds of completely conserved sequences that are identical in humans and in fish. These sequences are adjacent to genes that are active and that code for proteins, and therefore we assume that they control these genes' activity, and are essential for that reason. We've detected identical conserved sequences in the human genome in all of the human races with a length of at least five hundred nucleotides that don't code for proteins. To the best of our understanding, these sequences don't fulfill any active role, and yet they're both long and completely conserved. We compared these sequences among different and relatively isolated human populations, and although their entire vicinity has changed, these sequences are identical among all the human races we tested.

"Ever since then, I've been very interested in conserved DNA sequences. I believe that understanding their importance, and the mechanisms that conserve them beyond the constraints of evolution, can contribute significantly to the fight against disease. I've previously applied for several research grants to study this topic, unsuccessfully. This year I succeeded, despite many obstacles."

This would have been the time to tell Rick about Ronnie, the preserved humanoid they had discovered, whose DNA had revealed a long sequence completely identical to those found in all the human races examined, and of course, about the sequence radiation experiments, and the strange results obtained in them. He also wouldn't mention the new proteins being produced right now from various segments of the sequence and its immediate vicinity. No, he wouldn't mention any of that. He would confine himself solely to a general outline. The scientific details would only make sense to researchers in the field, anyway. His duty of confidentiality toward the university, the desire to take credit, along with his team, for future discoveries, as well as the thought that this information was not pertinent in any way to the murder investigation, all precluded him from mentioning the entire matter even in a casual way. *But maybe*, he thought apprehensively, *these unusual studies were the intruder's goal, rather than the longevity-enhancement study?* No, he would not expose any further details. No reason to go looking for trouble. And thus he ignored the entire topic in his explanations to Rick.

"As part of our research, we comprehensively compare human DNA to chimpanzee DNA, as well as comparing various human races. Our working hypothesis is that since the genetic difference between us is about 1 percent, the differences we discover will be expressed via slight changes in the genome. As expected, we're discovering conserved DNA sequences unique to humans, and have been working on those. For years now, science has established the existence of proteins in cells whose sole role is to recreate code segments that have been damaged for whatever reason. They're similar to bits used to enhance every piece of data in a computer's memory, and whose entire function is to note any change in data. Sometimes, with a significant addition of bits, you can even repair data that's been impaired. These proteins, which are actually called 'DNA-repairing proteins,' have rather limited capacities, which is not a bad thing. What do you think, Detective Heller—in light of the large quantities of unnecessary DNA in the genome, why didn't evolution develop more potent repair proteins that would fix every error?"

Rick stared at Tom, thinking, *What engineer wouldn't want software that detects every mistake or error in their designs, and then proceeds to fix it?* It sounded like every designer's idea of heaven. Only last month, it had been revealed that the new space shuttle on its way to Jupiter's moon Europa would be able to reach its destination and land successfully, but due to a design error, would be unable to carry out its mission to drill a hole in in the ice cover enveloping the moon. Two billion dollars had gone down the drain.

"Evolution was unsuccessful," Rick said. "Even evolution has limited capacities. If it were omnipotent, there wouldn't be so many diseases, and our life would be much better."

"Maybe," Tom replied. "Let's think about it together. If the repair mechanisms were even slightly more efficient, they'd fix some of the mutations and the replication errors, and life on Earth would look entirely different. Perhaps life would have remained on the unicellular level and would never have evolved into the diverse life that exists today."

"I'm starting to understand some of the challenges medicine has to deal with," Rick muttered. "On the one hand, you're telling me that evolution, and consequently the diverse life around us, depends on the occurrence of errors and mutations, meaning they're essential. On the other hand, you have repair mechanisms, which can't be too efficient, either. All in all, it sounds like life really is a miracle."

"That's very true. Life is an array of balances between numerous and often contradictory factors. If there were no repair mechanisms, apparently life would be quite paltry. But if the repair mechanisms are too efficient, again, no complex life evolves. The repair mechanisms, like most evolutionary solutions, aren't perfect but rather just good enough—bordering on barely sufficient, but just squeaking by—and the complex life forms around us are the proof. The large quantity of junk DNA is very strange, but helpful to us researchers. Our assumption is that understanding the unique process that conserves specific DNA sequences might help us find cures for diseases caused by distortions to the genetic information during replication, such as cancer, diseases related to aging, and many others."

"You must be referring to those scientists who claim that all varieties of cancer stem from a single factor, and once we find a cure for it, every variety of cancer can be eliminated," Rick commented.

"I wouldn't go that far, but that direction has certainly been investigated extensively, and further research is required."

Rick nodded in comprehension, signaling Tom to continue. *No more indirect questions*, Tom thought. Had he passed the detective's trustworthiness test? Without dedicating another thought to this topic, he resumed his lecture.

"Much to my surprise, although this direction seemed interesting and undoubtedly unique, I encountered strong objections to my application for a research grant from Professor

Paul Longstrom, the dean of the university, of all people. In light of the many years during which these diseases have been researched with no significant breakthroughs, I had expected a new research direction focusing on all diseases caused by genetic changes—possibly including aging itself—to be received with open arms. The dean came up with a variety of highly unconvincing reasons to reject the study. Some of them were so bad that they actually provided ammunition for the study's supporters, but indeed, as you've already realized, the study was approved, and we've been working on it for about a year and a half."

"It sounds interesting. What kind of findings have you obtained?" Rick asked.

"Well..." Tom cleared his throat.

I've touched a sore spot, Rick thought. *Tom no longer feels like a clever lecturer standing before an ignoramus; he feels a lot less comfortable talking about his results than giving general lectures. Apparently, he hasn't obtained any significant findings yet.*

For a brief moment, Tom felt tempted to tell Rick about their discoveries. However, he came to his senses immediately and reverted to the official version they had adopted when presenting the study to anyone on the outside.

"We've mapped the conserved DNA sequences that were discovered by other groups in the past. Since a significant part of the work was carried out years ago, we decided to re-examine the genome using recently developed new technology. And indeed, as of today, we have positively detected about four hundred conserved DNA sequences at a length of at least two hundred nucleotides that were previously undiscovered. These sequences were found in their entirety in all primates, meaning all apes."

"Even though I'm just a police detective, I know very well what a primate is," Rick interrupted him.

"I didn't mean to patronize you. I just don't know how fluent you are in these topics, and as I'm sure you've noticed, I'm trying to be as clear and understandable as possible, although the technical terms we use in our everyday research aren't familiar to anyone who doesn't work in our specific field. To get back to it, we're in the process of verifying several hundred more sequences about which we're still not entirely certain. However, most of them have undergone multiple rounds of testing and verification, and look promising."

"Sounds like you're doing a pretty good job," Rick said, before clearing his throat. He looked and sounded extremely tired, but actually found the topic fascinating. In an exhausted tone, he said, "This is a very interesting subject, and I'm sure I'll have lots of questions later. But it's been a long night, I'm beat, and I still have a long, busy workday awaiting me. Give me some time to take in everything I've learned from you tonight. I'm sure we'll have some more long scientific conversations, hopefully at a more convenient time and under more pleasant circumstances."

"I'll be happy to be done with this investigation," Tom replied. "This is the longest interrogation I've ever been through, definitely when it comes to a crucial topic like murder. If the subject of genetic research interests you on a scientific level, and not just as a means of cracking the murder, we really can meet some other time to discuss it at leisure."

"That's it for tonight," Rick said. "You can pick up your personal assistant at the entrance. I suggest you go back to your fascinating studies and leave the rest of the investigation to us. And yes, don't worry, we'll update you on every important development, and we'll probably have more questions. Good night, or more accurately, good morning, Dr. Lester. It's already almost nine a.m. If you wish, you're invited to freshen up in our showers. You'll find towels and a shaving kit there."

"I enjoyed being questioned and, even more, presenting my research, as I'm sure you've already noticed. Anyway, you can call me Tom. Everyone else does."

CHAPTER 5

Rick

Chicago, Wednesday, July 16, 2036

Rick, exhausted, looked at the pages of the investigation report detailing Tom and Steve's questioning, which he had spread out all over his desk. Both subjects had sounded trustworthy and shocked, as expected from people uninvolved in criminal affairs following such a close encounter with crime. This was particularly true in regard to the murder of a coworker, a man stationed at the site where he was murdered solely in order to protect them from harm. For a moment, it seemed to him as if Oleg had been cannon fodder for the security apparatus. An outrageous thought, and perhaps a true one, as well.

Tom and Steve had replied to all his questions immediately, revealing no hesitation or any fear of the encounter with him as the investigating officer, of the intimidating interrogation room, or of the long, exhausting nighttime questioning. Each of them had felt at some point that they were suspects; however, this did not undermine their self-confidence. Yes, there was no doubt in his heart that both had been speaking completely honestly.

Rick didn't understand a thing about science, not to mention genetics. His entire life revolved around his demanding job on the police force, and around the remainder of his family, which had broken up following his divorce, and now included only his son and daughter. Pure scientific research with no apparent commercial intent was entirely incomprehensible to him. *Why would people invest their time and energy to explore hidden, unknown corners of the world?* he thought. It was obvious to him that the break-in into Tom's lab had not been a random act. The lab had been targeted for a very specific reason. At first look, the longevity-enhancement research seemed like a good reason for a break-in. The immense financial potential could justify quite a few crimes. However, the research was divided among many labs, and if he could take Tom's word for it, which at this stage he had no reason not to do, even Tom himself didn't know much about the direction in which the research was going.

His experience had taught him that quite frequently, the approach that initially seemed to make less sense actually turned out to be right. Were there aspects of Tom's theoretical research that might be of interest to criminal elements? And perhaps criminal elements were not at the heart of the matter at all; perhaps the criminals had been sent by scientists. And perhaps there were additional aspects to the study that Tom hadn't mentioned. Could he be concealing essential findings that were of interest to others? Throughout the investigation, had Tom behaved as if he was hiding information or lying? Usually, Rick's extensive experience would have allowed him to answer this question immediately and very confidently; this time, he wasn't sure. He was very tired, and might have ignored some important details.

In addition, the burglar hadn't been a petty criminal who, if caught red-handed during the burglary, could have skated by with a slap on the wrist by claiming he'd broken in to steal equipment or that he had been sent by a third party whose identity was unknown to him. Burglars intending to steal property didn't usually carry guns, and definitely not ones with silencers, as evidenced by the corpse's wound. Such a burglar wouldn't risk committing a murder, a grievous crime.

Another option that occurred to him was that the murder had been a result of panic. However, the fact that the guard's body had been found near the main entrance to the building rather than inside the lab indicated that the intruder had been waiting for the security guard, apparently because he heard him approaching or opening the door to the building. He had waited behind the door, intending to kill him, most likely to avoid identification. This was evidenced by Oleg's tidy uniform, which gave no indication of a physical struggle. The killer hadn't even tried to escape. And assuming the small red stain on Tom's desk was a bloodstain, it appeared the killer had returned to the desk after the murder, probably to complete the task that had motivated the break-in and the murder. The killer's cold-blooded conduct in returning to the lab after the murder was an indication of an unusual, goal-oriented personality; this particular goal appeared to be of ultimate importance to him.

Rick wondered whether lab results would indeed confirm that the red stain was the blood of the murdered security guard. The deeper he delved into the findings from the incident, the more strongly he felt that the characteristics of the break-in were not congruent with a crime motivated by property theft, or even industrial espionage, which was very common in the high-tech industry. His well-honed senses told him this was a highly unusual case, on which he should definitely focus in order to crack it as quickly as possible.

Tiredness got the better of Rick, who was dozing in his chair when suddenly, he startled awake. Something was bothering him. The phrase "university lab break-in" sounded familiar to him. He had heard of a similar occurrence quite recently. His fatigue evaporated without a trace. A new burst of energy throbbed within his chest, like a man who had just received an adrenaline shot.

He recalled that several weeks ago, he had read in the police log about a break-in at a lab at Northwestern University in Evanston. The complaint had been odd because nothing had been taken, and in fact, the police investigator handling the case had suspected the complaint might have been false, although there had been no logical reason for this.

The new computer system did not let him down. Its cost, over $200 million, the uproar it had evoked, and the development that had lasted two years longer than expected had all proved worthwhile. Within seconds, he was scrolling down a list of four break-ins to university labs in the Chicago metro area that had been reported since the beginning of the year. In all of them, nothing had been taken, and the complaints had been archived due to lack of public interest. Expanding the search to the United States as a whole yielded eight more break-ins with similar characteristics. The incidents undoubtedly displayed an obvious pattern: clean break-ins into university labs, in which nothing was taken and no equipment was destroyed. Apparently, he had detected something much larger than a random break-in that had gone awry and ended in murder.

The upcoming wave of new appointments at the Chicago Police Department beckoned to Rick. Perhaps this discovery and the ensuing investigation would finally mark him as a candidate for the promotion he so desired after more than five years as a police field investigator.

Running another search on the police computer system, this time instructing it to find previously inputted listings of clean break-ins to labs of any kind, both public and private, in the United States within the preceding five years, yielded interesting results. No events of this kind had been registered during the years 2032 and 2033. The first event was noted on October 2, 2034. Six events were noted in 2035, and since the beginning of 2036, twelve more break-ins had been added to the list, not counting this last one. Therefore, the pattern of clean break-ins had begun with one incident at the end of 2034, six more throughout 2035, and now twelve break-ins in only the first seven months of the year.

Another shared characteristic was prominent in the listing of incidents: all of the break-ins had taken place at biology labs in universities and research institutes dealing with genetic studies. Rick had no doubt that he had uncovered an unusual common denominator. Someone was very interested in what was currently going on in the field of biology, and was investing plenty of resources in monitoring recent developments, while undertaking significant risks to do so.

For a moment, Rick considered approaching precinct commander Mike Robertson and presenting his findings to him. But this moment passed quickly. No, he wouldn't let such a golden opportunity slip between his fingers. This case would be his ladder up the chain of command, his ticket out of fieldwork and into a command position with commensurate wages and benefits. He won't run to his commander with the raw material like a rookie. He would investigate the case on his own, as part of the leeway granted to an officer of his rank, and only when he had gathered enough proof and put together a clear case would he present it. And then, maybe his long-standing dream—a promotion and freedom from Sisyphean fieldwork—would finally come true.

CHAPTER 6

Aaron

Chicago, Thursday, July 17, 2036

This time, it had been very close, Aaron thought. His luck hadn't held out, the way it had in all his previous break-ins to date, including the previous one into this very lab, which hadn't been discovered at all. This time, he had come very close to getting caught by a guard. He had had no intention of killing the guard, but the brawny man had completely prevented any possibility of escape, and the result would have been apprehension by the police, the end of his career, and most importantly, a lead guiding the police to the entire organization, which was not an option, at any cost. No, he'd had no other choice. This was the first time he'd had to kill in order to carry out his mission. Although he was willing to sacrifice his life if it became necessary, killing another person, the thought that he had taken the life of an innocent man, shocked him.

He would raise a proposal to pay compensation to the victim's family—completely anonymously, of course. Obscuring the origins of such payments or financial support by attributing them to various charities was always a possibility. First, of course, he must receive the group's authorization. He didn't think there would be any problem with the payment. It had often been made clear to him that funding was unlimited. The Guardians had defined goals, and they would do anything required to carry them out, while minimizing collateral damage to people in general and to innocent bystanders, in particular. Secrecy was always a top priority; it was made clear to everyone that any price must be paid to ensure their activities were not uncovered. Yes, he would also have to relocate; he couldn't risk a police investigation finding its way back to him. Who knew how many cameras had recorded his presence, although he had taken care to obstruct the ones of which he was aware, or what revealing clues he had left behind, despite having done his best to change his appearance and the way he moved.

In spite of their generous funding, the organization's activities were low-key in their execution, and involved minimal expenses. They should think of alternatives to the multiple break-ins, as they entailed significant danger. However, the information he discovered when he went over the material he had copied from Dr. Lester's computer had been enough to reveal that the study focused on locating conserved sequences that were identical among the various human races, and that among other discoveries, they had already noted the Message. Since the researchers weren't aware of its meaning, though, they did not attribute any special distinction to it. In any case, their work had brought them too close to it, and therefore, they had to be monitored on an ongoing basis. As things stood, chances were that the research team would merely add the

Message sequence to the list of conserved sequences appearing in humans only, and not in other animals.

All that notwithstanding, Tom was known as a talented, thorough researcher. His track record indicated that he would not be satisfied with merely discovering an identical, particularly lengthy sequence that was unique to humans and that did not code for any protein. He would do anything within his ability to investigate such a phenomenon in depth. It seemed highly likely that after a thorough analysis of his results, he would come up with various research directions, some of which might lead him to the worst possible outcome, the prohibited discovery that they must prevent at any cost.

It was a good thing that he'd had time to substitute a tiny camera for one of the screws holding up the image of the DNA double helix that covered a large part of the lab's northern wall. He'd also had time to make sure the camera could observe most of the area in the lab. Aaron was concerned that he hadn't managed to erase the traces of his search from the computer. The murder of the security guard had upset him, and he had left the premises immediately once he'd finished installing the camera and copying the research files.

Up to this point, he had managed to completely eliminate all traces of his presence after every break-in. He wondered what conclusions the investigators would reach. Aaron assumed they would come to the conclusion that the intruder had been interested in the longevity-enhancement study, which had tremendous commercial potential, and which he had also copied from the computer. Maybe, just to be on the safe side, Aaron thought, they should think of an active way of leading the investigators to this conclusion. The last thing Aaron and his handlers wanted was to lead the investigators in the right direction. They must make sure the investigators focused on the financial angle!

Well, he still had the morning hours to prepare for the cell meeting. Only now did he have the time to examine the scratch on his right elbow, sustained while he had hurriedly turned on the lab computer. He really had been under immense pressure. The murder of the security guard had undermined his confidence and his equilibrium. Apparently, the scratch still hadn't scabbed over, so he covered it with a light dressing. The long, tense night made him feel highly alert. He had exactly as much time as he needed to prepare the material. The cell meeting had been scheduled for Thursday morning. Generally, everyone was available for urgent meetings at any time. It was lucky he had had time to go over the material copied from Tom's computer, interpret it, and understand it.

At precisely eight thirty, the intercom buzzer rang and Takumi's round face appeared on the screen. Without exchanging greetings or any other words, Takumi and Chinatsu sat in two end chairs lined up on one side of the desk, which stood in the middle of the living room. The desk and chairs were the only pieces of furniture in the room. Aaron sat in the middle chair, opposite the computer screen.

The presentation was very short. It included four brief excerpts from the reports copied from Dr. Lester's computer.

"The long sequence was not found in any of the primates whose genome was available for immediate comparison. In contrast, it is completely identical in all the human races we have examined. We will continue examining more human races. Lise is also supervising a temporary assistant assigned to us to help with conducting varying radiation of the sequence in order to assess its strength. We have no idea about the role of this sequence...

"The primary question is whether this sequence has been conserved at random, or whether it's vital to a degree that any change will be eliminated from the genome. If this is the case, discovering its role is of great importance. Perhaps a yet-unknown factor is protecting it to such an extreme degree...

"In any case, pinpointing the reason for its conservation might lead to significant medical advances...

"Ronnie also possesses an identical sequence..."

"Who's Ronnie?" Chinatsu interjected.

"I don't know. That's the first time I've heard that name. I didn't find any other reference to Ronnie tonight. I'll read carefully through the material I copied one more time. Maybe I'll find something, or maybe the camera I planted will help me find out what's going on," Aaron replied.

The minutes ticked by without anyone saying a word, until Takumi looked up and said, "We don't know what they're calling 'the long sequence.' Based on what they're saying, there's a chance they're working on The Forbidden Message, the sequence whose discovery our activity is intended to prevent, primarily due to the result that it could yield. However, at the moment, it doesn't seem as if there's a concrete risk that they might follow a route that would lead to the discovery of The Forbidden Message. They're interested in the medical potential of the sequence, which is a good thing. I agree they should be consistently monitored, but despite their discovery, the next transition requires an unusual cognitive leap that is not in accordance with their current line of thought. Still, they're only two levels away from a discovery. Something should be done."

"I propose we escalate to Level 2," Aaron said.

Once again, several silent minutes went by, until Takumi resumed speaking. "We've escalated to Level 2. Chinatsu is responsible for focusing the police investigation and interest within the lab on the longevity-enhancement research. Think of a way and make it happen. We'll know about it."

A nearly imperceptible nod from Chinatsu confirmed he had accepted the task and would carry it out.

"Level 2," Takumi repeated, turning to Aaron, who nodded back. All three rose from their seats.

Only then did Aaron turn to Takumi and say, "During the break-in yesterday, I had to shoot a security guard, who died instantly."

Both men's eyes turned to him immediately, their expression conveying immense grief.

Takumi said, "I am sorry. It's obvious to all of us that this is not what we wanted, but there's no going back. We'll make sure the security guard's family is generously compensated from our resources."

Aaron bowed in gratitude to Takumi, who turned, along with Chinatsu, toward the front door, while Aaron made a note to himself to delete the evidence from his computer after immersing himself in the material once more. They never retained any documentation of their activities.

***

Level 2, Aaron thought, was just one level before "Let me die with the Philistines"-type activity commenced, a stage in which the most extreme measures were put into action in an attempt to stop unwanted revelations. At Level 2, the gathering of information continued, but was reinforced with misdirection activity. In cases where the research could not be distorted or stopped, there was also an attempt to actively subvert it by investing in alternate studies, tempting job offers, and threats, and by staging "accidents."

Aaron remembered his first meeting with Takumi and Chinatsu vividly. As a child, he had never visited his father's workplace. Even when he'd begged his dad to take him to work like the fathers of his classmates did, his father always found various excuses to refuse. Aaron was about eighteen when he received the news that, against all odds, he had been accepted to study law at the prestigious Loyola University. In his fantasies, he could already envision himself as a senior partner at a large law firm in Chicago, living in a big, fancy house, unlike the modest apartment in which his parents lived with his younger sister Meirav. However, his father had had other plans for him.

"All of us in the family, meaning the men, have studied the history of the Middle East and Far East, as well as the sciences. I expect you to follow in our footsteps and not to disrupt our long family tradition."

"And where has all that brought you?" Aaron had dared to ask, untypically bold in the presence of his father. "To a little apartment in a godforsaken suburb. I have friends who live in big, fancy houses, who frequently go on long vacations abroad. I'm not any less talented than they are. I could attain their kind of lifestyle if I studied law or some other major occupation. With history, the most I could achieve is becoming a schoolteacher, and continuing to live the way we do now."

He had uttered the words in one long breath, sensing that he had hurt his father by speaking them. Much to his surprise, a subtle smile surfaced upon his father's face.

"That's okay, son," his father said. "At the time, I reacted just like you did. I also wanted to study law and focus on my career. As you well know, I'm not a legal expert, and we live modestly in regard to finances. I'll make sure you get a chance to meet with some of the people I work with. They'll convince you to study topics that seem unimportant to you today." With these words, he left the room.

During the next two days, the topic of his studies was not raised in conversations around the house, and life continued as usual. On the third evening, he received a call from someone whose voice was unfamiliar.

"Hi, Aaron." He heard a deep voice that sounded as if it belonged to an older man. "I work with your father. We should talk— the sooner the better. Could you meet me this evening at my room at the Sheraton Grand Chicago on the river?"

The authoritative voice, along with Aaron's need to prove to his father that he could not be swayed, resulted in an immediate reply.

"Sure. When?"

"I'm waiting for you in room 1124. Get going."

That was the first time he had met Takumi and Chinatsu.

CHAPTER 7

Melissa

Chicago, Thursday, July 17, 2036

Exhausted after a sleepless night, exposure to a murder, and a long interrogation, Tom debated whether to go back to the university or drive home for a short nap. It was almost nine in the morning, a time when the streets, trains, and roads filled with cars and people hurrying to their workplaces.

No, it wasn't right for him to ignore the murder and go to sleep. There was no other choice; he had to return to the university, to update management as well as the students on recent events. It was lucky that Rick had made sure to drive him to the police station; he shouldn't be driving in his current state of fatigue, even in autonomous mode.

The train car was full of passengers. It was not easy to work his way inside and get settled next to a post, against which he leaned his back, his hands burrowing deep in the pockets of his coat. His sorrowful thoughts wandered from the murdered Oleg to the man's grieving wife and children, for whom Oleg had been the sole provider, and who would now be dealing with new difficulties.

He was also bothered by the fact that he hadn't told Rick a thing about Ronnie. Had he done the right thing? How would the detective react if he discovered that Tom had withheld information that might prove important? After all, the Ronnie study placed the long sequence in a completely different context. Perhaps he should go back to the precinct, apologize, and tell the truth, even if this would deprive the university of the major surprise they were planning to spring on the scientific community. No, he wouldn't go back to the detective. He would give it some thought.

He wondered about the motivation of the intruder, and of those who had sent him. Yes, without a doubt, the break-in did not seem to have been initiated by a lone-wolf burglar. What exactly was of interest to those who had initiated it? Who was so wary of exposure that he was willing to murder someone in order to prevent it from happening?

The conclusion was clear: either the murderous intruder was a public figure, or those who had sent him were. The more he delved into thinking about the event and analyzing it, the more mysterious it appeared. He had a hard time discerning the assistant's ring in the general bustle of the train; when it registered, it withdrew him from his state of contemplation.

"Guess which files were copied from your computer?" he heard Rick's voice in his ear.

That really is a tough question, Tom thought sarcastically. Who the hell was interested in research that, at first glance, seemed purely academic and tedious, about resilience to change in human

DNA sequences? Even the university barely exhibited any interest in that study. He had fought so hard to get authorization and funding for his research. Only fanatics delved into the esoteric nooks and crannies of human DNA analysis.

Most researchers focused on genes that triggered disease, extended life, enhanced IQ, strengthened the immune system, and so forth. These were the breakthrough studies that were generously funded and to which brilliant researchers and students flocked. Tom had no doubt that the longevity-extension research, part of which had been allocated to his lab, was the reason for the break-in.

"Longevity," he replied loudly, trying to overcome the background noise of the train. He felt a strong urge to add that succeeding in this research would truly overturn the world, while the mutation-resistance study was purely theoretical and probably held no interest for people outside academia. In any case, academic researchers didn't break into labs, and they certainly weren't killers. However, he held back. This was not the place for a conversation of that kind.

The ongoing silence in the assistant's receiver made Tom think the call had been disconnected, especially since the train was going through a tunnel. Then he heard a slight throat clearing before Rick replied, "Very interesting." Another long pause stretched out before he continued. "You're right. The entire research file on longevity extension was copied from the computer."

Rick's answer so thoroughly fulfilled Tom's expectations that he didn't even bother to ask him whether the mutation-resistance study had been copied as well.

***

The corridor in the lab building was abuzz with voices coming from every lab. Everyone was talking about the break-in and the murder. Mike and Lise, the two graduate students who assisted him, as well as the two lab techs, Lynn and Amy, were already at the lab when he arrived.

"Professor Longstrom and Dr. Colin asked that you go see them when you arrive," Lise said as he dropped into the one threadbare armchair in the lab. "They've been looking for you for about an hour now."

Only when he exited the building did he notice that Mike and Lise were following him.

"Dr. Colin asked the two of us to come along as well," Lise responded to his querying expression.

As they walked down the campus pathways, he suddenly remembered that he hadn't called his wife, who still didn't know a thing, as news of the murder had not been released yet. At most, she was worried about why he hadn't returned home last night. She probably thought he had been held up, and had decided to stay on at the university for the workday.

Kate replied on the first ring. "What's going on?" she asked, sounding more curious than concerned. Kate wasn't the kind of woman who tended to worry and stress out easily; she was more the type who allowed things to work themselves out, the way they usually did. Tom updated her with a few brief statements. It was another trait of hers that he appreciated; a short summary was generally sufficient for her. She would fill in the rest with her vivid imagination and sharp intellect.

"Don't stay until the end of the day," she advised. "I bet you're completely exhausted."

The severe gaze of Dr. Ron Colin, the university director who was standing at the entrance to the administration building, drove Tom to quickly end the conversation with his wife. Wordlessly, the director accompanied them to a small conference room adjacent to his office. On the way, he barked to his secretary to notify the dean of the arrival of Tom and his team.

The atmosphere in the room was tense enough to cut with a knife. Tom was exhausted as well, although the difficult recent events had also flooded him with adrenaline. No one had any interest in getting started before the arrival of Dean Paul Longstrom.

Tom surveyed the attendees. Mike Easter and Lise Oliver had recently completed their Master's degrees in molecular biology, cum laude, at the university, and had come to him to work on their PhDs.

Mike, an idealist, strove to work in ecological research. His wealthy family enabled him to dedicate his work to pure science. Tom's longevity-enhancement study greatly appealed to him, and he had applied to work on it even before they had received the grant. Mike looked like the type who had never been involved in a fight, much less a violent scuffle. He was probably deeply shaken by the thought that a killer had been walking around in the lab where he worked, touching the equipment with which he worked, perhaps even sitting in his chair.

Was Mike the one who had supplied the intruder with the access code to the computer? It was hard to think of Mike as an accessory to a crime. He was the very antithesis of the criminal archetype. On the other hand, most criminals probably didn't look like you'd expect them to. No, if Mike had provided the computer access code, he had surely been duped into doing so, and had not known he was enabling a criminal. Mike wouldn't break the law or cooperate with someone who did.

Lise was Mike's complete opposite: ambitious, self-centered, assertive, and determined to achieve her goals. Talented Lise would definitely have studied computer engineering had she been born thirty years earlier, the way her father had done in his youth.

A "Daddy's girl" her entire life, she yearned to prove herself to her father. A compliment from him about any of her achievements justified any effort and investment on her part, effectively oiling her gears for further action. She had studied biology because she believed she would be able to find her place in a senior role at a large international conglomerate. She was motivated to excel at any task, large or small, constantly positioning herself at center stage. She always had something to say, although she usually made significant contributions to any discussion.

She would undoubtedly have preferred to work on the longevity-enhancement study, on which Mike was already working when she joined the lab. To Tom's surprise, however, Lise had not hesitated and immediately accepted his offer to work on the mutation-resilience study. Apparently, she saw her work at the university as merely a springboard to the real world—working for an international pharmaceutical corporation.

Professor Longstrom's silhouette appeared at the entrance of the conference room. He was over six feet tall, his sturdy form and short, well-groomed beard lending him a respectable look somewhat in contrast to his clownish face and ruddy cheeks.

Tom recalled the professor's fierce opposition to his grant request before the research committee. "A waste of money, a boring topic, no PhD candidate will want to work on this," were some of his assertions.

Nevertheless, once the grant had been approved by a slim majority of committee members, the professor appeared strangely relieved. He had congratulated Tom warmly for receiving the grant, even embracing him affectionately and paternally—a direct contrast to his behavior during the discussion. Tom wondered about the reason for his sweeping objection, but mainly why his conduct had changed once the grant was approved.

Even before he sat down, the professor nodded at Tom and said, “Tell me.”

Tom succinctly recreated the events from the moment the assistant’s ring woke him in the wee hours of the night, emphasizing his discovery that his computer was still warm, his assessment that the longevity-enhancement study had been the intruder’s goal, and Detective Heller’s confirmation that the reports for that study had indeed been copied from the computer. No one interrupted him, and no questions were asked throughout his presentation of the incident.

Dr. Colin was the first to break the silence. “In what phase is the longevity-enhancement study?”

Mike’s tortured glance conveyed a wordless message to Tom. Mike didn’t like to find himself at the center of attention, especially in front of the university’s major players.

“We’re pretty much just starting out,” Tom said. “The people at Glenhill gave us all the material pertinent to the direction our research would take, based on the work carried out at their labs on the subject before they decided to allocate the work to other labs. They got quite stuck in developing molecules that could detect irregular development of new blood vessels created by cancerous cells; this detection process is vital for the next stages of the research. They conveyed to us that we weren’t the only ones tasked with this assignment. Naturally, they’ll go forward with the best solution developed. We’re betting on them working with placental cells, due to their rapid development rate and since they're rich in blood vessels."

"Do the researchers at Glenhill know exactly what stage we've reached?" Dr. Colin asked.

Tom nodded at Mike, who had calmed down in the interim.

"They know the direction we're taking and have authorized it. The latest update they got was about a month ago," Mike replied, his voice newly confident.

Tom's fatigue was beginning to take over. He listened to the discussion and participated in it, but his thoughts wandered as he assessed the status of the study for the umpteenth time in an attempt to speculate who might be interested in it. The team worked slowly, but thoroughly and methodically as well. They had invested considerable time in studying everything that had been done in Glenhill, while simultaneously examining new options for the molecule. The truth was that after inspecting and discussing the options raised, they had initially felt they had hit a dead end, that they could not discover a new breakthrough that had not been attempted by Glenhill in the past.

It had been during one of those moments of crisis when the discussion fell apart, the conference room growing silent as the attendees looked down and avoided one another's eyes, that Lise's whispering, hesitant voice was heard. "Mammals' placental cells could be an interesting direction. They develop quickly, surrounding themselves with a tissue that's very rich in blood vessels. Why don't we look into what activates them?"

Tom recalled how, gradually, heads were raised and occasional sparks of life reawakened in the attendees' eyes. A few seconds later, the entire room erupted into sound, with everyone speaking at once, to each other but mostly to themselves. It had indeed proved to be a quantum leap, the kind that tends to occur sometimes when it appears that all hope is lost. The sensation of breakthrough and the light at the end of the tunnel had ignited in all of their hearts.

From that moment on, work began to progress in an orderly manner. Research plans were composed and experiments were designed. Even then, problems continued to pile up. The cells responsible for creating the surplus of blood vessels had to be detected, and within them, the pertinent genes and the specific molecules had to be synthesized. The new direction received the blessing of Glenhill's people, who complimented the team and even rewarded them with a weekend in sunny Florida.

What a shame that now, following the break-in, their original work had been taken from them. He had already been dreaming of a paper in a respected scientific journal, and perhaps even a story in the mainstream daily press.

Something had changed in the conference room. Tom, immersed in his own thoughts, noticed it and turned his attention to his surroundings. The conversation had stopped, and everyone's gazes were turned in his direction. Apparently, a question had been asked, and he had failed to answer it.

"I'm sorry, my mind drifted. I'm really exhausted."

"That's very understandable," Dr. Colin replied. "Since the police are working on solving the murder and the break-in, I don't see any need to waste our time. I suggest we end this discussion. Dr. Lester will go home and get some rest, and Mike Easter and Lise Oliver will return to their work at the lab. I'll make sure Dr. Lester's computer is returned before the end of the day, so that he can resume his work tomorrow. We'll make sure to enhance the security level of the university's labs to prevent additional break-ins."

Everyone rose to leave. However, Tom found his path blocked by Dr. Colin, who was gathering his papers with uncharacteristic slowness. Something in his covert glance caused Tom to realize that he should wait patiently.

Once everyone had left the conference room, Colin turned to Tom and said, “Stay here for a minute,” closing the conference room’s door.

Tom was certain he was about to be severely reprimanded for failing to listen to the briefing, especially since Colin’s expression was quite grave.

“Did the intruder succeed in accessing the Ronnie study?” he asked.

“Not at all,” Tom replied. “All the material on Ronnie is still on the computer in the locked lab in which Ronnie’s kept in cold storage. We’re still not keeping any material that pertains to him in our main lab. Anyway, the intruder only accessed the material protected by the general lab password, the one that’s familiar to all lab employees and is also listed with the department secretary, just in case.”

“Excellent,” Colin said. “And where are you in the Ronnie study?”

“I’d say we have over 80 percent of his DNA sequence.”

“That’s great. Way to go! We have to continue to maintain the utmost confidentiality. Have you already compared it to the human genome?”

“We’re doing that right now. The DNA isn’t sequential but fragmented, so the comparison will take a while longer,” Tom replied.

“Update me in person the moment you know anything. You and I have to find out who provided the intruder with the computer password and the entrance codes to the building and to the lab. Someone at the university was an accessory to the break-in. I suspect everyone, and I don't want anyone to know that we're conducting an investigation as well. We'll make sure to meet using various excuses as necessary."

Tom nodded and exited the room. It was now after noon. The house would be empty at this time, he thought, and he couldn't sleep anyway considering his agitated state of mind. It would be better if he went back to the lab and talked to his team. But the best option in his current condition was to meet Melissa, who lived near the university.

"Yes, of course, I'm waiting for you," Melissa replied when he called her assistant. It turned out she had been working all night on funded research, and so she had gotten out of bed late.

Her entire body was still sleep-warm. All Tom's fatigue evaporated and disappeared when his body submerged into the soft, caressing, fragrant warmth of his lover. The two moved together wordlessly until reaching their peaks, disproving the most basic laws of mathematics by establishing that one plus one could equal much more than two. The sweet hour of slumber that followed and the sandwich she prepared for him charged him with renewed energy.

***

He spent the short route back to the university pondering recent events. Melissa hadn't asked a single question about the incident he had recounted for her. She seemed satisfied with his brief description, and said she would not burden him with questions at a time like this. Odd, he thought, and not like her at all.

The bustle outside the lab building and within its corridors had subsided. Apparently, everyone had returned to their own tasks. He hoped he would be able to sit quietly in the lab and talk to his team.

However, when he opened the door, he was startled to find the lab full of people whose eyes all turned toward him. Tom recognized researchers and assistants from neighboring labs, as well as several administrative employees. Other than Lise, who was talking quietly to a researcher from an adjacent lab whose name he couldn't remember, everyone else seemed glum and silent. It occurred to Tom to ask them politely to leave the lab. However, this turned out to be unnecessary since, one by one, the guests departed quietly, leaving behind only his team, whose eyes were still turned in his direction.

Tom dragged his chair to the open area in the middle of the lab and sat down. Everyone followed his lead, creating a half-circle around him. The facts were known to everyone; there was no point repeating them.

Tom looked directly at those around him and said, "The most terrible thing is a human life cut short by a murderer. The police will take care of the investigation. Our contribution will take two forms. First, we'll visit Oleg's family and help them receive any sort of help they might need."

"We can sort of adopt his two kids and bring them to classes at the university, or help them with their schoolwork," Lynn suggested.

"Great idea," he agreed. "Second, we have to do our best to assist the police investigative team, both by answering their questions and by conducting any mental analysis we can carry out ourselves. There's no doubt the killer used inside information pertaining to the university and the lab. Someone here helped the perpetrator, knowingly or unknowingly. We could help uncover his potential accessories, and thus provide the investigators with a lead that might eventually expose the killer."

His eyes met Amy's. She swallowed visibly. Apparently, up until that moment, it hadn't occurred to her that she was being viewed as a possible accessory to murder. It seemed as if even contemplating this was extremely hard for her. Mike and Lise maintained their solemn expressions. They had come to this realization themselves, or perhaps it had been hinted at during the meeting with the dean and the university director, while Tom had drifted away on his own train of thought and lost touch with what was happening in the room. Lynn's frozen stare did not provide any indication about what was going on in her mind. Tom could not penetrate her glazed expression.

"I suggest that tomorrow morning, we begin our weekly discussion with the subject of the murder. Later in the day, each of us will try to come up with circumstances in which we might have revealed the password to the lab's central computer."

***

It was after six p.m. when he got home. Kate hugged him tightly, sat him down at the kitchen table, and said, "Let's start with family stuff. We can discuss what happened later."

As he sat down, Jennifer, their youngest daughter, and Lynn, their eldest, galloped in and assumed their usual places, Jennifer on his left leg and Lynn on his right. Both of them immediately began to recount their experiences from the day, without listening to each other, naturally. He had often wondered why they stuck so faithfully to this exact seating arrangement.

By the time they had finished tending to the girls and could finally sit and talk quietly, it was after nine o'clock. Tom summarized the main events within several minutes. Kate was quiet as she processed what she had just heard.

"It looks like you covered all the main investigation directions I can think of. You must be exhausted after a sleepless night and going through all that. Go to bed. I'll take care of the kitchen and the house."

Tom fell asleep before his body even hit the bed.

CHAPTER 8

Ethan

Chicago, Friday, July 18, 2036

Dr. Ethan Almog couldn't believe his eyes. The calibration and testing phase of the space telescope array had ended recently, and the three-dimensional image representing a volume of space with a radius of about a thousand light-years was hovering right in front of him. Based on a very conservative estimate, this volume of space contained more than ten million stars, about a fourth of them M-type stars like Earth's sun, and a third of them K-type stars that are smaller than the sun.

Slowly, he typed in "STA264987," the temporary name given to the star in the Cygnus constellation, revealed only through the space telescope array. Astronomers would need many years to classify the abundance of stars that the space telescope had detected, some of which barely emitted light.

The display began to change. The effect resembled the motion of a spaceship through the universe, with stars passing quickly and disappearing until the motion slowed down, focusing on a bright star similar to others floating across the display area. Several pale planets could be clearly discerned at varying distances from the star. He still hadn't gotten used to the space telescope array's amazing capabilities. The ability to actually watch planets located hundreds of light-years away had been considered science fiction up to this point. Briefly, he savored the sight, and then typed in "STA264987B."

The spaceship resumed its motion, focusing on the planet that was second-closest to the sun. The planet slowly transformed from a dim spot of light to a pale circle, growing gradually until it looked like a bluish, blurry marble, about a half inch in diameter. *I wonder what life looks like over there,* he thought. Indeed, scientists were certain it did contain carbon-based life forms. The spectrum of the planet's atmosphere indicated the presence of oxygen and carbon dioxide, corroborating this conclusion. That was all they knew at this stage.

Even during the lifespan of Hubble, the first space telescope, scientists and engineers who dreamed of directly observing distant planets began to toss around an idea that seemed to verge on science fiction: an immense array of telescopes deployed across space, over an area of ten square kilometers (about four square miles). The resolution of such an array would exceed Hubble's by a factor of more than ten million. Calculations showed that the resolution enabled by the array's immense scale and the use of enhanced imaging techniques would allow direct observations of planets whose size approximated Earth's that were located hundreds of light-years away, which could then be viewed at a quality similar to viewing Jupiter with the Hubble telescope.

In light of the large number of planets discovered using transit photometry, which reveals only about 1 percent of a star's possible planets, the expectation was to find a deluge of Earth-like planets for which the chances of discovering signs of life were significant. The spectroscopic (Doppler) method was also suitable for only 40 percent of the possible planets per star. Most feasible planets were outside the range of the traditional methods of detection. The space telescope array (STA) was designed to discover any feasible planet, regardless of its orbital plane around its host star, as well as to analyze its atmosphere. Gradually, the dream became reality. All components of the STA had been in orbit for about two years now. The necessary calibration and initialization process was long and exhaustive, due to the almost unimaginable precision required.

The observation data—analyzed and deciphered since the array was deployed, and even more intensely in recent months—had become a daily news item in many papers throughout the world. The data showed that most sun-like stars had well-developed planetary systems. An analysis of their atmosphere showed that many were gigantic gas stars resembling Jupiter and Saturn and even exceeding them in size. Many others had atmospheres resembling those of the ancient Earth: water vapor, carbon dioxide, and nitrogen. However, the major surprise was the scarcity of planets with an atmosphere containing significant amounts of oxygen, indicating the presence of biological life processes resembling life on Earth. In fact, in the entire, immense volume of space that had been scanned, only two planets were found with atmospheres resembling that of Earth, with significant amounts of oxygen and not much carbon dioxide. Both were found in the "Goldilocks" or habitable zone, the orbital range in which distance from the sun enabled surface temperatures that allowed the existence of water in a liquid state.

How disappointing, he thought, *two planets exhibiting signs of life orbiting only two out of a hundred thousand suns.* Even odder was the fact that the orbits of the two planets as well as the other planets within their solar system were almost circular, a clear contrast to the eccentric orbits in most other planetary systems.

At the beginning of the era of planetary discovery, only particularly heavy planets, whose distance from their sun was short and whose orbital year was brief, lasting several days or fewer, had been discovered. Initially, this had been attributed to the method of detection, relying on the Doppler Effect, which revealed the oscillation of the sun observed in relation to Earth. The low sensitivity of the equipment available at the time enabled only the discovery of planets that deflected their suns significantly and in a short, rapid cycle. Small planets similar to Earth in size, with an orbital year resembling our own in length, could not be detected by such means.

The second era was characterized by dedicated telescopes designed to detect planets whose orbits obscured their suns, as seen from Earth. At the forefront of this movement was the Kepler space observatory, which had discovered thousands of planets of this kind, despite the minute probability of detection.

At the time, astronomers had been surprised by the high prevalence of planetary systems in general, and in particular by the large number of multiplanetary systems. In light of this fact, some astronomers came to the conclusion that life was highly common in the universe, and that soon humanity would join the greater community of cultures in the Milky Way galaxy.

Only two planets with signs of life other than Earth in such an immense volume of space; so little life in the universe, Ethan thought glumly. *And now, try to figure out how many such planets were needed in order for sentient life to develop on one of them.* It was indeed highly disappointing. His face tinted with displeasure, he continued to watch the bluish planet.

As he walked to the large conference room in preparation for the weekly team meeting, he recalled a recent statement from Gerry, a fellow astronomer, who claimed to have come across a discovery that would have a major impact on the human race. *I wonder what he's found that could impact humanity,* he reflected. During the past year, since observations of a previously unprecedented quality had begun coming in, Gerry had started to isolate himself, hardly talking to those around him. He had behaved like someone studying a unique topic that he did not wish to share with others until it was verified beyond a doubt. *What revolutionary discovery was possible in asteroid research?* Ethan thought to himself.

As usual, the meeting was conducted by Robert Shepard, head of NASA's Extraterrestrial Life Study Division, or, as it was affectionately known, LGM (short for Little Green Men), a nickname with which the division was saddled in light of the meager results of the search for extraterrestrial intelligent life forms. The research had been going on for decades, entailing an immense investment of resources, and unfortunately, yielding no results.

There was very little that was new to be found in the reports of the various presenters. Most of the attendees were already familiar with the majority of data, although during the meeting, it was arranged and presented in the appropriate factual order. Only five minutes were allocated to the last item on the agenda. Everyone was already exhausted after two hours of a meeting regurgitating known facts when Bob instructed Gerry to take over. Only then did the attendees notice that Gerry was not present at the meeting.

"That's odd," Bob said. "Gerry was so insistent about speaking to us. It's strange that he never showed up for the meeting."

No one present seemed to bemoan the absence of one more presentation, and everyone was happy to disperse a few minutes early. *It is very strange*, Ethan thought. Gerry had seemed highly eager to present his findings. He also wasn't the absentminded type who would forget to show up for the meeting. Perhaps he had uncovered an error in his calculations and changed his mind, or was totally immersed in recalculating his discovery. *It makes sense to check his office*, he thought, turning toward it. The door to Gerry's office was locked, which was odd as well. Only unusual circumstances could have caused him not to show up on a day in which he was scheduled to present his work to all of the teams.

CHAPTER 9

Gerry

Chicago, Friday, July 18, 2036

Gerry woke up and tried to open his eyes. The effort produced a sharp pain in his right eye. He tried again, unsuccessfully. He was engulfed by darkness. Gradually, recent events surfaced in his memory, as he tried to process what had happened to him. The last thing he remembered clearly was stopping briefly in front of the bakery whose delicacies he was so fond of, although he usually tended to avoid them. At that moment, he had felt as if he deserved a treat.

This was the day on which he was going to make history. This was the day when he would unveil the discovery on which he had been working over the last few years at the team meeting. The work had intensified during the last year, since amazingly precise images of objects in Earth's solar system had begun to be generated by the

STA. Humanity would never look the same again. His presentation, which included the observation data saved online, was his invitation to the annals of the human race.

At that point, he remembered the vehicle that had hit him as he'd exited his car. True, he hadn't exactly been focused on his surroundings, but he was always careful. Caution was an autonomous function within him. He didn't have to focus on leaving his vehicle carefully.

It had been a light delivery van, of the kind often seen on the streets. Apparently, its driver had also been trying to stop parallel to the cars parked at the side of the road, and therefore had driven too close to Gerry's vehicle and ended up hitting him.

He cautiously moved his right hand, brushing it across his face. His entire head appeared to be bandaged. Bandages also covered his chest and his left thigh. His hand could not reach any further. Any attempt to touch his feet was unsuccessful. He couldn't bend forward. Vaguely, he heard indistinct sounds of speech around him. He focused his full attention on trying to understand what was being said, but could not manage to do so; the sounds resembled a jumble of words in a foreign language. He tried to call out to the speakers, but a sharp stab of pain in his left ribs made it clear to him that he'd be better off keeping his silence. In his distress, Gerry moved his hand up and down, wiggling his fingers in the hope that someone would approach him.

The sounds of mumbling stopped briefly, replaced by voices that grew louder and more distinct. "He's awake," he managed to make out, hearing a familiar female voice. A soft hand gripped his own, and the voice of his daughter, now clear again, whispered next to his right ear.

"How are you, Dad? What happened?"

He touched his bandaged mouth with the finger of his right hand, signaling that he couldn't talk.

"You were injured, Dad. We still can't remove the bandage on your head. I'll get hold of some paper and a pen right now, so you can write it down for me."

Within seconds, he felt a pen being thrust into his hand, as the hand was elevated and placed on a surface apparently containing a piece of paper. With considerable effort, he managed to steady his hand and write.

Condition my is?

"A car hit you while going full speed, and threw you about fifteen feet forward. Luckily for you, there wasn't too much traffic at the time," Elaine said. "You have a head injury that caused a brain hemorrhage. You were unconscious for half a day; the doctors couldn't estimate the extent of brain damage. They said that if you woke up and communicated, that would prove your brain had overcome the pressure that had affected it. That's also why your ears aren't bandaged. I think you'll survive the accident. Other than the head injury, you also have cuts on your face and lips, a crack in your left thighbone, and four cracked ribs. Other than that, you're just fine," she added sarcastically.

When talk? he wrote.

"The bandages will be taken off your head in a day," she replied. "Your general condition is stable. You won't have to be hospitalized for too long."

Suddenly, he experienced a wave of alertness and mental clarity that felt unprecedented. The white van that had been following him since the moment he left his home. The vehicle he could see in his rearview mirror every time he looked, but to which he paid no attention. The vehicle that had slowed down when he had slowed down, stopping to buy a pastry. It was the same van that had apparently sped up when he exited his car, and hit him.

The vividness of the memory was amazing. The images were etched into his mind, as if he were watching a movie, or more accurately, as if he were experiencing them again precisely at any moment he wanted to do so. He could focus on any detail of the event. He could clearly see the scratches in the paint on the front of the van, and the dusty windshield, through which he could see the silhouette of the dark-skinned driver. He could even read the license plate from any direction, as if it were literally in front of his eyes!

It hadn't been an accident at all. He had been hit deliberately! This immediately reminded him of the strange assistant call from last week, which he had tried to repress. The seemingly polite call, insinuating a threat not to distribute the results of his research. His shock when he realized that although he had maintained strict secrecy in regard to the details of his work and certainly about his findings, someone had found out about it. Someone was willing to go very far, including physical injury or even murder, to silence him.

Who had been following his work, and why? True, he hadn't gone overboard in maintaining confidentiality about his research. The material was saved on the computer, guarded by its general protections. And other than the single encoded copy he had carefully concealed, he had made no additional copies. He had not discussed the details of his work with anyone beyond the bare minimum required by NASA.

Who had access to NASA's general database? He was well acquainted with Jim and Larry, the maintenance engineers for the main server farm. Due to the workload that had expanded beyond their capacity to handle it, a third engineer, Robert, had recently been hired. Gerry hadn't had the chance to get to know him due to the many hours he'd been dedicating to his work during the last year. In fact, some gossip had surrounded Robert's hiring. The details floated in front of his eyes. More than twenty highly experienced candidates, both internal and external, had applied for the bid. The appointment of Robert, an inexperienced external candidate, had been met with much astonishment. Two experienced NASA employees who had applied for the job protested the odd choice, but he couldn't recall any reaction to their grievance. The entire story simply faded away, and had not been mentioned since. Strange indeed.

Had the purpose of injuring him been to murder him under the pretense of a car accident, or had it been another warning? Perhaps it was the last warning before he was truly eliminated? If it had been a murder attempt, the perpetrator surely knew of his condition, and that he had survived. The obvious conclusion was that his life was in danger now that he had awakened from his coma. Could he hide his recovery from this person?

On the other hand, if the assailant had wanted to finish him off, it seemed safe to assume he could have done so. Apparently, therefore, his attacker wasn't eager to commit murder. Perhaps he would assume that Gerry had been sufficiently warned, and would heed the unsubtle hint given to him, and avoid publishing his work. He wondered if the work was still saved in its entirety. Was the presentation he had prepared for the staff meeting still stored on the server? It was hard to know, although it made sense to assume that anyone who had uncovered the contents of his work could also delete it.

His lips curved in a brief smile. This was the epitome of irony.

The person who had injured him in an attempt to prevent his work from being published had probably deleted it as well. But his assailant hadn't foreseen the change in his brain which, among other things, had granted him a perfect eidetic memory. He could now easily reconstruct his work. The entire project hovered in front of his eyes as if he were watching it page by page, slide by slide. All he'd been missing was the images from the telescopes, but he remembered their archival references with utter precision, and so others could easily attach them.

The most important, urgent question was whether the incident had been a warning or an unsuccessful attempt at murder. What should he do if it had been attempted murder? How could he protect himself? Perhaps he should pretend to be a brain-damaged amnesiac? And perhaps he should add on a significant reduction of his mental capacities, as well. Would an announcement that he couldn't continue his research due to his head injury satisfy the assassin? Even if the man had tried to murder him, it seemed reasonable to assume that under such circumstances, he would now leave him alone. Perhaps he would continue to follow Gerry for a while until he came to the conclusion that he no longer posed a threat? Yes, that would be the path he would choose. No one had to know what his capacities were. He would behave toward everyone as if he had become brain damaged, his abilities diminished. He didn't consider abandoning his research even for a moment. He would find a way to publish his findings.

He wondered who was interested in suppressing such a groundbreaking discovery. Perhaps it wasn't a single individual? Could it be an organized group that would be harmed in some way by his revelation? He couldn't think of anyone that could be harmed by the discovery to an extent that would justify such investment and such risk. Who would be bothered by something taking place millions of miles away from Earth? Any attempt to delve further into this question only brought him to a dead end.

He found himself in a very odd position. On the one hand, his life was in danger, he was recuperating from a major accident, covered in bandages, including his eyes, and barely able to move his hands. On the other hand, he had been endowed with a major sense of illumination, cognitive sharpness and mnemonic capabilities at a level he had never possessed before. If he had been blessed with such abilities when he was a student, he could have finished his PhD thesis in one year instead of the four years he had ended up dedicating to it.

Perhaps this was how humanity's prominent geniuses—Newton, Einstein, and others—saw their environment. He didn't need the pages of his work in order to see its contents, the observations and orbital calculations that had led him to his oh-so-strange conclusion. He tried to mentally survey the calculations again, but other than slight inaccuracies in negligible terms, he could find no fault in them. The conclusion was unequivocal. This might be how Stephen Hawking had felt while working for years on the theoretical discovery of black hole radiation, all while being unable to move any part of his body other than his eyes and lips.

It was odd not to need an implement for writing such as a blackboard, paper, or computer. As he neared the end of his computations, he dedicated some time to assessing the latest astronomical discoveries, hoping to find further corroboration for his conclusions in previously unexplained astronomical phenomena. Unfortunately, he had been unable to dedicate sufficient time to such studies due to his intensive work. Now that he had the time, what he yearned for most was a computer terminal that would allow him to peruse astronomical websites and seek similar phenomena. If he did it at the hospital, he could not pretend to be brain damaged. He had to get out of there as soon as possible, and find anonymous access to the Web.

CHAPTER 10

The Funeral

Chicago, Friday, July 18, 2036

On his way to the university, Tom debated how to discuss the murder with his team. Should he gather them all for one meeting, or see each of them separately, one-on-one? Start today, or try to re-establish a routine, and deal with the murder occasionally during the week? He decided to talk to each of them personally in order to minimize the disruption to their work.

Fridays were usually his favorite days: the weekly summary meeting, everyone talking and snacking on offerings each of them had prepared, joking around and laughing a lot, and even going home early. It seemed unlikely that any of the team members had brought any treats today, which was a shame. Tom was very fond of the communal gathering, which also often yielded good pragmatic results. It wasn't a waste of time in the slightest. *Too bad it won't be like that today*, he thought. The meeting would probably run until the time of Oleg's funeral. *When you choose to embark on an academic career, the last thing you think about is being involved in a murder*.

Wrapped up in his own thoughts, Tom didn't notice the gray vehicle that had been tracking him since shortly after he had left his home. He also failed to register the gaze of the attractive female driver, which focused upon him at the traffic light before the entrance to the lab building.

His back bent and face flushed, he walked into the lab. Much to his surprise, he saw the conference table laid out as it was every Friday morning, with the entire team assembled around it.

"We decided to go back to our work routine as soon as possible," Lise said.

Tom, who didn't even try to hide his surprise, smiled and said, "I didn't know we were studying telepathy genes, and that we were the guinea pigs. You managed to precisely read my mind. We'll get back to the matter of the murder next week. But for now, on to the weekly summaries. Mike, get us started, please."

"We've identified several control sequences near genes producing blood vessels. We're looking into which of them is responsible for increased production of blood vessels. We're very optimistic about attaining a positive identification for at least one of them. A positive result here would be an important breakthrough."

The lively technical discussion developing in response to Mike's statement was exactly what they needed in order to get back to the atmosphere of the days preceding the murder. Lynn provided a detailed description of the Sisyphean work required to examine the effect of each control sequence on the gene's function, the environmental data in the experiments, and the anguish of each failure. Tom's thoughts couldn't help but drift to the not-so-distant days in which researchers had to physically examine the effect of each sequence. The number of options was astronomical, and each study of this kind lasted years and employed numerous researchers. Today there were computers capable of eliminating most of the improbable options within a short time, thus leaving researchers with only a tiny portion of the original ocean of possibilities.

The discussion and the snacking continued until Tom put a stop to them. "It's noon. We have to leave for the funeral. I'd be happy if someone would accompany me. We don't need more than two people, so as not to burden the family."

The change of atmosphere was a tough one. The alert, lively crew in which everyone offered contributions and opinions instantly became unanimously silent and morose.

On their way to the parking lot, Tom and Lise passed through the administrative offices. Once he heard of their destination, Steve asked to join them in his capacity as Oleg's direct manager. Tom's personal assistant guided him among the cars in the parking lot until he found the university vehicle allocated to him. He didn't need a key; the assistant communicated with the car, allowing him access to it.

The funeral procession departed from the clearing in front of the lab building. A short caravan of cars accompanied the vehicle bearing the coffin all the way to Oak Woods Cemetery. The ceremony was understated and brief. Eddie, Oleg's brother, spoke on behalf of the family. With a distinct Russian accent, yet in eloquent English that surprised the funeral-goers, Eddie portrayed his brother as loyal and dedicated to his family. He described how hard it had been for him to support his family after he had been forced to leave his home, his job, and his assets in Ukraine and arrive penniless in the United States. He expressed his hope that Oleg's employer would take on the care of his family and children.

Tom, who eulogized Oleg on behalf of the employees of the lab building in which the murder had taken place, aimed his comments at law enforcement authorities and expressed his certainty that they would do everything in their power to catch the killer. The last speaker, university dean Professor Paul Longstrom, promised a full scholarship at the university for both of Oleg's sons, in whichever faculty they chose to study.

Once the ceremony was over, as they were headed for their vehicles, Eddie approached Tom, thanking him warmly for taking part in the funeral and for what he had said in his eulogy.

"All of us at the lab will do whatever we can to help Oleg's sons. It's the least we could do," Tom promised. "I didn't know a thing about you before this. What do you do?"

"Like many others, you were probably surprised by my fluent English."

"I was," Tom replied.

"I was head of the English department at Odessa University in Ukraine, where I was also a professor of linguistics."

"Very impressive," Tom said. "And what do you do here in the States?"

"I'm a linguistics lecturer at Loyola University. I'm also a member of NASA's think tank on communication with extraterrestrial life forms, which is preparing for the time when such contact materializes."

"Definitely impressive," Tom responded, and parted from Eddie with a friendly handshake. There was no point in going back to the university after such a barrage of events; nothing would happen if he cut his workday short today and returned home earlier than usual.

On his way home, after the funeral and after saying goodbye to Steve and Lise, he found himself envisioning the faces of Oleg's two small children as they realized their father would never return from work. It was undoubtedly the hardest moment in that long, exhausting 24-hour period.

As he approached his home, he noticed that the entrance to the garage was blocked by a supermarket delivery truck, which was unloading cartons at the entrance to the house. For a moment, he couldn't understand what they were doing here, until he recalled that Kate was hosting a garden party at their home on Saturday afternoon. Having no other choice, he was parking his car on the other side of the road when the assistant rang. Lise was on the other end of the line.

"I sent you a news item from CNN. It's important that you read it."

"What is it exactly? I just got home. I'll read it when I have the time," Tom replied.

"No. This is very urgent!" Lise was almost shouting, her voice loud and tense. "You have to drop everything and read it immediately."

"Murder in Academia" and "The Life of Methuselah, Available to All" were only two of the prominent headers in the story. "The pharmaceutical industry, in cooperation with various academic partners, is developing a process that will double the human lifespan," read the sub-header in a story that opened with a description of the murder that had taken place at the University of Chicago and immediately proceeded to describe the far-reaching repercussions of research to expand human longevity. The story was by Robert Collins, the *Chicago Tribune*'s science writer, and did not include any clue to the source of the information. Neither did it mention the University of Chicago by name in the context of the scientific research, leaving any connection to be made by the reader, rather than the reporter.

Tom leaned back in his chair, closing his eyes. The story did not mention any names. It seemed informative, and other than a few words regarding the murder of the security guard, did not appear related to the break-in, other than its timing. Should he inform Detective Heller of this? Interrogate the reporter himself regarding his sources? Do both?

Kate's loud address drew him out of his thoughts, returning him to reality. "Hey, Tommy, what's going on? You look upset, and you've barely said hi to me. Did another terrible thing happen?"

"There's an item on CNN about the murder at the university. They wrote about a study aimed to significantly enhance human longevity being carried out in various labs. There are no names mentioned, no technical details, and no reference to us," Tom concluded.

The topic did not come up again throughout the evening or the next day.

CHAPTER 11

Gerry at the Hospital

Chicago, Friday, July 18, 2036

No doubt about it—no one must know about his new abilities, Gerry decided. This included Elaine, his beloved daughter, although if he continued to act confused, it would cause her much pain. But he had no other choice. Later, when he felt his life and perhaps the lives of his loved ones as well were no longer in danger, he would tell her. He justified his actions to himself, thinking that the bottom line was that he was also protecting her. This was it. He had to start constructing his image as someone who was brain damaged.

Tell me sings, he scrawled on the sheet of paper.

"When they called me from the hospital, I left a conference at work and got here as soon as I could. They didn't tell me what your condition was, only that you'd been injured in a car accident, and that they couldn't yet determine the extent of the long-term damage."

He didn't have to make an effort to scrawl illegibly. His condition after the accident, in combination with writing from a prone position while unable to see the page, was enough. Only the spelling and style errors were intentional, meant to demonstrate the damage his brain had sustained.

Were I m? The truth was that he had soon grown accustomed to his writing pose, but had to keep up the pretense that he could not think clearly. Therefore, he wrote slowly. Although he could not see what or how he was writing, he could still sense when he was writing over a previously written word. In short, he adopted the sort of confused writing appropriate for the kind of condition he wanted to impersonate.

Right hopsital wich?

"You're at the new Johns Hopkins Hospital. Everything's shiny and new here. The doctors are young, too, talented and up-to-date on everything. You're getting excellent treatment, Dad."

Gerry continued to scrawl out words without acknowledging her. *Cantremember nothin always care,* he jotted.

"Dad, you're tired. You should probably rest and not overdo it. You're still disoriented from the accident and from the sedatives they gave you. I'm staying at the hospital, but please try to get some rest."

He would continue to play dumb, he resolved.

Wanthom home, he scribbled.

The doctor had warned her of the most awful of possibilities, that her father, the smartest man she knew, the astronomy professor whose sharp mind was admired by all of his students, might lie here, injured and helpless, scribbling confused words. But perhaps things might get better. He was still under the influence of the anesthesia. It was a good idea to wait a bit, and see how he behaved in a day or two. In the meantime, he should continue to have company, and be encouraged to interact with his surroundings as much as possible, considering his limitations.

"Dad, what do you remember about the accident and what happened right before it?"

This time, the scrawl was a bit clearer. Apparently, he was getting accustomed to writing despite being unable to see the written words.

Acident alwayscareful hohome.

Her heart contracted painfully within her. Her elderly father behaving like a little boy. Although some of this was expected, she found the reality itself very hard to handle. She was flooded by childhood memories. She was holding the hand of her big, strong father, who towered high, high above her as he took her to nursery school. How she had been startled when the neighbor's dog from across the street barked at her, causing her to burst into tears, and then her big daddy had swept her up in the air, hugged and kissed her until she calmed down. In his sturdy arms, she was not afraid of the dog. She was protected by this big, strong man.

And now, the man she so admired, the smartest man in the world, was covered in bandages, unable to move, and scrawling muddled words, while she, the little one, was playing the part of the responsible adult. She found the role reversal hard to handle. Even as her father grew older and even a bit aged, and while she herself gained knowledge, working in the company of brilliant people, her father was still one of the smartest people she knew, and she continued to admire him for his wisdom and the unconditional support he provided her. He was always there for her. Always listening attentively to what she had to say, always willing to advise and explain and persuade. He never imposed his opinion on her. When he disagreed with her, he always tried to convince her, and even when he was unsuccessful, he never withheld his support or his encouragement.

"Dad, you're always careful. I'm sure you were driving carefully this time, too. The police investigators are still looking into the circumstances of the accident. I'm sure they'll discover it wasn't your fault at all. But unfortunately, accidents happen because of other, less cautious drivers. You're still under the influence of sedatives and painkillers. It's important for the doctors to monitor you at the hospital for a day or two until your condition stabilizes. And as I've said, I'll be by your side until they release you from the hospital, so you'll feel almost like you're home anyway. The way it used to be, a long time ago, when I was little and the entire family was home together."

The mention of family reminded her that she had yet to inform her mother and her brother of the accident. She had to let them know immediately. Her level-headed, calm mother asked a few questions about Gerry's condition and immediately let her know that she was on her way to pick up her brother, and would go from there to the hospital.

Her father's slow, steady breathing indicated that he had fallen asleep. *Good*, she thought. Let him rest until her mother and brother arrived. He would need plenty of energy in order to deal with them.

***

She was awakened by the low murmur of speech. Her mother and Ben were standing next to her father's bed, whispering to each other. For a moment, she considered feigning sleep, so she would not be required to explain everything she knew and withstand her inquisitive mother's cross-examination. However, this option faded away once her brother noticed she had opened her eyes.

Slowly and quietly, they left the room for the corridor, where she told them everything she knew. About the accident, the injuries, the doctors' uncertainty about the extent of the damage to his brain, and particularly about his confused state, which she believed and hoped was a result of the anesthetics that were still affecting his system. Uncharacteristically, her mother asked no questions. Apparently, the shock she had suffered was still affecting her.

Without exchanging another word, the three of them returned quietly to the hospital room, standing opposite her father's bed. About ten minutes later, a tall, dark-skinned doctor entered the room, wearing a suit under his white lab coat. He nodded at them, skimmed through the chart affixed to the bed, checked the flow in the IV, and left without saying a word.

Elaine's mother, Ramona, was the first to react. "What kind of attitude is that? A doctor comes in, examines the patient, sees his family members standing there waiting upon his every word, doesn't say a thing, and just takes off?"

"How do you know he's a doctor?" Ben whispered slowly. The two women's eyes flitted to him briefly.

"Of course, he's a doctor." Her mother raised her voice somewhat. "He has to be a doctor. Why would just anyone be examining Dad at the hospital? He's also old enough, wearing a suit and a white lab coat. Of course, he's a doctor. I don't think an orderly or a male nurse would wear a suit to work. He must be your dad's attending physician," she concluded. This was probably more in order to convince herself than out of actual certainty, Elaine thought.

“His ID badge was upside down. You couldn’t read his name or his position,” Ben said, emphasizing every word.

“What do you mean?” Ramona asked.

“I don’t mean anything. I’m just listing the facts.”

“Let’s all ask to talk to the attending physician. We’ll learn a lot that way,” Elaine urged her family.

“You’ll have to wait about half an hour,” a nurse at the nurses’ station informed them. “No, there’s no tall, dark-skinned doctor in this unit. There’s also no reason for a doctor from a different unit to go into one of our patients’ rooms without coordinating with us.”

“That’s very strange. What could all this be about?” Ramona asked, but received no reply. Both her children were uncommunicative, concerned about their father and now also apprehensive about this new unclear development. Who was the man? Was he even a doctor? If so, who had sent him, and why? And perhaps he was not a doctor at all? What, then, had he been checking? Had he wanted to harm their father, and only their presence had saved him?

“This is really weird,” Ben told the nurse. “A few minutes ago, that man entered my father’s room wearing a white lab coat, with his ID tag turned the wrong way. He checked the patient chart and the IV, then left. He never said a word.”

“Wait here. I’ll call Security.”

“Dad has to be watched constantly until we know what’s going on here,” Ben said, turning back toward his father’s room.

Elaine and her mother sat down in the soft seats of the waiting room adjacent to the nurses’ station. A few minutes later, the hospital’s head of security arrived, introducing himself as Larry. Ramona described the odd visit in her husband’s room to him, and conveyed the family's concern regarding a possible assault.

"Is there anyone in his room right now?" he asked.

"My son is there."

"Okay, he should stay there for now. Meanwhile, I'll set up constant monitoring of his room and raise his security level."

Following a few keystrokes on the assistant, a hologram of Gerry's room appeared in front of their eyes. Elaine could be seen entering the room. Gerry was writing something with considerable effort, to which Elaine was replying.

"You can move back and forth in time until we see the strange doctor," Larry said.

Elaine fast-forwarded the hologram until she could freeze a clear visual hologram image of the man. A few more keystrokes resulted in his images beginning to appear throughout the hospital. He was seen coming in through the main entrance, wearing a suit and holding a small cloth bag in his hand. His image then appeared in several locations on his way to Gerry's room. He was spotted opposite the restroom, and in the next hologram was seen exiting it wearing a white lab coat and a badge, but without his bag. Larry paused the holograms' progress and asked his subordinate to locate the bag, which had apparently been left in the restroom, hoping he would find some clue there.

He then proceeded to the holograms from the parking lots and the entrance. The best hologram showed the man in the suit opening the door of a taxi.

"That's great. We can locate the taxi and scan its camera. That way we can find out where he was driving the man. There might also be some clue in the bag he left in the restroom."

Elaine loved her mother, appreciated her wisdom, and shared her own life with her, but she also suffered from her mother's critical nature, her excessive nosiness, and her relentless stream of questions on any topic, however trivial. Elaine often avoided consulting her on various issues. This was a trait in which she truly didn't wish to resemble her. This time, however, her mother was sitting silently, wrapped up in her own thoughts. Although she did not withhold her critical barbs from her husband, she loved him very much and was having a hard time coping with his condition.

The doctor who arrived to update them looked nothing like the imposter who had come in to check up on her father. Elaine asked Ben to join them, and the three of them stood in the corridor across from the door to Gerry's room, listening as the doctor repeated the diagnosis Elaine had already conveyed to them almost word for word.

"You probably want to hear some possible assessments of how his condition is going to change in the short and long term."

"Right. That's all that matters right now," Ramona said.

"Well, the physical damage to his body isn't very severe, and he's expected to recuperate at least somewhat within several days. We'll be removing most of the bandages tomorrow morning, so he will be able to see, talk, and of course eat. His mobility will be limited because of the cracked bones. We're not planning to put any casts on any part of his body. He'll receive treatment to accelerate the reknitting of bones, and within a day or two, his discomfort when moving will decrease.

"As for the head injury, the internal hemorrhage in the brain has been addressed. We drained the blood that accumulated in his skull, and now we have to wait for him to bounce back. At this stage, it's hard to assess the damage his brain has sustained."

"I communicated with him," Elaine interrupted him. "I talked to him and he answered me in writing, on a piece of paper. His writing was confused, but generally comprehensible. I think our dialogue tired him out, and he fell asleep. I hope the confusion is a result of the anesthesia he was under, and not permanent brain damage."

"Sounds excellent," the doctor said. "In our experience, brain cells are flexible, and can withstand temporary pressure compressing them for a short period of time. We'll know a lot more tomorrow. I'll be happy to talk to you again then."

The three of them returned to the room quietly, but apparently, the sound of the closing door woke Gerry, who waved hello.

"Hi, Dad," Elaine and Ben called out almost simultaneously.

"Hi, Gerry," Ramona exclaimed.

He reacted immediately, signaling them to come to him. Elaine thrust a pen into his hand and laid a sheet of paper under it.

Mona Bn hi, Gerry wrote, and then continued to scribble. *Got hert car hitme cant ta lk howaryou?*

Elaine's eyes met Ramona's.

"We came as soon as Elaine let us know," Ramona began. "We talked to the doctor. They'll be taking most of your bandages off tomorrow and you'll be able to see us and talk, too. Does anything hurt? Do you want us to ask the nurse or the doctor for anything? Should I bring you anything from home tomorrow?"

Doing good, dontneed nothing, justhome, he scrawled.

"Maybe, if he really is doing so much better, the doctor will let him go home as soon as tomorrow?" Elaine asked, speaking to herself more than to anyone else.

The family continued to conduct a slow, confused exchange with Gerry. The man whose writing had been immaculate, without a single spelling mistake, was now writing with multiple spelling and grammatical errors, some of which were a result of being unable to see what he was writing, while others apparently resulted from mental confusion. He was interested to know whether anyone from the university had called.

"Actually, no one there knows about the accident. Ethan tried to contact me, but I rejected the call," Ramona said. "Tomorrow's Saturday. I'll let Ethan know tonight." She wanted to know Gerry's opinion of Ethan. "Should I tell him everything and encourage him to come visit, or would you prefer some peace and quiet here?" she asked.

Not here, justhome, he scrawled.

"Okay, I'll let him know you were injured, that you'll be released from the hospital soon, and that in the meantime, you want to rest as much as possible. There's no rush."

Gerry confirmed this with a hand gesture. *What is she thinking?* he wondered. *Is she buying my confusion? She's known me for decades now. I wonder if I can fool her, too. I have to do everything I can to get out of here as soon as possible.*

Wanthome, he scribbled.

Ramona leaned in toward him and whispered in his ear. "I love you and I want you home. I'll make sure you come home the moment it's an option. In the meantime, try to rest and sleep as much as you can. You've worked very hard in the last year. At least make use of this time to get some rest. We'll let you be. We'll take turns staying here so there's always a family member at the hospital. That's it. Good night."

Ramona urged her children to leave the room with her. A security guard armed with a gun was already stationed across from the entrance, along with a technician who was preparing to install a security lock on the door to the room.

Outside in the waiting area, Ramona told her children she

would stay at the hospital to keep watch, and that they should call her tomorrow morning. Her good friend Lucy would book a room for her at the hotel operated by the hospital.

Ramona returned to Gerry's room and sat down in an armchair. Her man looked so quiet and helpless, she thought, examining him. This was the first time he had ever been admitted to a hospital, and she was the one in charge of him. Up to now, their roles had been reversed. She was the one who had been hospitalized three times, for two births and an appendectomy. He had been so worried every time, so devoted to her, running off immediately to fulfill her every wish. Now he was lying there, injured all over, and who knew when and how he would get better.

On their way out, all of them left their contact information at the front desk, just in case.

Despite the late hour on a Friday evening, Ethan answered immediately. Ramona gave him a brief update and encouraged him to call at any time.

Saturday, July 19, 2036

The moment she woke up at the hotel, Ramona called the hospital.

"It was a quiet night. No point in arriving before ten o'clock, since he'll be undergoing treatment. Yes, the security guard is still stationed at the door. Don't worry," were the answers she received.

The guard was a different man than the one she had seen yesterday; apparently, there had been a change of shift. He let her in only after thoroughly verifying her identity as well as receiving video confirmation from Larry, the head of security, who insisted on taking a good look at her before authorizing her entry. She decided she found the security arrangements satisfactory, and quietly opened the door to the room.

At first, she thought she had entered the wrong room. She found Gerry propped up on the bed, which was raised into a sitting position, with all his bandages gone. The only indications of the accident he had been through were several small Band-Aids on his head and face and his somewhat swollen left hand. His broad grin expressed the pleasure he felt at her surprise.

"Wow," she blurted out. "What a transformation!"

"I c-c-can even t-t-talk," he replied, his voice shaky and weak.

Ramona was stunned. On the one hand, he looked much better without all the bandages that had covered most of his body. On the other hand, she had expected the confusion he exhibited yesterday to dissipate. However, although she was starting to feel worried, she decided to express joy and encourage him to talk, hoping that the more he talked, the sooner he would return to himself, the brilliant, eloquent man with whom she'd been living for many years now.

"I can't believe it. What an amazing recovery. Way to go, modern medicine! How do you feel? Are you in pain? Can you move?"

"N-n-no p-p-pain. They said m-m-my en-entire chest was s-s-stabilized. C-c-can't t-t-turn over b-by my-myself. Want h-h-h-ome; want h-h-home now!" Gerry concluded loudly.

"I'll go check with the nurse about when I can take you home."

Gerry concurred with a nod, adding loudly, "Q-q-quick, q-q-quick."

That's really all I need now, Ramona thought. *To bring home someone who is that brain-damaged.* Who knew how long it would take him to get better? Would his mind ever return to what it once was, or had his brain been irreparably damaged, and instead of a brilliant scientist, she was now stuck with a childish, stuttering, mentally challenged man for a husband? Also, had he winked at her while he was stammering, or had that been her imagination? Something in her well-developed female intuition sensed something, she wasn't sure what, but she felt that things weren't quite as they appeared. She would keep her eyes open and try to pick up on any small, unusual details. If Gerry was a part of some intrigue, he should be the one to determine the rules of the game.

"The hospital's Continuing Care department is currently rounding up all the equipment you'll need at home. They'll drive him home in about an hour," the nurse informed her.

She returned to give him the good news, with mixed feelings. "I'll let the kids know they should come home, rather than to the hospital, and that they can take their time. They can go on with their lives until this evening. I'll go home immediately to get your bed set up and to organize the house for your arrival."

On the way home, she talked to Ben and Elaine, who were happy about their father's rapid release from the hospital. Elaine wanted to know what his speech was like.

"The same way he was writing yesterday. He gets stuck and stutters when he's talking, too. I hope all these neurological symptoms are temporary, and Dad will be back to his old self soon." She did not consider, even for a minute, sharing her suspicions with them. She would not say a word to anyone, including to Gerry himself, but would continue monitoring him until she knew what was going on.

The hospital staff members were efficient and well practiced. He was transferred to a wheelchair very gently, with the assistance of a lifting robot, which elevated him gradually and slid him into the chair softly. This was significant progress indeed compared to the era when this work had been done by people, who often jostled and hurt the patients. The drive home was also smooth, with no bumping or pain. The innovative ambulances were equipped with shock absorbers and especially soft tires that glided over any bump on the road.

Within minutes of the time he arrived home, Gerry found himself relaxing in his bed in Ben's room, which had been converted into a study since Ben had left home. It was very roomy, especially after Ben had moved the large bed he so loved to his own apartment. Eventually, they had installed a twin bed in the room, where Gerry would sometimes nap.

"Did getting moved around, the ride, and being jostled hurt you?" Ramona asked as she sat down in the chair across from him and held his hand.

"N-n-not at all," he replied. "Ev-everything went c-c-completely s-s-smoothly." Once again, she fancied she saw the shadow of a cynical smile at the corner of his eye. "Is e-e-everyone gone?" he asked.

"Yes, we're finally alone again," she said, hoping he would react and solve the mystery. However, Gerry didn't respond and appeared to be nodding off. The transition seemed to have tired him out. She waited with his hand in hers until his breathing indicated he had fallen asleep, then let go of his hand and left the room.

CHAPTER 12

Gaya

Chicago, Saturday, July 19, 2036

Everyone was immersed in family meals and preparations for the garden party. Simple domestic preoccupations soothed Tom to such an extent that the topics of his work and the recent tragic events did not trouble him until the moment he found Mike standing at the threshold. For a moment, his surprise left him breathless. Once he came to his senses, he shook Mike's hand warmly, wondering who had invited him to the party. Kate was the only likely candidate; she was in charge of the invitations and the organization. However, Mike was not included in their usual coterie of guests. Apparently, Kate had decided to surprise him. And indeed, he found himself startled again several minutes later when Lise showed up, immediately followed by Lynn and Amy and their dates. He briefly had time to wonder what Kate's intentions had been in inviting his team before he was dragged off by his friends.

It was at the height of the party, while the juicy steaks were emitting an irresistible aroma, that his personal assistant rang.

"Am I speaking to Dr. Thomas Lester?" he heard an assertive female voice.

"You are," he replied, trying unsuccessfully to identify the speaker.

"I'm sorry to disrupt your weekend with business matters, but this is urgent. My name is Gaya. I represent a large organization with plenty of financial resources. We're well aware of the nature of your work. It's important that we meet soon and confer."

"I'm sorry. We're not allowed to discuss our work outside the university, especially in light of recent events. You'll have to contact me through the appropriate channels," he replied, reaching out to end the call. *Who would bug me with business concerns during the weekend?* he wondered, and then heard the woman's voice resuming.

"Don't hang up, Dr. Lester. Talk to me."

He returned the assistant to his ear very slowly, saying, "I don't have anything to add."

"We're aware of all the topics of your work. We're also familiar with your family, and in fact, with every aspect of your life. Meeting us won't cause you any harm. We have an offer I'm sure you'll be very interested in. Give us a chance to present it to you."

The reference to his family, as well as her tone, convinced him that complying would be advisable. He could always tell Rick or the dean all about it.

"Okay," he blurted out.

"When your wife is in hearing range, set up a game of golf with your cousin Bob for tomorrow, Sunday, at four p.m. at your usual course at the Beverly Country Club. Don't tell anyone about the meeting. Your car's computer has already been programmed with the route, including a vacant parking spot that will be waiting for you. From there, continue walking up the street in the same direction until you reach Bob's Pub. I'll be waiting for you there."

"And how will I recognize you?" he asked.

"Don't worry, you'll know it's me," she replied.

"How did you program the route into my car? You don't have the access code."

"See you tomorrow," she responded, ending the call.

"Who was that on the assistant?" Kate asked.

"Bob booked us a course for tomorrow afternoon," he answered. These people knew that he sometimes played golf with his cousin at Beverly Country Club. What else did they know about him?

Although he tried to immerse himself in domestic and familial matters, Tom could not stop thinking of the implied threat conveyed in the conversation. His greatest fear was that his work would end up harming his family.

Sunday, July 20, 2036

Their day of rest was a leisurely one. Everyone slept in, as was their custom on Sundays when they had no particular plans. To an outside observer, the house and its inhabitants appeared quite ordinary, resembling millions of other households in the United States.

It was several minutes after three thirty. Tom estimated he would arrive at the meeting shortly before four. Feeling utterly incredulous, he checked the navigation software. Indeed, the log featured a new route named "Gaya." Although he drove the way he did habitually, he found himself peering in the rearview mirror a lot more frequently than usual. *Which turns out to be a very good idea*, he thought as he noticed a vehicle following him. *They're tracking me.*

Kate and the kids were safe now, according to the plan he had worked out at night with Kate after he had told her about the call and his ensuing fears. She and the girls would be leaving in several minutes, supposedly to visit relatives in Manteno, a small, peaceful town about fifty miles south of Chicago. The home computer had been programmed to turn on the lights and the TV once evening came.

They kept an ancient, decrepit house in Manteno that Kate had inherited from her grandmother, and which they rarely used. The last time they had visited it was about two years ago. Laura, a childhood friend of Kate's, also lived in town with her family, and was always happy to have them over.

Kate hadn't challenged his proposal to disappear along with their children. The murder and the implied threat were enough to make both of them realize they were unwilling to put the girls' lives in danger. They had decided that she and the girls would board the train at a small station that was far from their home, where she could observe anyone else boarding, at a time when the train was generally not crowded. From there, they would continue to her friends' house in town so as not to reveal that her old house was inhabited once more.

The car tailing him disappeared at some point, only to be replaced by a different car that continued the surveillance. The people following him were serious, and had invested quite a lot in their actions, Tom thought. *Apparently, it's very important to them that I show up for the meeting*. However, if they were putting so many resources into tracking him, it was possible that Kate and the girls were under surveillance, too. This thought perturbed him. Kate was supposed to take a good look at the faces of the people boarding at the Van Buren Station and compare them to the people getting off the train at Manteno. In any case, it was a good idea for his family to be far away from him.

The automatic driver brought him to a typical middle-class residential neighborhood, featuring well-tended duplexes. The street resembled other streets in the neighborhood, and a parking spot opened at the exact moment the vehicle navigator announced that they had reached their destination. Bob's Pub was located at the beginning of a small high-end commercial strip that was a natural fit for the bucolic street.

Once his eyes had grown accustomed to the dimness inside, he discovered a small, intimate pub in which he immediately identified Gaya, who was awaiting his arrival. She was the only patron in the pub, which contained only a handful of tables, and her inviting gaze instantly made everything clear.

She was of Asian descent, probably Japanese, pretty but not particularly beautiful. She seemed ageless, the way many Asian women appear to Westerners, somewhere between thirty and fifty. Her face displayed no makeup, and she was wearing an athletic outfit: leggings, sneakers, and a sweatshirt, over which she wore a light jacket. She seemed ready for her afternoon jog. She definitely didn't look like the type to turn men's heads. However, her appearance was pleasant and her face friendly and unintimidating, in complete contrast to her manner of speaking on the assistant.

Her gestures as she rose and extended her hand to be shaken were flowing and catlike. Tom was surprised by her firm and powerful grasp, which differed significantly from the gentleness and fragility he expected from an Asian woman.

"Sit down, please," she said, sitting down across from him. She definitely seemed accustomed to issuing orders. "I'll get right to it," she said, in the voice of someone used to being obeyed. "As I'm sure you've realized, we've researched your personal history thoroughly. We're aware of your financial affairs and, of course, have been following your work closely. We have no doubt that a scientist of your caliber could go very far in his research.

"What we're suggesting is combining your scientific development with an environment that would also contribute to your family's standard of living. We're offering you a job at a leading company with the best-equipped labs imaginable. You can establish a lab of your own there, expand and equip it as you see fit, with no limitations. You'd have absolute freedom in your work, so long as you focus on the company's goals, which are not essentially different from your current areas of focus at work. Your initial salary would be exactly ten times your current salary. In addition, you'd be entitled to royalties for the products of your research. Some of the researchers working for us have happily substituted an additional half of a percent of royalties for half their salaries. We don't expect you to give us an answer immediately, but we'd be happy to get one soon."

For a moment, Tom felt as if his eyes were about to pop out of his face and that he had swallowed his tongue. A yearly salary of nearly two million dollars was definitely tempting, especially with the addition of royalties, which might yield him a lot more. *Wow. What to do?* In spite of his surprise and the appeal of the offer, he managed to avoid displaying his enthusiasm, and in a businesslike voice, thanked Gaya for the offer, adding, "I need time to think, of course. My work at the university is important to me in a way that goes far beyond financial compensation. I've rejected tempting offers before. How can I get back to you?"

"Don't bother, I'll call you," she said, rising from her seat to signal the end of the brief meeting.

Tom had been an academic his whole life. He'd never been involved in business and had never had to fight for his salary conditions. Naturally, the events of the last few days had only exacerbated his anxieties. He couldn't see himself waging battle and putting himself, and more importantly, his family, in danger for some study or other. Not to mention the generous bonus entailed in accepting the offer, a bonus that could secure his future and that of his children, to whom he was primarily and utterly committed. The new framework would still allow him to work in research, and anyone willing to pay such a high salary was guaranteed to employ him to perform lucrative scientific work situated at the forefront of technological development. It was true that his academic career would come to a halt. However, despite this, the price he would be paying seemed worth it, considering the returns.

Although his answer was obvious to him, he would not chase Gaya. He would let her call him. In the meantime, he had to call Kate immediately in order to stop her from fleeing with their daughters and urge her to return home. But perhaps he should wait a little, and first consult the most appropriate person?

Melissa answered on the first ring. Apparently, she was waiting for an urgent call. He wondered who it was from.

"Yes, of course, I'm waiting for you," she responded to his urgent request to see her.

This time, he would tell her the entire story. It was odd that she hadn't asked any questions when he had visited her on the day of the murder. He wondered what insights the conversation with her might yield. As he imagined her in his arms, he set out with a smile of expectation on his face.

The warm curves of Melissa's body clinging to his entire length, her sensual lips, and the flick of her tongue in his mouth made him forget all his thoughts and plans. Only when their passion had abated and they were lying calmly in each other's arms did the events of the last few days return to him.

His personal assistant sent Melissa's assistant the pertinent sites regarding longevity enhancement, to which he added several brief explanations before moving on to focus on the details of his meeting with Gaya.

"I still haven't told Kate anything. She doesn't know about the offer I received."

"How serious does this offer look to you?"

"I have no way to evaluate it. I don't know who the woman is, what company she represents, or what her role there is. As long as I haven't been offered a contract similar to what she described to me today, I'm not leaving my current position."

"That seems to imply you're interested in the offer," she said slowly.

"Regardless of the work I'll be doing for this company, am I entitled to reject such a generous offer, which could mean so much to my family?"

"There's no doubt you have a duty to your family. But let's not forget that they're not hungry for food or lacking for clothing right now, either. The question is whether you're willing to sacrifice an academic career that gives you plenty of freedom in return for work at a commercial company that will ultimately dictate the research you get to work on."

"Is a wage earner with a family like me even allowed to refuse a yearly salary of two million dollars and an option for royalties on products I'll develop, which are likely to prove commercially successful? It's true, I've never thought of leaving the university, although I've seen a few people turn to commercial ventures and reap major success. Sometimes I've even felt a bit of envy, but I've never initiated any action in that direction. No, I have no doubt I'll accept the offer, after looking into it thoroughly, of course. Assuming the offer is serious, I'm there!"

"I completely agree with you. I wouldn't hesitate to accept an offer like that, either."

"What do you think is behind it? Obviously, they could hire researchers of my caliber for a lot less. This offer reflects significant interest in my current research on someone's part, and if you want to get into conspiracy theories, that massive interest may also have been the motive for the murder. Imagine that—I might find myself working for an institution that was directly or indirectly responsible for the murder of the security guard. How could I live with that? And while we're at it, maybe all they want is to get me away from my work, at any price. They didn't negotiate about the wage. They just put out an offer so high that I couldn't possibly refuse it."

"Don't belittle yourself, and don't be too modest," she said with a seductive smile, as she held him tight and bestowed a lip-smacking kiss upon his mouth. "You're unusually talented, and the university can't afford to reward you financially the way it should. It is true, though, that a salary this high seems to imply that whoever extended the offer is specifically interested in you and your qualifications."

"Could you sniff around and see what's behind this offer, the moment we know who made it?"

"I promise to try," she said as she draped herself over him, inserting her tongue into his mouth and thus effectively preventing him from saying any more. "Aren't you in a hurry to get back home?" she asked.

"Kate took the girls to visit friends in Manteno. Considering the implied threat in what Gaya told me, we agreed she'd stay away from the house until things calmed down. We also agreed to suspend communication for a while. She's not expecting to hear from me in the next few days. We have the whole evening and night to ourselves."

"Wow," Melissa cheered. "You're sleeping with me tonight. I can't remember the last time that happened. Do you want to order dinner, or should we cook our own meal?"

"I like the idea of cooking. It would calm me down and let me think. How about you?"

"That works for me, too."

CHAPTER 13

Gerry at Home

Chicago, Sunday, July 20, 2036

Gerry was frightened when he opened his eyes and couldn't see a thing. For a moment, he thought the blindness was a delayed effect of the accident. Then he noticed the dim lighting around him. He had simply slept for many hours and awakened during the night. He tried to sit up in bed, but couldn't manage it. His entire body screamed with pain, and he gave up on any further attempt to get up. What should he do?

Apparently, his attempt to sit up and moans of pain woke Ramona up, or else she had not been sleeping at all. Within moments, she was standing by his bed, holding his hand. He tugged at her hand until she bent down, bringing her ear close to his mouth.

"I tried to sit up, but I couldn't. My entire body hurts," he whispered in her ear.

Ramona straightened at once, her face glowing with joy. She almost burst out into loud cheers. The depressing stammer was gone. Lucid Gerry, her life partner, was back. The accident hadn't harmed his mental capacities.

"Shh," he continued whispering. "Don't react. Keep acting like before. Don't show any indication of the improvement in my condition. I'm in danger, and that's the reason for the mentally challenged speech I've been exhibiting since I woke up. We have to keep pretending until the threat is over."

Her face grew immediately sober, and in a normal speaking voice, she said, "Don't try to speak. You have to get some more rest."

Just like that, his sharp-witted wife had understood instantly and joined the game of misdirection.

"I c-c-can't s-sleep an-anymore. C-c-come lie wi-with m-me," he said out loud.

Ramona snuggled in beside him, hugging him so that her mouth was just across from his ear. "What's going on here?" she whispered.

Gerry turned his head slowly while Ramona lowered her head so that her ear was just against his mouth. "Don't react with shock or change your previous behavior in any way, in spite of everything I'm about to tell you," he whispered. "It wasn't an accident. Someone tried to run me over."

Ramona shifted and, while pretending to alter her position in the bed in relation to him, brought her mouth up to his ear and asked, "How do you know? Do you have any proof, or is it just intuition, which I'm not dismissing in any way?"

This time, it was Gerry who shifted slightly, tilting his face up toward her ear. "The vehicle that hit me was following me in the minutes before I stopped to buy some pastries at my favorite bakery. It stopped right behind me when I did, but started driving madly toward me the moment I left my car."

Once again, Ramona moved subtly to whisper in his ear. "How did you see all that? Since when do you have eyes in the back of your head?"

Another execution of his half dance, half unconscious motion, and his mouth was next to her ear again. For a brief moment, he was nearly tempted to tell her about the unusual alertness and mental clarity he had been experiencing since he had first awakened after the accident, but he came to his senses immediately. She wouldn't believe him, would think he had lost it and was hallucinating. She would then link this with what she might view as his newly developed paranoia, the stutter and the seeming confusion he had imposed on his speech and writing. In the meantime, it was better if no one knew anything.

"I don't, but let me finish telling you this. In the last few days, I've been particularly suspicious. About a week ago, I got a strange assistant call I didn't tell you about. The caller knew what I was working on, and apparently understood the groundbreaking nature of my work."

"What are you talking about?" Ramona burst out.

"W-w-what's wrong w-w-with you? I l-l-ove you," he answered loudly. Ramona realized her error instantly and grew silent.

"I know," Gerry continued whispering, "that you have no idea what I've been focusing on for the last few years. The truth is that I haven't shared it with anyone. At first it was because I was having a hard time processing the conclusion implied by the observations. Only repeated testing convinced me that it was true, but then I began to fear the far-reaching implications of making it public. And no, I don't intend to tell you about it, so you're not an accessory to this secret. The less you know, the safer you'll be.

"Anyway, the caller demanded that I delete all my work and avoid publishing it or talking about it. He didn't explicitly threaten me with any retribution, but he sounded very assertive. Like the kind of person other people obey without asking questions. I think that what looked like an accident was an attempt to convince me to listen to the caller. I know you, and I know what you're thinking. No, I don't think the assailant tried to kill me. I believe that if that had been his intention, he would have succeeded. The fact that I survived and that, all in all, my condition's not that bad, testifies to that."

"What are you going to do?" she whispered.

"I'm sure the caller already took care to delete my work at the university. In my condition, I can't do a lot without the proof contained in my work, so to a certain extent, he's already achieved what he set out to do."

He didn't consider even for a moment telling her about the copy he had prepared and hidden away, and of course, he didn't tell her that in fact he didn't need a copy, due to his miraculous memory. He had to soothe his wife and convince her that he had succumbed to the caller's demands and had given up his work in order to guarantee his well-being.

"In the meantime, I have to continue appearing mentally challenged due to the accident in order to make the caller feel at ease. We'll think beyond that later."

"Do we tell the truth to the kids or to our friends?"

"No way! My life, and perhaps other people's lives, are in danger. I debated whether to even tell you, because by doing so I'm putting you at risk. Until things grow clearer, only the two of us can be in the know. In regard to the kids and the rest of the world, we'll continue our charade, without even the slightest hint that might arouse their suspicion. We don't know where the person who initiated the assault is getting his information, but if he managed to find out what I'm working on, although I was very secretive about it, he must have channels of information that shouldn't be underestimated."

"So what do we do in the meantime?" she asked.

An excellent question, he thought. *What do we do?* How would he gain access to a computer without exposing himself and undermining his image as someone who was brain damaged to the point of near retardation? Was it worth the effort and maybe the risk of reclaiming the copy he had stashed in his private toolbox at the Metalwork Division workshop?

Metalwork was one of his active hobbies. At the beginning and end of each major assignment, he would spend many hours at the workshop, where he had access to most of the metal processing machinery. The copy had been hidden in the handle of an old, battered screwdriver.

And if he did get his hands on it, where would he hide it? Retrieving the hidden copy would save him plenty of reconstruction work, which would also require an effort to conceal.

And what to do later? Should he publish the work, knowing that this was equivalent to a death sentence for him and perhaps for Ramona as well? Or should he avoid publishing it, as the anonymous caller had ordered? In short, what should he do?

"To tell you the truth, I have no idea what I can do under the circumstances I'm in. I think that during the next few days, we shouldn't do anything. I have to calm the assailant down. We have to think of a way to let him know about my compromised condition and my head injury. He has to believe the damage is permanent, and then maybe he'll leave me alone."

Apparently, the effort and the sustained speech had exhausted his energy. His breath grew measured and even, and he fell asleep.

***

Ethan called while Ramona was busy with household tasks. He didn't want to bother her, but just wanted to ask how things were going at home. He knew Gerry had been discharged; he had gotten an update directly from the hospital. He would be happy to visit Gerry at home at any time.

"He's feeling a lot better," Ramona said. "He fell asleep just a short time ago. I think you can come see him in the afternoon. Anyway, don't be shocked by his condition. As you know, he sustained a serious blow to the head, and it looks like his brain was damaged. It's hard for him to communicate with those around him. But why am I prattling at you, anyway? Come visit him and see for yourself."

"I'll come in the afternoon," he said. "Should I bring anything? Would he like to see more people? There are other colleagues at the department who are worried about him."

"No, it's too early for a mass visit. You can come see him. As for the others, we'll wait a few days."

"Thanks. I'll be there," he concluded, and hung up.

***

Although he was head of NASA's astronomy division, deep in his heart, astrophysics was Ethan's true love. Perhaps this was because his first two academic degrees had been in physics, and only his PhD was in astronomy, mostly because he had received a full scholarship and had even been offered a teaching assistant position.

Gerry, in contrast, was a born astronomer. A bookshelf in his office still displayed the four-inch telescope he had received as a gift from his grandfather, as he was eager to tell anyone who asked about it. It had been the most precious gift he'd ever received. He'd spent so many long nights with his grandfather, observing the planets and the moon. He had especially adored watching Saturn's breathtaking rings.

At age five, he could already recite the names of all the planets in the solar system, starting with the one nearest to the sun and ending with the farthest, as well as classify them by size. He would also recount how, when he had been in first grade, he had volunteered his grandfather to lecture to the students about astronomy. He liked to describe the preparations the two of them made for the class, and especially how his grandfather had allowed him to help present the lesson.

Ethan preferred long-term research, was very interested in astrophysics, and was up-to-date on the minute details of the various studies carried out by NASA. Gerry had told him more than once that he respected him for his hardworking nature, his leadership qualities, and mostly for the complete support he granted his subordinate researchers. He gave them full freedom to choose the topics of their research, so long as they fit in with the general spirit of NASA. Gerry's current research was a case in point. All Ethan knew was that Gerry was investigating the relative motion of large asteroids in the asteroid belt between Mars and Jupiter. However, not infrequently, Ethan felt some discomfort in Gerry's company. It might have resulted from the unbridgeable gap between those in love with their work, like Gerry, and those who worked to earn a living, no matter how well they performed this work.

Once Ethan arrived, Ramona prepared him for his meeting with Gerry. She asked him to ignore the stutter, to focus on what was going on at NASA rather than asking Gerry questions, and in general, to keep the visit short, as Gerry tended to grow tired quickly.

She updated Ethan as she led him to Gerry's room. "He's still very weak and needs a lot of rest, which will also have a positive effect on his brain. In the meantime, we haven't observed any improvement in his mental state since the accident."

She didn't want to sit in the room with them, although she was curious to know how their conversation would develop and whether Gerry would manage to fool Ethan, who was considered particularly intelligent. In order to satisfy her curiosity, she sat in the giant armchair in Elaine's room, which was adjacent to Gerry's. The open doors of both rooms made eavesdropping easier.

The ensuing conversation between the two appeared to be relaxed and easy. Ethan ignored Gerry's stammer and told him how worried his colleagues were, how much they'd been surprised on Friday when he hadn't shown up for the meeting, and that they all wished him a speedy recovery.

"W-w-what hap-happened in the m-m-meeting on F-F-Friday?" Gerry asked.

Ethan described the contents of the meeting in detail, his report peppered with countless words Ramona didn't understand. She had heard most of them numerous times, but had never dedicated any thought to their meanings. Astronomy didn't particularly interest her.

Occasionally, Gerry interrupted Ethan with a stammered

question that sounded completely authentic. She found his pretense believable, and didn't think it would raise Ethan's suspicion. Ramona immersed herself in her thoughts of Gerry, and stopped listening in on the conversation in the adjacent room. Only when she emerged from her contemplation did she notice that the dialogue, or more accurately the monologue, had come to a stop. *What's going on there?* she thought. Just as she was rising from her seat, Ethan appeared in the doorway.

"He fell asleep. I guess I tired him out. There's no point in me staying."

"I did let you know," she replied. "He gets tired very quickly and sleeps a lot. The doctor recommended that he get a lot of sleep."

"I don't want to burden the two of you. I'll call in the next few days to keep a close eye on his condition. Do you have any idea what your husband was working on? He promised me a discovery with global implications."

"I really have no idea. Astronomy has never interested me. In our many years together, I've learned a lot of terms, but I never really bothered to take an interest in the specific topics he was working on. This suited Gerry, who never bothered to share his work with me. I only know that during the last year, the information from the new array of telescopes was very helpful to him. He was very impressed by the quality of the data it provided, and mentioned it frequently. During the last year, he'd also say from time to time that the array was placing discoveries on our doorstep that we've been searching for, from a great distance, for decades. He was preoccupied with thoughts about his presentation at the meeting, and I guess he wasn't careful enough."

Only after Ethan had said goodbye did she find herself considering, for the first time, the mystery engulfing Gerry's work. Until that moment, she had treated the whole matter of the discovery with equanimity. Gerry loved his work, and this wasn't the first time he thought he had uncovered an extraordinary discovery. During the last incident she recalled, the "discovery" had fallen apart while he was presenting it to a colleague, the moment he understood where he had gone wrong. She wondered how certain he was of his discovery this time. Perhaps his lack of confidence had affected his caution. But this time, he had used the most innovative telescopes, which could present precise images and data at a previously unprecedented level. Maybe this time, there actually was something there?

Apparently, the person who might have followed Gerry and was responsible for his injury knew that he had uncovered a groundbreaking discovery. But who cared about an astronomic discovery, no matter how groundbreaking? How could an astronomic discovery even be parlayed into a financial profit? Why would anyone try to prevent any sort of revelation concerning astronomy, when so few people were interested in this field?

Perhaps he had found an asteroid entirely made of gold or diamond or some other precious mineral, as she knew he had been researching asteroids lately. She was certain of this because he had mentioned them frequently during the last year. He had also made repeated references to changes of trajectory. Perhaps he really had been investigating the possibility of changing the trajectory of a diamond asteroid and bringing it to Earth. An idea like that truly could have interested plenty of people. But then why hurt him? On the contrary, anyone who uncovered the details of his research should have collaborated with him and taken the best possible care of him—the complete opposite of what they had actually done. No, that wasn't the right scenario.

What exactly had Gerry been hiding from her? What revolutionary discovery that might affect humanity as a whole had he come across? What revolutionary thing could possibly be discovered about a barren chunk of rock moving around in frozen outer space? She didn't have the faintest idea.

CHAPTER 14

KYRA

CHICAGO, MONDAY, JULY 21, 2036

That morning at the lab appeared totally mundane. The events of the previous week were not mentioned, and everyone was busy with their work. Tom repressed any thought of the offer he had received. So long as he was at the university, he would continue working at full steam.

A brief glance in Lise's direction revealed that she seemed unusually preoccupied. Her gestures were jerky, and she seemed to be checking the same data again and again. *She'll come see me when the time is right*, he thought. Mike didn't seem to be at his best, either. He was introverted, as usual, but today his gaze seemed downcast as well. Perhaps the events of last week had had a severe effect on him, and he still hadn't managed to shake them off.

Tom ate lunch with his colleague Paul from the physics

department, as usual. Their fields of concentration were so different that they generally did not discuss work matters, which suited both of them very well.

He debated whether to offer Lise his help or let her be. She seemed very busy, so he decided to hold off and wait. Mike, in contrast, seemed even worse off than he had that morning. He appeared at loose ends and very tense.

"What's going on, Mike?" Tom asked him gently. Despite Mike's somewhat odd character, his frightened expression made Tom feel a sense of suffocation. "Let's talk," he said, placing his hand softly on Mike's shoulder.

Tom's office was small but cozy, creating a calm atmosphere. The quiet classical music that piped in once they entered the room enhanced the relaxed environment. Tom gestured for Mike to sit in the small armchair and walked over to make coffee for himself and cocoa for Mike, a preference of which everyone was aware.

The relaxed atmosphere, the music, the cocoa, and Tom's positive, mellow demeanor had a cumulative effect that calmed Mike down. Tom sat down across from him, focusing on his coffee cup, without saying a word.

"I feel like I have to talk," Mike suddenly blurted out.

"You should feel free to do that. We're not in a hurry, there are no recording devices here, and anything you tell me will stay between the two of us."

"My girlfriend, Kyra, has disappeared."

Shy Mike's stunning girlfriend was a frequent topic of gossip at the lab, as well as the focus of many jokes. Everyone believed Kyra was the first girlfriend Mike had ever had. The relationship between them seemed odd. Kyra, a slim blonde possessing the body, the face, and the confidence of a supermodel, was a clear contrast to bashful, introverted Mike, who seemed like the ultimate geek, the type whose existence tended to be ignored by women, especially the prettier among them. The women in the lab would have been willing to pay a lot in order to find out what Kyra saw in Mike.

"What do you mean she's disappeared? She's not answering her assistant? Maybe something's happened to her?" Tom queried.

"She's not answering her assistant or messages of any kind. That's really not like her. We usually communicate daily. Since we've been a couple, we've spent every single weekend together. It's only now that I noticed that other than her assistant address, I don't have any idea how to find her. I don't know where she lives or where she works. We always hung out at my place. She would initiate and plan our meetings and our outings. I never suggested going to her house, so as not to oppose her suggestions. I just accepted her the way she was. I never thought she might disappear from my life in an instant. I don't know how to even start looking for her. I contacted the addresses for the two entries I found in the assistant directory, but neither of those people knew anyone with her name. I feel completely helpless. I think about her all the time. I just can't focus on work."

"When was the last time you talked?" Tom asked.

"We talked on the assistant on Wednesday afternoon. Kyra asked if I had any ideas for the upcoming weekend. As usual, I didn't, and she laughed and said she would think of something. I tried to call her several times on Thursday, but she was unavailable every time. That's never happened to me. Kyra usually answered every one of my calls almost immediately."

Tom thought for a moment, and then said, "I'm sure you remember how you two met."

"That was strange, too. Her job is selling general equipment and materials to chemistry labs. She tried to interest me in purchasing high-precision scales. Even though I told her our lab was well equipped when it came to scales and that I wasn't the one making purchasing decisions anyway, she insisted on coming to see me at the lab and presenting the company's products to me. I remember I tried to get her not to waste her time and asked her to send me a catalog of the products by mail so I could peruse them, but it did no good. She explained away the visit by saying she was seeing several clients at the university that day anyway, and that it would be no hassle at all."

"Do you still have the catalog?"

"No, she showed it to me on her computer. In fact, I searched my place from top to bottom for clothes or papers she might have left behind, and I couldn't find a thing. For all intents and purposes, she might as well have never been in my house. I don't even have her toothbrush. She'd always come with a packed bag and wouldn't leave anything behind."

Tom considered what he had just heard for another moment. A growing suspicion caused him to ask, "When exactly did you meet, and how did you make the transition from business acquaintances to having a personal relationship?"

"We've been a couple for about two months," Mike replied. "In fact, even the business meeting felt very warm and personal. Kyra told me that she was single, and that after a series of boyfriends who were the partying type, she had come to the conclusion that the next guy she met would be the exact opposite. She described a serious man working at the forefront of science who would be an interesting conversationalist. In fact, she described me. It was the first time such a beautiful girl had even acknowledged my existence, much less flattered me like that.

"At the end of the meeting, she told me she'd love to keep talking to me under less formal circumstances. It took me a day to realize that in fact, she expected me to ask her out on a date, and it took me two more days to find the courage to ask her out. We met two days later, and from there, everything flowed way quicker than I'd hoped, even in my wildest dreams."

Tom's apprehension was gradually taking shape and solidifying. The entire story seemed more like a cheesy Bollywood movie than real life. Kyra had targeted Mike a short time before the break-in and the murder, and disappeared without a trace after those events had occurred. She definitely had an agenda in initiating the relationship, and might have actually achieved her goal.

Motivated by his growing suspicion, he turned to Mike and asked, "Does the material you take home from the lab include the access codes to the lab building and to our lab?"

"Yes, of course. I have a file in which I keep all my secret passwords."

"Has Kyra seen them?"

"I don't think so, although she worked on my home computer quite a few times. She'd always giggle and say it was a lot more convenient than her bulky computer. I always gave her complete privacy when she said she had to finish this or that for work."

"What do you think of this scenario: Kyra was sent by whoever's behind the break-in and the murder. She came to the lab seeking easy prey, made a connection with you, obtained all the secret passwords from your computer, and once the murder took place, disappeared without a trace?"

Mike's gape of astonishment said it all. His surprise was absolute, or at least appeared to be so.

"I suggest we update Detective Rick Heller, the investigating detective, immediately. If possible, he'll locate Kyra, and maybe she'll provide a lead to finding the killer."

Mike swallowed heavily. Tom imagined how hard it was for him to realize that Kyra had had no interest in him as a man or as a boyfriend, to think that she was connected to the break-in and the murder and had also taken advantage of his innocence. His fragile male ego was probably on the verge of shattering into a million pieces. *I wonder*, he thought, *which part is harder for Mike to accept: the fact that Kyra conned him or that she might be connected to the perpetrators of the murder.*

"Maybe...maybe we should wait another day or two," Mike said. "Maybe she'll still show up."

It was hard for Tom to watch Mike falling apart. "Okay. We'll give her another day to show up. If by noon tomorrow I don't get an update from you that Kyra's gotten in touch, I'll contact Rick."

Mike nodded glumly, bowing his head.

Tom wondered whether he should rush off to tell Dr. Colin about his suspicions. But this would be a betrayal of his promise to Mike. No, Dr. Ron Colin could wait until noon tomorrow as well. Tom had no doubt that Kyra had disappeared because she had been involved in the murder in some manner.

He was in no hurry to get back to his empty house, so he stayed at the lab late into the evening. Eventually, he and Lise were the only ones still working. She seemed to have calmed down a bit, as she was focused on the computer before her. Around eight o'clock—an hour that was unusually late for Lise, whose evenings tended to be packed with various activities—she approached him and asked to review some findings. At that exact moment, her assistant rang.

"When?" she asked, and after apparently receiving an answer, replied, "I'm on my way.

"I can't stay tonight," she told him. "Could we continue this tomorrow?"

"That's fine," he replied.

Lise gathered her purse and left.

On his way home, Tom wondered when Gaya might call again to receive his answer. In light of her pressure to meet over the weekend, he had expected her to call during the day. Perhaps she wanted to give him time to consider the offer, or to consult others. He had already planned what he would say to her: he would want to receive an official offer, specifying the place of employment, the company's general structure, the fields in which he would work, his role in the research, the team and budget at his disposal, what other studies the company was working on, and of course, his wages and other benefits. He wouldn't accept the offer, but rather would display interest and inquire about the details, as would behoove a senior researcher who was considering factors beyond mere financial profit.

It was now after nine p.m.; it seemed she wouldn't be calling before tomorrow. *That's good; apparently, they're not under too much time pressure, which works for me*, he thought.

The assistant rang just as he was sprawling out on the couch, in a comfortable pose somewhere between sitting and lying down.

"Dr. Lester?" He recognized her voice.

"Speaking."

"This is Gaya. I forgot to tell you during our last meeting that our offer is valid for a few days only. That's why I'm calling you today. Have you happened to come to a decision on the matter?"

"I've come to a decision not to reject the offer for the time being. In order to move forward, I'll need to receive a proper, official offer that includes information on the work I'll be carrying out, my team, the budget, and other such details. Of course, I'll also be interested in meeting the people onsite."

"That's very understandable. I'll make sure you're invited for a meeting, where you can formulate an opinion on the offer and its originators. I have no doubt you'll be won over and will decide to accept the offer. I want to note that you're taking the logical course of action." Despite the flattering words, she made the statement sound like a threat to be reckoned with.

The quiet, empty house reminded him that he still hadn't talked to Kate. In fact, as long as he had not come to an agreement with the company making the offer, whose identity was still unknown to him, and signed an agreement that he found satisfactory, nothing was certain. No, the safe location of his loved ones would give him greater freedom and leverage in the negotiations with his potential new employer.

CHAPTER 15

LIA

CALIFORNIA, MONDAY, JULY 21, 2036

In the wee hours of the night, Professor Lia Rosen, exhausted, looked up from a summary of the test results. Her study, usually in immaculate order, now looked almost as it had when she had first moved into her current home. Piles of journals and books were strewn around everywhere. Coffee cups whose contents had dried up long ago and takeout pizza boxes were scattered about chaotically, with no one bothering to pick them up. Cobwebs and the dusty floor also testified to the long neglect the room had suffered.

However, Lia did not see any of it. Recently, her life had been conducted on an utterly different plane. She was entirely focused on her discovery. In recent months, she had abandoned anything that could be put off and checked the results of her work again and again. Dozens of times, she had tested and retested the data arriving from the James Webb and STA space telescopes, repeatedly verifying the automatic calculations performed by the computer and their results. She didn't confine herself to her own calculations, but also consulted colleagues specializing in quantum physics and astrophysics. Naturally, she did not expose the reason for her queries, fearing they might condemn her as a believer in gods or miracles, or accuse her of ignoring a key detail that would alter the entire picture. Even worse, they might snatch away her earth-shattering scoop if her discovery did turn out to be valid.

Each calculation had been verified dozens of times, and the result was always identical: the pale star in the constellation of Virgo, STA331047A and its companion, the white dwarf STA331047B, as well as the binary star STA333654A and its companion, the white dwarf STA333654B. One in the Aquarius constellation, at a distance of 360 light-years, and the other in the Tucana constellation, 290 light-years away. The white dwarfs in both pairs were surely absorbing mass from the large star adjacent to them, and should already have exploded in a massive supernova. That is, unless they were found to rotate around their axes at an unbelievable rate.

All mass measurements she had carried out for these stars indicated that each had an exact mass of 1.76 solar masses, with a possible measurement error of ±0.07. The measurements showed conclusively that the mass of the two white dwarfs had significantly exceeded the Chandrasekhar limit of 1.44 solar masses, beyond which stars exploded in a massive supernova. Nevertheless, neither of them had exploded.

Several decades ago, astronomers had worked out the characteristics of such a supernova, called an Ia supernova, which occurred when a pair of stars—a white dwarf and a red giant or a star in its main sequence—orbit each other. The red giant is a star nearing the end of its life, past the main sequence phase. At this stage, it expands to immense dimensions of more than one hundred million kilometers (over sixty million miles).

The white dwarf is also reaching the end of its lifespan, having already passed the red dwarf phase and contracted into a small, dense star that no longer generates energy. Due to its proximity to the star, the gravitational pull of the white dwarf attracts and absorbs mass from the red giant, gradually increasing its own mass until its increasing gravitation overcomes its electron pressure. At that point, the dwarf explodes, projecting immense amounts of energy into space within a very short time. The luminous intensity of the exploding star is at the same scale as the luminous intensity of an entire galaxy.

As the explosion takes place, when the mass of the white dwarf reaches a set value, the absolute luminous intensity is also fixed and identical for all Ia supernovas. The only factor known to science that can affect this process is rapid rotation of the white dwarf around its axis, which creates centrifugal force, decreasing the gravitational effect, and therefore the pressure on the star's core.

Measuring the luminous intensity reaching Earth enabled a precise calculation of the distance of the star from Earth. Astronomers finally had access to the absolute astronomical gauge, which allowed them to accurately determine the Earth's distance from faraway galaxies. This understanding paved the way to the groundbreaking discovery that the rate of the universe's expansion is accelerating, in contrast to any known physical logic, ultimately resulting in a Nobel Prize granted to the scientists who discovered it, Saul Perlmutter, Brian Schmidt, and Adam Riess, in 2011.

Something unclear was taking place in those two binary

systems. Something that wasn't in accordance with the known laws of physics, which had been tested on more than a hundred Ia supernovas discovered in the Milky Way and in distant galaxies. The infinitesimal chance that each of the white dwarfs revolved around its axis at precisely the rate that would cause an equal decrease in the pressure of gravitational force, allowing both to reach the exact same mass without exploding, didn't merit serious consideration.

Newton's equations of motion accurately described observations on Earth and in the solar system. Einstein's theory of relativity predicted different results than Newton's equations, but only at speeds approaching the speed of light. The predictions of the theory of relativity and its observational verification required sophisticated measuring equipment.

However, for all intents and purposes, for motion at speeds significantly below the speed of light, Newton's equations provided plenty of accuracy, and were still in use. Yet they did not seem to apply to the phenomena on STA331047B and STA333654B. The red giants adjacent to these stars were still at their peak, and contained massive amounts of gas, in contrast to the leading theory, which had been verified many times. Such a significant difference should have been discovered long ago, had it been a common phenomenon.

No, there was no doubt that these stars exhibited unusual phenomena, which were unclear to astrophysicists. Discovering the factor that allowed two relatively close stars to reach the same large mass without exploding might have a significant impact on the entire science of astronomy. She had to measure the rate in which they revolved around their axes, a complex task that would probably cause more than one raised eyebrow among the operators of the STA. Although by now they were probably used to her occasionally odd requests.

Her investigation had brought her to Professor Avi Tsur from the Weizmann Institute of Science in Israel, who was considered one of the leading experts in the world on the development and death of stars. His youthful appearance and casual way of dressing had surprised Lia.

"Have you ever encountered a white dwarf in a binary system whose mass significantly exceeded the Chandrasekhar limit, but that didn't explode? If so, do you have an explanation for this phenomenon?" Lia chose to read directly from her notes when speaking to Avi, in order not to miss any significant words, and mostly in order not to hint at her discovery.

Avi's immediate response hit her like a sledgehammer. "You must mean STA331047B." Lia nearly collapsed. "I've been tracking it for a few months now. I've rechecked the observations and the calculations again and again, but I haven't found any explanation for the phenomenon. The only possible explanation would be an especially high rate of revolving around its axis, which I can't measure."

Lia was stunned. How the hell had Tsur obtained the observations? He wasn't an American. The STA observations weren't even being distributed to American astronomers, other than those who worked with the array. Foreign astronomers weren't even supposed to know the temporary names of the stars the STA had discovered, and certainly did not have access to its observations. She couldn't hold back.

"How do you have information about the STA observations? As far as I know, this information still hasn't been shared with the American astronomy community as a whole, much less with astronomers outside my country?"

There was no answer from her interlocutor. Thinking the call had been disconnected, she asked, "Are you still on the line?"

"Yes, of course, and I'll be happy to collaborate with you on this subject," he replied, completely ignoring her question.

Professor Tsur's open, cooperative approach made her bounce back from her shock quickly. She decided to accept his offer, and leave the question of his sources of information for a later stage in the proceedings.

"I went through the exact same thing with STA331047B. Did you find any other stars that behaved in the same manner?" she asked.

"Not at all. The truth is that the results surprised me so much that I've dedicated most of my time to exploring the phenomenon. I find it hard to believe that after so many years of observations, which have always revealed similar results, we've discovered such a strange star."

Lia hesitated briefly. Should she tell Avi about STA333654B, or keep the discovery to herself? No, in light of his openness and willingness to cooperate, and despite his reluctance to expose his sources of information, she could not hide such pertinent information, which he would surely find fascinating.

"Have you looked into STA333654B?" she asked.

"No, not at all. Why? What distinguishes it?" he asked.

"It behaves precisely like STA331047B. Each of them has the same mass, which has significantly surpassed the Chandrasekhar limit, but neither of them is exploding."

"I don't believe I could have missed something like that." She heard the surprise in Avi's voice. "I have to check this out thoroughly. Let me get back to you in a few days."

How does he have all the information? she wondered. He must have access to the STA observations if he could immediately investigate any star the array had discovered. Although he had concealed the sources of his information from her, she still felt comfortable continuing to collaborate with him. Something about his voice projected trustworthiness. Perhaps she would discover where he was getting his information at some future time.

"Let me help you. I'm sending you a summary of my work, and will wait for your call once you've studied it," she replied quickly, startled by the speed at which she'd transitioned from suspicion and secrecy to full cooperation.

"It's late night your time, but around noon here. I suggest you call me when it's morning for you, so I'll have time to go over the material later today."

"I'll call then. Have a good day," she responded.

"Have a good night," Avi replied, ending the call.

***

Despite her extreme fatigue, Lia could not sleep that night. She found herself twisting and turning in bed. Had more astrophysicists discovered the anomaly in these stars? Until very recently, she had been certain that she was the only one. How had Avi Tsur even managed to expose the anomaly without having access to the STA observations, which in the meantime were reserved only for a select group of American astronomers? Was there a leak among the STA scientists? Or perhaps the Israelis, known for their advanced technological capabilities, possessed sophisticated means of observation that were unknown to the rest of the world? That would indeed be like them. But if that was the answer, it was truly illogical that Avi would be using the same names for the stars.

The more she thought about it, the more she grew convinced

that Avi had open access to the STA observations. What would happen if someone beat her to the finish line, and published the results before she did? Up to this point, she had been careful to maintain confidentiality. Even when she turned to her colleagues for assistance, she had made sure not to include too much information. And now others knew of her discovery as well. With a sense that she had no control over the revelations, she fell into a restless sleep.

CHAPTER 16

Goldon and the Structures

Chicago, Tuesday, July 22, 2036

Without the usual familial bustle of morning, including breakfast and sandwiches for everyone, Tom found himself leaving for work earlier than usual. *That's great*, he thought. Finally, he could work uninterrupted until the first researchers arrived. His commute was also considerably shorter before the masses swarmed the roads.

To his surprise, he found Lise already so immersed in her work that she didn't hear him enter the lab. He cleared his throat to alert her to his presence.

Lise turned to him with a tense glance, blurting out, "I'll be with you in a second."

Unexpectedly, Lise insisted they sit in the small isolated conference room adjacent to the lab. Almost all team meetings were held in the lab itself. Tom tried to maintain a spirit of openness and transparency among everyone at work. Other than personal issues, everyone knew—or at least could know—about everyone else's work.

"I'm going to tell you a strange story. Please don't ask me any questions until I'm done," Lise began. "This is the first time I've ever experienced a murder of someone I knew and respected. Oleg always smiled at me and always asked how I was doing. In the chaos after the murder, I was completely disoriented and couldn't focus on my work.

"Once I calmed down at home, I tried to reconstruct the order of the different amylase enzymes I'd added to the petri dishes containing various proteins produced from the long sequence, after adding initiators and terminators to it, and leaving the dishes in the incubator. But I couldn't remember. I was convinced I'd made a mistake and that I had to rerun the experiment. Yesterday morning, I was about to throw the petri dishes away when suddenly I found myself thinking, *I wonder what happened there?* And I looked at the results."

Lise swallowed heavily, produced several pages from a slim portfolio with the blank side turned up, and continued. "These are single images from the microscope." She flipped one of the pages over and handed it to Tom.

Tom was proud of the new quantum microscope, which could capture images of atoms and molecules with high resolution. It was a vital tool in their biological research. At first glance, the images looked exactly like hundreds and thousands of the usual images of strange amorphous proteins. But then he noticed multiple series of symmetrical, three-dimensional geometrical structures. He saw balls, cubes, pyramids, cylinders, and toroids. He swiveled the page around, looking at it intensely as Lise handed him another page. The angle at which the image was taken differed from the first photo, and the structures looked significantly more prominent. His reaction, mouth gaped open in amazement, was apparently exactly what she was expecting as she handed him another image. This one displayed a large matrix comprising numerous structures. The entire complex was reminiscent of a portion of a DNA molecule. It was confined by two vertical columns, with what appeared to be horizontal rows of symmetrical structures floating between them.

As he continued to look, Lise handed him another image, this one zoomed out. It showed an immense maze of similar groups of structures. Apparently, a large portion of the tested sample had transformed into matrixes of geometrical structures.

"This can't be happening," Tom finally managed to spit out. "It can't be. There's got to be a biological explanation. We're familiar with several spatial carbon-based geometrical structures. Maybe what we've discovered here are some more kinds of carbon-based organizing principles? On the other hand, this form of arrangement just doesn't make sense for a biological system. I'm stunned," Tom concluded, leaning back in his chair and staring out into space.

"Who else have you shown these results to?" he asked.

"No one but you. I'm stunned, too, and I don't know what to do with this."

"First, we have to figure out exactly what we did that resulted in these structures. The moment we do that, we'll continue from there. Although, on second thought, even if we can't replicate this strange outcome, the very fact that it occurred requires comprehensive investigation. From an operative standpoint, we shouldn't share this finding with anyone else. We'll replicate the experiment as accurately as possible, then think about it some more."

Lise nodded in agreement, but remained in her seat. Her voice so quiet it was nearly inaudible, she asked, "And if the finding is real, and we manage to replicate it? What does that mean? What are we doing? Have others discovered this before us? And if so, why haven't we heard about it? Maybe discoveries like this are silenced? I'm scared."

"Before we get all fearful for no good reason, let's maintain utter secrecy, run the experiment again, and most of all, calm down." Apparently, Tom's confidence had an effect upon her. She looked up, briefly resembling the strong Lise he knew.

The ringing of his personal assistant brought both of them back to reality. "Dr. Lester?" asked a woman's voice.

"Speaking," he replied.

"This is Karen, Professor Andrew Goldon's secretary. Are you free to talk to him now?"

Tom was briefly unable to breathe. He couldn't believe his ears. Professor Andrew Goldon was the CEO of the BL Corporation, currently the major developer worldwide of products based on the human genome. The most well-known of these were CardioBoost, for rejuvenating the tissues of the human heart; LungBoost, for rejuvenating human lungs; and PlaqueDissolve, for clearing plaque from human blood vessels. The company was also known to be developing products to maintain human skin at the level of a person in his or her thirties, as well as systemic treatments for the human immune system.

"Yes, of course," he replied, stammering a bit.

He heard a short beep, followed by a deep, pleasant baritone voice. "Hi, Tom."

He really sounds like an opera singer, Tom thought.

"I hope I'm not interrupting you in the middle of anything important. If you prefer to talk in the evening rather than during work hours, that's not a problem."

"No, now is fine. I'll just step out for a moment," Tom replied. "Okay, I'm with you," he said, once he was out of Lise's hearing range.

"I'll get right to it," the opera singer continued. "We're in urgent need of a lead researcher for a prominent project in the field of genetics. Your name came up when we were looking into potential candidates. How do you feel about coming to see me so I can describe the project to you?"

"I'd love to," Tom answered, without a moment's hesitation.

"My secretary will coordinate with you. It's been nice talking to you, and I'd be even happier to see you on our leading team."

Immediately, he heard the voice of Karen the secretary, as if she had been listening in on the conversation and interrupted it at precisely the right second. "Professor Goldon would be happy to see you as soon as possible. Could you come right now?"

"Can I get back to you in the next hour?" he asked.

"We prefer not to wait that long. I'll call you back in five minutes."

Lise apparently understood immediately that he had drifted away to another world, and that the call he'd received wasn't a routine one; it seemed as if something important had happened. However, despite this realization, probably due to the extreme strangeness of the experiment results, she did not give up, saying, "Okay, in the next few days I'll try to recreate the combination that led to the result we just saw. In the meantime, I don't intend to discuss the experiment with anyone until I can precisely replicate it, and then we'll sit down and think it over." With that, she turned back to her lab table.

***

BL Labs was located in Bedford Park, more than an hour's drive from the university. Judging by the rate at which events were developing, Goldon might pressure him into giving him an answer on the spot. Working at BL Labs was the wet dream of every biologist: unlimited budgets, the most fascinating research, and of course, a handsome salary. Work like that would definitely justify the long, exhausting years of study. On the other hand, Gaya, with her offer that couldn't be refused, still hadn't called, and he had no way to get in touch with her; moreover, the implicit threat in her proposition couldn't be ignored. Should he give up an offer from Goldon in favor of an offer from Gaya that still hadn't materialized?

A glance at the clock in the car told him it was noon, reminding him that Mike still hadn't called about his girlfriend, Kyra. It seemed safe to assume she hadn't gotten in touch. That was it—he had to notify Rick.

The detective answered immediately. *Working with police officers is so convenient*, Tom thought. *They're accessible twenty-four hours a day, you can wake them up at night without feeling guilty or getting reprimanded, and they 're immediately alert when they answer.*

He briefly explained about Kyra's disappearance as well as his suspicions, asking Rick to locate her.

"I'll ask Mike for all the information he has on her. I'll get on it immediately," came the reply, followed by the clear sound of the call being disconnected. Policemen were indeed efficient.

As Tom continued deliberating, with no resolution in sight, the distant view of the giant BL Corporation sign shot a wave of adrenaline through him. He would listen to any offer made, ask for some time to make up his mind, and in the meantime, would wait for a call from Gaya. If he was making the transition to the business world, at least he would have the added perspective of another offer.

***

Karen, wearing a casual outfit, was waiting for him in the luxurious lobby of the management building. She had already taken care of the entry authorizations he required. They turned to an elevator located some distance away from the public bank of elevators, by which some people were waiting. It was smaller, with room for no more than six passengers and a door that opened automatically as they approached. There were no control buttons. Once they had entered, the door closed, only to open again several seconds later. Tom was certain some mishap had occurred, as he had not felt any acceleration or motion. To his surprise, the door opened directly into a large lab packed with equipment.

"This is a very informal company. Mr. Goldon likes to do some research himself." With a smile, she added, "Don't be surprised."

The office of BL Corporation's CEO was in fact a sprawling biology lab, with wide work tables and shelves laden with equipment that Tom could only dream about. For a moment, he thought the lab was empty, but then he noticed Professor Goldon tending to the newest and most expensive model of quantum microscope currently available.

Tom had never met Professor Goldon, but recognized him instantly from online photos and from the few interviews in which he had taken part. The professor was a short, slim man who looked to be about forty-five, dressed in a lab coat and a cleanroom hood, as was appropriate in a clean lab. He definitely did not look like one of the most influential CEOs of his era. Despite his youthful appearance, it was a known fact that his seventieth birthday had come and gone. In one of his interviews, the professor had attributed this youthful appearance to his lifestyle, including a strict vegan diet and BL's nutritional supplements. Apparently, even physical exercise would no longer be necessary in the future with Aerobion, a product that had still not been approved for general use, and which affected the body similarly to engaging in intensive aerobic activity for an hour a day. There were also rumors of another additive currently under development that would serve as a substitute for anaerobic activity, preserving muscle tone as well as bone density and strength, at the level of a person engaging in regular exercise.

Goldon's appearance made him a walking advertisement for BL. The company could have saved a lot of money had he agreed to be the spokesmodel for its products.

"How are you?" he called out, briefly disengaging from the screen at which he had been gazing intently. "I'll be right with you."

Signaling Tom to approach, he pointed at the eyepiece of the 3D microscope, bringing his finger to his lips in order to instruct him to keep quiet.

For the second time that day, Tom's mouth gaped open in amazement. In the three-dimensional space in front of his eyes, he saw the structures that Lise had showed him about an hour ago. However, through the microscope, they truly appeared three-dimensional. It was a wondrous sight. Goldon activated controls that rotated the structure in space, enlarging and contracting it so that it could be examined from every angle. When he zoomed out, the image revealed about ten identical structures, far fewer than the quantity revealed in Lise's image.

"Wow, time flies," Professor Goldon said. "I didn't notice it was already lunchtime. You've been on the road for more than an hour. I bet you're hungry."

Tom began to reply that he wasn't hungry, but Goldon shushed him immediately. "We don't discuss business here with a growling stomach. Come on—my treat." He extracted the sample from the microscope's plate, locked it in a small safe embedded in the lab's wall, grabbed his coat and signaled Tom to follow him.

Once the elevator door closed, Tom said, "I've already seen—"

"Of course you have," Goldon interjected rudely. "If we didn't know what you were working on, we wouldn't have approached you. But, as I've already said, we don't talk on an empty stomach. Let's eat, and then we can talk comfortably."

It was obvious to Tom that the professor was intentionally avoiding discussing what they had just seen through the microscope. What exactly had he meant when he silenced him? Was he referring to the identical patterns he had seen for the first time in his life only mere hours ago, and up to this moment, had believed were known only to Lise and him? If this was true, it implied that Professor Goldon had access to everything that took place in his lab, which was impossible. It was a shocking thought, but perhaps...? *No, no, impossible.* Goldon couldn't know about the structures that Lise had just shown him. Or perhaps the photographic material generated by his lab was under surveillance? He decided not to initiate any questions on the matter, and to allow Goldon to reveal his cards.

Tom was surprised when Goldon led him to a popular health-food restaurant, which was teeming with office workers who had come down to grab a quick, nutritious meal. He had been sure he would be invited to some fine-dining establishment where they would be assigned to a quiet table isolated from other diners. A place that would allow them to talk without any attentive ears around them.

The computer at the host station displayed a map of the restaurant with available tables clearly designated. The moment Goldon selected a table, they were approached by a pear-shaped robot, which invited them to follow it. Tom actually liked the new generation of robots designed in various shapes, which had begun to show up in restaurants and other locations where people needed to be directed or ask frequently repeated questions. The pear robot was quite popular and amusing, suitable for casual-dining restaurants.

When it stopped opposite the corner table he had selected, the professor sat so that he faced the entrance. From his own seat, Tom could only see Goldon, or watch the entrance in the mirror covering its northern wall. The electronic menu on their table depicted Tuesday's specials in words and mostly in tantalizing images. The professor was either familiar with the place or in a big hurry. He immediately touched the image of a sandwich and a beverage rich with digestive enhancers. Tom interpreted this as a hint, and rather than reading through the entire menu, as was his custom, chose one of the first three sandwiches. The table thanked them for their order and promised them it would arrive within four minutes. A large timer appeared on the screen and began the countdown.

Goldon didn't say a word as he ate his entrée. His gaze roamed alertly and constantly over the entire restaurant, returning persistently to the front door, as if he was waiting for someone. Tom cooperated by maintaining the silence.

Once they were finished eating, Goldon took care of the payment and appeared calmer, even allowing himself to briefly stop scanning the restaurant and focus his gaze on Tom.

"Shall we go?" he asked, rising from his seat.

The avenue bustled with pedestrians, employees of the many companies in the prestigious industrial park. The sunshine, the pleasant temperature, and the blue sky drove many people to the various restaurants.

"What is it that you think you saw through the microscope?" Goldon asked.

Tom didn't know whether to try one more time to tell Goldon that he had already seen a similar molecular organization. He didn't want to be silenced again. "It's still hard for me to process that image," he replied. "I've never seen such a symmetrical structure in biological matter. We're all familiar with carbon cage molecules, the fullerenes, and their famous representative Carbon 60 or Buckminster fullerene, and similar molecules, but they all possess only spherical symmetry. We've never seen pyramidal molecules, cubic ones, or any others. Do you know what those structures are?"

Goldon looked at him strangely, as if deliberating and trying to decide what to say. "No, we don't know what these structures are," he said, his intonation slow and drawn out, as if considering each word before pronouncing it. "No, neither we—nor, of course, you—know what these structures are," he repeated, emphasizing every syllable.

This seemed like a clear confirmation of Tom's fears that Professor Goldon was aware of Lise's bizarre results. But Lise had said she hadn't told anyone about her findings. How, then, did Professor Goldon know about it? Or did he keep track of everything that took place in the lab by bugging it? All Tom had to do was locate the bug and prevent any possibility of information leaks. He would have to think of a way to do so when he returned to the lab.

"I doubt that is a natural form of organization," Tom continued. "Nature tends to favor structures that bestow some advantage—

spheres, for example, or teardrops. But I can't conceive of any biological advantages for these patterns. I still don't know how these structures would affect living matter. Considering all that, how they were formed and..."

At that moment, he noticed that the professor's gaze had focused upon a tall, dark-skinned man wearing a suit who was walking across from them. Although they did not exchange greetings, Tom had no doubt that they were acquainted. This seemingly random encounter amused Goldon. For a moment, he looked as if he was attempting to conceal a mischievous smile, but snapped out of it immediately.

"How and for what purpose were these structures formed?" Tom continued. "We might look into the option that this is a natural occurrence, despite the low probability. We could raise the question with the biologist community—maybe someone's come across something similar."

"Believe me," Goldon replied, "that's the last thing you want to do. What would you say about the patterns you've seen?"

"Nothing other than that we should keep investigating them," Tom replied.

"Back to business matters," the professor continued. "As I've already told you, we're interested in having you lead a new project in a field I'm not even allowed to tell you about. The study is based on a scientific breakthrough we've achieved in the last two years, and which has just now ripened to the point where it can be used for product development. You'll build the team as you see fit, subject to information security considerations. You won't be limited in regard to purchasing equipment or any other expenses you believe will expedite or enhance product development.

"Since the projected market is estimated at many billions of dollars, it should be clear to you that we will invest whatever it takes in order to ensure rapid production of reliable products. I can't even describe the degree of urgency to you. We're not sure that we're the only ones working in this direction. Being the first on the market has enormous financial significance, not to mention the publicity achieved once the story breaks."

"I've got a potential problem," Tom began. "I'm waiting to hear about another excellent offer that, at least from a certain perspective, I've already committed to."

"You must be referring to the offer you got from Erie," Goldon said.

"Who's Erie?" Tom asked.

"Erie is the woman you met at Bob's Pub on Sunday."

"I met a woman named Gaya there." Tom looked at Goldon incredulously. "How do you know about the meeting?"

"Yes, she likes Greek names, and uses them freely. I don't know her real name. I know her as Erie."

The blood drained from Tom's face. Goldon hadn't even bothered to answer his question. The pleasant and charming Professor Goldon was an accessory to the threat Gaya had made during their meeting. Gaya and Goldon were partners in crime. *That's it—the cat is out of the bag*. BL was connected to the threat he had received, the one that had caused him to send his entire family into hiding in order to protect their well-being. Suddenly, he found the professor's pleasant demeanor artificial and repellent.

At least he no longer had to debate between two different offers. What was the project he would have to work on, which the professor couldn't even tell him about? On the other hand, for an annual salary of two million dollars, he would also be willing to work on a less interesting project for a certain time.

The lab was under constant surveillance. Professor Goldon knew exactly what Lise had discovered. Apparently, the conference room was bugged as well. What did they know about the strange structures that they weren't revealing? Were the structures related to the project he would be assigned to work on? This seemed logical; otherwise, why was Professor Goldon in such a rush to show them to him while attempting to lure him into the company? Tom found himself flooded by a sea of questions that continued to pile on, without any hint of an answer.

He took a deep breath and decided to stick to practicalities. "Will my salary be what Gaya proposed it would be?"

"Definitely. Gaya, as you know her—or Erie, as I know her—coordinated everything with me."

CHAPTER 17

Sheffy

California, Tuesday, July 22, 2036

Lia's sleep was restless. Again and again, she dreamed of Professor Tsur explaining to her the measurement errors that both of them had made, how a mistake in interpreting the spectrum emitted by the star was the cause for all the chaos she had experienced in the last few months. She called him even before breakfast.

"Good morning, Avi, have you had time to at least skim through part of the material?" she asked, feeling weak in the knees.

"Part of it? I've gone over all of it thoroughly," he replied immediately. She had to make a massive effort not to interrupt him. "Your measurement data regarding STA331047B is more up-to-date than mine. Naturally, I was surprised to discover that there's an identical situation in STA333654B as well. I'd still like to check the measurements there myself, which will require another day. I don't think this is the time for scientific hypotheses regarding what's causing this condition. The very fact that it exists at all is an essential shock to science in general, and to physicists in particular. Two stars like that is a different matter entirely. I don't have any sort of physical explanation for the phenomenon. It's definitely irregular, as evidenced by the fact that to this day, we haven't encountered a white dwarf with a similar mass among the hundreds of white dwarfs we've investigated. How do you plan to continue your research?"

"I'm basically stuck in the uncertainty phase I presented to you," she replied. "It's frustrating that even with all the resources I could recruit for a more in-depth investigation into this topic, I just can't think of any practical research angle that might produce an answer. Do you have any such research directions?"

"Not at the moment. I just haven't given it any thought. What does occur to me is to contact—with your permission, of course—Benjamin Sheffy, my colleague at Tel Aviv University. I'm sure you've heard his name. He specializes in Cepheids and Ia supernovas. If someone can help here, it would be him."

For the second time within twenty-four hours, she had to confront the question of confidentiality. Should she expand the circle of collaborators on the discovery that, until yesterday, she had been certain was exclusively hers? On the other hand, even with all her experience on the subject, Professor Sheffy had a stellar reputation as one of the major experts on supernovas in general and Ia supernovas, in particular.

Moreover, she also felt as if she had exhausted her research capabilities. Yes, she desperately needed to expand the cadre of scientists investigating the anomaly. Something in Avi's personality made her feel confident he would not con her, nor would Professor

Sheffy, and that when the research reached the publication stage, neither of them would claim to have made the initial discovery. Yes, she did feel that she could trust him and any researchers he recommended.

"That's perfectly fine with me. Please ask him to give me a call and to maintain confidentiality about the whole issue."

Absentmindedly, she shuffled into the kitchen and inserted two frozen slices of bread into the toaster, boiled some water, and made herself a cup of morning tea. The hot, refreshing tea woke her up somewhat. Her thoughts veered between a desire to sum up the entire study and publish an article that would shock the astrophysics community, and the more conservative option of continuing the research with the help of other scientists, aiming for a paper with more facts and proof and fewer open questions. It was only as she extracted the still-frozen slices from the toaster that she realized how distracted she was.

The assistant rang less than fifteen minutes after she had concluded her conversation with Avi. The call was from Professor Benjamin Sheffy himself. Yes, he would be happy to help. He was aware of the anomaly Avi Tsur had cited on star STA331047B. He hadn't dedicated too much thought to the subject, as he had attributed the result to imprecise measurements, as was often the case with telescopes. Professor Sheffy didn't know of another star with similar data. This sounded odd to him, perhaps justifying an examination of the means by which the measurements had been obtained.

"Where are you now?" he asked.

"At home," she replied.

"No, where are you geographically?" he asked.

"Berkeley, California."

"You're not going to believe this. I'm currently in Berkeley too, on my way to a conference on Ia supernovas that continues until the weekend. How do you feel about coming to the conference? We'll get a chance to meet, and you'll also hear about the latest discoveries in the field."

Lia couldn't believe her ears. Finally, she would get a chance to talk to an expert in the field who might illuminate her on her own cognitive or measurement errors, as well as to learn about the topic directly from the experts, in a concentrated manner. She wasn't surprised in the slightest that she had not heard of the conference taking place at her own university. Her obsessive preoccupation with accurately measuring the mass of the two stars had shielded her from everything going on around her that did not directly affect her research, including countless messages and emails she hadn't bothered to open.

CHAPTER 18

Will

Chicago, Tuesday, July 22, 2036

Will was proud of his long list of acquaintances. He had dedicated plenty of time and thought to nurturing his relationships with them. He always attended the weddings and birthday parties to which they invited him, always brought worthy gifts, and always took care to conduct long conversations with his friends and acquaintances. After all, they were the source for many interesting leads that he had come up with long before other reporters suspected a thing.

In that regard, Detective Rick was no exception. They would occasionally play squash and then sit down for a light meal and a gossip session that encompassed the entire world. Rick was frustrated, due to the problems in his personal life and the fact that he had been stuck in one job for too long. This job ate up most of his hours, and was apparently also the straw that had broken his wife's back when she had decided to separate from him.

Yesterday evening's squash game was no different than the ones that had preceded it. This time, Rick thoroughly demolished him, although Will had done his best to win. The victorious grin remained affixed to Rick's face, and as they sat down to eat, he talked incessantly. As usual, Will was all ears. After all, he might learn something interesting. He had no doubt that Rick had uncovered a promising investigation. It had been a while since Will had seen him so confident, or so talkative.

He could sense when the experienced Rick was being elusive, taking care not to reveal any confidential details. Will knew he was investigating the murder case at the University of Chicago; the media had reported on this fact. His enthusiasm couldn't have resulted merely from being appointed lead investigator on the case. He had already investigated similar major crimes in the past. Yes, there was something much bigger at work here, something he hadn't shared with anyone, even other cops.

On the night after the game, sitting at his home computer, Will stared ahead while gnawing on the end of his pen. Something Rick had said during the conversation struck him as a possible lead, but had later been forgotten. Something that might enable him to start his search. Rick had completely avoided discussing any findings from the crime scene, as behooved an investigating officer. No, the thing to spark Rick's enthusiasm hadn't been any particular piece of evidence, but rather an idea he had come up with himself, which had proved to be correct. This idea had been related to a broader perspective on the case.

Will began by characterizing the incident. Someone had broken into a university lab. The security guard had been killed with a gun equipped with a silencer. Nothing had been taken, and no evidence had been found on the scene.

Suddenly, the lead flashed out at him. Rick had made a reference to “scientists,” plural, when he had discussed his investigation into the incident. Similar incidents had taken place. There was a pattern here. This case wasn’t confined to a single occurrence involving a researcher.

Will scrambled for the computer. Within seconds, he was scrolling down an impressive list of criminal cases and accidents in which scientists, researchers, labs, and research institutions were directly or indirectly involved. The last of these to conform to the general characteristics he had defined in his search had taken place last Friday, only two days after the murder at the University of Chicago. He really hadn’t expected to discover a similar event in which a scientist crossed paths with the police taking place so soon after the previous one. This time, it was an astronomer who had been run over by a van on a fairly quiet street. Assuming there was a common denominator to these incidents, what did a biologist and an astronomer have in common?

He found an official description of the studies taking place in Dr. Thomas Lester’s lab on the University of Chicago website, while NASA’s website provided details on the research conducted by Dr. Gerald Apexton, who had been injured in the accident.

Dr. Thomas Lester was involved in the hot field of developing a means of expanding the human lifespan. His lab was also studying some unclear, esoteric research angle related to the human genome. At first look, it seemed obvious that the lifespan-enhancement study might have been the reason for the break-in, despite the large number of labs looking into this topic. After all, anyone who would find and implement a practical solution would reap a lot of money.

However, Will couldn’t think of any reason to harm a senior

astronomer, assuming that he had been intentionally assaulted. An astronomer specializing in analyzing the routes of asteroids and comets, a field that, by its nature, interested only a small minority of people and involved no obvious commercial applications, as the NASA website made clear. Unless Dr. Apexton had discovered an unusual asteroid, perhaps one made entirely of diamond or even metal. Will had read about the possibility of such an asteroid. There had also been some commercial ventures to locate and mine asteroids, although, as of today, he had not heard of any developments concerning these ventures. Despite his experience in finding hidden connections between seemingly disparate events, this time he could not come up with any ideas.

Dr. Apexton had dedicated plenty of work to analyzing the complex movements of asteroids in the asteroid belt between Mars and Jupiter, as well as celestial bodies entering the solar system from the surrounding Kuiper belt. He was also interested in the reasons why the immense collection of fragments in the asteroid belt had never coalesced into a whole planet, as had happened to the other terrestrial planets closer to the sun. There was no mention of an attempt to identify the matter from which such asteroids were comprised. This definitely was not a topic with commercial potential that might justify attempting to harm someone.

Will was facing a dead end. He could not come up with a single idea to explain Detective Rick's satisfaction and improved mood. The prominent correlation linking the list of criminal incidents was a significant majority of biology labs. Other than the murder at the University of Chicago and Dr. Apexton's accident, there were five biology labs on the list. He assumed a more thorough search might uncover more incidents. In the meantime, he decided to focus on his current list.

The aromatic cup of coffee he made and the quiet music allowed him to focus for most of the night on mapping the various areas of research taking place at the labs in which the break-ins occurred. The biology labs focused mainly on various aspects of genetic engineering, such as enhancing crops by improving their nutritional value per growth area unit, so that they would contain a greater concentration of vitamins, minerals, and calories essential to humans and animals. However, all five labs were also active in the field of the human genome. Will was entirely convinced that the break-ins were intended to obtain information on behalf of manufacturers of food and chemicals.

***

His aching back and the sharp pain in his forehead woke him up from the nap that had overtaken him as he sat in his chair. A quick glance at his assistant revealed it was now early morning.

As he held a fresh cup of coffee in one hand, he read the morning news on his terminal. For quite a while now, the hot topic dominating headlines all over the world was energy costs, a topic of essential global importance. Everyone was interested in the price of a barrel of biological oil, as the new fuel was called, a designation also reflected in its pricing. The aftershocks following the global upset caused by the war in the Middle East continued. Most countries in the region had taken part in the war, and the major superpowers—China, the United States, and Russia—were involved in it as well. Major damage was still apparent in many cities in the region, and focused terrorist activity continued to disrupt the everyday life of their citizens and had unfortunately become a routine aspect of life.

The extreme fluctuations in oil distribution and its raging price motivated massive investment in developing alternatives. The most promising solutions were based on the impressive advances in genetic engineering. Colossal ponds installed in sunny areas had been filled with bacteria genetically engineered to produce long sequences of carbon directly from water and air. These sequences were then used to produce cheap and efficient biological fuel substitutes.

The current price of a barrel of biological oil was $24.65, about one quarter of the price of an original barrel of oil before the war broke out. The global significance of the countries producing traditional oil was gradually decreasing.

The second scientific story whose headline caught his eye dealt with predicting the results of the many studies on genetically engineered food. The story focused on research at the forefront of this field. The future did look greener, cheaper, and a lot healthier, involving more quality food per growth area unit. The studies were already bearing practical results. The efficiency of current crops had more than quadrupled compared to the beginning of the century. The story also briefly referenced new areas of research, aiming to replace agricultural crops with industrial processes. *Indeed, it's the end of the world as we know it*, he thought.

At his request, the terminal displayed a long list of large corporations dealing with genetically engineered crops. He had to talk to Melissa—she knew this industry from the inside. Melissa, or rather Dr. Melissa Colette, was an independent and unaffiliated advisor in the field of genetic engineering, and had also played a major role in the development of grain varieties that could be irrigated with seawater. The endless pastures of grains in the Sahara Desert were a testimony to her abilities. She was personally acquainted with many people in the field, and could tell him some behind-the-scenes tales regarding the industry. With her help, he could compile a short list of companies that might be behind the break-in and the murder.

For most people he knew, 6:10 a.m. was not a reasonable hour to call. However, Melissa was an exception, and she answered immediately.

"I can only see you after ten thirty," she replied when he requested to meet her as soon as possible.

He understood that she could not put off her morning meeting under such short notice. Well, this would allow him to get more than three hours of sleep before the meeting, as well as update the paper's editorial board.

***

The assistant call received by Martin Patterson, head of the *Chicago Chronicle*'s investigative department, was brief. "Some interesting developments are afoot. Still investigating. I'll update you later."

The call came from Will Thorne, one of the young, determined investigative reporters he managed. Will had a track record of finding topics to investigate on his own. Usually, he worked the field independently and would report back only when he achieved a breakthrough. His specialty was finding connections and patterns in seemingly unrelated events. His last investigation had uncovered a series of financial actions taken by the Muslim organization Al Jamaa in an attempt to undermine the value of the euro, which had already decreased significantly following the collapse of about half the countries comprising the European Union and had yet to bounce back. This time, the editorial board had not heard from him for more than seven days.

Martin also did not know what Will was working on at the moment, but he wasn't concerned. Quite the opposite. On days when Will was hanging around the paper's offices, Martin knew he had nothing to investigate. When he disappeared for several days, Martin knew he had uncovered some interesting lead, and was digging into it in depth among his mysterious sources.

***

The prestigious Dempsey's Bar downtown was busy at all hours of the day and night. It had been a while since he'd last met Melissa, and more than two years since they'd broken up. Everything had been fine between them, but their demanding and very different careers had not left them enough time and energy to invest in a relationship that had gradually declined. He wondered how she felt about him today. Since they had gone their separate ways, he had not been involved in any relationship worth mentioning.

Without thinking, he sat down at a table for two, in the chair facing the entrance, but only for a brief moment. This was Melissa he was meeting, after all. She would never sit with her back to the entrance. This was one more small habit he had had a hard time getting used to when they were going out.

He found an appropriate table at the far end of the restaurant. From here, he could watch the door with a slight turn of his head, and more importantly, Melissa would feel at ease. He found himself smiling with pleasure as he recalled her small and sometimes amusing idiosyncrasies. He ordered himself a glass of carrot and pomegranate juice, and a cup of coffee with no sugar and a little soy milk, the way she liked it, for her. Melissa always arrived five minutes late to her appointments. The coffee wouldn't grow too cold, especially since she didn't like it very warm.

As he sat there, absently observing the people coming in and pleasantly recalling her various habits, she came storming in, in her typical manner. Sensations he had not experienced in a while reawakened within him. No doubt about it. His feelings toward her had not diminished. He still loved her.

Melissa noticed him immediately and headed quickly in his direction. This was how it had always been. She had a special ability to recognize someone within a sea of faces within a split second. The expression in her green eyes and her sexy, provocative walk flooded him with sweet memories. Will straightened in his seat, his arms stretching out to embrace Melissa in a warm, loving hug. Her embrace in return seemed much more than a friendly gesture. Yes, she was still attached to him as well. Maybe, he found himself thinking, maybe they could get back together?

Melissa pushed him away to get a better look at him. "You haven't changed at all. Actually, you look even better. Something's different. Wow, you shaved off your awful mustache. Way to go," she said, sitting down. She reacted with pleasure to the coffee on the table, prepared the way she'd always liked it, and, as usual, quickly transitioned to the matter at hand.

Will had summarized his research on a single page, which he laid out before her.

Melissa needed no more than two minutes of browsing in order to look up and say, "This is only the tip of the iceberg. The action behind the scenes is at least as extensive as what takes place on the surface. It's a very hot field. Every breakthrough entails the potential for enormous profits to the developer, but also catastrophic losses to the previous technology, whose infrastructure required an investment of immense sums. The corporations working on this are very large, and are spread out all over the areas of the globe subject to intense sun radiation. Behind closed doors, there's often collaboration between competitors to delay new discoveries, sometimes for long periods of time. Companies pay significant sums to their competitors in order to delay distribution of new technologies. This covert system works in spite of the competition because, due to the rate of innovations, each of them will need favors from the others at some point."

"Are break-ins and murder also considered legitimate in this covert relationship?" he asked.

"I'm not aware of any incidents of murder," she replied. "Espionage, and everything it entails, is in very common use. I don't know what kind of boundaries the corporations set out for those acting on their behalf. Murder might certainly take place if someone loses control. There are major agendas at work, with commensurate payments to the investigators who get results."

Will gazed at her face, his expression amused. *Why not kill two birds with one stone?* he thought. Why not ask Melissa to join him and Detective Rick to work as a team on solving the murder, and perhaps some of the other break-ins as well? He would finally get a chance to work with her, which would enable them to look into the option of resuming their relationship. Everyone would benefit from their collaboration. He and the detective would receive a reliable, professional, inside perspective on the world of genetic engineering, and get to know the players behind the scenes, the power clashes, the egos, and the machinations.

Apparently, Melissa was still interested in him and might be pleased to be offered a collaboration that would allow them to work together. And the project might also help her to advance her career. Although her work had brought about breakthroughs in engineered crops, which had yielded handsome profits for the companies she worked for, she had not personally enjoyed the financial rewards of her research, and definitely needed the income.

Will emerged from his thoughts when he noticed that the flow of Melissa's speech had come to a stop. Apparently, she had noticed that he wasn't listening to her. She didn't need to say a thing; he knew her too well. The look she gave him conveyed a question mark. He smiled for several more seconds.

Just as he saw her look of query about to transform into one of admonition, he said, "I've come up with an idea: How would you feel about collaborating with me as part of a small team including you, Rick, and me, which would delve into the biological topic in an attempt to understand who the major players are, and what's motivating them?"

"Who's Rick?" she asked.

"Rick Heller is the police detective responsible for investigating the murder at the University of Chicago. I'm convinced he's found a promising lead. It might be the direction I'm also moving in, or it may be something completely different. Anyway, since he's a police officer, he has access to considerable resources that might help in the investigation. Especially since, despite my experience, my research has been largely limited to what I could access online and through my connections. Rick's investigative options are a lot more diverse, and working together, our chances of success increase significantly."

Will expected Melissa to allow her fertile mind to ruminate on the offer, to ask for time to consider it, to request further clarifications in the days to come, as was her custom. To his great surprise, she responded with a decisive, "I agree."

Her immediate consent could only mean one thing: she was

already familiar with the topic or the story, in whole or in part. She had been ready to delve into the matter even before he had approached her but, apparently, didn't know how to go about it. He had provided her with exactly what she wanted—the possibility of taking part in a fascinating inquiry in which she'd been interested even before their meeting, under appealing conditions. He wouldn't ask her about this directly. If she had wanted to disclose any of it to him, she would have done it by now. She might still tell him about her involvement later. At this stage, he had achieved his goal, and all that was left now was to proceed as quickly as possible.

Still gazing at her, he asked the assistant to contact Detective Rick, who replied immediately with an amicable, "Hi, Will. How are you?"

"I'm sitting at Dempsey's Bar with Melissa Colette, a doctor of genetic engineering as well as my ex-girlfriend, whom I've told you a lot about. Melissa's fluent in current research in the field, and I'm sure she could offer a lot of help. I propose that the three of us meet soon."

"Does twenty minutes from now work for you two?" Rick asked.

When Will consulted her, Melissa nodded her assent. "That works for us. We'll be waiting for you."

Will and Melissa were engrossed in a friendly, intimate conversation, and did not notice as the minutes ticked by, until they sensed someone standing at Will's side. It was a young boy whom they had failed to notice until that moment.

"I was asked to give this to the lady," he said, extending a large manila envelope in front of Will's face. As Will reached out tentatively for the envelope, intending to pass it to Melissa, she leaped from her chair and snatched it out of the boy's hand.

"Thanks, that's okay," she said, sitting down again as she

clutched the envelope.

The strange event, which lasted only a few seconds, strengthened his impression that Melissa had covert dealings behind the scenes concerning the topics she wouldn't discuss openly. The incident certainly necessitated an explanation from her. He decided to use the efficient method of applying pressure that he had practiced many times before: stare at the person sitting across from you and don't say a thing. Melissa undoubtedly realized that her jittery response required an explanation. She looked down at the envelope, not bothering to open it. Her behavior clearly indicated that the delivery of the envelope had not surprised her, and that she might know its contents, as well.

Apparently, Will's piercing gaze had caused her to open her mouth to say something. But then her mouth continued to open, her eyes reflecting an expression of fright. Will's first thought was that Melissa was in immediate danger, and that he should leap in her direction and remove her from the line of fire of a gun aimed at her. However, he came to his senses immediately. No one would shoot a gun in such a crowded location in the middle of the day. No, such extreme behavior was not required. He spun quickly in the direction Melissa was facing. The restaurant looked utterly routine and mundane—people eating and drinking, robotic waiters scurrying between the tables, and not a single human waiter in sight. When his wandering gaze met the eyes of a tall, dark-skinned man wearing a suit who was standing at the hostess station, the man turned on his heels and left the restaurant.

Will immediately turned to Melissa, only to see her looking away from the restaurant door. His questions multiplied instantly.

Melissa opened her mouth again. "Well—." when Detective Rick approached the table and introduced himself to her.

After ordering an extra-strong coffee, Rick consulted the assistant screen in front of him and addressed Melissa. "Dr. Melissa Colette. A PhD from Northwestern University in Evanston. Four years on the genetic engineering faculty, in Professor Harel's department, until the professor decided to go back to Israel and his position became available. Surprising quite a few people, refused to accept the position of department head offered to her, and preferred to retire, although she was associated more than anyone else with the department's current research goals and its rapid development. Worked for the Monsanto company for five years, focusing on genetically engineering grains, and from then to the present time, an independent consultant. Pretty impressive.

"Dr. Colette, are you aware of what's going on in research labs in the areas in which Dr. Thomas Lester is working?" He quickly brought up the matter at hand.

"I advise several labs on various biological topics, but I'm not an expert on longevity enhancement. I know Dr. Lester well, I'm aware of his work, and I know some of the players in the field. The immense scale of the potential market leads to massive investments in the research. There's constant, impressive progress in regard to small mammals. All of us experience these small enhancements in our daily lives; life capacity has surpassed one hundred years on average for people in a modern environment. However, it doesn't feel like a breakthrough.

"My area of expertise is genetically engineering crops and manufacturing food industrially, a field that has seen significant ongoing progress for many years now. My colleagues and I believe there's still room for significant progress, which justifies an investment of resources. The bulk of the research focuses on increasing nutritional value in crops per area unit, and in developing industrially manufactured substitutes for various crops and meat types."

The concentration with which the two men listened to her indicated that they understood the gist of her presentation thus far.

"I assume you're mostly interested in knowing how the potential of Dr. Lester's research rates in comparison with other research being conducted, and assuming he's made more progress, which of his competitors might potentially be behind the break-in and the murder. Will also showed me a list of several labs that were broken into in the last year with nothing being stolen and with no leads as to the identity of the intruders."

Surprised, Rick glanced briefly at Will, and then flashed him a quick smile of satisfaction. This was all Will required. He realized he had indeed intuited Rick's main direction in the investigation. Turning back to Melissa, Rick quietly instructed, "Go on, please."

"The wave of break-ins into biology labs has been going on for about two years now. The break-ins are generally clean—nothing is taken, no equipment is vandalized, doors are opened using the appropriate keys. Everything points to collaboration with insiders. The break-ins aren't always detected. Sometimes it appears as if someone just forgot to lock the door to the lab. The labs targeted deal with a variety of advanced biological topics.

"If you look online, you can find articles on work carried out in university labs on behalf of—and using funding from—commercial elements, in a variety of areas. In general, investment in the various fields of biology is currently significantly more extensive than investment in computation topics, which once far outpaced other topics. The focus, naturally, is on expanding longevity, improving health, enhancing cognitive ability, improving and increasing global food manufacturing capabilities, and of course, developing more efficient synthetic fuel. The interesting thing is that most of these articles aren't written by well-known scientists, but by complete unknowns.

"I've made several attempts to contact the writers, to no avail. I found myself talking to young, inexperienced researchers. I believe there's a well-connected, powerful element behind the scenes that is following developments in certain areas and is interested in focusing public and scientific opinion on research aimed at longevity enhancement. Not that they have to try that hard. The public yearns for every glimmer of hope regarding progress on this front. Everyone wants to live for many years, in good health. To me, it looks like intentional misdirection, at least to some extent. It's still unclear to me what these articles are trying to steer the scientific establishment and the public away from, but I'm pretty sure that's what's going on."

"We'll have to compile a detailed list of all the studies taking place in the labs that were broken into...or seemingly broken into," Will said, turning to Rick. "Only you guys in the police have access to that kind of information."

"Once we have the list, we'll try to find the common denominator and focus on who might be interested in it," Melissa summed up the topic.

"I'm on it," was Rick's only reaction. As he rose from his seat, he instructed his assistant to pay his share of the bill. He shook Melissa's hand, saying, "I enjoyed meeting you. I hope we'll have a fruitful collaboration," then left the restaurant.

"Truly a fascinating conversationalist," Melissa whispered, as if she were afraid he would hear her.

Will replied, "He's a good guy, but he's a cop. He thinks like a cop and he can get a lot done. If you handle him correctly, you could go far with him." He had no doubt that Melissa was indeed involved, and was more intimately acquainted with what was going on than she had let on.

The frightened look she had directed at the dark-skinned man made him think she was afraid of getting hurt. The murder of the security guard had already made it clear that their opponents, whoever they were, had no inhibitions when it came to attaining their goals. To some extent, he had begun to fear for his own life. Of course, he had no intention of backing off. On the contrary, the scent of danger only raised his adrenaline level. This was precisely the sensation to which he'd grown addicted, and which was occasionally provided by his work.

He would have preferred to stay and talk to Melissa about more personal matters, but meeting Rick and bringing up the murder of Oleg had sullied the ambiance. The silence that took over once Rick had left only added to the oppressive atmosphere. And, in a depressing conclusion to the meeting, Melissa sat up in her chair, mumbling that she had to run as she slipped the envelope, still sealed, into her purse.

Will didn't even try to change her mind. Briefly, he considered sticking around and planning his next moves, but then changed his mind abruptly. A quick glance revealed that Melissa had turned right after she'd exited the restaurant. He confirmed the bill and hurried out, just in time to see her crossing the street and opening the manila envelope. She extracted several large sheets of paper, perused each of them briefly, then tore them up, along with the envelope, and tossed them into a trash can. Pausing, she looked around as if searching for something, then quickly turned to a shady sitting nook, isolated from the bustle of the street.

Will stopped abruptly, almost causing the people rushing

down the street to bump into him. He leaned against a streetlight in a position that provided a good vantage point. Melissa sat down, burying her face in her hands. She seemed very tense. Something was going on with her. He wondered what she had gotten herself involved in.

Immediately, he turned around and continued up the street, submerged within the teeming sea of people.

No doubt about it. Melissa's involvement in the matter far exceeded the objective description with which she had provided them. He briefly considered sharing his apprehensions with Rick and asking for his help in having her followed. But if she ever discovered he had done so, this would ruin any chance of her returning to him.

On the other hand, the frightened look in her eyes at the restaurant indicated that she might be in danger, in which case his actions might save her. He was also perturbed by the fact that she had been in no hurry to open the envelope the young man had brought her. Apparently, she had been wary of doing so in his presence. She probably knew or suspected what it contained. Her nod as she examined the pages she extracted from the envelope also seemed like a confirmation of something she had known. Yes, Melissa was definitely in danger. It didn't matter what she would think of him—he couldn't ignore her signals of distress and just let her be. He had to act in order to save her. She might not be in immediate mortal danger, but there was no doubt she was in significant trouble.

As he walked down the pedestrian-laden boulevard, he called Rick, explaining why he had chosen to follow Melissa immediately as she left the restaurant, and giving him the location of the trash can as well as the bench on which she was sitting. He was certain of

Rick's ability to locate the pages and the envelope.

While continuing on his way, he felt himself being gently carried along by the pedestrians around him to the edge of the sidewalk, so that he found himself standing at the edge of the road opposite the traffic light, although he hadn't decided in which direction he was going, and wasn't certain that this was where he wanted to get across the intersection.

Once he grew aware of the circumstances, he started to turn around, but then felt a powerful shove propelling him into the road, directly in front of an oncoming garbage truck. The last thing he saw was the dark face of the man from the restaurant who had frightened Melissa so much, standing where he himself had just been standing. He then submerged into a deep, dark hole.

***

Out of the warm, soft darkness engulfing him, he managed to hear cars honking and distant human voices that seemed to be rapidly approaching. Subconsciously, he tried to suppress and ignore the voices and return to the sensation of a warm, protective womb.

Then he heard someone shouting, "He's alive. He's got a pulse!"

For a brief moment, he was disappointed. It had been so pleasant before, and now he had to deal with the loud, annoying voices. As he woke up, he felt a tremendous burst of pain on the right side of his head. The unbearable stab of pain produced an unprecedented cry of anguish from him before he submerged once more into the black hole, devoid of voices and concerns.

CHAPTER 19

Tom and the Structures

Chicago, Tuesday, July 22, 2036

Only when he set the autonomous driver to Relaxed Driving Mode on the quietest route leading back to the university could Tom focus once more on his meeting with Professor Goldon. What unknown elements were hiding behind the giant corporation? Which dark forces were exerting their influence over it, and what were their goals? Who was Professor Goldon? A sharp, brilliant, and pleasant man running a major company, as he was portrayed in the media and in accordance with the image he tried to project—or a criminal who would not stop at blackmail in order to attain his goals? And what, in fact, were his goals? Were they even legal? Was he going to work for an outlaw and help him attain objectives that would hurt numerous people? Who, or rather what, was Professor Goldon? What exactly would Tom be working on over there?

Plenty of questions and no answers, other than one single, obvious reality. He could not refuse the job offer. He couldn't put his family at risk. Perhaps in the course of his work for Goldon, he might understand more and be able to exert a positive influence.

The professor was definitely interested in him; however, throughout the meeting, Tom hadn't felt as if he was under any pressure to accept the offer. The atmosphere had been one of persuasion and enthusiasm rather than coercion. It was easy to understand how BL had managed to recruit the best scientists and researchers to join its ranks. The professor was blessed with the ability to make the person he was talking to feel so good that at the end of the meeting, that person would do anything to work with him. He hadn't even asked Tom what his decision was. From the first moment, he had acted as if he was Tom's employer, while Tom himself had made no effort to change this assumption. It was as if they both knew that Tom would be joining BL.

No, he would not be dealing with the geometrical structures discovered in both their labs. Only Goldon dealt with them, perhaps more out of personal interest than any business objective. It was true that the company had made considerable investments in general research that was not aimed at any commercial objectives. But in this specific case, the professor was the only one researching the topic.

Goldon had chosen not to elaborate much on the project he had designated for him. He did say that Tom could easily guess it if he looked into the company's current products and tried to speculate regarding its future ones. He only hinted that in a world in which medicine could promise the generation of children currently under ten a lifespan of 120 years, additional aspects of such a long life must also be considered. Tom was definitely not surprised that there were many ways of enhancing quality of life that were no less important than extending it.

For a moment, he thought that the best thing he could do was talk to Melissa. She might provide insight into some angles he had not considered. But then again, he would be working for BL regardless of the projects he would be assigned. Somewhere deep inside him, he did not want to accept the possibility that Professor Goldon was a criminal. Perhaps he, too, was being blackmailed by some dark, powerful element forcing him to behave in a corrupt manner. Everything he knew about Goldon, his demeanor and manner, did not fit in with what he expected from an arch-villain.

He made a conscious decision to abandon this line of thought and move on to considering the nature of his future work for BL. He hoped his assigned field would be interesting rather than merely commercially promising. Maybe...maybe he would even be invited to join the study of the strange structures.

At that moment, his thoughts refocused on the spatial geometrical structures. How had they been superseded by discovering Professor Goldon's involvement in the implied threat made by Gaya? And more importantly, how could he be delving into banal topics such as his next place of employment and his salary when he had been exposed to such amazing discoveries, discoveries that might alter the face of humanity forever? He no longer thought the structures might be an experimental error, as he'd initially suspected when Lise had showed them to him; Goldon had showed him identical structures. What could they be?

As part of his biology studies, he had learned quite a lot of chemistry. He had been very impressed by crystal structures, which through a microscope looked as if they had been designed and built by the most fastidious engineers and builders. They included giant crystals grown in space stations at zero gravity. Often, due to the slightest contamination in the crystallizing material, the normal process was disrupted, resulting in a collection of structures in various shapes and sizes that always made him think of a large, crowded city as seen from a great height. Perhaps Lise's vial had been contaminated in some way by an unknown component that changed the protein's three-dimensional structure and created the unusual formations?

Once again, he recalled the structures he'd seen. They looked solid, rendering only the outlines of geometrical shapes. They looked more like rods or columns of various lengths whose edges adjoined to form precise structures. No, those hadn't been crystals. Tom had already seen proteins that resembled straight or rounded rods, but they had never joined together to create such symmetrical, uniformly sized, three-dimensional structures. A double or single strand of DNA that had straightened for whatever reason could also fill the role of the rods he'd seen.

The first test to be carried out, he thought, should be identifying the ingredients of these rods in order to discover whether they were biological molecules or crystallized minerals. Anyway, there was no longer any need to recreate the experiment, as he'd asked Lise to do. Goldon had proved that it was not an experimental error; it was real.

Lise answered on the third ring. "What's going on? Are you on your way back to the university?"

Until that moment, Tom had not decided whether to return to the lab or go meet Melissa. However, the fact that his thoughts had drifted to his own private affairs while dealing with such an important discovery disturbed him, and he answered Lise's question with no hesitation. "Yes, I'm on my way to the lab."

Lise's sigh of relief was clearly audible through the assistant. She was definitely on pins and needles, and his abrupt departure to meet Professor Goldon had not contributed to her peace of mind. She sounded very tense, and it would take a considerable effort on his part to calm her down.

For a moment, he almost succumbed to the urge to provide some guidance that would allow her to get some work done before his arrival, but he came to his senses immediately. This was not an appropriate conversation for the assistant.

He was certain that in her agitated state, Lise hadn't had any lunch, and therefore told her, "I'll be on the road for at least another twenty minutes, and it'll take a few more minutes to park and walk. I suggest you take your lunch break before I arrive, so we can sit down with no interruptions."

"Okay," she replied. "I'll grab something quick and be back immediately."

"No need to rush," Tom said. "Take your time. I can't get there any quicker, anyway. Traffic is pretty slow."

CHAPTER 20

Will is Injured in an Accident

Chicago, Tuesday, July 22, 2036

On his way back to his office, Rick asked Lily, his efficient secretary, to set up protections against surveillance on Melissa's and Dr. Lester's assistants, using the usual technique that would also reveal to the police where the information was being relayed if the devices had indeed been bugged. She advised him that all the material Melissa had requested was already waiting for him. She always understood her assignments with minimal explanations, and had earned a reputation as the most competent of the precinct's administrative assistants, despite lacking the professional training that police officers received.

The table she had compiled listed thirteen break-ins and two more accidents and criminal incidents involving science personnel in the United States within the past twelve months, alongside a list of the studies conducted in each of the labs and the fields of specialization for each of the scientists involved in an accident. He thought the list of research topics resembled a collection of words randomly selected from a dictionary in an unfamiliar language. After a few failed attempts to call Will in order to ask him to forward the list to Melissa, he decided to try later. Just then, Lily entered his office, her expression troubled.

"What's wrong?" he asked.

"Is the Will you met today a reporter for the *Chicago Chronicle*?"

"He is," he replied.

She walked over to his desk, chose the summary of afternoon incidents on his terminal, and clicked on a headline featuring Will's name. Rick read through it quickly. Will Thorne, a reporter for the *Chicago Chronicle*, had been badly injured in a traffic accident and evacuated, still unconscious, to Rush University Medical Center. The driver who had hit him claimed he had been driving at a moderate speed when the victim simply flew at his vehicle out of a cluster of pedestrians on the street, from a distance that did not allow him time to brake. He believed the victim had been engaged in a confrontation with another pedestrian, who had pushed him in the driver's direction.

Rick leaped from his seat, informing Lily that he was on his way to the hospital as he left the office. She ran after him as he rushed through the hall, where dozens of preoccupied investigators toiled in their cubicles.

"Hold on a minute," Lily called out after him. "The results of the blood samples from the university also arrived." Her voice was unusually loud. "Just like you thought, the blood belonged to Oleg, the murdered security guard."

Rick turned toward her, saying, "I'd have been very surprised if it belonged to anyone else," before heading quickly toward the parking lot.

He preferred to drive himself rather than relaxing and letting the automatic driver take over. He felt so tense that relaxing wasn't an option, anyway, and he was unable to generate any productive thoughts the entire way, although usually manual driving allowed him to focus on the most urgent topics on his agenda.

Will definitely had quite a few enemies. Every scandal he had exposed increased their number to proportions that could definitely be considered threatening. However, up to this point, no lines had been crossed. Will did his work, and those harmed by his revelations hated and resented him. Some had even sued him and the paper in court, but they had never hurt him physically.

Some extreme covert activity was currently taking place. It had begun gradually in the past few years, but had accelerated during this last one. He had to sit down with Melissa or some other expert on biological research in order to better understand what was going on both openly and behind the scenes.

Rick briefly debated whether to assign security to watch over Will. Just how desperate was a person who would push another man to his death on a busy road in broad daylight, and what else might he be capable of? Or had it been merely a warning to Will, not to interfere in the topic the assailant was protecting? The department had recently hired several new cops who were not too busy. A surveillance and security task of this kind could provide useful practice for them, and most importantly, would ensure Will's safety.

The assistant's ring interrupted his train of thought. "We've looked into Kyra," Lily said. "We didn't find anyone by that name who fits the limited description Mike gave us. As far as the system is concerned, she doesn't even exist. Apparently, she gave him false information. Representatives of a forensics lab are on their way to Mike's home to collect biological traces, which should allow us to produce DNA and locate her in the police database. I assume that if her fingerprints are in any database, we can locate her by this evening."

"That's interesting, but also totally predictable. This case is expanding by the hour, to proportions I never even imagined when I left for the university last week."

"The material from the garbage can has been collected per your request and is on its way to you. The municipal officer who collected it reported that he found a torn envelope and a torn-up photo of an unidentified restaurant in which a man and a woman are sitting. We're trying to identify it based on the few details in the photo. There was also a torn-up print of a news article about the Muslim organization Al Jamaa."

"Too many of these paths are intersecting. We have to sit down and sort out a sea of information," Rick said. "Ask Brad to assign one of the new officers to protect Will. Ask him to keep it discreet. I don't want to make too much of a fuss about it at this stage."

After hanging up, he instructed the assistant, "Call Dr. Melissa Colette." It was a good thing the assistants had exchanged addresses, he thought. Within less than a minute, he heard the assistant's sexy programmed voice. "Dr. Melissa Colette is on the line."

"Hi, how are you?" came Melissa's calm, businesslike voice. It was obvious that she didn't know what had happened to Will. He had to let her know, he decided. Perhaps they could also meet at the hospital.

"I'm on my way to Rush Medical Center. Will's been hospitalized there after being involved in an accident. We don't know exactly what condition he's in."

"I'll be there as soon as I can," she responded.

"See you there," he replied.

As he parked his car, he saw that Lily had sent him a reminder to show Melissa the list she had requested. *That's a great idea*, he thought. Now Melissa might find the common denominator among the labs that had been broken into, and provide him with a list of companies working on these topics. This would enable him to focus the investigation.

At first look, this seemed like significant progress. On the other hand, his acquaintance with Melissa had been very brief. It was true that she had a longer relationship with Will, but should he trust someone he didn't know to such an extent? Should he provide her with such sensitive confidential information?

His deliberation ended once he got to the hospital. The assistant guided him from the parking lot through the hospital corridors to the neuro-surgical ward where Will was being held.

In the message window of the assistant, he saw that Lily had forwarded the photos. Despite his desire to reach Will quickly, he paused briefly to examine them. The first photo showed Melissa and Will sitting in a restaurant that resembled Dempsey's Bar, where he had met them that day. There was no doubt that the photographer had been focusing on them. The image had been lightly processed, so that the two of them were clearly displayed at its center, while its edges were somewhat blurred.

The second image displayed the newspaper article. Rick tried unsuccessfully to read the reporter's name; he could only discern that it comprised two short words. He gradually expanded the image several times, zooming in until Will Thorne's name filled half the screen. No doubt about it: the sender of the envelope was clearly implying that he knew exactly whom Melissa was meeting. It was a tangible threat, and assigning an officer to watch over Will now seemed like an especially good idea.

CHAPTER 21

Professor Benny Sheffy

California, Tuesday, July 22, 2036

At 12:15, precisely according to schedule, Lia entered the Berkeley Coffee Shop, which was overflowing with people. Exhaustion and stress had kept her from thinking about how she would identify Professor Sheffy. She assumed he would be the only one by himself at a table for two, but a quick glance did not reveal any solitary patrons. As she stood there, examining the people sitting around her, a handsome man in his sixties walked over to her, extended his hand, and introduced himself.

"Benjamin Sheffy." Her sigh of relief provided all the proof he needed that she was indeed the person he had been waiting for. "I managed to snag us a table," he said, leading her into the teeming café.

"How did you recognize me?" she asked after they sat down.

"You were the only woman who entered the restaurant alone at exactly the time we'd decided on." Privately, he also thought she looked absentminded, as expected from a professor who was so neck-deep in her research that she didn't even glance in the mirror before leaving the house. The amount of rouge she used would have been enough for a full week for any woman.

The small talk with Professor Sheffy flowed well and proved interesting. He had been working on Ia supernovas for many years, and was responsible for investigating some of the most distant ones.

Lia said, "I'm entitled to two hours of STA observation a week with no need for committee approval. I also have a lot of leeway in determining when the observation hours will be scheduled. If we could decide today which observations and measurements we need, we could have results as early as tomorrow morning."

"Sounds excellent," he replied. "Why don't you join me for today's lectures, which are scheduled until six? Then we could sit down for dinner and plan the observations."

"Great," she replied.

As they were on their way to the convention hall, she notified the department of an urgent observation request for that night. *These Israelis are an efficient, businesslike bunch*, she thought. She had just talked to Professor Tsur this morning, and he had already found her an expert on the topic that was most vital to her, who had contacted her immediately. Within hours, she would carry out a series of observations that would significantly advance her research into the anomaly in the two irregular stars she had discovered, after it had gotten stuck in recent weeks, confined to repeated examination of her latest data and calculations.

The lectures were interesting, but she had a hard time

concentrating, particularly on the most technical aspects, to which the majority of the time was dedicated. The audience was fluent in the most minute details, and nearly every mathematical derivation presented was subject to lively reactions.

Dinner, during which the professor insisted she call him Benny, was both productive and relaxed. Although he would be defending one of his articles the next day, he seemed entirely at ease. If Lia were in his shoes, she would have been feeling the pressure, and wouldn't have wasted time having dinner with strangers.

She recognized many of the restaurant's patrons as the conference's attendees and lecturers. Everyone was talking enthusiastically about the startling discoveries that the STA's accurate observations were expected to yield, as well as looking for a way to influence the observations and, of course, be the first to receive the results. Ideally, they wanted to receive them long before everyone else in order to have time to interpret them and write the expected groundbreaking papers.

Three hot topics attracted the attention of the conference attendees, monopolizing most of the discussions. The first was the increasing accuracy of measuring distances to Ia supernovas, and therefore, distances to the galaxies in which they were discovered.

The second was the extent to which the extraordinary resolution, the mechanisms preventing glare from the nearby suns and the stability of the measurement would allow unmediated observation of distant planets.

And the third was speculating about the limitations of the distance at which it would be possible to discover fluctuations in star locations, caused by planets orbiting around them in a plane perpendicular to the line of observation from Earth, which had prevented their discovery up until now.

The prediction was that this would enable the discovery of a particularly large number of near and distant planets that had been impossible to discover using transit photometry, which enabled discovery of less than 10 percent of possible planets. The Doppler method also did not facilitate discovery of more than 50 percent of the planets it could potentially locate, especially since its forte was discovering large, heavy planets.

All this had, of course, been made possible thanks to the STA, which the speakers praised wholeheartedly. All of them expected the STA to facilitate the breakthrough that the astronomers so avidly anticipated. The speakers compared these expected discoveries and breakthroughs to those made during the initial years of the Hubble telescope.

Benny asked to measure four binary systems, each of which contained a white dwarf absorbing gas from a nearby red giant whose mass should be approaching the Chandrasekhar limit. He suspected these dwarfs possessed irregular characteristics, and Lia could provide him with an immediate window of observation. He also requested to repeat Lia's observations on the same occasion.

Benny transferred the data for the stars to Lia's assistant, from which they were immediately conveyed to the Observation Department. She had already observed two of these stars without noticing any irregular characteristics, but was not familiar with the other two.

I wonder what we'll find out, she thought. Apparently, she would not be sleeping well tonight, either.

CHAPTER 22

The Guardians Under Pressure

Chicago, Tuesday, July 22, 2036

The atmosphere in the room was somewhat tense. Aaron opened the meeting, while Takumi and Chinatsu sat stiffly in their seats, their expressions frozen.

"Although we've declared a Level 2, the situation in the field forced me to implement a higher level. Still not Level 1, but definitely higher than 2." Aaron briefly described the need for physical intervention, though it still wasn't extreme to the point of necessitating murder or causing key people to disappear.

"I'm seeing irregular activity in Dr. Lester's lab. Unfortunately, I can't hear what's being said, probably due to some technical glitch in the camera I hastily installed. One of his PhD students has discovered something that's very upsetting to her. I don't know what she's discovered, but we have to act on the assumption that the worst has happened. I'm assuming she's discovered the geometrical structures, realized how unusual they are, and panicked. It's safe to assume she's shown them to Dr. Lester. Erie has set up a meeting between Dr. Lester and Professor Goldon, who was supposed to make him an offer he couldn't refuse.

"Now for the latest updates. Dr. Gerald Apexton was on his way to report his latest findings at the weekly NASA meeting. To my knowledge, those findings include his discovery of the true role of the asteroid belt between Mars and Jupiter. STA observations are providing scientists with plenty of information, which will lead to extraordinary insights about the space around us.

"Dr. Ethan Almog has already seen the summary of STA observations citing the presence of two solar systems with planets orbiting within the Goldilocks Zone, meaning they support life, within a radius of hundreds of light-years from Earth. Dr. Apexton's unequivocal observational proof has an earth-shattering potential beyond our containment abilities. I had to stage a car accident that resulted in Dr. Apexton's hospitalization, unconscious and suffering from a head injury. I also visited him in the hospital, masquerading as a doctor. Based on his physical condition, I don't think he'll be continuing his research in the years to come.

"It turns out that Dr. Melissa Colette, whom I occasionally use as a consultant in the field of genetic research, has recently met with Will Thorne, one of the more talented investigative reporters at the *Chicago Chronicle*. I 'helped' Will take a fall, resulting in his being hit by a vehicle and then rushed to the hospital.

"This recent spate of revelations might not be surprising, but is certainly very troubling. Observations from the new telescopes might reveal many more disturbing aspects. I still don't feel comfortable asking that we declare a Level 1, but it's a good idea to prepare for this unprecedented occurrence."

As usual, after Aaron had finished speaking, all three sat quietly for several minutes until Chinatsu summed up the meeting by saying, "The situation is deteriorating. Current technology is enabling discoveries that weren't possible until a short time ago. I'm not sure we can continue handling the troubling news that still awaits us. I propose that Takumi consult with the Leading Gentleman."

Both turned to Takumi, who remained in his seat, his expression unreadable. Not even a mosquito's buzz disturbed the silence that took over the room as they all contemplated the latest statements.

After an interval that seemed longer than usual to Aaron, Takumi straightened in his chair, declaring, "I'll talk to the Leading Gentleman. I'll report back soon."

After getting up, he turned around and exited the apartment immediately. The two men left behind maintained their silence until Chinatsu, too, rose from his seat and left.

Things are falling apart quickly, Takumi thought as he walked to the train station. He did not consider, even for a moment, calling the Leading Gentleman. The Gentleman would confirm any decision he made, as always. His status in the organization had long become so well established that he no longer needed authorization from any senior element.

After all, during the course of the last year, he had frequently heard whispers that he was the one designated to replace the Leading Gentleman once he retired. Although he had talked to him occasionally, both one-on-one and in conference calls, Takumi had never actually met him. They avoided video feed during the conference calls as well, mostly in order to maintain confidentiality, or at least that's what he was told.

I wonder who the Leading Gentleman is, he found himself thinking. He wasn't Japanese, of that he was certain. His accent was clear and well-enunciated, as was often the case with someone who had acquired the complex language at an advanced age. He could not guess the Leading Gentleman's national origin from his accent.

CHAPTER 23

Jack

Chicago, Tuesday, July 22, 2036

Rick was rushing determinedly to Will's room, but was stopped by a sturdy nurse from her post at the nurse station.

"We don't allow visitors to enter the ward freely. Where do you think you're going?" she asked, stationing herself in front of him and effectively arresting his progress. The police badge he flashed at her softened her only slightly; however, she continued to block his path, her gaze impenetrable.

"Will and I are old friends. I was with him at a restaurant just a few hours ago. The accident happened after I left. I'm very concerned. I promise not to disturb him," Rick begged.

"Friends are allowed to go in. I thought you might be here on police business. I wouldn't let the cops go in and harass him. Anyway, I'll come with you so you're not tempted to bug him with police matters. Your friend is lucky to be alive. He sustained a serious head injury, but apparently, he's got an extra-strong skull. The doctors managed to quickly drain the internal hemorrhage that resulted in pressure on his brain, as well as repair the damaged artery. Now we just have to give him time to recuperate. He might recover completely, although certain aspects of his memory might be affected."

At a waiting nook in the corridor, Rick spotted one of the new officers, whose name he couldn't recall. He was wearing a blue hospital gown and reading a newspaper. The officer slanted a brief glance at Rick, but his expression didn't change in the slightest, although he had definitely recognized him. Rick was pleased. They were indeed keeping a low profile, and not raising any unnecessary questions.

Despite the dimness of the room, Rick noticed bandages on Will's right hand, chest, and head. Thankfully, all the bandages were smaller than he'd expected. Will looked more like someone who had slipped on the street and sustained some light contusions than a man who had just been in a serious traffic accident.

The nurse, who noticed his startled look, responded by saying, "There's no need for the clunky bandages we used in the past. Modern dressing protects the site of the injury from infection, while simultaneously supplying nutrients to accelerate tissue regeneration and healing. Other than the major head injury, the damage to other parts of his body is relatively superficial. Draining the blood from the brain and repairing the artery were also done through two minute openings. In the past, doctors had to remove a section of the skull to enable the kind of treatment that took place here."

The nurse allowed Rick to approach the head of Will's bed and take a closer look at him. Will, still under sedation, did not stir or react in any way.

“He was unconscious when he got here. The holes in his scalp were drilled using only local anesthesia. Immediately after the internal pressure was reduced by draining the blood, he woke up, and stayed awake until the conclusion of the surgery. Later, he was sedated in order to expedite the healing process. All in all, his condition is stable and quite good.”

Surveying the various monitors in the room, Rick noted that the screens of the pulse and breathing monitors depicted both measures as stable. Other instruments tracked medical functions that were unfamiliar to him, but the display was monotonous and steady on all of them.

He drew away from the bed, whispering to the nurse, “How long will he be sedated?”

“I don’t know. In any case, even when he’s awake, I’m not sure the doctors will allow him to be interrogated, if that’s what you mean.”

It was now late in the afternoon. On his way out of the ward, he heard the sound signaling an incoming message. He paused briefly, debating whether to drive home or wait for Melissa at the hospital. His deliberation was cut short when Melissa appeared in front of him. He gave her a succinct update regarding Will’s condition.

“Thanks. I’d like to see him,” she said.

“You’ll have to go through the nurses. I’ll wait for you in the open area in front of the ward,” he said.

The message awaiting him contained a transcript of the interrogation of the driver who had hit Will. He had been very frightened, and did whatever he could to cooperate with the officers questioning him. He claimed his slow driving had saved the victim from being injured more severely. The victim seemed to have tripped or been pushed into the road from a couple of feet away. At the time of impact, the driver had been pressing the brake as hard as he could. He said he had seen a dark-skinned man wearing a light suit in the place where the victim had been standing previously.

Melissa returned several minutes later. Apparently, seeing Will, as well as his condition, made it hard for her to stay any longer in his room, or perhaps the ward nurse had made her leave. The grim look in her eyes reflected her turbulent emotional state.

She dropped into the seat next to Rick on the couch, buried her face in her hands, and began to weep quietly. Rick grasped her shoulder and hugged her to him. She succumbed to his touch, leaning into him as her tears gradually subsided. After a while, she stopped crying, freed herself from his grasp, wiped her face with the tissue he handed her, then turned to him.

"He looked so fragile," she said, her voice breaking. "As you know, we were a couple for almost two years. He's a charming person who's true to his values. What exactly happened out there? What are the doctors saying? What are his chances of recovery? What precisely are his injuries, and how serious are they?"

"Will's a strong guy with an especially thick skull. Luckily for him, he arrived at the hospital quickly. The doctors drained a hemorrhage in his brain and repaired a damaged artery. He's under sedation now to expedite his recuperation. The nurse in the ward said he's got a good chance of making a full recovery. His other bodily injuries are superficial, and shouldn't worry you."

He briefly debated whether to tell her that Will had been following her as she left the restaurant, before deciding to go for it. He would tell her everything while closely examining her reaction. He trusted his ability to read people.

"Will called me when he left the restaurant. He followed you after you left."

"Why?" she asked. "What made him follow me? He knew I'm always okay, and that I know how to take care of myself."

"He noticed your frightened look when you saw the dark-skinned man wearing a light suit who was standing near the door of the restaurant, and decided that someone was threatening you. He also got the impression that the unmarked envelope you received while the two of you were sitting there upset you, and that's why he decided to follow you. We tracked the two attempts you made to call him, and also picked up the ripped envelope and its contents, which you threw away."

"Wait a second, are you having me followed? And how did you know about the story with the envelope, and why did you collect it after I tore it up?" Apparently, Melissa had completely gotten over her bout of weeping and sentimentality, and had resumed functioning at full capacity.

"Will was worried. He let us know, and we acted immediately. And why did you call him just a few minutes after you parted at the restaurant?" he asked.

"Will's instincts were right," she replied. "I did feel threatened, and if you've seen the contents of the envelope, you can surely understand that I was worried about him. I tried to warn him to be very careful."

"We've questioned the driver of the truck that hit him. He said Will was pushed into his path by a dark-skinned man wearing a suit. Could this be the man who frightened you and caused Will to follow you?" Rick stopped there, deciding to confine himself to a general question in order to encourage her to say more. Under the current circumstances, she was being less guarded than usual.

He was likely to learn a lot the more he maintained his silence and allowed her to speak freely.

She watched him quietly. Rick's gaze was understanding and sympathetic, but he did not say a word.

She'll talk, he thought. *You bet she will. She'll reveal everything.* She knew plenty of details that she had intentionally refrained from revealing to him, and perhaps hadn't told anyone. All he had to do was keep quiet. *Don't break down, keep your mouth shut. She'll talk.*

Indeed, eventually she breathed deeply, and then let out a sigh.

"The dark-skinned man in the suit introduced himself to me as Jack, though I don't believe that's his real name. He told me he was a member of a very ancient religious sect that was deeply concerned about the fate of humanity, especially in light of increasing intervention by scientists in genetic altering of plants and animals. They're highly wary of the accelerated trend of developing genetically based drugs, which they believe may very quickly lead to intentionally genetically altering human DNA, and from there to other unpredictable consequences. They have been continuously tracking genetic research in the leading labs in the world since intensive genetic studies first began. The organization has considerable resources, which it uses to try and limit the creation of mutations by manipulating public opinion against using genetically engineered food products, or by tempting the leading scientists to switch to other fields.

"Jack didn't bother telling me which god they believe in, but did tell me that it was a religious organization that believes all living beings were created by a higher power, and therefore mere mortals are forbidden from altering them."

Rick debated whether to use the brief pause in her speech to ask her about the nature of her relationship with Jack, but didn't want to interrupt her train of thought and decided to maintain his silence, which, as always, paid off when Melissa resumed speaking.

"Jack approached me as an expert on genetic engineering and asked for my help in tracking and monitoring current projects in university labs. He asked me to focus primarily on any studies related to the human genome. Occasionally, he also passed on information about studies that couldn't be found online and required confidential sources of information. My role was to assess the goals of the study, the means the researchers used to analyze and understand the genome, and—in cases of an attempt to alter the genome—to describe the techniques the scientists were using in these attempts.

"I got paid very well. I billed them by the hour, and there were no questions or arguments. I believe I'm not the only one carrying out this job for them. On several occasions, I met Jack at cafés, so he could ask me for clarifications about my analysis. He would reference material on his computer that apparently analyzed the same studies in a different way than I did. Jack was an excellent source of income for me. The hours were convenient, and payment was immediate and generous."

"Why are you using past tense?" Rick couldn't refrain from asking.

"Because after the murder of the security guard at the University of Chicago, I got very scared. You see, on Wednesday morning, I'd given him my most recent analysis of Dr. Lester's research. Up till then, I hadn't had any suspicions about the organization, but when I found out about the murder, I cross-referenced the analysis of research institutions I'd carried out for them with criminal incidents in the same institutions, and discovered a correlation that scared me. To tell you the truth, I decided to stop working for him. Other than the payment transferred to my account yesterday, I haven't had any contact with him since he asked me to look into what was going on in Dr. Lester's lab.

"You can understand how upset I was when Jack showed up at the restaurant where I was sitting with Will. At that moment, I didn't know that Jack knew Will. I assumed he would think we were just two friends chatting. I don't know how he found out we were meeting. I wouldn't be surprised to find out he was having me followed. That man knows way too much. The photo and the newspaper article prove it, and once I saw them, I started fearing him even more.

"That's why I called Will. I wanted to warn him about Jack. I guess he didn't hear the assistant ring. I only hope that the fact that I didn't keep trying won't end up causing him any irreversible damage. I could never forgive myself if that happened. I really hope he comes back to us soon." She seemed to be having a hard time dealing with the thought that she might have been able to save Will had she tried harder, and started crying once more.

Rick was pleased, as much as one could be pleased under such circumstances, when a close friend was hospitalized with a head injury. He now had an initial lead for his investigation, rather than a collection of seemingly unrelated details. At last, he had found his villain, and Melissa even had a way of getting in touch with him. The precinct could easily locate Jack, or whatever his real name was. There was also no need to bother Melissa with the list of studies carried out by labs that had been "lucky" enough to receive a visit from Jack. It made sense to assume that his own list was very similar to those compiled by Will and Melissa.

The random details were starting to coalesce into a coherent picture. Jack's ancient sect, with its abundant resources, would do anything to discover what, specifically, the research labs in the fields of biology and genetic engineering were up to. The murder of the security guard might have been an unplanned act of manslaughter, but pushing Will into the busy road had been a deliberate act. Perhaps it wasn't intended to kill him, but it was definitely aimed at hurting him and his work, which they could guess involved an investigation into their activities. Perhaps this staged "accident" was also intended to signal to Melissa that she shouldn't mess with them.

At that moment, he realized that Melissa herself might now be in considerable danger. They definitely knew that she had gone to the hospital and, in fact, that she was talking to him, a representative of the law. Melissa must be protected from this moment on. It was fortunate that they hadn't hurt her thus far.

A chilling thought flitted through his mind. *No, that's impossible.* Rick suppressed the idea immediately. He was too accustomed to working with criminals, and consequently, had come up with an extreme notion. *Perhaps Melissa hadn't been harmed because she was part of Jack's apparatus!* Could Melissa be in collusion with Jack and with the organization that had carried out the break-ins and murdered the security guard? It was hard to believe, but criminal investigations often revealed that the most seemingly trustworthy person involved in the case was, in fact, the perpetrator. He wouldn't ignore this extreme possibility completely, in order to entrap her if she actually was cooperating with the sect beyond the involvement she had described thus far. He would also maintain contact with her in order not to make her surmise that she herself was a potential suspect in his eyes.

He briefly debated whether to let her know of his decision to assign security personnel to protect her, but immediately dismissed this option. She would behave less freely if she was aware of this fact. It was better not to tell her. If she discovered what was going on and complained to him, he could always come up with some security-related justification. Claiming he had to visit the restroom, Rick drifted away from Melissa.

Lily answered immediately. "I want to assign a security detail to Dr. Melissa Colette. The goal is to protect her from physical assault, as well as to track her movements. Tell whoever's assigned to the job that there might be someone else tailing her, so he or she should be extra-careful. If a tail is detected, assign another detective to follow that person immediately. Is there anyone with experience who's immediately available to get on it?"

"Yoni would be a great fit. He's also free, and has been bugging me every day for a week now to find him an interesting assignment."

"Great," Rick said. "Send him to Rush Medical Center immediately. Give him all the information we have on Melissa, including photos so he can identify her. I'll try to keep her here at the hospital until he arrives. Instruct him not to call me or address me when he finds us."

"I'll get right to it," she replied, in her pragmatic tone. Lily was capable of handling dozens of matters simultaneously, with amazing efficiency and without exhibiting any stress whatsoever. She never implied that she was busy with something else, and always competently performed whatever he assigned her to do with a smile. She was the complete opposite of his ex-wife.

"And speaking of security details," Rick added, "I saw the agent watching over Will here at the hospital. He was very discreet."

Melissa wouldn't leave without saying goodbye to him. This was a good opportunity to stall until Yoni arrived. Rick approached her again.

"We'll need your help locating Jack's address," he mentioned casually while observing her reaction.

"Of course," she replied immediately and with no hesitation. "Could you send a computer expert to my house this evening? I don't have anything urgent to do tomorrow morning, but I prefer to keep those hours free, so I can spend as much time as possible in the hospital with Will. Has anyone notified his family or the paper where he works that he's been injured?"

"The hospital's taking care of it," Rick replied. "His parents live in New York. I'm sure they'll be here tomorrow morning. As for your home computer, there's no need to send an expert to your home, unless you insist on dealing with an actual human," he said, smiling in amusement.

"No, I really don't, but how will we find out Jack's address?"

"Don't worry. Send any email you received from Jack to the address I'll give you, and our experts will do the rest. Do you want anything from the cafeteria? I'm going to get a cup of coffee for me, anyway."

"Thanks, I'd like some coffee," she replied.

It was very important to make sure she didn't leave the hospital until Yoni could follow her. Rick took a deliberately long time fetching the coffee, making sure that it was very hot. Melissa would have to wait until it cooled down a bit, thus giving Yoni more time to arrive. Indeed, several minutes after he sat down next to Melissa, Yoni passed them by. He was now free to go home. Melissa was safely protected.

***

The assistant rang as he was on his way home.

"Good evening," he heard Lily's leisurely voice. "You're not going to believe it. Kyra's DNA print wasn't found in any of the databases we have access to. That means Kyra doesn't have any credit cards or a driver's license, has never been employed by any government office or major corporation, doesn't have a passport, and has never been admitted to any hospital. In short, Kyra is unidentifiable here in the United States or in any of the countries whose databases we have access to. Another option is that Kyra belongs to a top-secret branch of some covert organization—the CIA or the FBI."

"That's okay," Rick replied. "We already have a lead that should bring us to the killer, as well as to the man who pushed Will into the road. We can continue looking into the Kyra angle at a later stage."

CHAPTER 24

Eddie and the Structures

Chicago, Tuesday, July 22, 2036

The first thing that caught Tom's eye as he entered the lab was Lise's form as she sat staring at the computer displaying her favorite screensaver—a photo of her family. She didn't even hear the door opening. However, the sound of its slamming startled her, and when she turned toward him, he saw that her eyes were red and weepy. It was troubling to think she had spent the last two hours crying. Apparently, her fears had gotten the better of her. He should have stayed with her and soothed her once he realized how much her discovery had frightened her.

"I'm sorry I had to leave. I tried to keep it as short as I could. Let's go sit down," he said. On his way back, he had spent quite a while deliberating whether to tell Lise about the structures he had seen at BL. On the one hand, it might calm her down. Conversely, the chance of a groundbreaking scientific discovery, and the acclaim it would entail, had decreased significantly. Judging by her behavior, the important thing at the moment was to calm her down. Yes, he thought, he would tell her that he had seen the same structures in a different lab. She didn't have to know he had visited BL, and definitely not whom he had met there.

When he saw her walking into the conference room, holding the prints, he curved his lips in a warm smile, which, as usual, achieved the desired effect. Lise did quirk her eyebrow in surprise, but also responded with a faint smile of her own. *Much better than nothing*, he thought.

"Sit down. I understand your emotional reaction and your fears," he began. "I was also somewhat upset when you showed me the structures. But, as they say, truth is stranger than fiction. In the meeting I was just invited to, they showed me the same structures! It's unbelievable that I've seen such a surprising, extraordinary, and unique phenomenon twice on the same day."

"Where did you see it?" Lise burst out.

"In another lab, whose name I prefer to keep to myself for now," he replied.

"What did the structures you saw look like? How similar are they to the structures I've discovered? How did they produce them at the other lab? Did they try to recreate the experiment? What were the results?"

"Hold on a minute, hold on." Tom tried to stop the barrage of questions. "I saw very little, and I know even less about the structures and the processes they went through. The structures are very similar to the ones you've discovered, perhaps even identical. I only looked at them for a few seconds. To the best of my recollection, they're identical. The people there didn't provide any more explanations about how they discovered the phenomenon or of any continuation of the research. But considering that the phenomenon has also been observed elsewhere, we can't attribute it to a laboratory error, and there's also no need to put a lot of effort into recreating it. It does exist! The question is what to do now."

"Do you have a possible explanation for the phenomenon?" she asked.

"Unfortunately, I don't."

"Did your host at the other lab express his opinion about a possible explanation for the phenomenon?"

"He really didn't. He showed me the structures through a microscope."

Tom briefly considered telling Lise that Professor Goldon was aware of her findings, but immediately relinquished the idea. The last thing Lise needed to know was that Goldon was tracking their progress at the lab in real time. Such knowledge would shatter the little confidence she had regained.

"He immediately dragged me to a quick lunch at a busy location where we could barely hear each other," he resumed, "and then moved on to other matters that the two of us might be dealing with."

"Why don't we initiate a meeting with him and discuss the findings together? He might know more than we do," she proposed.

"That's an excellent idea, but probably impractical."

"But why?" Lise asked urgently.

"I also proposed sharing the phenomenon with other researchers," Tom said, "since one of them might be able to come up with an explanation. But it was made clear to me that this matter should be kept as confidential as possible. This message was very clear and unequivocal. No, for now we have to prevent any leakage of the discovery. We'll be attentive and alert to any possible discovery by anyone else, and track what's going on. Anyway, the very fact that we're not the only ones to discover the phenomenon should calm us down." "Us" was indeed the most soothing word for Lise; he would lump the two of them together, thus making things easier for her.

"I feel a lot better about this," he continued. "It's also possible that the same techniques that allowed us to discover the phenomenon have only recently become widely accessible. Therefore, it makes sense that additional research teams will discover it soon. It's also possible that additional teams have discovered the phenomenon, started panicking, and like us, are sitting and waiting for the first lab to break the news. And if they haven't yet, they definitely will soon.

"Let's try to focus on the phenomenon. What do you think might have caused it?"

"I don't have the faintest idea," she replied. "Let's think about it together. Does it make sense for a control protein array for any gene to look so symmetrical? The spatial structures of proteins we're familiar with are more like miniature chemical plants—a random collection of containers and pipelines. But since we've discovered this sequence only in humans and not in other primates, it seems reasonable to assume that the structures serve one of the features that are unique to us, perhaps the brain. What do you think?"

"Your analysis sounds very reasonable. The problem is that we can't look into the effect of removing the sequence from the genome of a human subject."

"Hold on, I have an idea," Lise murmured slowly. "It makes sense that all the active proteins in the human body have been observed multiple times by countless researchers. If one or several of them had discovered such a unique phenomenon, it would have been published a long time ago. This implies that the phenomenon was only discovered recently. It happened here as a result of using the beta-amylase enzyme, which isn't even present in humans. Despite that, it's possible that some enzyme out of the thousands that are active in humans might also create a similar effect. I propose a project where we expose the unfolding protein to every known enzyme in the human body. I wonder what we'll come up with."

Tom was enthusiastic. "Lise, that's a really brilliant analysis, and an operative conclusion. I'd definitely try that route. Anyway, assuming no enzyme leads to the effect we observed, we have to think what conclusion we can draw from that."

Both of them became preoccupied with their own thoughts, and the room was utterly silent for quite a while.

Tom spread the prints out in front of them, and he and Lise stared at them wordlessly. As he usually did when facing a difficult problem or an unclear phenomenon, he tried to organize all the known details in his mind, while taking into account that they constituted only a random sample of the phenomenon's description, then tried to approach it from a completely different direction, considering what might have caused it. He was certain of one thing. The structures served no biological function.

Biological systems that have developed on an evolutionary basis for millions of years or more without a guiding force do not resemble a factory designed by an engineer who is governed by the efficiency of the process. Biological systems have a very disorganized spatial structure. They merely carry out their assigned role, using as few resources as possible.

Yes, the structures don't serve the cell or the organism. At best, they don't interfere with it. How, then, did they come to exist? It's also hard to believe that they had served some purpose in the distant past. No, the biological-evolutionary direction doesn't fit here.

The longer he stared at the structures, the more stymied he felt about their origin or role. Frustrated, he leaned back in his chair and raised two random prints to examine. Some of the structures were too orderly, resembling short rows of several structures arranged in a straight line. For some reason, this reminded him of a shopping list of the kind affixed to the refrigerator in his home, to which the entire family added items that needed to be purchased on the next shopping trip. There, too, family members used abbreviations that often resulted in odd, unnecessary purchases when the person shopping couldn't understand the abbreviation or the handwriting.

As he let his thoughts drift, recalling everything that had happened since the murder, an image of Oleg, the murdered security guard, surfaced in his mind's eye. He had never had a proper conversation with him. Oleg would make the rounds through every room in the building when he arrived at six in the evening every day. Rather than merely receive an update from the day-shift guard, he made a point of greeting all the workers in each of the rooms and ensuring they were all doing okay. He had never been late, and as far as Tom could recall, had never missed a day of work.

At the funeral, Tom had met Eddie, Oleg's brother, of whose existence he hadn't even been aware. Eddie's image now surfaced in front of his glazed eyes: Eddie eulogizing his brother in fluent English; the family members crying in a quiet, restrained manner; other mourners giving speeches in memory of the deceased, some of them in Russian, which most of the attendees spoke; and the dean promising scholarships for Oleg's children. Tom, too, had spoken and promised to provide any help the family might need. Meanwhile, Eddie's form had been in the background the entire time. Tom couldn't break free of it. He was shaking Eddie's hand. Glad to meet him. Eddie had said something important, something that might help him. How was Eddie connected to a shopping list, a list written in unfamiliar handwriting? What had Eddie said? What had he said that might help?

Then it came to him. Eddie was a linguist! His work involved developing ways of communicating with foreign cultures, deciphering and understanding extraterrestrial forms of communication, including, certainly, unfamiliar forms of writing. That was it. Eddie could help. Eddie would be happy to help.

For a moment, he considered sharing the idea with Lise, but immediately decided against it. All Lise needed to know for the time being was that she was not the only one who had discovered the structures, that others were investigating them as well, and that perhaps an explanation would soon be found. He would deal with Eddie on his own.

Out loud, Tom said, "I think we've exhausted the topic for today. We have a lot of work to do investigating the direction you suggested. I suggest you start with the preparations."

As she was getting up, she began to gather the printed images when Tom reached out for them, as if requesting to take them. She nearly tossed them into his hands, as if she were disposing of disgusting trash she was glad to be rid of.

Tom waited until she left the room before exiting in the direction of his car. He preferred to conduct this conversation outside the lab. The assistant located Eddie in less than a minute at his office at Loyola University.

***

"Yes, of course, I'd be happy to help," he replied with no hesitation. "What time works for you?" he asked.

"I don't want to inconvenience you. What if I pop over to see you now? I can be at your office in less than... an hour." The assistant supplied the timeframe.

"Excellent. We can talk at a nice little café not far from my office."

"No, I ate not that long ago, and I don't want to waste your time. I also prefer to talk without having other people around me."

"No problem. I'll be waiting for you." Eddie signed off.

The assistant notified Tom that it had instructed the autonomous driver to choose the quickest route, allowing him to lean back comfortably in his seat.

His thoughts kept returning to the strange structures. Although in his youth he had enjoyed reading science fiction and had also seen quite a few movies in that genre, in his working life he preferred replicable scientific facts, rather than unsubstantiated tales of people who had seen flying saucers or aliens but for some reason could not supply any conclusive proof. For a moment, he thought the structures might serve as a good opening for a science fiction story whose next portions he couldn't predict. He simply could not conceive of a natural process leading to such results. This implied that the phenomenon went beyond nature as it had been perceived up to this point.

He wondered what Eddie's reaction to the structures would be. Tom had to come up with a cover story regarding their origins. He definitely did not want to tell Eddie about the actual circumstances under which the structures had been discovered. What could he tell him? He needed the sort of cover story that would not raise any unnecessary questions. To an untrained eye, the structures didn't look biological in nature, but they also did not resemble, to any extent, any familiar structures from everyday life. They did not even look like ancient structures. On the contrary, they were immaculate and shiny.

Perhaps an image from Mars or Venus, which had finally been visited by a roving vehicle capable of dealing with the incredibly high temperatures and pressure. Venus actually seemed like an appropriate idea. The story of the soft landing and the roving vehicle had dominated the news for a week. The view on Venus looked like it had been taken from Dante's vision of Hell. It could definitely work. However, since he worked for NASA, Eddie had much better access to images of the planet than Tom did. No, that wouldn't fly. Back to square one.

What should he tell Eddie? It would be better if the cover story was close to the truth. Perhaps he should say that after several labs had managed to produce simple geometrical structures from proteins, the researchers had decided to have some fun, and had sent him and a competing lab an image of the series of structures they had created, accompanied by a question mark. He was very interested in being the first one to respond intelligently to their prompt. Not a brilliant story, but it should do the trick.

In any case, he was now approaching the university, and this was the best idea he had come up with. Therefore, it would have to do.

Life with fourth-gen personal assistants and autonomous vehicles is so convenient, he thought. He didn't even need to take part in the communication between assistants, which resulted in his assistant being loaded with instructions for reaching the nearest parking lot, and, of course, for exiting the lot and finding his way to Eddie's office within the giant building. All of it had taken place immediately after his conversation with Eddie.

Once he drew near the parking lot, the lot's automated system directed his car to a free parking spot, in which the car parked itself without his intervention. The various assistants spared people so much hassle and precious time. They made everyday life infinitely easier.

Eddie was warm and pleasant, just as Tom remembered him from the funeral. After a brief exchange about Oleg and his family, Tom gave him a short summary of the latest developments in creating a wild variety of new proteins. He added that, at the tail end of this process, a kind of jocular competition had emerged between the different labs, with each of them developing proteins possessing strange three-dimensional structures.

Eddie listened politely; however, Tom sensed that he wasn't buying the story. In any case, it was too late to retreat now. Staring intently at Eddie's expression and relying on his social instincts to interpret his reaction, he slid over an image showing several clusters of structures arranged in short rows of sorts. Eddie's eyebrow raised in wonderment and the shadow of a smile on his lips said it all. Tom didn't need any further proof. He had come to the right place.

Tom maintained his silence. Continuing to smile, Eddie swiveled the prints and then separated them into two piles, one containing the images portraying the collection of structures that did, indeed, look like a shopping list, and the other with the rest of the images, which he shifted aside. He slowly spread out the images in the shopping-list stack all over the desk, occasionally hesitating as well as swapping around the various images to create an order that seemed thought out, rather than random. Tom watched him, trying to discern any logic in the order of the images. Eddie appeared to have clear intentions regarding this order. He was sequencing the prints in accordance with a logic that was obvious only to him.

Linguistics had never been Tom's strong suit, nor his favorite topic. Was there some linguistic logic behind the arrangement of the images, or perhaps an aesthetic principle? Perhaps Eddie viewed the prints merely as images with a certain visual beauty. As he continued to speculate, he noticed that Eddie had finished arranging the images, and was examining them with a focused gaze.

Slowly, his inquisitive, probing expression turned relaxed and satisfied, finally transforming into a kind of victorious smile. For Eddie, the collection of strange images was a coherent statement. Something was entirely obvious to him. Something that Tom had not even noticed.

"Very interesting," Eddie said, his expression conveying achievement and gratification. "I don't know how your colleagues created this arrangement of molecules, since I'm not a biologist, but at least one of them works with, or is interested in, some of the more basic aspects of computers."

"I have no idea what you mean," Tom responded. "What kind of logic do you see in these images?"

"I don't want to rush. I do have a certain direction in approaching this that originates, of course, in my profession. I do see a certain order here, but let me work on it for a while. I also need to consult a certain professional expert."

"I don't want to expose the images to anyone," Tom blurted out urgently.

"Don't worry," Eddie replied. "Your secret and the images won't be exposed. I need some specific information from the field of computing. If my assessment is correct, I can provide you with an elegant solution to this series of images, or at least to some of them."

"When do you estimate you can complete it?"

"Before the end of the week, so long as my current speculation is correct. All I need is confirmation of that, and some details I'm not fluent in. I'll also need to keep just one print, if you agree."

Tom was surprised. He had not for a moment considered that he might have to part with one of the prints. What to do? There was no choice but to keep going.

"Please use it as little as possible. Don't show it to more than one person, and make sure that person is someone you trust completely."

The image Eddie selected, with no hesitation, was no different than the others. Tom wondered what its distinction was.

On his way home, Tom mentally surveyed the meeting with Eddie. There was no doubt that Eddie had seen something in the prints that Tom and Lise had not. Had Professor Goldon seen something in them as well? Had Goldon and Eddie seen the same thing? This was an excellent, essential question. If they had, what had they seen in the strange series of structures in the images? He felt as if he had hit a dead end, and did not think further consideration would contribute to his understanding. He would wait for Eddie's verdict, hoping he would come up with a compelling solution. Perhaps it wouldn't be a bad idea to disengage from the images in general, and move on to other topics. His subconscious might end up providing a solution.

It was time to deal with bringing Kate and the girls home. The kids had already missed two days of school, and the school's administrative office had contacted him asking about their whereabouts. He had ignored the call, not knowing how to reply. Kate probably hadn't responded, either.

It was true that they had access to all the material, including classroom presentations, but socializing with other students and the educational implications of this process were just as important. It was a good idea not to miss too many days of school. Even if they decided to come home, it would happen tomorrow at the earliest, resulting in three days of absence from school. The main question he had to answer was whether they were still in danger.

The implied threat Gaya had conveyed had been enclosed in a rustling cellophane wrapping—the promise of a wage increase, the kind he had never even dreamed of. As of now, he had no conclusive proof of any connection between Goldon's people and the lab break-in that had culminated in the murder of the security guard, other than the temporal proximity of the events. However, Goldon was tracking the developments in his lab. He had sent Gaya, and was probably complicit in the threat she had delivered. And the murder? Had Goldon sent the intruder who had copied files from Tom's work computer and killed Oleg? Too much circumstantial evidence linked Goldon to the murder. *Who knows what else he's capable of?*

Or perhaps there was no actual connection between Goldon and the executors of the break-in and the murder, and the proximity of the events was merely a coincidence? *Who knows?*

However, if he started working at BL like Goldon wanted, would that appease him and remove the threat from Tom and his family? There was still too much uncertainty to instruct his family to return home, potentially exposing them to dangers he couldn't even conceive of. There was no other choice; he would have to wait. In the meantime, it would be a good idea to consult with Melissa.

When contacted, her assistant replied that she was at a lecture and inquired whether the matter was urgent and she should be interrupted; otherwise, it would connect them once the lecture ended at eight p.m.

Tom replied that he would wait for her at her home, requesting that he be allowed to do so until she returned. Once he had settled down comfortably in her apartment, he found himself debating what to tell her. Should he mention the strange structures he had seen twice now? Or the connection between Professor Goldon and Gaya?

They had only been lovers for a year. They had happened to sit next to each other at one of the routine conferences in their field. The ice-breaker between them took place the moment the saltshaker she had asked him to pass her slipped between his fingers, straight into her soup bowl. Nothing works to create intimacy quite like uninhibited laughter.

By the end of the meal, they were on a first-name basis, and their assistants had exchanged addresses. Only when they were the last two people left in the cafeteria did they emerge from their conversation and start laughing again.

The connection between them was perfect. He could not remember ever having such a pleasant, fascinating conversation with anyone. Quickly, they transitioned into a secret relationship. They talked about everything, yet he still knew very little about her past. The truth was that he wasn't really interested. He enjoyed their situation the way it was. For the first time since they had met, he wondered to what extent he could trust her.

Despite the late hour, she was alert and energetic, and as usual, immediately discerned his distress.

"You seem really troubled. Sit down, talk," she half-said, half-commanded, sitting down in the armchair across from him.

Choosing his words carefully, he updated her on everything that had happened to him since the beginning of the week. It was unbelievable how much had transpired in the two days since he'd last seen her. He told her everything, without omitting a thing, feeling that he trusted her completely. He described the strange, precise geometrical structures that had developed in the lab as a result of enzyme activation. He told her that Professor Goldon had invited him for a meeting and in fact offered him the position that Gaya, who had threatened his family, had first brought up. He revealed that Goldon had shown him the same structures, and even knew that Tom had seen them in his own lab. He described Lise's fears and the disappearance of Kyra, who was apparently Mike's first-ever girlfriend. He told her about Eddie, the linguist, and his mysterious smile when he saw the images of the structures. Finally, he mentioned that he had not spoken to Kate since she had left, and was debating whether to ask her to return with their daughters, as well as whether to accept Goldon's job offer.

Melissa didn't say a word. She let him express himself as long as he saw fit. She didn't ask any questions, merely encouraging him to go on, with her curious eyes. The two of them were silent for a long time.

CHAPTER 25

Melissa is a Suspect

Chicago, Tuesday, July 22, 2036

The monotonous ride provided by the autonomous car, along with his cumulative exhaustion, put Rick to sleep. Apparently, the assistant in the vehicle rang quite a few times before he woke up.

Lily had grown concerned. “Melissa’s looking for you.”

“Okay, put her through,” he said, half-asleep. “Hi, Melissa.”

“Hi, Rick. I just got another delivery of material to be researched from Jack. What should I do with it? He already knows about my connection with Will, and might know that I met you, too. I’m really worried and scared.”

“Let’s think about it together,” he replied. What Melissa had just told him woke him up completely. Things were growing complicated. It appeared that, just like in a game of chess, he had to think several moves ahead and consider the implications before every step he took.

"You know, Will and I have been friends for years and we've traded quite a few stories. Let's meet where you and Will met on your first date. Do you remember?"

"Are you sure?" she asked, barely suppressing her laughter.

"Meet you there in half an hour," he said. "And don't forget to bring the material you received."

"Of course, I'll bring everything. See you there."

Rick glanced at the car's clock. He would have time to buy some refreshments and get to Will's aunt's house in time. It was the last place anyone listening in on their conversation would think to monitor.

Will had told him that he had really wanted to see Melissa, but his aunt had been ill, and his mother had asked him to move in and take care of her. Melissa hadn't hesitated at all, and agreed immediately to the oddest site for a meeting that she could imagine. In retrospect, it turned out to be an ideal location. The aunt slept through most of their meeting, and no one else bothered them. Rick asked Lily to inform Yoni to be hypervigilant about verifying whether anyone else was following Melissa, as well as to inform the aunt of their visit.

The aunt turned out to be a handsome, modern woman. She directed them to the living room while she herself retired to the bedroom. Melissa showed Rick the material she had received from Jack.

"We have to consider the possibility that Jack is baiting you to test your loyalty," Rick said. "How well do you know Dr. Tom Lester?"

Melissa's brief hesitation registered immediately with the experienced detective. *She knows something that hasn't been brought up yet*. Rick's suspicion that Melissa was in collusion with whoever had hurt Will surged once more, and his focus on her every word and gesture increased.

After her momentary hesitation, Melissa sighed heavily and said, "I have to make a full disclosure that didn't seem necessary up to this point."

Rick tensed. *She's about to confess*. What would he do? Arrest her and take her to the precinct?

"Well, I'm not proud of what I'm about to tell you, but that's how things worked out, and I'm not sorry about it. Dr. Lester—Tom—and I have been lovers for about a year now. I'm well aware of his work, his family, and other aspects of his life."

Rick was quite surprised. He had not linked her, even for a moment, with Tom. However, at that moment, he had expected Melissa's confession to concern additional business connections within her profession, rather than personal romantic affairs.

"I should have mentioned it when we met, but I didn't feel comfortable making this kind of disclosure in Will's presence. You see, we were together for a long time. We broke up about two years ago, even though we loved each other and got along well. Our busy careers simply put a strain on the relationship. When I met him yesterday...actually this morning—this day has been so packed with events that it feels like I met him yesterday—anyway, during the meeting, some old emotions rekindled in me. I hope you understand what even I can't quite understand."

"Wow," Rick exhaled audibly. "And I thought our problem was complicated. Your life is no walk in the park, either. Anyway, since I'm no expert on relationships—I'm divorced, in case you didn't know—who am I to tell you what to do?

"To return to our own business here, it's important that we

go over all of the new information. We have lists of lab break-ins during the last year, as well as accidents or criminal incidents involving scientists that you, Will, and I compiled. We have the research topics the labs are investigating, and of course, the latest material you received from Jack. All we need is for you to identify the common denominator among all the events. I won't bother you. I'll make some coffee, and I've got some pastries I bought on the way here," he concluded, heading for the kitchen.

Rick's matter-of-fact approach and his non-judgmental acceptance of her personal relationship helped Melissa feel much more at ease, allowing her to focus her thoughts. She didn't require much time. Briefly skimming the new material from Jack at home, as well as everything she had learned thus far, allowed her to form quite a clear picture. Browsing the material again in conjunction with Rick's list strengthened her conviction.

When Rick entered, bearing a tray with cups of coffee and pastries, Melissa leaned back in her chair, smiling, and said, "I have a pretty reasonable and well-supported assessment of what's going on here. Let's both take a look at it."

"So quick? That's great," he cheered.

"The broadest common denominator is human genetic research in general. Within that extensive field, the studies have focused on two more-or-less specific areas. The first is the hot topic of longevity enhancement, and developing general immunity to all varieties of cancer and various generative diseases. The second area includes research concerning the human genome and comparison of various human races in the past and at present, as well as comparing the human genome to that of various higher animals, mostly other primates. At first glance, it seems that both subjects interest the perpetrators of the break-ins and the murder. But if we assume that Jack and his gang are behind the break-ins and the murder, an interesting picture emerges."

"What makes you think Jack is linked to the break-ins?" Rick asked.

"It's much more than female intuition. Every assignment I got from him included a preface intended to guide my work, which directed me specifically to research concerning junk DNA. I don't know how familiar you are with this topic..."

"I'm fairly familiar with it," he replied. "While Dr. Lester was being questioned after the murder and the break-in, he told me what they were researching, and also got into some of the scientific topics."

"Well, as you can probably guess, the majority of studies focus on the active sections of the DNA. The junk areas are largely ignored. All of the labs researching human DNA that have been broken into, including Tom's, study the quite esoteric field of junk DNA, and as I said, Jack was interested in this subject as well. But—and this is a big *but*—those were Jack's assignments to me until recently. The one that came when Jack already knew of my connection to Will is focused on enhancing human longevity."

"Well," Rick sputtered impatiently, "what does that mean?"

"It means that Jack is trying to divert me away from researching junk DNA to researching longevity enhancement! Don't you see? Jack is interested in studies concerning junk DNA, and is now orchestrating a diversion to lure us away from his target and distract us with extending longevity."

Rick's intense look did not disclose what was on his mind.

What's going on here? Does she think I'm stupid? Is she trying to divert me from the obvious direction? What kind of interest could any kind of violent group have in academic research, as opposed to studies with the sort of commercial potential that can't even be expressed in words? People would be willing to pay any sum, and even commit murder, in order to extend their lives even a little.

This was it. If, up to this point, he'd still doubted where Melissa's loyalty lay, now the answer seemed obvious. *Melissa's not with us*. The maneuver was too transparent. Perhaps she was the one who initiated or even sent herself this latest assignment from Jack. After all, logic dictated that after discovering her connections with Will the journalist, the last thing Jack would do would be to send her any additional material. Rick had to quickly decide how to proceed.

Still immersed in her own line of thought, Melissa continued. "Research on junk DNA is so marginal, yet it was the focus of Jack's interest, so it seems crystal clear that Jack is probably behind the break-ins and the murder," she concluded triumphantly.

All that notwithstanding, Rick thought, the logical sequence she was presenting was well constructed, and sounded convincing enough to warrant his attention. The only one who could solve his dilemma was Will, who knew Melissa well and who Rick trusted. However, Will had not been in touch with her for about two years. How would he know what she had been up to since they had broken up? At most, he could vouch for her trustworthiness and integrity. But, as he knew well, integrity could also be bought. In short, he would continue to treat her respectfully without relinquishing his suspicions.

It was also possible that her recent confession concerning Tom might prove helpful. She had said they had a long-term, intimate relationship. Tom should be questioned as soon as possible in order to find out what side Melissa was on. Perhaps Yoni would find something out while following her, or else the answer might come by itself, as it often did, as a result of unforeseen events.

He still had to address Melissa's question regarding how she should reply to Jack.

"Assuming you're right," Rick began, "the last thing we want is for Jack to suspect that something has changed on your end, that you've been monitoring the topics he's asked you to look into, that you can discern a clear pattern, or that you're linking him to the murder. It's also possible that the assignment he sent you was intended to test your reaction and maybe, as you said, to feed you with bogus information in order to steer us away from the right direction. Your work now should match your work for him in the past, business as usual, while we keep going, regardless of recent events."

"Okay," she said. "I'll prepare the analysis for him and bill him as usual."

"That's great. Okay, it's getting pretty late. I suggest you go home and get on with your life as usual. I'll talk to you tomorrow morning."

"Okay," she said. "Is it safe for us to talk on the assistant? You know how easy it is to intercept those calls."

"Of course," he replied. "We've installed security measures preventing any sort of surveillance on your assistant. Don't worry."

Rick was the first to leave the house, pausing briefly as he pretended to tinker with his assistant and simulated making a call, when in fact he was watching the front door until he saw Melissa leave and enter her car. Immediately after she took off, another vehicle departed, followed by one more. He hoped Yoni was the second tail, rather than the first.

This was interesting. If they were following her, this meant she was on the straight and narrow, and not their accomplice. *Unless, unless, they had noticed her police escorts and were trying to clear her name by tailing her, a sort of reverse psychology. I really am paranoid*, he found himself thinking.

In any case, the surveillance would continue, and he still had to warn Yoni. He did so before setting out for home.

CHAPTER 26

Sheffy's Stars

California, Wednesday, July 23, 2036

Lia suffered from insomnia that night as well, although she had still not overcome her fatigue from the night before. This time, her research in its entirety was about to be tested by another expert who was unbiased and who was not motivated by a desire for acclaim, like she was.

If her conclusions regarding STA331047B and STA333654B were collaborated by another round of measurements, and if some of the stars Professor Sheffy had wanted to observe were to exhibit the same behavior, she would be in seventh heaven. At last, after many years of work, she would be the one who had uncovered another layer in the human race's long journey to discover the secrets of the universe, and would go down in the pantheon of humankind's greatest scientific pioneers.

It was too bad Professor Sheffy couldn't go over the results of the night's observations with her. He was delivering his lecture this morning, and would then be taking part in a panel that was so long, they wouldn't even be able to meet for lunch. He estimated he would only have time for their project this evening.

As for her, she couldn't sit around at the conference all day, although she was interested in the topics being discussed and truly wanted to listen to Sheffy's lecture. After nine a.m., she would be able to access the telescope's night observations, once the material had been sorted through and sent to the various astronomers who had requested observations.

She didn't wait even one extra minute. All she had asked was to receive the change in position for her two stars and Sheffy's four stars, with the highest degree of precision possible from the STA. She had requested two measurements for the six stars: one at the beginning of the night's observations and one at the end, so that all in all, she had to interpret twelve observations. Such observations, measuring the position of a star located hundreds of light-years away, at a level of precision enabling the detection of motion on a plane perpendicular to the line of observation from Earth, had not been possible with the telescopes preceding the STA.

When she had first calculated the orbits and masses of "her" stars, she couldn't believe the results, and had repeated the calculations again and again. She had worried that the minute variations in position she had found, which constituted the basis for her extraordinary conclusions, could have resulted from the STA's stabilization system.

In fact, this had been her main fear, and in order to eliminate it, she had studied the stabilization system in depth. Only then was her mind set at ease, as the time constants of the stabilization system were significantly different from those she had obtained for the motion of the stars. Nevertheless, she felt that she must receive additional confirmation from other researchers.

The STA data, as well as many other measurements gathered by telescopes utilizing different spectral ranges, allowed her to assess her results from additional perspectives as well, to calculate the stars' orbital periods and the mass of each of the companions. And indeed, the results confirmed what she already knew.

Among the four stars Sheffy had cited, only two exhibited measurable position changes. The other two could be single stars or, if they were binary, could have long orbital periods that caused their changes of position over one night to be too small for the STA to measure.

With a rising sense of excitement, she activated the software she had developed to calculate the mass of the two new stars. The result she received for both was hair-raising. The mass for each was precisely 1.76 solar masses—exactly the same result obtained for the stars STA331047B and STA333654B!

Cold sweat covered her forehead. She had discovered a yet-unknown physical phenomenon that allowed a star to gradually expand beyond the Chandrasekhar limit of 1.44 solar masses, a result that had never been observed before, and which also violated the reigning theory, found to be reliable for thousands of stars. This could lead to a real scientific uproar, one in which she would find herself center stage. *Sounds pretty exciting*, she thought, her face illuminated by a brief smile. Proper compensation for many hours of working in the dark.

On the other hand, how could the reigning theory—which had produced numerous scientific discoveries, primarily the proof that not only was the universe expanding, but that its expansion had been accelerating for the last seven billion years—require reassessment, and perhaps even collapse? She might turn out to be the one to drive researchers to re-examine their assumptions. They might even reach the conclusion that the universe's expansion was not accelerating, thus eliminating the need for the abstract, unclear concept termed "dark energy," which so many scientists over the years had attempted to unravel, to no avail. Perhaps a simple solution to this quandary had now been found.

What should I do now? she thought. Sheffy would only be free this evening. How would she manage to wait that long, with such an immense discovery at her fingertips? Actually, Sheffy would also want to know about it, even in the middle of the conference.

That's it. She would go to the conference and update him during the first break. And so she did. With uncharacteristic speed, she made the necessary preparations and drove to the main hall where Sheffy was scheduled to deliver his lecture.

Based on the current content of his lecture, she must have arrived only a few minutes after it began. Sheffy started by presenting a succinct version of Chandrasekhar's calculations, emphasizing the famous Chandrasekhar equation.

Suddenly, she realized he must be laying the groundwork for a scientific explanation of her discovery. Did he know the results of the night's observations? No, that was impossible. No external researcher had access to the data. But maybe, like many Israelis, he had some friend who was a member of the STA team and who had leaked the results to him. Or perhaps he was merely relying on her results for the two stars that she had presented to him only the day before.

Lia was stunned. She had trusted him completely. He projected so much trustworthiness that she had not even bothered looking into his personal history. Feeling immensely upset, she disengaged from the lecture and was immersed in her own thoughts, when loud applause from the audience brought her back to reality. She couldn't understand the first thing about the mathematical analysis on the board. Apologizing to the person sitting beside her for not paying attention, she asked what was going on. The man, who was also applauding enthusiastically, replied without stopping his clapping. "Can't you see? He managed to derive the Chandrasekhar equation from classic thermodynamic considerations, rather than quantum mechanics. We've never seen such an elegant mathematical derivation. He's a virtuoso who definitely deserves the applause."

Lia was certain everyone could hear her immense sigh of relief as her tension eased, and she blushed briefly. Sheffy hadn't even mentioned their topic. She waited impatiently for the end of his lecture, delving into her own thoughts once more.

Her hope of sitting down somewhere quiet with Sheffy and telling him about her findings soon faded away. From the moment he descended from the lectern, he was besieged by a crowd of scientists who would not leave him alone. At some point, after being asked by many of them about the mathematical proof he had demonstrated, they all climbed onto the stage, where, facing the giant whiteboard, Sheffy explained his lecture again, using more complex mathematical terms. Only then did the group seem appeased. It split up into smaller factions, which began to discuss the various points on the board. Only two scientists stayed with Sheffy, initiating a discussion that seemed quite volatile, judging by their hand gestures and their scrawling on the board.

Lia sat down again, waiting for the arguments to subside. The scientists dispersed gradually. Hunger might have motivated them to take off, or perhaps Sheffy had promised to continue the discussion on a different occasion. The two last stubborn stragglers finally concluded their conversation with him, parted from him with a warm handshake, and walked away. He didn't look exhausted in the slightest; on the contrary, he seemed refreshed and ready to return for another lecture. Apparently, the scientists' reaction to his lecture had energized him.

"Are the results in?" he asked the moment he approached her.

"They are."

"Well?" he challenged.

"Well..." she replied, asking with a smile, "What are you expecting?"

"Come on, don't leave me hanging. You wouldn't have bothered coming here, sitting quietly with a mysterious smile on your face and waiting while everyone interrogated me to the point of exhaustion unless you had some interesting news."

"I do have amazing results, but let's sit down somewhere and discuss them."

"This lecture hall is going to be the quietest place in the next hour. Everyone's rushing off to eat, and no one will be here."

"What about you? Aren't you hungry?"

"Who could think about food now? Come on, what did you discover?"

Lia instructed her assistant to display the results of the night's observations, starting with her own two stars and proceeding to the two stars he had requested for which no motion was observed. Sheffy dwelled for a bit on the results for STA331047B and STA333654B, apparently not finding anything new there, but wanting to further confirm her conclusions. He didn't seem disappointed by the lack of motion of the two stars for which he had requested measurements.

"I'm still convinced those two stars are also absorbing mass from their companions, and that their mass has also surpassed the Chandrasekhar limit. Apparently, their orbital period is too long to produce a measurable motion in one night, even with the STA. We should measure them again in a few days."

"Please go on to the two remaining stars," she prodded him.

His gaze focused on the results of the latest calculations showing that the mass of the two stars was exactly 1.76 solar masses. Lia had expected his face to light up, or perhaps a roar of exhilaration. However, his actual reaction was quite different. Sheffy slowly examined the STA measurements for the last two stars, and then thoroughly went over the detailed calculations performed by the software Lia had written to facilitate her work. Only at that point, when she already feared that he had discovered a flaw in her calculations, did he look up, his face illuminated with joy.

"HOORAY!" he declared loudly. "There's something real here. As of now, I don't have the faintest idea what we've found. How about you? You've been thinking about this for a while now. Surely you've considered some possible physical explanations for your results?"

"Unfortunately, I really haven't," she replied. "I was so immersed in measurements and calculations that I didn't put a lot of thought into possible explanations, especially since I think the answer should be provided by theoretical astrophysicists and not by astronomers like me."

"You're probably right, but I don't have any idea what's going on here either, even though I am a theoretical astrophysicist. This is very interesting. Can you see anything these four stars have in common?"

"Other than the clear fact that all of them are, of course, in our galaxy, the only shared and somewhat irregular trait I can see is that they're all fairly close to us. Unlike the supernovas that have exploded in other galaxies and whose occurrence per galaxy is a lot rarer. Assuming each one of these has the potential to become a supernova, we have too many potential supernovas in a relatively small area of space. That really is odd."

With a strange, childish smile on his face, he said, "Well, didn't you consider the possibility that some extraordinary power is preventing these stars from exploding because, due to their proximity, the consequences of any of them exploding would almost certainly be the total annihilation of all life on Earth?"

The expression of disdain in her eyes was precisely the reaction he had been expecting.

"Right," he said, laughing out loud. "I didn't think so, either. But it seemed worth it to check your reaction. Which brings us back to the theoretical astrophysicists. How do you think we should proceed from here? Would you like us to continue looking into this discovery with my research group in Israel? I have an excellent team seeking an interesting project. I'm sure they'll dive right in. Or maybe you have a different team or a different idea in mind? The discovery is all yours, and you have the right to decide. Of course, I'd be very happy if you did us the honor of allowing us to investigate such a unique finding, but I'll respect any other decision as well, and support you and your research."

Lia did not reply, looking pensive.

"You don't have to answer me right now. Take your time. You also have to make a decision about publishing the discovery, or refraining from publishing it. I'm sure you understand such a publication would have major reverberations in the astrophysicist community, and possibly in the mass media as well. Consider the implications."

"You've given me a lot of things to think about and decide on. The truth is, I'm a little confused. So many decisions to make, and all of them are top priority. You've said the conference ends tomorrow afternoon, and that you'll be sticking around for another few days. Give me a day or two to think about it, and I'll certainly want to meet you and decide on a resolution before you return to your home country."

"Excellent. I'll be happy to meet with you and help you come to a resolution."

Sheffy walked her out of the lecture hall, where he parted from her with a warm handshake. Lia turned around and began to walk away when she stopped abruptly, spun on her heels, closed the distance between them and hugged him warmly, whispering in his ear, "Thank you from the bottom of my heart for your help and your friendship. You've been immensely helpful. I'll get back to you soon."

Benny did not try to hide his joy, replying, "Like I told you, I'll always be happy to help."

Lia had been baptized as an infant, but had never had any interest in Christianity and was not a churchgoer. Like most of her friends, her only connection to religion was during holidays and the vacations that accompanied them. She knew that Israelis had a deeper connection to the Jewish religion, and recalled asking a colleague about the meaning of the little cap that a few Israeli students at the university wore. She remembered him replying that the small cap symbolized the extent of their belief in the Jewish religion. He had also told her that different communities wore different kinds of hats; each of these communities had a different degree of religious devotion and observance.

Sheffy did not wear anything on his head, and so she could not assess the extent of his devoutness or belief in an omnipotent creator. She had found his comment regarding the possibility of an extraordinary power preventing the stars from exploding odd, although her dismissive reaction had merely made him laugh. She would never have come up with such an idea. It would be interesting to discuss this topic in the future if they did end up working together.

In any case, it was obvious to her that she was going to compose a detailed scientific paper regarding the discovery. She would credit Professor Sheffy as a research partner, and of course, carefully look into the work team he had mentioned. She might even visit the Weizmann Institute of Science and personally assess the researchers and their capabilities. Yes, she wouldn't delay the publication for too long. She'd cooperate with Sheffy in verifying the article and, once they were satisfied with it, she would publish it, which would surely contribute to her career at the university. She would not let Sheffy wait too long for an answer. She would get back to him this very evening, she decided.

CHAPTER 27

Gerry Resigns

Chicago, Wednesday, July 23, 2036

The six days since the accident had been highly beneficial for Gerry. All the bandages had been removed and the cuts on his face were in the final stages of healing, thanks to the tissue regeneration cream he had applied daily. Had he suffered such injuries even in the near past, he would have had to stay in bed for weeks while his cracked bones knitted together. His thigh probably would have been in a cast for weeks as well, which would have limited his mobility significantly.

Today there were no signs of the cracking in his ribs and thighbone, thanks to the electrodes he was required to place upon them, which reactivated the growth factors in the cracked bones. No surgery was necessary. All he had to do was run the device in his home for half an hour daily over three days. Truly amazing.

He ate, rested, and grew stronger, able to move freely around the house. He had regained his wife's full trust, while with everyone else, including his children, he maintained the façade of a man suffering from a brain injury.

However, despite the physical improvement, his spirits were at an unprecedented low. He was eager to continue on the path from which the accident had diverted him. The academic desire to publish his discovery became almost an existential need for him. Every day that went by without any progress in this regard tormented him and left him sleepless. He was not perturbed regarding the risk to his own life. He didn't care if they murdered him after the publication. The world would look completely different by then, in any case. Only the fear that his wife and children would be harmed prevented him from publishing his discovery immediately.

This was the first day he had dared go online since the accident. He did so from his wife's computer, and made sure his Web surfing would not look too professional. During the first few days, he tested his new abilities, successfully facing every challenge he posed for himself. Recalling yesterday's paper, he saw page after page surfacing in his mind's eye, and immediately compared them to the pages saved online. He could read any story or article, even starting at the end and going backward—the image in his mind was that clear.

He mentally paged through the last book concerning quantum theory, which he had finished reading a month ago. He could see the page numbers, the images, and the diagrams, as if the book had actually been placed in front of him. *Interesting*, he thought. He could remember events that had taken place prior to the accident with absolute precision, such as the details of the car that had hit him, a book he had read long before the accident. *It turns out our brain stores all the details of every image we see in our lives. We simply can't usually retrieve this information.* He wondered how far into the past he could delve and still retrieve such full details. He would have to test this soon.

Returning to more urgent matters, he decided his first priority was to regain possession of the hidden copy of his work, a protection against any future complication that might compromise him. His physical condition now allowed him to leave the house, and of course, the first place he wanted to go was work. He wouldn't be able to drive comfortably, but Ramona would be happy to do the driving for him. Yes, he would come for a social visit, meet his colleagues, and among other things, retrieve several tools from his toolbox, including the screwdriver in which he had hidden the copy of his presentation. He would use the excuse that some light household tasks might do him good.

Ramona organized and coordinated everything. Ethan and Gerry's other coworkers were glad, encouraging her to come soon, even immediately. Yes, they would clear their schedules entirely, so long as they could see him soon. Indeed, everyone loved Gerry.

The drive went by easily, and he felt almost no pain in his ribs. The innovative medication to facilitate bone healing was working quickly and efficiently. His ribs still hurt a bit occasionally, and his thigh pained him with every step. The doctor had confirmed to Ramona that the more he moved around, carefully and with no sudden motions, the more his condition would improve.

His friends met him in the department's conference room, which was set up in a way that was somewhat too festive, in his opinion. Everyone was smiling and expressing their eagerness to hear him describe everything that had happened. And so he found himself sitting at the head of the table, with all his colleagues expectantly waiting for whatever he had to say.

Briefly, he considered giving them a complete account of everything he had been through since the accident: waking up in the hospital in utter darkness, the initial impression that he was in hell, his aching ribs, and feeling his bandaged face, indicating that he was alive but injured, recalling the accident, his daughter describing the extent of his injuries, and his rapid recuperation, bringing him to the point where he was able to come and see them.

Of course, it never occurred to him to mention his work, or the unusual mental acuity he was experiencing. He'd never say a word about the threatening call before the accident, or about his suspicion that the incident had been intentionally staged.

However, he had to continue the masquerade that he had suffered a brain injury. Therefore, in a quiet, stammering voice, using somewhat inarticulate language, he began to describe what had befallen him during the last week. The attendees' smiles and jovial expressions evaporated gradually. He was well aware of the glances they exchanged, which contained plenty of sadness and pity.

They were good people, working at the forefront of technology and cosmology. Each was a world leader in his or her own field. It was hard for them to watch a colleague who, only several days ago, had been researching observations from the most sophisticated, costly apparatus that humanity had ever constructed, but today faced them with a brain injury that had stolen away his entire future as a scientist, all because of one brief accident.

It became clear to him that there was no point continuing to describe the recent events in detail. They wouldn't be able to stand it, and it would be hard for him, as well. Therefore, he gave them a brief summary of what he'd gone through, emphasizing his speedy recovery and his hope for an improvement in his cognitive state. His coworkers' uncomfortable fidgeting and whispering made it clear to him that they had exhausted their ability to listen. This was the moment he had been waiting for.

He stopped speaking, raising himself slowly from his seat. His assembled colleagues stopped squirming and whispering, their eyes focusing upon him.

"I w-w-want to in-inform you that d-d-due to my c-c-condition, I'm re-resigning be-because I d-d-don't want to b-b-be in your w-w-way," he concluded, sitting down again.

Everyone was clearly surprised. They were not expecting this, although they appeared to appreciate his decision. Ramona, who had been sitting quietly on the sidelines throughout, also seemed surprised. Slowly, his coworkers rose from their seats, shook Gerry's hand warmly, and left. No one touched the refreshments.

Once everyone but Ethan had left, Gerry and Ramona got up as well, heading for the door, when Ethan pulled him aside and said, "You still owe us a presentation about your last research topic. You'd mentioned a discovery that would affect humanity as a whole. Considering the improvement in your condition, maybe you can tell me about it briefly now, or sometime soon?"

Gerry wasn't surprised. He had been anticipating this question, and had prepared his answer in advance.

"I w-w-want to st-still ch-check it f-f-first. M-m-might he-help m-m-my br-brain."

That's it. He sighed internally. The hard part was behind him. He had handed in his resignation. Whoever had known about his work and had hurt him would surely find out that he had quit and, even more importantly, about his cognitive condition, and perhaps he would be able to go on with his life without fear, at least until the moment he published his discovery.

"I'm really sorry," Ethan replied. "I hope you get better soon and can come back to us. We'll always have a place for someone like you."

"I sin-sincere-l-ly th-thank you," Gerry responded, shaking Ethan's extended hand then exiting the room, with Ramona following.

As they headed out, Gerry turned in the direction of the mechanics' workshop. The place was nearly empty other than two technicians he knew, who were tuning the milling machine and paused to greet him. It appeared as if no one had touched his toolbox, which lay on the right side of the second shelf next to two other toolboxes, exactly where he had left it several days ago.

He opened it and extracted the long pliers and two regular screwdrivers. He handed these to Ramona, who put them in her purse. Finally, he reached out for the old, worn-down Phillips screwdriver in which, about a week ago, he had hidden a copy of the presentation, just in case.

Suddenly, Gerry realized he was still entrenched in the patterns characterizing his former life. He didn't even need the presentation he had hidden. With his enhanced brain and his perfect memory, he could reconstruct all of it, down to the smallest detail. He briefly considered returning the screwdriver to its place, but on second thought, handed it to Ramona, who buried it in her purse among the other tools and the entire inventory of items that filled every woman's handbag.

Who knew what might happen to him? Perhaps he hadn't managed to fool those who had injured him. Perhaps they knew about his new cognitive abilities. They might try to harm him again, this time intending to kill him rather than merely warn him. He would do anything to ensure his work was not lost; he would not relinquish its publication even if it cost him his life. He would tell Ramona about the screwdriver and the presentation, and ask her to give it to Ethan if he was hurt or unable to function for any reason. Hand in hand, the two of them slowly headed out to their car.

"Since we're already out and about, and I see that you're not exhausted, how about eating out somewhere? It might do you good to be around people," she suggested.

Gerry nodded in affirmation. He preferred not to talk when there were so many people around.

The illustrious Alinea was one of the restaurants that did not follow the latest technological trends. In its distant past, it had been rated one of the ten best restaurants in the world, and had even received three Michelin stars. At its peak, it had been booked six or eight months in advance.

But the passing years and new ownership had had a cumulative effect. It was still considered a good restaurant today, but it was now possible to find a free table for lunch during the week. It did not feature robot waiters or electronic menus, but rather human waiters and printed menus. Surprisingly, the patrons were not exclusively older people. Apparently, there were quite a few young people who enjoyed the restaurant's old-fashioned, more personal style. Perhaps, to them, it resembled a visit to a museum of history.

Gerry was about to give the young waitress his order. Briefly, he debated whether even here, away from his home and work, where no one knew him, he still had to keep pretending to be brain damaged in order to fool a possible tail. The temptation to resume regular human speech was great, enhanced by the calm environment in his home during the last few days.

He had already opened his mouth, having decided to speak

normally and order whatever he wanted, when a dark-skinned man wearing a suit entered the restaurant. Gerry ignored him for a split second. Then, from the outskirts of his mind, the image of the van that had been following him and later hit him, as seen in his rearview mirror, floated to the surface of his consciousness. He had been able to see a blurry image of the driver through the windshield. His skin had been dusky and he had been wearing a suit, or at least a formal jacket.

He found himself wondering momentarily whether this was the driver who had hit him. Gerry attempted to mentally survey the driver's features. Just like in a computerized image-processing application, he managed to enlarge the driver's face, gradually eliminating the blurring caused by the window and the sun's flickering upon it, until the image appeared sharp and clear in his mind. It had indeed been the man who had just entered the restaurant, briefly gazed at him, then left. He was absolutely certain of it. The driver who had intentionally hit him had just signaled to him that he was still under surveillance.

He had to continue to pretend to be brain damaged. Who knew what else the person following him was capable of? Perhaps he might come to the conclusion that his warning hadn't had the desired effect on Gerry. He might plan another assault, and this time, the injury might be fatal.

Gerry wasn't afraid of death. All he wanted was to publish his work first. Anything that happened after publication didn't matter. Publishing his research would bring on the inevitable change.

At that moment, he came to a decision. He wouldn't waste the remainder of his life, which might prove very short, on fear and hiding. On the contrary, he would publish his findings, and would happily pay any price the publication might entail, including his own life. But in the next few hours, he must go online, get up to speed on the news of the week he had skipped, and then recreate the presentation based on his eidetic memory, rather than retrieving it from the Cloud. He would leave the original presentation hidden in the screwdriver in Ramona's purse. He had to inform her of its importance.

Ramona, who noticed the flurry of emotions passing across his face, did not want to make things any harder for him and asked, "Should I order for you, so you can keep thinking?"

Gerry nodded distractedly. His wife knew him well. This wasn't the first time he had retreated into his own thoughts and disengaged from the world around him, like the classic absentminded professor. At the beginning of their relationship, such reactions would hurt her. She would think she was boring him, and feel angry. However, over time, as she had grown to appreciate him, she had also learned to accept him the way he was, including his little eccentricities.

They ate quietly, without exchanging a word. She was certain he had no idea what he was eating, and that had she switched the plates on him midmeal, he would never had noticed. He was too wrapped up in his thoughts.

Gerry mentally reconstructed the presentation, while debating what his target audience should be. Originally, the presentation had been intended for his colleagues, NASA astronomers and astrophysicists. It was quite technical, and included plenty of mathematics. Should he leave it the way it was and pass it on to Ethan, hoping he would distribute it using the appropriate forum at work? But perhaps Ethan was being threatened as well, and would be afraid to distribute the study. No, he couldn't take that chance. He might not be around for much longer.

Briefly, he considered posting his work on one of the astronomy blogs, from which it would eventually spread to the entire scientific community. Or perhaps he should post it on a general science blog, or even address it to the mass media. Any venue he chose would require making some adjustments to the presentation. If he started working immediately once he returned home, by evening he could have a perfect general presentation. In the course of the afternoon, he would have to come to a decision regarding his means of publication, and rewrite the presentation accordingly.

On the way home, he decided to take the risk and visit some astronomy websites for the first time since the accident in order to read the latest updates. He would do so from Ramona's computer, an act he had been avoiding until now. Of course, he would do it only after he finished writing up his research. A long, busy, and dangerous evening was awaiting him. He wondered how long he had left before his final encounter with the assailant.

CHAPTER 28

Aaron is Suspected of Murder

Chicago, Wednesday, July 23, 2036

The night was uneventful as far as Rick was concerned. Yoni didn't call. Apparently, there had been no progress with the other person tailing Melissa, which might be a good thing. Lily called as Rick was on his way to the precinct in order to update him on the search for Kyra. She had set up an early morning meeting for him with their regional FBI contact. Perhaps they would manage to locate her. Rick would have to request that they do so in the course of the meeting, in order to emphasize the importance of the matter.

James, their regional FBI affiliate, worked from an office in a typical professional building outside the city. As usual, Lily had determined it would be more convenient for him to swing by there on his way to the precinct in the morning, thus saving travel time as well as allowing him to reach the city after rush hour had ended.

Rick liked the efficient, detail-oriented way she worked. Her job was her life; she enjoyed every moment of it, and her performance reflected this.

A random passerby would never have imagined that the sign "James Morrison, Small Business CPA" fronted the office of the liaison between the FBI and Chicago Police Department headquarters. Rick and James convened frequently. The friction between the local police force and the FBI was inevitable, but both men knew how to compromise and tamp down the flames between their respective bureaus, often exacerbated by the field officers, who enjoyed the inter-agency competition.

Rick was certain that James would conduct the investigation in the best way possible. He was always highly efficient. However, Rick was not particularly hopeful about the search. He believed Kyra was a member of the organization responsible for the murder and perhaps for many of the lab break-ins. It was very easy to infiltrate academic institutions, which were not naturally suspicious and did not invest enough resources in protecting and securing their information. Using a pretty young woman to seduce an employee was an old, established method. *Mike wasn't the first and certainly won't be the last to fall for it*, he thought on his way.

The meeting with James was short and to the point, as usual. Both of them were busy people, and it was in both their best interest to cooperate without stirring up unnecessary difficulties. James promised to check all the classified organizations to which the FBI had access immediately after Rick's office sent over the records of the investigation they had conducted.

It was only when Rick got up to leave James's office that James called him back, saying with a grin, "Sit down—don't go yet. Lily already sent us all the material you've gathered, although, in fact, we didn't actually need it."

Rick's perplexed look only made James's grin grow wider. "What's going on here?" he asked.

In response, James whispered into the assistant, "Ask her to come in now."

The office door opened and a beautiful young woman came in. She walked over to Rick, extended her hand, and said, "Laura, at your service. Or, as you've heard me referred to, Kyra, at your service."

Rick's awkward gaze bounced between her and James. The moment he noted the smiles on both their faces, he understood everything.

"Kyra's your agent," he said. "And we were so certain she would be the lead who would help us locate the killer."

"Sit down, please," James told Laura. "I'm sure Rick has countless questions. You can get started here and continue wherever you want. Only please take into account that Laura works at the FBI branch in San Francisco and is only here on loan for this assignment. We transfer employees between the various branches as part of our policy of misdirection and safeguards in regard to exposing agents to national threats."

"Before you begin questioning me," Laura said, "I want to say a few things, both to you and to James, who wasn't familiar with the details of the operation. I'm sure what I have to say will also spare you quite a few questions that are on your mind."

Rick nodded his consent, feeling primarily grateful. His surprise was so immense that he had yet to fully process what was going on, and certainly hadn't had time to come up with a coherent set of questions.

"Well," Laura began, "I was sent on loan to the Chicago office, as James just told you, for a specific assignment, after the Bureau discerned a recurring pattern of break-ins into biology labs all over the country that were a bit too clean."

Rick felt momentarily breathless, his inhalation labored. The FBI had already discovered the pattern of break-ins. Well, there went his glory and his promotion. On the other hand, if he couldn't be promoted, at least he could cooperate with the FBI in a nationwide investigation.

"Based on the characteristics of the labs broken into, primarily their areas of research, our investigative team compiled a list of labs that the team assessed might be targeted for a break-in in the near future. These labs were rated based on the probability of a break-in, and agents—specifically female agents with an extensive knowledge of biology, an appropriate personal appearance, and, of course, seduction skills—were sent to the three labs topping the list from several FBI offices throughout the United States. I personally have degrees in biology and computer science from Harvard University.

"It was clear to the investigative team that the intruders' goal was specific biological information, the nature of which we were tasked with discovering. Mike was a very easy target. Please don't judge me for taking advantage of him in order to protect national interests. I'll get back to him later.

"I'm not part of the investigative team, so I didn't have access to all the information collected. My role was to discover exactly what the lab did, and pass the reports on to headquarters.

"Mike didn't discuss his work much, so I had to burrow into his computer. Of course, I discovered all the security passwords, which I passed on to headquarters, although I didn't make any further use of them. I provided as many details as possible regarding the longevity-enhancement research from the material on Mike's computer."

The two men listened attentively. Rick had received all the answers he needed. His hope to make use of Kyra had faded away, but what he heard from Laura would save him much time and effort. He was about to thank her when she continued speaking.

"I promised to get back to Mike. Although I carried out my assignment, and I don't apologize in the slightest for taking advantage of Mike's naïveté, I found him to be a warm, genuine person, and I'd be happy to transform our relationship into an authentically romantic one. I'd firmly request that both of you keep the personal aspects of what's been said here between us. I'll find a way to get back to Mike, and who knows? One of these days, you might be invited to Declarations. Now that I'm done, I'll be happy to answer any questions I can."

"What's Declarations?" Rick asked.

"I've heard something about it," James began to reply. "Some trendy California thing."

"Allow me to explain," Laura said. "Declarations ceremonies are popular among loving couples in San Francisco. For years, couples simply lived together without marriage, had children, and sometimes even grew old together, but without any official mutual commitment that would replace the old institution of marriage. I don't know who the first pioneers were, but it took off like a house on fire. The couple throws a party, culminating with each of them reading out loud a series of declarations and commitments that he or she will take on within the relationship. These commitments are also distributed to the guests, and thus the couple is considered 'declared.'

"This ceremony proved appealing not just to new couples, but to many established ones, who saw it as a declaration of commitment to their partners. Within several years, thousands of couples were 'declared' in the city and around it. From there, the idea spread to many areas all over the nation, and I heard it's been adopted by many couples in Europe as well. This might be our generation's rebellion against our parents, many of whom still got married in religious ceremonies."

Rick's eyes roamed between Laura and James. Laura/Kyra had eliminated the need for any additional questions.

"Thanks for sharing the information. I get the picture, although I was hoping for a different sort of picture. I don't have any questions at the moment. I understand Tom doesn't need to know about what was said here today, either," he concluded.

"Of course, Tom can't know anything about this. Don't worry, he'll be summoned too, when the time is right," she stated, with a grin that further emphasized her attractive features.

***

Back at the precinct, Lily came into Rick's office, and he briefed her on the topic of Kyra.

She responded, "That's just like the FBI. They're very effective. Very little slips by them. I hadn't anticipated this development, though."

On his desk were the two lists of organizations and individuals potentially interested in the research being conducted in the labs, as compiled separately by Tom and Melissa. At first glance, the lists were similar in length but consisted of different names. Only a more comprehensive assessment made it clear to him that, other than the order in which the names were listed, the lists were quite similar.

Apparently, everyone in the field was familiar with everyone else.

"Anything new with the blood sample?" he asked.

"We found a match," she replied quietly. "Ben's been working on it alone. Here's the person's info." She handed him a note specifying a name, a physical address, and an assistant address.

"Why isn't there a photo as well?" he asked.

"We didn't want to leave any evidence of the search for him in the computers," she replied. "All of the work was done with no documentation, as we agreed, with only a few people involved."

"And what do we know about him? Background, activity?"

"Actually, there's nothing. We have no records of any activity concerning this man. As far as we know, he's an anonymous figure who's always stayed under the radar. Going through Melissa's computer didn't add anything, either," she added. "Aaron has been concealing himself effectively, and no further information is available."

"Has anyone here at the precinct displayed any interest in or talked about the murder of the security guard?" he asked.

"Not really. The truth is that I have a hard time believing anyone in the department or in the precinct is involved in this."

"I also hope the precautions we've been taking are unnecessary. In any case, assuming the intruder and murderer was unaware of the blood stain, I believe his mind should be somewhat at ease right now." More loudly, he added, "Actually, I'm not too busy right now. I might go out for an early lunch. I got up very early this morning, and I'm really hungry." With these words, he left his office.

On his way, he fumbled for the note with the killer's information. Once he had reached his car, he looked up the address. Carefully, he disconnected the vehicle's internal GPS and set out without requesting navigational assistance. He wanted to make perfectly sure that his route would not be detected. He wasn't sure that the car's system was free of malware, which might report his destination to an unwanted interceptor.

He often found himself debating whether his work had made him paranoid. The thought that he had concealed his actual destination from Lily as well made him uncomfortable. In retrospect, he discerned that this was often his custom—to share information with others only when strictly necessary, and to conceal his actions as much as possible.

The residential building at which he arrived was one of several in a crowded, unappealing complex. Aaron Gorong lived in the most derelict of the buildings. The front door had been torn out and tossed outside the building's lobby quite a while ago, based on the vegetation growing through its cracks. Everything was in a state of neglect.

For a moment, he was briefly tempted to use the elevator. It was not much fun to climb seven flights of stairs.

The staircase matched the building and its façade in its neglected state, with old chairs lying here and there, perhaps to allow those climbing the stairs to rest between floors. Apparently, the elevator had seen better days. There was no illumination in the seventh-floor hallway. A dim light originated beyond the bend in the corridor.

Holding his stun gun in his extended hand, he walked carefully to the end of the corridor. The light emanated from an open apartment door. A glance at the numbers of the apartments leading to the open door confirmed his suspicion. His destination was the apartment whose gaping, uninviting entrance was now facing him.

He debated briefly whether to summon backup and await its arrival. Once, in the distant past, he would not have hesitated to storm inside on his own. Now that he was older and knew quite a few cops who had been hurt by such reckless behavior, he paused first. He wondered whether the security guard's murderer was waiting for him in the apartment with his gun drawn, but for some reason, rejected this scenario.

He believed the killing of the security guard had been an accident, rather than a premeditated act. The open door also clearly indicated that someone knew he was on his way. Someone—male or female—had leaked the fact that he had discovered the killer's identity, despite all his precautions and misdirection. The killer was probably far away from here.

Nevertheless, he proceeded with extreme caution, entering slowly. The apartment was empty. Not abandoned, simply empty. He found nothing inside except a basic table and three plastic chairs. The refrigerator had been unplugged, its door wide open and its interior completely dry. Well, at least he didn't need to worry that someone had leaked the information regarding the blood stain. The killer had left the apartment at least several days ago, perhaps immediately following the murder.

This was the time for an extensive police investigation regarding the apartment and its recent resident. The investigation, as well as locating the killer, could now be made an official assignment. Lily would distribute the killer's information, as well as his photo, among the detectives. The suspect was several steps ahead of them, but now there was no reason to conceal anything from him. Actually, he thought, he hadn't seen the suspect's photo either. Within moments, the assistant screen displayed a photo of the killer, a dark-skinned man in his late forties.

His stomach reminded him that it was lunchtime, a conclusion confirmed by the time shown on his assistant. Why not go through the hospital and visit Will on his way back? That would work out well. Perhaps he would even meet Melissa there, and they could dine together. He would have an opportunity to get to know her better, and perhaps make some progress.

The moment he spoke Will's name, the assistant consulted a current traffic map, guiding the automatic driver along the optimal route in the maze of traffic jams within the big city.

Melissa answered immediately. Yes, she was at the hospital, and had good news. Will was completely awake and doing well. Apparently, there was no brain damage. He was talking slowly and laboriously, but the doctors were certain that once the swelling in his face was reduced, he would resume speaking normally. He might also be discharged in the next few days. She would be happy to meet him there and have lunch with him.

The automatic driving, which didn't require any effort from him, flooded his mind with the type of thoughts he preferred to repress, sweeping him into the realm of paranoia, namely how he didn't trust anyone, including those closest to him. It was true, he had been burned more than once by those near to him, whom he'd trusted unreservedly. And in this case, Melissa remained a suspect until her trustworthiness was proved. Were his suspicions excessive when it came to her? There was no way of knowing. Perhaps their shared lunch would provide an answer. Until then, he would maintain his suspicions.

Up to this point, he had seen Melissa during the business meeting with Will, when she seemed assertive, pragmatic, and in full control. Later, he had met a frightened, tense, borderline hysterical woman when she had arrived at the hospital before seeing Will. When she had left his room, he had seen a broken woman on the verge of collapse. In the evening, she had been businesslike and sharp again. On the assistant, she sounded full of vitality. He wondered which Melissa he was about to meet.

As he hurried down the hospital corridors, he recalled the sight of Will bandaged and sedated, with existential uncertainties hanging over his head. What would he see in a moment?

In the waiting nook in the corridor was a different officer this time. He, too, was wearing a patient's gown, and he also ignored Rick completely. Brad, his deputy, had indeed trained them well.

Will was sitting up in his bed. His face was slightly swollen, but it lit up with a broad smile the moment he saw Rick.

"Sit down," he said. "Dad, vring a chair for Detective Rick flease," he addressed the older man sitting next to an older woman, apparently his parents. "Flease meet my farents. Dad, Mom, this is Detective Rick I was just telling you avout."

Melissa, who had been sitting across from his bed, rose to warmly shake his hand. "I don't need a chair. I can't stay long," Rick said. "I see resting has done you some good, and you're back to running the world around you. Let your father be. How are you?"

"Other than a few vandages and my face veing a little swollen, mostly my lifs, which is distorting my sfeech, I'm vack to my old self."

"When are you being discharged?"

"Frovavly today or tomorrow," he replied.

"Great. I'm glad to see you on the mend so quickly, and I can't wait for our next game. Don't worry—I won't go easy on you just because you're injured." Everyone smiled and nodded.

Rick said goodbye to Will and his parents and left the room, along with Melissa. In the commercial floor of the hospital were various restaurants. Rick chose one that looked pricey, where it seemed most likely they could find a quiet, isolated place to sit, to the extent possible at such a busy hour.

On their way there, he discovered a new Melissa, different than the ones he had seen so far. It seemed as if a major weight had been lifted off her shoulders. She was jolly and happy. The guilt that had been oppressing her had melted away. Will would recuperate and return to his old self. She was simply overjoyed and charming. *How did Will let her get away*, he wondered. Well, perhaps he had discovered something that Rick still didn't know. *I really am incorrigibly paranoid*, he found himself thinking.

Rick told her that they were proceeding with the murder investigation, and had found a suspect named Aaron Gorong. The name did not sound familiar to Melissa. But when he showed her the photo, her appealing face jerked briefly. She was no longer a happy, cheerful woman.

"That's Jack," she blurted quickly, her expression becoming fearful. "How did you find him? Where is he? Do you have him under arrest?"

"Don't get upset, and don't rush into anything. We found him as part of the murder investigation. He's under considerable suspicion, but we don't have him yet. Searching your computer didn't help us. Aaron Gorong, or Jack, as you know him, was very good at concealing any ties he might have. How exactly is he paying you?" he asked.

"Money transfers, of course."

"Have you ever checked where the money comes from?"

"I really haven't. I made sure the money came, and that was the only thing that interested me. It really is too bad that I didn't bother to look into it, but you can. I'll give you access to check out my bank account."

"We'll look into it, although it's also very easy to conceal the source of the funds. We'll give it a try, anyway."

Rick connected Melissa to the precinct, and she relayed her bank account details and immediately instructed the bank to give the police access.

"What's happening with the assignment Jack gave you?" he asked.

"I'll finish it today and send it to him."

"Wait before you send it," he interrupted her. "Our communication expert will give you instructions when the material is ready."

"What exactly are you going to do?" she burst out.

His suspicions mounted instantly. She was wary regarding what the police could do to discover the route through which the material was conveyed. He had just told her they hadn't caught Aaron, and obviously, this was now the focus of their efforts. He was not ready to relinquish his suspicions.

On the other hand, she had told him that their suspect was also her contact person. She certainly could have chosen not to betray him. Or had it been a slip of the tongue that she had instantly regretted? The possibility that sophisticated Melissa, with her evident self-control, had acted so thoughtlessly did not fit in with the image he had constructed for her. Or perhaps she was preparing for the moment Aaron was caught, when she would have had a hard time explaining why she hadn't recognized him? No, he would continue to consider her a suspect at this stage.

"We'll add a component to your reply that will relay all the intersections through which the material passes, which will allow us to instantly detect its final destination."

"Wow," she exhaled, with an expression of wonder. "I didn't know you could do that."

"It's not simple, but we have Internet experts who can get to him." He knew that in fact, they could only access the last intersection from which Aaron retrieved the reply, which could indicate quite a large area. But he was very interested in having her believe that this feat was indeed possible. Her fear of the possibility that Aaron would be caught soon would force her to tell him about the surveillance, thus allowing them to intercept the warning message she would send him.

That's great, he thought. *She's swallowed the bait*. Her assistant communications were being monitored anyway. The only thing left was to locate the warning message.

He found himself cheering internally. He wasn't actually paranoid, he decided, but simply had sharp instincts when it came to detecting imposters. But what if sophistication wasn't exclusively the domain of the police? Perhaps she had other means of communication other than the assistant and the Internet. The more he thought about it, the more he grew convinced that this was indeed true. And since he didn't know what this additional method of communication was, his people would probably be unable to intercept her warning message. What a shame. It was a waste of a golden opportunity to trap her, or to ease his suspicions. He would now have to return to his office feeling even more uncertain about her.

***

Will was engaged in a lively conversation with his parents when Melissa entered the room.

"I'm sorry, I don't want to interrupt you. I'll try to come back this evening," she said.

"You're not interrupting us," his mother replied. "The doctor is ready to discharge him. We want him to come to New York with us so he can rest for a few days, but he insists on recuperating alone in his own home. He's always been a stubborn boy."

"I feel a lot vetter, and more imfortantly, I feel stronger vy the hour, and my sfeech is imfroving, too. At this rate, I can go vack to work this week. There's no foint in going to New York just to return immediately."

"I'll keep an eye on him," Melissa interfered in the familial argument. "We've known each other for a long time. I know him well, and I'll be happy to come over and help him until he's feeling better," she continued, flashing her winning smile.

Will's nod confirmed that he had been won over by her line of reasoning.

"I know how he likes his coffee, what he likes to eat during the day, and in general, we have a lot of common interests to talk about. I'm sure that resting in his own home, without the hassles of flying, would be better for him, and will bring him back to us quickly."

Apparently, her arguments had the desired effect. The parents exchanged knowing glances and removed their objections to allowing Will to stay home.

Once they had left, Melissa stretched out in the only armchair in the room and asked with a mischievous smile, "Well, what can I do for you?"

The two of us are finally in a room all by ourselves, Will thought. *Too bad it's under such harsh circumstances.*

"I see you're in close contact with Rick," he began. "I assume there's veen some frogress in the murder investigation. And to answer your question, the only thing I can do in my current condition is study and think. How do you feel avout ufdating me on everything you've learned avout the investigation?"

For a moment, it seemed to him as if Melissa hesitated. Her gaze, previously fixed upon him, was now averted. Something was preventing her from erupting in her usual fluent monologue, enumerating and elaborating on everything that had happened during the twenty-four hours in which he had been out of commission. Perhaps she had nothing to tell him. Perhaps nothing had happened.

How odd, he thought.

But then Melissa squirmed in her seat, her eyes focused upon him once more, and she let out a gradual sigh. "You have no idea what kind of Pandora's box you've opened. I'm trying to structure what I'm about to say in a way that will sound logical, as much as possible, although I doubt I'll succeed. I hope you've bounced back enough to process what I'm about to tell you.

"I know the man who pushed you under the truck that hit you. It's the same man you saw looking at us at the restaurant, the one who scared me. His real name is Aaron Gorong, although he introduced himself to me as Jack. He took photos of us at the restaurant, and then sent me the photos in the envelope during our meeting.

"When I left the restaurant, and saw the photos, along with an old newspaper article you'd written, I understood that he'd recognized you and knew you were an investigative reporter, and most importantly, I realized you were in danger. I tried to warn you a few times, to no avail. I know you followed me to make sure I wasn't hurt, and I'm grateful. I believe he pushed you to warn you not to mess with him. You set out to protect me from the unknown and put yourself at risk, while I, the person responsible for the entire mess in the first place, couldn't even manage to warn you. I feel guilty about what happened to you, and I've barely slept since that night.

"I wrote quite a few assessments for him about what's happening at the forefront of research concerning various topics related to human DNA. He introduced himself to me as a member of an ancient sect attempting to prevent scientists from altering the human genome. I was frightened when I saw him watching us at the restaurant because, just a day before the murder, I'd given him my analysis of the research taking place in Dr. Thomas Lester's lab, where the murder of the security guard happened."

Will's lips parted in response, and his eyes gradually widened.

"And that's not the end of the story. Detective Rick and I met—you're not going to believe where. At your old aunt's house."

"I don't velieve it," he burst out. "Why? What haffened?"

"Rick was concerned that Jack was listening in on us. He knew we'd met there on our first date, so we could set up a meeting without mentioning an address."

"Vut why did you meet?" he asked.

"Despite your accident and all this chaos, Jack sent me more work. Maybe he wanted to continue the game, or maybe he had some other reason. We met to come up with an action plan and decide how to respond. Anyway, Rick was the one who recognized Jack as Aaron Gorong, apparently of East Asian descent, although he still hasn't been arrested."

"Wow, what a convoluted affair," he responded. "Now I understand why Rick was in such a good mood. He's on to something vig here, way vigger than the random murder of a security guard."

The wealth of information Melissa had just provided him, in combination with the enforced rest, ignited his vivid imagination.

The puzzle pieces began to hover in his consciousness, occasionally trying to come together, only to drift apart and recombine in new ways. He had no idea what the final picture was or how many pieces the puzzle had. It was also possible that he wouldn't manage to obtain them all and might have to guess some, and, similarly to questions in a math test, speculate on the missing puzzle pieces based on clues or fragments of clues.

Relatively well-secured biology labs dealing with human DNA research had been broken into lately, sometimes cleanly, with no apparent damage, nothing stolen or broken. The intruders weren't common thieves or junkies. The profile seemed to fit that of an inside job, in which the intruders were aided by lab workers who might have supplied entry codes. One of the break-ins apparently had gone awry and ended with the murder of the security guard. The perpetrator's fear of being caught had led to the murder.

There was a promising suspect for the break-ins and the murder—Jack and his ancient religious cult, which monitored studies that might affect and alter human DNA. Or perhaps this was a cover story for a business group interested in studies that would result in longevity enhancement, or any other area with major commercial potential. This seemed much more convincing than the story of the ancient cult.

There was also his own staged accident. A work-related accident while breaking into a university lab was one thing; it made sense to assume the murder had not been premeditated. But in his case, there had been a clear initiative to harm him, perhaps to kill him. Why? The killer was aware of his occupation, proving it with the photo he'd sent Melissa. He was probably afraid of a damning story about him and the activity of his organization.

Now that he thought about it, perhaps the event involving the

NASA astronomer hadn't been an accident, either. But what was the link between astronomy—asteroids and comets—and biological research? No, apparently, his house of cards had grown too tall. There was no connection between the events. But if the astronomer had discovered an asteroid made entirely of diamond or any metal, even iron or aluminum, its value would be unimaginable, and might well interest businesspeople, like a treatment to extend the human lifespan would. However, why hurt the person who had discovered it, instead of cooperating with him? Or perhaps they had gotten the information they needed, and since he was blackmailing them for an excessive finder's fee, they decided to silence him in this manner?

He had to meet the astronomer. Thinking about him and about NASA, his place of employment, brought back a recent memory about an investigation he had conducted about two years ago involving subterfuge, bribes, and embezzlement, all taking place at the renowned institution. The person who had given him the initial lead was Dan Auster, who had been forced out of NASA. After the exposure of the embezzlement and the firing of those responsible for it, Dan had promptly been reinstated and, ever since then, had felt as if he owed Will a personal debt. Why not talk to him? He would be happy to help.

Should he wait until Melissa left, or share his suspicions and inquiries with her? He had to consider it carefully. Only at that moment did he notice that she had grown silent. She had probably noticed that he had become immersed in his own thoughts and drifted away from her. She knew him so well.

"Sorry, I got distracted. I was trying to fut all the crumbs of information together into a coherent ficture, with very little success. I'm missing too many ingredients. Anyway, I interrufted you. Flease go on. You said the man who fushed me still hasn't veen arrested?"

"That's right," she continued. "I'm sure Rick will do anything he can to find and apprehend him."

"That means I'm still in danger and he might try to finish what he started when he fushed me into the road?"

Her relaxed expression instantly became intimidated and frightened. "I didn't think even for a moment that you might still be in danger. I was glad you weren't too badly harmed in the accident, as we initially believed it to be, and I thought that was the end of it. I have to tell Rick about it, so he can consider what to do."

She called Rick immediately. "He promised to think about it," she said. "What are you doing?" she raised her voice when she saw Will twisting around in bed, attempting to sit up.

"That's it, I've had enough. I'm trying to get out of ved," he said.

"Why don't we call a nurse who can confirm whether you're allowed to get up? If she does, I can help you."

"That's exactly what I don't want," he replied. "I feel like I can get uf, so I don't care what the nurse thinks."

"You haven't changed," she said with a smile. "You're still stubborn and opinionated." She watched him with wonder as he took two tentative steps, after which he straightened and took several more steadier ones.

"Way to go," she said softly. "I didn't believe you'd get better so quickly. I'm really glad to see it."

"That's it. I'm going home today," he said, setting out for the nurses' station, with Melissa following. As they walked, they continued to argue whether they should go to his place or to hers. "The doctor confirmed that I don't need any physical sufort or sufervision."

"Yes, that's right—he did, but only based on a remote assessment. I'm not sure I'd trust an examination from a doctor who never physically touched the patient."

"Things have changed," he replied. "Remote assessments vy doctors are in use in every hosfital. Instead of making the doctor rush around vetween fatients, wasting his time, the doctor can assess the entire course of the disease and treatment, and through a sfecialized system, can frovide the vest diagnosis. I'm certain, of course, that I can get along by myself, although I'd ve very haffy if you came with me."

CHAPTER 29

Lia Publishes the Anomaly

California, Wednesday, July 23, 2036

Briefly, Lia considered staying for the rest of the interesting lectures at the conference, perhaps sitting down with Sheffy and brainstorming some more. But she was too agitated. She had to keep going and publish the anomaly as soon as possible. Throughout the course of her work, she had invested plenty of time in writing the scientific paper. All that was needed now were some brief additions and a final fine-tuning.

There was no point in returning home. A brief roam revealed a quiet area consisting of several small conference rooms, most of which were occupied. The empty room she found suited her purposes. It was very small, guaranteeing that it would be of interest to few people, and therefore, that her work would not be interrupted.

Within less than an hour, she was looking at a properly phrased scientific article, laden with the names of stars, measurement data, and detailed calculations. But she was not tempted, even for a moment, to submit it yet. She had to get Sheffy's opinion.

It's interesting, she thought. Until yesterday, she had not even known him, and had occasionally published papers in astronomy on her own, without needing the opinion or approval of any colleagues. What had happened this time to make her feel insecure? As if she needed Professor Sheffy's approval to publish. It's true, she had included his name in the credits, and therefore required his consent for that reason alone. But even if she hadn't included his name, she would still feel that she needed his approval. Somehow, she felt that such a dramatic paper required plenty of support and another critical perspective, especially by a reputable, experienced scientist such as Professor Sheffy.

After one more pass, she sent him the article. He might have time to read it during one of his breaks. It wasn't too long, and could be skimmed in about fifteen minutes.

Now all she had to do was recruit all the patience she could muster and wait for his response, which, much to her surprise, arrived before she even had time to sit down in the nice café she knew in the neighborhood.

It's true, he told her, he was attending a lecture that was quite interesting, but he was impatient as well, and had been certain she would get back to him fairly quickly. The article was good, precise and succinct. Its publication would make waves within the astronomy community, primarily among the astrophysicists. It would be a field day for the astronomers. Her discovery would open up a new quest to seek similar stars in the universe. The astrophysicists would have to come up with a fresh theory capable of explaining this new data. Things would get interesting within the scientific community.

He was happy, of course, to be credited for the paper, although he did not think he deserved this honor. “In fact, I didn’t help you in any way,” he repeated several times. “You did all the work. You discovered the anomaly. All I did was confirm your findings.”

“You have no idea how much you helped me. It’s such a strange phenomenon that I was afraid I was missing something major. It takes courage to publish such groundbreaking findings. I needed support and confirmation from a leading scientist. Thanks to you, I’m not afraid of publication.”

“Shall we celebrate over dinner, and wait together for the reactions?” he asked, half joking and half serious.

“I’m posting it right now,” she said slowly, and in a clear, confident voice, added, “And...Send.” The article glided into the virtual astronomy community.

“I’ll pick you up at eight,” he said. “My treat. It’s not every day that a scientist uncovers the sort of discovery that might change the face of science, and maybe even humanity as a whole.”

“Aren’t you getting carried away?” she asked. “All we actually discovered was an anomaly in the part of the universe that’s closer to us. Who knows how many similar phenomena are still hidden away in the immense universe?”

“That’s true,” he said. “The universe truly is wondrous and enormous. Who knows what else we might find.”

Lia glanced at her assistant. It was now 6:43 p.m. “I wonder what the reaction time of our astronomer colleagues will be.”

“I wonder who’ll be the first to react,” Sheffy responded. “Astronomers, astrophysicists, or physicists? My bet is on the astrophysicists. They’ll want to get their hands on the raw data of the unprocessed measurements. They don’t trust anyone, especially when it comes to disproving a well-established theory that's been around for years. Then we'll hear from the physicists, who'll claim measurement errors or some other form of error. I don't think the astronomers will react. They tend to leave the quantum physics to others."

"I guess we'll wait and see. I'm starting to time it right now," she said, activating the timer.

Once again, there was no point in driving home. She would take a leisurely stroll down the campus's broad walkways. This would be her first hours of relaxation for many months now. Previously, even when walking down the street, she could not see a thing. Not the wintry sun shining through in the afternoon, or the beauty of the rain-drenched flowers illuminated by the streetlights. Sheffy could collect her from wherever she ended up by dinnertime.

She wondered when the reactions would start to appear, and what they would be. When she peered at her assistant again, it was already 7:22. More than half an hour had gone by with no responses. They must be going over her calculations and planning their replies. Who might be the first to respond? Everyone on the East Coast had already gone home for the day. Europe was fast asleep. Only in the Far East, China, Japan, and Australia were people working now.

Actually, there was no reason for stress. Her calculations were correct, and had been verified by a reputable scientist. The telescope measurements had been reconfirmed again and again. She had done her part. From this point on, the hot potato had been tossed at the scientific community. They could knock themselves out. She wasn't an expert on quantum physics, anyway.

Sheffy had found the time to change into a more casual outfit, and looked much younger than his age. The early spring evening seemed suited to their celebratory feeling. He had skipped lunch, and preferred to avoid filling up on snacks, and was therefore very hungry. They decided to go wild. After all, it wasn't every day that a theory that had been working reliably for many years, providing accurate predictions, was challenged. Their discovery would shake up the understanding of a basic physical process. It would provide research fodder for many scientists and researchers attempting to develop a better, more accurate, and more comprehensive theory.

This was the way physics worked. Many theories had been considered excellent for quite a while, until emerging cracks in their predictive ability, sometimes very slight ones, had led to in-depth research resulting in the emergence of better theories. However, ultimately, they were only theories. The universe was apparently too complex for simple theories, with the best example, of course, being Einstein's general theory of relativity, which had generated more accurate predictions than Newton's laws, previously dominating science for many years.

The assistant proposed two good restaurants within walking distance.

"Today we're celebrating," Sheffy said, "and when you celebrate, you eat the best food. Which of those two is more expensive?"

"I have no idea. I've never been to either of them."

"Susannah's is pricier and has better reviews," the baritone voice of his assistant rang out.

Sheffy responded with an impish smile and a nod. "Off we go to Susannah's," he cheered, and they were on their way.

Sheffy did indeed celebrate. The bottle of wine he ordered was among the most expensive on the menu.

As the waiter poured the costly wine into their glasses, Sheffy asked, "Where do you think the first response will come from?"

"People aren't at work yet anywhere other than the Far East, from India eastward. If we get anything this evening, it'll be from there."

The wine was wonderful; Sheffy had chosen well. As they sipped it leisurely, her assistant beeped. One quick glance at it effectively ended the celebration. The wine goblets were placed back on the table. Lia sent the message to his assistant, and they both immersed themselves in reading it.

Dr. Sabrang Chandrasekhar, grandson of Subrahmanyan Chandrasekhar, from New Delhi, had written that he was stunned and frustrated, unable to understand what was going on. He was certain that some error in the observations or calculations would eventually emerge. It was impossible that his grandfather, winner of a Nobel Prize in physics, after whom the maximum possible mass for a white dwarf had been named, had been wrong, especially in light of the multiple verifications of his calculations since they were initially made.

"What do we do?" she asked.

"Nothing. You'll get plenty of responses of this kind, which don't merit a reply. There'll also be harsher reactions from physicists and astrophysicists who will propose convoluted and unclear explanations and mathematical derivations. The storm hasn't even started yet. Just wait for the scientists from Russia and Israel. They won't be polite and pleasant like Chandrasekhar's grandson. They'll be followed by the Europeans and the Americans.

"I wonder why Chandrasekhar's grandson returned to the East. His grandfather actually spent most of his life in the States after leaving his homeland of Pakistan. Anyway, there's no point in letting it spoil your mood. Let's order. I'm starving. I'm also silencing my assistant, and I suggest you do the same. We're allowed to disengage from the world for one evening. The responses can wait."

CHAPTER 30

Benny Has an Idea

California, Thursday, July 24, 2036

It was a good thing he had anticipated what was about to happen, Benny thought as he glanced at his inbox. It was bursting with emails from Avi Tsur, from his colleagues at the Weizmann Institute of Science, from several of the department's PhD students, from prominent scientists throughout Europe, some of whom he knew well, and even two scientists from Boston, apparently early risers.

He had been right to propose that Lia silence her assistant as well; otherwise, there was no chance they would have been able to sleep. He wondered how many messages she had received, and briefly considered asking her. Perhaps she still hadn't woken up. After all, this was her first night of rest since she had immersed herself in working on the discovery.

Finally, however, he was unable to overcome his desire to find out who had responded, and how many responses had arrived. Yes, she said, she had been up for a while. Although she could finally sleep peacefully, she was excited to see the first global reactions. She'd even had time to read some of them in the blogs and in various astronomy and general scientific columns. She had slept very little, and had already skimmed some of the many emails she had received. No, she wasn't interested in competing with him over the number of responses, but would be happy to meet him soon to go over the responses together, and perhaps start planning the next stages.

She had time to book a small, comfortable conference room for them, brew some coffee, and make sure the projector was tuned and linked to the computer, just as Benny showed up with a bag containing several pastries and sandwiches from the hotel's dining room. As they snacked and sipped, they started by perusing several science and astronomy columns that cited the study and quoted parts of it. These did not include any criticism, but focused on the facts, as befitting respected scientific publications.

The personal responses arriving via email were different in nature. Lia and Benny divided them into several categories. More than half of them questioned the accuracy of the measurements, dismissing the conclusion without even attempting to explain it or deal with its possible implications. Benny nicknamed this category "The Fixated," those for whom a good day was one that resembled the day before as much as possible, with no significant changes, no alarms, and no surprises, and mostly, no need to deal with any new challenges. As he sarcastically phrased it, they preferred to "go with the flow and not to make waves."

About a quarter of the responses did not state any position. They asked to receive the raw, unprocessed measurement data, as it had been received from the telescope. Some even asked for the specifications of the mirrors and the stabilization systems, as well as the STA's degree of accuracy. Benny termed these "The Serious Researchers": thoughtful, cautious people who did not shoot from the hip. They were willing and able to dedicate significant time to testing the precision of the measurements, and would contact the manufacturers of the telescope's components and the providers of its raw materials in order to interrogate them, as well.

"The Thorough Overachievers," Lia suggested with a smile.

That left two smaller groups, "The Enthusiasts," as Benny called them, researchers yearning for information or a discovery that would excite and shock them, challenging them to investigate fresh new directions in which no research had been conducted. Some of them began with a thorough examination of the calculations, while others turned to the most difficult option—a renewed, careful re-examination of the calculations of Noble Prize winner Professor Subrahmanyan Chandrasekhar. The last two responses were from the Weizmann Institute. One was from a group of colleagues and PhD students, while the last was from his own graduate students, who congratulated them for the discovery and expressed their hopes that it would withstand the scrutiny from other scientists.

"Not even one response that accepts the findings and tries to explain them," Benny said.

"Would you act differently? Or more precisely, how would you respond if you were surprised by a discovery like this, the way the others were?" she asked.

"That's a good question. I think I would respond the way my Israeli colleagues did, by expressing my hope that the findings are indeed valid. Simultaneously, I'd do all I could to check the accuracy of the measurements and the calculations that led to it. Only after I was convinced would I delve into the possible physical reasons for those very large masses.

"You have to remember that this disproves a theory that has been dominant in astrophysics for decades now, and was a cornerstone for the conclusion that not only is the universe's expansion not slowing down, as expected, but it's actually accelerating. This is a phenomenon that's been investigated for decades, and its cause still remains unclear. There's also something else that we mentioned briefly yesterday, and has been bothering me since."

"What are you talking about?" she asked.

"You know, my detractors have often claimed that I hover at forty thousand feet, the altitude at which commercial aircraft fly, and look down at the ground from there. This comment is usually intended to insult me, and to emphasize that I'm disconnected from the sea of details that constitutes reality. There's something to that claim. I think that from a low altitude, you can see an abundance of tiny details whose importance I'm not dismissing, but from a high altitude, it's an entirely different picture. It's more inclusive, and often provides essentially different insights than the ones seen from a lower altitude."

"What are you getting at?" she asked, sounding concerned. "What are you seeing that I can't see?"

"You know what? I have an idea. Try to summarize the discovery in a few words. Write them down on a piece of paper and focus on them. Try to avoid thinking about the long path that brought you here, and the countless details that kept you busy on the way. Just focus solely on the facts describing your discovery. I'm sure that in a short time, you'll see what I see."

Lia's nerves felt as if they were too frayed to withstand the test with which he now challenged them. "Look," she said tensely, "what you've just said is stressful and disturbing to me. Yesterday we both published an article that, assuming all the measurements and calculations it's based on are accurate, should shock the global physics and astrophysics community, and lead to further studies whose results are impossible to predict. On the other hand, if we were wrong, we'll be depicted as empty vessels, and our entire academic future will be swallowed up by a black hole. At a time that's so rife with pressure, you remember that you didn't talk to me about an idea concerning the discovery, and expect me to relax and think outside the box? You really think so? Either tell me immediately what your idea is, or I'll promptly lose my mind," she concluded, her lungs entirely drained of air.

"Do you remember how both of us were laughing yesterday at the possibility that God wasn't allowing those stars to explode so as not to destroy life on Earth?"

"Of course I remember. Please don't tell me you think the best explanation science can find for this phenomenon is that God is preventing the stars from exploding," she retorted with a distant, condescending smile.

"I've been dealing with physics, and mainly with astrophysics, for decades now," Benny began to reply, his speech unusually drawn out. "Collapsing and exploding stars are actually the research lab for us astrophysicists, because naturally, we can't carry out similar experiments in a lab. I've explored the Chandrasekhar equations from multiple angles, one of which I introduced at the conference yesterday, and it was received with massive applause."

"I know. I was there. I heard and saw the enthusiasm, but I'm not fluent in the math involved."

"Yes, I know you're not a mathematician or a physicist. All I'm trying to say is that the Chandrasekhar equations have been examined and verified by many physicists, including me, and they're correct and accurate. That's why I'm so perturbed, and I keep going back to some factor outside the realm of known physics that is preventing these stars from exploding. Doesn't it seem strange to you that not only are the masses of the four stars we've discovered significantly larger than the mass that should trigger their explosion according to Chandrasekhar, but that their masses are also identical, within the boundaries of our ability to accurately measure them?"

The gaping of Lia's mouth and the widening of her eyes were her only discernible responses.

CHAPTER 31

Gerry's Research

Chicago, Thursday, July 24, 2036

A warm, familiar feeling enveloped Will that morning as he woke up in his bed and remembered that Melissa was sleeping in the guest room. Since they had broken up two years ago, he hadn't been in a serious relationship. In fact, their relationship had been the most significant and longest one he had ever been in. He had suggested that she sleep with him, but she politely declined, saying she would bother him, that she might aggravate his injuries, that he needed a bed where he could stretch out, and that in general, it had been so long since they'd split up that she didn't feel comfortable sleeping in his bed, although it had been clear that he meant the word 'sleep' literally.

Getting out of bed was easier and nearly painless. Melissa was already engrossed in the morning news, with a cup of coffee next to her. He wondered what she was feeling. Last night, he'd had time to talk to Dan from NASA, who had promised to inquire about the astronomer who had been injured in the accident, and to update him later.

"Good morning," she said brightly. "You look almost like a new man. I think that after a shower and with normal clothes, you'll only look like someone who cut himself slightly while shaving. Should I make you breakfast? I still remember what you like in the morning," she concluded, heading toward him.

Her hug was gentle and maternal, definitely not a lover's embrace. Had he misread the way she had hugged him at Dempsey's Bar? That seemed like it had happened a month ago, although in fact it had only been two days. Perhaps she was afraid of hurting him by hugging him too tightly, he tried to console himself.

"That would be great," he replied. "I'd love my usual breakfast. You'll find everything in its usual place in the kitchen. I haven't changed a thing."

The buzz of the assistant caused his eyes to focus on the photo of Dan from NASA. He was momentarily surprised, thinking it was too early in the morning, but a quick glance at the large analog clock on the kitchen wall revealed that it was almost nine a.m., still early for many office workers, although he recalled that many of the NASA employees started their day at an early hour. That was what tended to happen when people loved their jobs, especially when that job entailed investigating the mysteries of the universe.

"Good morning. I hope I didn't wake you up. How are you feeling? How are your injuries?" Dan asked.

"Good morning to you, too. I'm feeling a lot better, almost like new, and of course you didn't wake me. What's going on?"

"I sent your assistant Dr. Ethan Almog's address. He'll be

happy to talk to you, and I think a conversation with him will prove beneficial. If you need any more help, don't hesitate. I'm always at your service," he said in conclusion.

Will didn't wait for the look of inquiry he was used to getting from Melissa, and told her about Dan, his friend from NASA, whom he had contacted to find out some details about Dr. Gerald Apexton.

"Who's Dr. Apexton? Yesterday you were still laid out in the hospital, and today you're already working again?" she asked.

"I think Dr. Apexton is connected to this whole thing. My gut tells me it'll be interesting to meet him."

"Ah, the doctor recommended resting at home, but you're already rushing off to a work meeting. I know I sound like your mother, but I promised your parents—and actually, myself as well—that I'd keep an eye on you."

"It's okay. We won't rush. We'll walk slowly, and I'll take it easy, I promise," he said with a smile. "And as for Dr. Apexton, I think we might learn some things that go beyond the scope of my work. Anyway, I have to talk to his supervisor at NASA, and then we'll decide."

Dr. Almog was happy to speak to him. He described the serious accident Gerry had been through, his cognitive state, and his surprising resignation from NASA, which had not been anticipated, but was understandable. In response to Will's question, he told him that Gerry's specialization had been the study of asteroids, and that he was considered a prominent researcher in his field.

Will thanked Dr. Almog and was about to end the conversation when the doctor continued.

"I remembered another interesting detail about Gerry. On the morning of the day when the accident happened, he was scheduled to present a research project he'd been working on recently and was being quite secretive about. If I remember correctly, he said it would have global impact, or something along those lines. I was really looking forward to his presentation, both because he'd aroused my interest and because I hadn't been involved in the research. Gerry took full advantage of his bi-annual privilege to conduct research that was not monitored by the system. I'd be glad to know what he was working on, if you find out."

Will thanked him and turned to Melissa. He instructed his assistant to relay the conversation to her, thus sparing himself the need to repeat everything that had been said.

Hearing the conversation played back did not eliminate her querying expression, but actually intensified it. "What's the connection between an astronomer studying asteroids and our case?" she asked.

"Like I said, it's more of a gut feeling. I don't have a rational explanation. You're welcome to join me. We might actually be able to meet him this morning."

***

It was closer to noon when he and Melissa walked to Dr. Apexton's modest, utilitarian house. The paved path leading to the entrance cut through a small lawn surrounded by a little patch of flowers, without the garish lawn ornaments common in many gardens. A pragmatic décor of the kind expected from a scientist floating somewhere between the stars and the asteroids.

When Will had called in the morning, Ramona, the astronomer's wife, had summarily rejected the prospect of a meeting with her husband. She said his condition still didn't allow him to meet people, that he had been through a major accident and was still having trouble speaking, and that his ability to listen was significantly impaired. All of Will's attempts at persuasion did no good; she would not budge.

In his distress, he had contacted Rick, who had to meet her in person in order to convince her to allow the meeting to take place. His winning argument was that the meeting might advance the inquiry into the accident, as the astronomer's accident shared certain characteristics with Will's own. She was truly eager to see the driver who had hit her husband locked up.

Ramona and Rick greeted them at the entrance to the house. Rick was surprised by Will's condition and appearance, and stopped himself at the very last moment from clapping him on the back.

"You look great! How did you manage it? Just two days ago, you looked as if you weren't going to survive the accident, and now you're back on your feet and hard at work again. Maybe Ms. Colette had something to do with it," he said, with a grin directed at Melissa.

"Come to Gerry's room. He gets tired quickly and he's waiting for you," Ramona said after introducing herself.

Dr. Apexton also didn't look like someone who, just a week ago, had been through a major accident, which might well have ended badly. He had three Band-Aids on his face that seemed more like the result of a shaving mishap than a serious traffic accident. Sitting in a regular chair seemed to demand an effort from him. He was seated in a large armchair lined with extra pillows, and did not get up when they arrived.

In a voice that was cracked and slow but clear, he asked Will to describe anything he could remember from the accident, requesting him to specify any detail he could remember, no matter how trivial. He delved into the small, minor details to an extent that bothered Will, whose curiosity regarding the research had propelled him to leave his home and come all the way here. Dr. Apexton spent some time inquiring into Jack's appearance, and once he understood that Melissa had met him face-to-face, asked her to describe Jack as well. The astronomer nodded with satisfaction in response to her detailed description; apparently, the details matched his own mental impression.

Will's patience was about to run out as Dr. Apexton, who seemed to be wrapped up in his own thoughts, showed no indication of intending to talk about his research. Perhaps he had changed his mind and would now ask them to leave. Will bit his lip until he had almost caused it to bleed. However, his patience and restraint paid off.

Dr. Apexton straightened somewhat in his armchair, cleared his throat and said, "We have to wait a few minutes. With your permission, I've also invited Dr. Ethan Almog, who until recently was my supervisor at NASA, where I carried out my latest research. Although I don't have any obligation to them, it would be appropriate to receive the institution's authorization for any publication. This also applies to anything you publish regarding what you're about to hear today."

"That's fine with me," Will replied. "Any publication citing your research will be coordinated with you and with NASA."

***

Dr. Almog looked familiar to Will. Apparently, he had met him while visiting Dan at NASA. After the customary handshakes and introductions, Gerry asked all of them to assemble around him. Ethan looked extremely surprised, as Gerry expected. After all, when they'd met just the day before, Gerry had stammered and been unable to utter even a single fluent sentence.

I wonder if he realizes that yesterday's meeting was a masquerade, he thought. *If so, I'm sure he's very eager to know why*.

Everyone sat down around him, their gazes focused upon him. Gerry's eyes surveyed their faces. All of them looked tense, awaiting his every word.

He began by saying, "Dr. Almog, I asked you to join us for the first time I present the research I've been working on over the last year. Although I've resigned from NASA, I'm willing to seek the institution's authorization for any publication of my research. Mr. Thorne, who's a journalist, has also given his consent to this condition." Both Ethan and Will nodded their assent.

"My second point also concerns my supervisor, Dr. Almog, who yesterday, saw me as a broken, damaged man who couldn't utter even one clear sentence, which was the reason for my resignation from NASA, while today he sees a person in full possession of all of his faculties.

"Ethan, my friend, when I woke up in the hospital after the accident feeling entirely lucid, I mentally reconstructed it, to the best of my recollection." Oh, how he wanted to tell them exactly what the best of his recollection currently was. How, not only had his brain not been damaged in the accident, but on the contrary, his cognitive abilities had been upgraded to a level he had never experience before, and which might even exceed anything than any human had ever experienced. However, of course, he had no intention of doing so. He would make sure to phrase things in the conventional manner, always taking care to add expressions of uncertainly in regard to his memory, as any scientist would do.

A sip of water also helped cool his desire to expose his new abilities. He continued, “I came to the conclusion that the accident in which I was injured was no random accident, but a premeditated assault.”

Ethan’s face conveyed surprise and anger. A brief smile flickered across the journalist’s face, directed at the woman who had come with him, and who also looked startled. *Apparently, the journalist had already guessed what happened*, Gerry thought. *Clever guy*. The detective didn’t seem particularly surprised, either.

“Today, when Mr. Thorne described to me the details of the accident in which he was involved, it turned out that its characteristics were similar to the one in which I was injured. Apparently, both assaults were carried out by the same man, whose motives I don’t know.”

Rick produced an envelope from his bag, from which he extracted a photo and handed it to the astronomer. Gerry nodded, and then resumed speaking.

“Detective Heller has just showed me the photo of the man who injured me and Mr. Thorne. He also talked me and my wife into having this meeting. I haven’t mentioned this so far, but about a week before the accident, which I should probably now call an assault or a murder attempt, I received an assistant call that implied I should abandon my research and avoid publishing it. Of course, I ignored the call and continued my work, even informing Dr. Almog that I intended to present it at the department’s weekly meeting. Ladies and gentlemen, someone knows the topic of my research and has tried twice now to prevent its publication. Perhaps the recent accident—or more precisely, the assault—on Mr. Thorne, the investigative journalist, was also intended to prevent some publication by him.

“I decided to present myself as a brain-damaged man who

could no longer cause any trouble, in order to hopefully prevent another conclusive and fatal assault by this man. Even my family members, other than my wife, didn't know the truth.

"You must be asking yourself what caused me to end the charade. Well, yesterday after the visit at NASA, in which I pretended to be brain damaged and also announced my resignation, in order to signal to the assailant that I posed no danger to him, he peered into the restaurant in which I was sitting with my wife. I'm absolutely certain of that. I understood that my life was in danger, and that this time the assailant wouldn't stop at a warning or an unsuccessful attempt at murder. Therefore, I decided that I needed to publish my research as soon as possible, as my days on Earth were numbered, anyway."

"Not if we have anything to do with it," the detective said. "We'll do whatever it takes to protect you."

The assembled guests shifted nervously in their seats. Ramona looked frightened and upset.

"Dr. Almog, can I assume I have your permission to describe my research to the select group assembled here? I'm sure Dr. Colette and, of course, my wife, Ramona, will do whatever they can to preserve the utter secrecy of what's about to be revealed here."

Ethan's gaze bounced between Ms. Colette, Ramona, and Will several times before nodding his consent in Gerry's direction.

"Well, then," Gerry continued. "I won't go into complex scientific details here. The summary of my research, including all the scientific details, was sent to Dr. Almog several minutes before you got here. This research was made possible thanks to the STA observations, which are of a quality that was previously impossible.

"This research uncovered a surprising, improbable phenomenon that contradicts the known laws of physics, which impelled me to reconfirm the observations and the results multiple times. But the results recurred precisely.

“I need to preface this with one more statement: I assume everyone here knows that asteroids have hit the Earth before, multiple times, resulting in destructive impact upon the planet. Perhaps the most famous strike is the one that occurred about sixty-five million years ago, which caused the extinction of the dinosaurs who had ruled the Earth for about two hundred million years. This opened the door for mammals, which started out as puny creatures forced to hide from the wrath of the dinosaurs, to evolve into a variety of species, including the human race.”

A brief nod from the entire group confirmed that they were indeed familiar with the topic.

“You’re probably also aware of the existence of the asteroid belt between Mars and Jupiter, which contains thousands of asteroids of various sizes, some of them massive enough to destroy life on Earth, or at least fatally impact it. The human race, after such a strike, would in no way resemble humanity in its current form.

“For the benefit of those of you who aren’t astronomers, I’ll mention that at the outskirts of our solar system is the Kuiper belt, and beyond it is the Oort Cloud, which stretches out to an immense distance. Both of them are teeming with countless asteroids, which are the remainder of the material from which all planets were formed, thus ‘cleaning out’ the system, except for the known celestial bodies of which the belt is comprised. For various reasons, asteroids occasionally diverge from their stable, distant orbit and penetrate deep into the solar system, where they might occasionally hit the inner planets, including Earth.

“We’ve all seen the images from the surface of the moon, which is pitted with millions of craters, resulting from the impact of millions of asteroids over billions of years. Many theories have tried to explain the decrease in the frequency of strikes over time. The most popular among them is that the large planets, with their significant mass and high gravity, attract the asteroids that infiltrate the system and 'sweep' them away, thus preventing many collisions."

Will was fascinated. He liked to watch science shows, but only the more popular, accessible ones, and most of what he was hearing was new to him.

Apparently, the astronomer had grown tired. The flow of his speech dried up, and he leaned back slightly, seeming exhausted by the effort. His listeners leaned back as well, also absorbed and tense.

After a minute or so, during which he sipped some water and his breath grew less labored, Gerry continued. "The theory sounds so good that in fact, its feasibility has never been tested. There were plenty of other, more fascinating subjects to deal with.

"Clusters of asteroids in the asteroid belt were chosen as a means of calibrating the new telescope array, the STA, in its initial stages of operation. As I've said, the variety of asteroids is immense, from the tiniest to fairly massive ones. Most astronomers had no interest in the photos and films shot, sometimes for several consecutive days. But I, of course, couldn't wait to get my hands on this photographic material, and immediately proceeded to study and process it.

"At some point, I noticed an asteroid moving within the inner part of the belt and heading toward the sun, a direction highly untypical of the belt's asteroids. It looked like one of those that had managed to evade the giants' 'sweepers.' Calculating its previous path showed that it had actually passed by Jupiter, which had diverted it inward, deeper into the solar system. The asteroid's path toward the center of the solar system was clear; there was nothing in its way. Even the third generation of WISE, the telescope intended to locate asteroids that might strike Earth, hadn't detected it yet.

"Calculating its path indicated that it would pass by Earth at a distance that wouldn't be dangerous, unless it was diverted by Mars on its way to us. Looking into the proximity of its path to Mars's orbit showed that it would indeed be affected by the gravitational pull of the last planet before Earth, causing it to strike us with a probability of more than 95 percent. Taking its mass into consideration, the impact of the collision would be on the same scale as that of the asteroid that caused the extinction of the dinosaurs. This realization made me shudder, covering my face with cold sweat. What to do?"

Gerry surveyed the faces of those around him, one by one. Curiosity and tension were at a peak. None of them were leaning back leisurely in their chairs. Instead, they were leaning forward, perhaps competing over who would be the first to hear the all-clear. Every instant was crucial. What solution had the astronomer found to prevent the annihilation of the human race?

Gerry cleared his throat briefly, sipped some water and continued. "I decided to let the subject go for a few days, and then ask for an observation directed at the asteroid, which I named 'Hannibal.' My calculations had been based on a short portion of its path. I was hoping that calculations based on a longer segment would yield more accurate results, which might indicate that all is well and that Hannibal would pass us by somewhere deep in space, without hitting Earth.

"I remember the perplexed expression on Dr. Almog's face when I made my request. The telescope team faced an endless list of tests, as well as a promised deadline for its routine operation, which the entire astronomy community was awaiting with bated breath. Just imagine... A space telescope that cost about two trillion dollars and which would allow us, for the first time in the history of humanity, to actually see planets located hundreds of light-years away, rather than just guessing at their existence based on minute variations of illumination in the suns they orbit. Meanwhile, I was bugging him about tracking a chunk of rock in our own little solar system. I was sure his immediate reaction would be a gesture of impatience and then completely ignoring me and my strange request, and I was already working on a list of arguments to convince him. But then, his perplexed expression gradually dissolved, replaced by curiosity and the adrenaline of pursuing a challenge. His bafflement turned into interest, and a desire to discover another layer in the delicate balance of life on Earth.

"The first two days of observation out of the four I was allocated, carried out with a four-day gap from the next two, provided all I needed to accurately calculate the asteroid's path. The result was horrifying and unequivocal. The asteroid would definitely strike Earth! I knew exactly where and when it would strike. The disaster facing humanity was utterly indescribable.

"My first thought, of course, was to contact the administrator of NASA. But then, due to the scope of the discovery and its implications, I decided to wait and examine the last two days of observation in order to obtain further confirmation. The asteroid had nearly traversed the asteroid belt. There was no problem observing it, because the belt is quite sparse. Analyzing the final measurements indicated a minute deviation in the asteroid's trajectory compared to the calculation based on the first two days of observation.

"At first, I attributed it to the gravitational pull of other asteroids in the belt, although this should have been negligible. I couldn't stop thinking about it, and after a few days, decided to request—or more precisely, demand—another series of observations on the asteroid. I prepared myself for an immediate rejection from Dr. Almog. I composed a reasoned presentation justifying the observation that contained no reference to my main reason, the possibility of a strike on Earth. This wasn't how I wanted to reveal my discovery. To my surprise, I didn't need any of it. It turned out that the telescope crew wanted additional close, focused observations, of any kind, and Hannibal was the most appropriate option. Within several hours, I received the first observation, and additional ones began to flow every four hours."

A slight gesture by the astronomer activated a three-dimensional holographic projector aimed at the middle of the circle created by the attendees. The light in the room grew dim due to a gradual tilting of the room's blinds. The entire event had been meticulously planned. As the illumination faded away, the holographic projection began to reveal more details, made up of tiny, luminous points of light.

"First, to help those of you who aren't astronomers, I'll present our solar system." The solar system was depicted from an external, perpendicular perspective, as it was traditionally portrayed in textbooks for beginners. The sun could be seen at its center, surrounded by four points of light representing the familiar inner planets, followed by a pale circle, after which Jupiter and Saturn were clearly depicted.

"The pale circle is the asteroid belt, which is actually so sparse that it's invisible to the naked eye. Now we'll zoom in on a small section of the belt, which we'll gradually expand."

The sun and the other planets dissolved into the margins of the hologram as it gradually focused on an area in which there were only a few points of light.

"These are the images I received from the telescope," Gerry continued. "This is Hannibal," he noted, and one of the dots began to flicker lightly. "And now we'll see a red line beginning above the asteroid belt and continuing up to Hannibal and beyond it. This is the path that I estimate Hannibal traveled after being diverted by Jupiter to the inner part of the solar system.

"The extension of this line is the path Hannibal should have taken after it crossed the belt, and as I've noted, this trajectory would have brought it in close proximity to Mars, and ultimately, to crash into Earth. And now..." Hannibal began to move along a green line, which gradually diverged from the red line. "...the short green line that just appeared denotes Hannibal's actual path."

"What's going on here?" Dr. Almog interjected urgently. "What's diverting the asteroid?"

"Does this mean it won't crash into Earth?" Rick asked.

A pandemonium of voices filled the room. One by one, each member of the group realized they had just been spared a certain death. The structured technical lecture was replaced by a variety of voices, all expressing a combination of indescribable relief along with a barrage of questions directed at the astronomer. What had caused the path of the asteroid to change?

Dr. Apexton allowed the voices to die down. But, once he seemed ready to proceed, Dr. Almog's voice rang out. "To the best of my knowledge, none of the asteroids in the belt that are visible in this image are large enough to trigger such a change of course. Something here doesn't make sense. What could have caused such a significant change of course in such a short time? What are you hiding from us, Dr. Apexton?"

Everyone faced the astronomer, their expressions conveying a single emotion—tension, replacing the previous looks of fear.

"Please allow me to finish," he requested. "Here I should mention an element of chance. For reasons I can't explain, I continued to receive observations documenting the trajectory of Hannibal's path every four hours. In fact, it's still going on as we speak. The continuation of the green line forming in front of your eyes right now represents three days of observation." The emerging green line was gradually veering away from the red one. "It's clear to all of us that Hannibal has been diverted from its collision path with us to some other trajectory.

"There are two essential questions facing us. The first is what's diverting it, and the second, most important one—what will its new path be? How close to Earth will it pass and, after it sweeps by the Earth, will it be diverted by it and come back to strike it?"

"Why would it come back?" Melissa asked.

"Passing in close proximity to us could pull it into an unstable orbit around the Earth that might gradually converge until it strikes us in the future," Ethan replied.

"What can we do?" Will asked.

"Maybe the time we gain while it orbits around us will allow us to hit and destroy it?" Rick whispered.

Their gazes turned to the astronomer once more. "Your concern is understandable. However, you've ignored the first question—what's diverting it?" Gerry replied. "Maybe an in-depth analysis of the reason would provide answers about its future path."

Now that the fear of an imminent deadly strike had passed, his listeners were becoming more curious.

"And do you have an answer to that question?" Ethan asked. A quick nod by everyone present confirmed their urgent need to find out the factor that had saved them.

"Well, I've calculated the mass and the location of the attractor that caused the observable change. My base assumption, of course, was that this was caused by the gravitational pull of a massive asteroid in the belt."

In the hologram, a yellow line formed directly from the center of the green line's arc to a very pale spot in the asteroid belt.

"What immense luck," Ramona called out. "Imagine what would have happened if it wasn't for that asteroid. Life here is so fragile and precarious. As a believer, I'd like to pray now," she concluded, her face glowing ecstatically.

That sounds logical, Will thought. Apparently, somewhere out there was a heavy asteroid that was pulling at Hannibal. Everyone seemed cheerful and full of smiles, other than Dr. Almog. Will didn't take his eyes off him. Something about the story bothered him.

Slowly and quietly, Ethan said, "I don't see a large asteroid at the end of the yellow line."

The smiles dissolved at once. Everyone focused on the hologram, attempting to see a large asteroid at the end of the yellow line, and when one could not be found, all eyes turned to Dr. Almog and from him to the astronomer. The euphoria and curiosity on their faces were instantly replaced with apprehension and a sweeping uncertainty. *What's going on here?* their faces asked wordlessly.

Gerry took a deep breath. He was enjoying every moment. After long months of work in secret, having no one with whom to share his discoveries, he was finally revealing them to others. And if the mysterious discovery wasn't enough by itself, there was also his finding from the past few days, which had just happened to fall into his lap.

"Friends, I'm only an astronomer dealing with discovering the mysteries of the universe. I don't have answers to a lot of questions. In addition, let me pile another riddle on top of the previous one. As I've said, I received the results of many more observations, and you can now see Hannibal's route for the next three days." The green line grew slightly longer, veering more emphatically toward the asteroid belt.

"At this stage, I calculated the new location of the attractor asteroid as it should be three days later, considering its orbital speed, its mass, and Hannibal's effect on it. I expected, of course, to confirm further curving of its trajectory, as the observations indicate." A short broken yellow line emerged from a point located at some distance from the initial yellow line. "But, to my surprise, the calculations did not match the observations." The end of the broken yellow line did not reach the midpoint of the new arc.

"In light of that, I performed a calculation identical to my initial one. I checked for the gravitational pull and location of any element that, in combination with the first element, could cause the observed deviation. You're looking at the results." A yellow line emerged gradually from the center of the line depicting the last portion of the asteroid's path, ending in another pale spot located at a distance from the broken yellow line.

That's odd, and entirely unclear, Will thought. *What else could attract Hannibal and divert it from its path of destruction?*

Apparently, the others were having similar thoughts, as they seemed to be waiting for further explanations from the astronomer. Gerry, meanwhile, had an odd smile on his face, and showed no intention of going on.

He's waiting for some question or comment, Will thought.

The only one who was still attentively examining the

hologram was Dr. Almog, who noted, “You have a few more days of observations. What did they provide?”

The astronomer smiled.

Apparently, this is the question he’s been waiting for, Will thought.

“I’ll show you the last segment,” the astronomer said, and the green line continued to curve toward the middle of the asteroid belt.

“I don’t want to bore you,” he continued. “Here, too, I found a new mass, the third to attract Hannibal and adjust its path to those of the other asteroids in the belt.”

Will felt himself growing increasingly confused. What was going on here? What was this series of large masses that could not be detected by the most sophisticated of telescopes, and which was diverting Hannibal from its path of impact with Earth? Apparently, the others found the description unclear as well. Their querying expressions made this evident. Someone had to explain what was going on, and only Dr. Apexton and Dr. Almog were equipped to do so. Slowly, everyone’s eyes turned to them, awaiting their every word. They needed a terrestrial explanation for what was happening in not-so-distant space, and which had existential significance for life on Earth.

The tense silence had a cumulative effect. Ethan cleared his throat and said, “Allow me to summarize what we’ve heard here. You’re saying the asteroid belt between Mars and Jupiter, which contains thousands of celestial bodies that today, with the STA, we’re capable of seeing, also contains small bodies that still have a very large mass, and are capable of attracting large asteroids with tremendous destructive potential in regard to Earth, and diverting them from their path?”

“I don’t know how many such celestial bodies the belt contains.

I assume that if I continue with my calculations, I'll discover a few more that are adjusting Hannibal's speed and trajectory to those of the other asteroids in the belt."

"What kind of elements could they be?" Will asked.

"I have no idea what they are, or how many of them exist in the belt," the astronomer replied with an impish smile. "And maybe all these celestial bodies are there just to save us from a big asteroid strike. Sounds very appealing, doesn't it? What do you think?"

Apparently, the implications were clear to everyone. No one spoke up. They all delved into their own thoughts, each in accordance with his or her own beliefs and education. Minutes ticked by in silence.

"I've presented everything I know on the subject to you," the astronomer whispered. "It's clear that our planet was saved from a strike by this Hannibal. Calculating its new path indicates that it's converging into the asteroid belt, where it could travel for many eons, so we can go on with our lives."

He concluded dramatically, "Until the next Hannibal, which will always arrive."

CHAPTER 32

THE LEADING GENTLEMAN

CHICAGO, THURSDAY, JULY 24, 2036

Aaron had no doubt. The man in civilian clothing who had entered his abandoned apartment with his gun drawn was definitely Detective Rick Heller, assigned to investigate the murder of the security guard at the university, as the media had noted. It had certainly been a good idea to leave the apartment immediately following the murder, after first concealing a motion-activated camera there.

Apparently, he had left revealing tracks at the university, leading the investigator to him. Well, from now on, he would be unable to walk around undisguised, and in general, it was best to avoid exposure as much as possible. Cameras and new monitoring systems were capable of identifying people not just based on their features but also based on their frames, their gestures, and their manners of walking.

The safe house in which he had been staying since he had left his home was smaller and more cramped. Not that his previous apartment had been roomy. On the contrary, it was tiny but comfortable. However, in light of the current circumstances, the apartment housing him now had justified its ongoing maintenance in a state of readiness over the last two years.

The emergency gathering he had initiated was proving to be stressful. In addition to Takumi and Chinatsu, the regular cell members, on this occasion, for the first time in many years since the cell's activity had commenced, the other local organization members were also scheduled to arrive. There were two of them: Professor Andrew Goldon, CEO of the BL Corporation, and Professor Paul Longstrom, the dean of the University of Chicago, neither of whom he had ever met.

Aaron decided he would stand during the meeting, although there was a low stool in the apartment at his disposal. This time, he thought, he had to stand up and tower above Takumi and Chinatsu. It's true, this was not in accordance with the protocol and decorum characterizing their meetings thus far. But this meeting was different than the ones that had preceded it for hundreds and thousands of years. This time, he had to fight for his opinion with all his might, even in the face of the fierce opposition he was expecting.

The order of his presentation and its outline were clear to him. He had dedicated plenty of thought to the subject, examining and considering numerous details that came together in his mind to form one clear picture, and the more he delved into the latest developments, the firmer his conviction grew. Unlike his usual custom, he had not come up with any alternatives. His opinion must prevail.

As in every meeting to date, at the appointed hour, on the dot, he heard a knock on the door. When he opened it, he saw Takumi standing alone. Aaron didn't even bother to close the apartment door once Takumi entered the small living room. And indeed, one after the other, with only a few seconds separating one arrival from the next, Chinatsu walked in, followed by Professor Goldon, whose face Aaron recognized from various scientific publications, and finally by another man who had to be Professor Longstrom, and who was utterly unfamiliar to Aaron.

Once everyone was sitting down, Chinatsu directed a commanding look at Aaron. This look conveyed two words: *sit down*. However, Aaron brazenly ignored it. It was clear that Takumi understood that Aaron was refusing to sit down. He, too, could see the low stool. No, Aaron would not be the first to speak. That would be a blatant, unnecessary violation of decorum. Takumi would quickly realize that he had to give in and would begin the meeting as usual. But he would surely think of some way to punish Aaron.

Indeed, Takumi opened by saying, "Aaron has summoned us for an urgent meeting. He asked for full attendance by our members in Chicago. Currently present are myself, Takumi, Chinatsu, Goldon, and Longstrom." He pointed at each member as he called his name. "Aaron has important things to say. We will allow him to do so."

Naturally, everything Aaron had learned by heart in order to remember it at the moment of truth evaporated and disappeared from his consciousness. The things he wanted to say were extremely harsh, especially for people who had dedicated decades of their lives to the cause, with no adequate compensation and with many sacrifices. Some of them had never established families, leading lonely, solitary lives. Their entire lives had been at the service of the organization. The words and sentences he had meticulously planned, statements creating a logical sequence, meant to explain and persuade, to change opinions grown rigid long ago, were all forgotten, vanished without a trace. Instead, he was swept up in the desire to call out, to roar like a deranged lion.

Then, just a fraction of a second from the time the stage was given over to him—an interval that seemed to him like an hour in which he was standing silently—but long before the attendees could realize what he was going through, the orderly words and sentences returned to their proper place in his mind. The words floated in front of his eyes, large, shiny, and clear. Perhaps he didn't even have to speak them. After all, surely they could see the words as well.

"My entire life, beginning with my childhood, has been dedicated to one single goal. I did all I could for it, while risking myself and others. The last few days have been full of events that have led me to a terrible conclusion. A conclusion I'm having a hard time saying out loud. It feels like a betrayal of my very essence. But enough beating around the bush. I'm convinced that today, we must allow humanity to deal with reality. Cease all our underground activity. The flow of scientific discoveries arriving from the various fields of science can no longer be suppressed."

That's it. The words had been said. Not as he'd planned them, without the extensive reasoning and logical analysis that had brought him to this extreme conclusion. But such a harsh conclusion could not be explained and justified calmly. He had to state it quickly and immediately once he began speaking, for fear he would be stricken by regret and retract it. Just like someone committing suicide by jumping from a high roof. There was no stopping. He just had to do the deed. No thinking.

For a moment, he thought he might actually be committing

suicide as well. He wouldn't have been surprised in the slightest if his blatant declaration of heresy before his companions on this long road had ended with a bullet from Takumi's gun blowing his head to smithereens. Takumi always carried a weapon, after all.

The utter silence in which his speech had been received surprised him. He had expected a sweeping assault from everyone present. He had expected them to throw decorum to the wind, and for the attendees to burst out in angry shouting, condemning him. But none of that happened. No voice was heard in the crowded room.

For a moment, he wondered if someone had masked the sound of his voice. Perhaps they never even heard him. Perhaps he hadn't even spoken out loud. Perhaps the intense pressure had made him imagine he was speaking, while in fact, his words had only echoed within the space of his skull, with the attendees still waiting for him to begin talking. Their eyes, focused upon him, did not shift in the slightest, their pupils remaining fixed.

Then came the first confirmation that he had, indeed, spoken and been heard. The two professors exchanged looks and both nodded swiftly.

Professor Longstrom's hand was raised slowly, as if he considered every minute motion before carrying it out, and he said, "Professor Goldon and I support Aaron's proposal."

Aaron couldn't believe his ears. He had not thought, even for a moment, that anyone would agree with him, and certainly never dreamed that more than half of the members present supported his opinion. It turned out he was not alone. Others felt the way he did.

All at once, he felt significantly better. He wondered what would happen now. The Guardians had never acted as a democracy. The sect was run as a complete dictatorship. Everything was determined from above. Everyone obeyed the instructions of the Leading Gentleman, with no hesitation or objection. This was how the Guardians had conducted themselves for thousands of years. No member dared question the authority of the Leading Gentleman. And this would be their conduct in the future, as well.

His rebellion would be dealt with, one way or another. Or perhaps, if his speech truly had convinced the two professors, they might be able to convince the Leading Gentleman as well. Perhaps the sect was ready for its first essential change in the thousands of years it had been in existence. Could it be?

And then Takumi and Chinatsu turned to look at each other. Their blank expressions revealed nothing of what was in their hearts. A nearly imperceptible nod, and they both rose to their feet simultaneously. *This is it*, the thought tore through Aaron's mind. *Takumi is about to draw his gun and shoot all of us*. He was certainly capable of shooting everyone present in an instant.

In his youth, Aaron had been present during Takumi's target practice. The man was a virtuoso when it came to shooting a weapon. Aaron decided he would not run or try to fight. He had betrayed the cause, and betrayal necessitated the gravest of punishments. He had known this when he summoned the meeting and was willing to bear the punishment.

But then the strangest thing happened. Both of them turned and exited the room.

No one else moved, and to Aaron it seemed as if none of them were breathing, either. The silence in the air could be cut with a sharp knife, or more accurately, hacked with an ax—it was that dense and hard. Hours seemed to go by until the silence, which had actually lasted only a few minutes, was interrupted by the ring of Professor Goldon's assistant.

It was impossible that the professor had forgotten to silence the assistant before the meeting. All of their assistant authorizations allowed only the most senior members of the organization to call at any time. Takumi must have called the Leading Gentleman, who was now calling Goldon. Aaron was very curious to know what was being said to Goldon, who listened intently for several seconds and then, much to Aaron's surprise, replied in fluent Japanese before ending the conversation.

There was no response to Aaron's and Longstrom's probing looks. Goldon continued to sit still, staring at the corner of the room. The silence was interrupted by a knock on the door, in the familiar code used by the Guardians. Aaron and Longstrom immediately turned their startled gazes to Goldon, who didn't react at all, as if he had heard nothing. Aaron opened the door, letting in Takumi and Chinatsu, who returned to their seats quite naturally, as if nothing at all had happened.

Apparently, everyone was trying to process what was going on. Why had the two returned? What would happen now? Takumi seemed uncomfortable in his chair. Aaron continued to stand, leaning against the kitchen counter. The air froze. A soft snapping of fingers was heard from Professor Goldon's direction, causing everyone's eyes to focus on him.

The professor turned his gaze to Aaron, still standing, and then, in the deepest and most assertive voice Aaron had ever heard, he said two words: "Sit down."

Aaron sat down immediately. He had obeyed mindlessly, without hearing the command, processing it, deliberating whether to comply, and then deciding to do so. It seemed as if the command had gone straight to his legs, bypassing and skipping his brain.

The professor's sharp-eyed gaze appraised each of them until pausing on Takumi, whom he addressed in Japanese. Takumi's face grew pale, to the extent that a Japanese man's face can do so. Once the professor stopped speaking, Takumi rose slightly from his chair, brought his palms together and bowed to him respectfully. At that moment, Chinatsu joined him, bowing to the professor as well, before the two men returned to their seats.

The cold, emotionless Takumi seemed truly shaken. His eyes darted back and forth as he surveyed each of the attendees in turn before stopping and fixing on Professor Goldon.

Takumi then began, "The Leading Gentleman has guided the Guardians' actions through me for many years now. Until this moment, I only knew his voice and had never actually met him. My friends, the Leading Gentleman is...Professor Andrew Goldon!"

Everyone's gazes instantly turned to the professor, whose eyes roamed between them leisurely. Aaron was stunned. He had heard so much about the Leading Gentleman, the figure who determined everything, and whose absolute authority was obeyed by all, with no objections. The one who shaped the sect's activity worldwide and managed the organization's massive resources. The one whom all the Guardians admired to the point of worship. At long last, the Leading Gentleman himself was sitting with them around a table in Aaron's little safe house.

Since joining the Guardians many years ago, he had only heard about the Leading Gentleman. At meetings, his opinion was often conveyed. His messages to the sect were read, usually focusing on encouraging his people to stick to their difficult and unrewarding path, as this was the ultimate dictum that they must obey. They were instructed to do all they could to ensure the success of their task, just as the Guardians had done for many generations.

In Aaron's imagination, he had pictured the Leading Gentleman as a tall man with fierce black eyes, so that anyone who encountered his gaze would be enchanted, carrying out whatever he was tasked with accomplishing. He always wore a light-colored suit. Perhaps that was why Aaron himself liked to wear light-colored suits as well. Perhaps, deep inside, he wanted to resemble the Leading Gentleman. This was a troubling yet interesting possibility.

During his first years in the sect, he had been keen to meet this admired personality. He often thought that if only he had gotten to meet the Leading Gentleman, this highly respected man he had never seen and whose name he never knew, face-to-face, even for a brief meeting lasting no more than several minutes, all his problems would be solved at that instant.

But his many years of service, along with growing older, diminished his yearning, which became an aspiration and a distant, unattainable dream, the kind to which people cleave during moments of crisis. The kind of dreams that are accessed in order to suppress disturbing thoughts and unsolvable distress.

And now, unbelievably and inconceivably, the Leading Gentleman himself, in the flesh, was sitting across from him, in his tiny apartment. For some reason, he had been certain that the Leading Gentleman was Japanese in origin and in appearance, although, of course, much taller. But the man facing him was a slender Westerner, an utter contrast to the fantasy. However, the man possessed great power, expressed in the way he had seated him instantly, despite his deliberate decision not to sit down.

Professor Goldon was an extraordinary man indeed. Or perhaps that wasn't even his real name? His thoughts drifted to the Better Life Corporation—or- as the public knew it, BL—founded fifteen years ago by Professor Andrew Goldon, who had also served as its CEO throughout this time. Initially a small, obscure company, it had expanded at record speed to the point where it had established itself as the leading pharmaceutical company worldwide, with sales over $200 billion a year.

BL didn't focus on cures for specific illnesses, but rather on drugs and treatments to strengthen the immune system as a whole, to balance the body's various systems, and to regenerate tissue and return the body's systems to their original healthy state, with none of the negative residue accumulating in the body over years and disrupting its optimal function. BL built upon the old saying that had been common toward the end of the twentieth century, "Sixty is the new forty," taking it one step forward to "Ninety is the new fifty."

The products generating most of the company's income were CardioBoost, to regenerate heart tissue; LungBoost, to rejuvenate the lungs; and the most popular of them all, PlaqueDissolve, which melted the layers of residue coating blood vessels, returning them to their original suppleness and volume once more.

Most of BL's products had been developed behind a thick wall of secrecy. The exception was a product that had yet to be approved for use, and which was intended to return the muscle tone of anyone taking it to a youthful state, without the need for exhausting physical exercise. The rumor mill, apparently fueled intentionally, promised that taking one pill a day, along with a healthy diet, would lead to shedding any excess weight and developing the kind of muscles normally requiring an hour-long, rigorous daily workout. The comments on the pertinent websites immediately inquired whether two, three, or four pills a day were equivalent to the same number of rigorous workout hours. Once people were freed of physical exercise, they immediately aspired to Mr. Universe-type muscles.

The more Aaron thought about it, the harder it seemed to explain BL's meteoric rise. The financial gossip columns had also often hinted at mammoth investments whose origin was unknown, despite plenty of efforts to uncover it. BL was the largest Western private company in the world. Despite its scope, the company did not reveal its profit-and-loss balances or any other data. Its shareholders were straw companies registered in various tax shelters. On this front as well, despite repeated, costly efforts, investigators were unable to discover anything about the source of the funds. Occasionally, usually following some prominent success achieved by one of the corporation's products, various investigators would increase their efforts, leading to a plethora of rumors regarding the origin of the funds. The rumors were quite diverse in the range of possibilities they covered, from laundered drug money and unknown oil tycoons, to the claim that Professor Goldon's physicist brother had developed a lucrative process for producing quality synthetic diamonds in commercial quantities.

Apparently, he was not the only one caught by surprise. All of the attendees' expressions wavered between astonishment and deep respect, although, here and there, there were also looks of disbelief. Apparently, the others had also expected a different sort of figure than the slight professor. It seemed to Aaron as if a long time had passed since the surprising declaration, an interval in which everyone held their breath, and which had not been interrupted by even the slightest of murmurs. Then, for the first time since the command that had seated him so quickly, the professor began to talk.

"Aaron said everything I had intended to say. The Guardians have been successfully active for 3,348 years, during which we've concealed findings and made sure to divert humanity's attention to the various religions. We didn't interfere, and didn't shape the believers' faith. Any religion was fine with us, as indeed they all were initially. We observed and reluctantly accepted those religions whose paths grew warped over time, terrible religions that led to millions of people being murdered in their name.

"Our mission was clear. We were not tasked with educating people. We were tasked with preventing certain revelations, or more accurately postponing them for as long as possible, and this is what we have done through the ages. We did so discreetly, without focusing attention on ourselves.

"People worshipped these gods or others, and were satisfied with the answers provided by religion. Blind faith was the answer to the difficult questions that popped up every once in a while. However, our original mission had a clearly defined ending, and today, this condition is fulfilled. A new religion has taken form. It's called science. No more consecrated beliefs that cannot be questioned, passed down from generation to generation. Religion is no longer accepted as the absolute, exclusive means of understanding our world.

"We've also acted extensively on the scientific front. We've diverted studies, distorted the results of research, and spread rumors that contradicted and sometimes mocked specific findings. Well, no more. As of this moment, we're allowing science to progress with no intervention on our part. Humanity—or, more precisely, its sane component—has grown up and consequently no longer blindly accepts conventions and historical 'truths.' On the contrary, science questions and constantly re-examines every such 'truth.'

"Over the past few days, we've had to act several times, and on one such occasion, an innocent man was even hurt and killed."

Aaron squirmed in his seat in discomfort, and although no one turned to look at him accusingly, he still keenly felt the stabbing of guilt. Oleg's family would be compensated, he'd been promised, but there was no way to compensate a little boy who had lost his father. He wished he could surrender to the authorities, but the sect's bylaws did not allow it.

Activists in a similar situation had relocated to another country or, even worse, committed suicide, all in order to avoid exposing the sect.

"Quite a few of our people have taken their own lives over many generations," the professor continued, and once again, Aaron felt an intense stab in his stomach.

Was the Leading Gentleman hinting at what he should do? Was this how he would end his life? And what would happen if he didn't kill himself? Would someone else take care of it? Would he be ordered to commit suicide? He would no longer be able to work openly here in Chicago, and probably anywhere in the United States, because sooner or later, he would be identified by one of the sophisticated monitoring systems and captured.

Perhaps he should request to be transferred to another country. He could assume a new identity; perhaps even undergo plastic surgery to change his appearance. Did he want this? To keep on living at any price, although he had taken the life of an innocent man? It was true that he had been acting on behalf of the organization and under its banner. In the fraction of a second in which he debated pulling the trigger, did the option of committing suicide cross his mind? No, he hadn't considered this possibility. The security guard had surprised him, leaving him no option of slipping away. If he hadn't shot him, he would have been arrested. The cops would have searched his home, and who knows what their investigation would have ended up uncovering.

He would give his life with no hesitation in return for the life of the security guard. What should he do now? Take the fast-acting poison pill out of the drawer and swallow it in front of everyone, or wait for the Leading Gentleman to finish speaking? And then what? Officially present the question to everyone? Let them decide his fate? Ask to speak with the Leading Gentleman? Perhaps he could propose something to him that was better than suicide?

Apparently, he had gotten too absorbed in his own thoughts and hadn't noticed the change in the room. The Leading Gentleman had stopped speaking, and when Aaron looked up, he saw that everyone else was looking at him. For a moment, he panicked. How could he have gotten wrapped up in his own affairs and stopped listening to the Leading Gentleman? What had happened in the room?

"I'm sorry, I wasn't listening," he said. "The mention of the security guard brought me back to that terrible night, and the unforgiveable thing I've done."

"You really weren't listening to what Professor Goldon was saying," said Professor Longstrom. "The Leading Gentleman said you were a very dedicated member, that you acted on behalf of the Guardians as well as you possibly could have, and that your encounter with Oleg, the security guard, was actually an encounter between the Guardians as a whole and the rest of humanity. You had no way out, and any other course of action might have been disastrous to the entire organization. Your act saved the organization."

"As of this moment, all your ties to the organization have been entirely blurred and obliterated," said the Leading Gentleman. "We've made sure you can live honorably as an independent person.

Starting today, you can continue on any path you choose. We'll make sure the security guard's family is handsomely compensated, and will never lack anything.

"As for where we go from here, I'm not convinced that humanity is mature enough for this major turning point; however, all that notwithstanding, as of this moment, we're allowing scientists to act with no monitoring or interference from us. The recent discoveries are already surfacing in the media, and soon all hell will break loose. Up to this point, we've done everything possible to put off and undermine the troubling discoveries by dismissing them and even mocking the new information we disapproved of. For now, we'll cease all active intervention, and dedicate ourselves solely to tracking what's going on via public sources and using the means and abilities we've developed over the years.

"We'll maintain the connections between us, and it's possible that every once in a while, we'll carry out a focused intervention, which I'm hoping won't require too much investment on your part. At this point, I want to thank you for your dedicated and loyal service. Your salaries, of course, will continue to be paid as usual, and you may live a normal life among other people."

No one got up. Perhaps, like Aaron, they were expecting more, an additional stressful assignment like the ones they had become used to for many years now, even if it was the last one. So long as they didn't have to stop, and could maintain the addictive tension. The abrupt transition to zero pressure, to no action, to a life out in the open with nothing to hide, didn't seem possible. The pressure and the secret lives were an essential part of their existence. How could they live without that?

The minutes went by with no words or gestures. For a moment, cynically, Aaron thought they looked like mourners at a cemetery, grieving the death of a beloved. After all, they had just received the ultimate gift—absolute freedom to do anything they wanted, with no need to work and no other obligations, but instead of cheering and celebrating, they were all glum and bleak. The ways of people were strange indeed.

CHAPTER 33

Tom Meets Aaron

Chicago, Thursday, July 24, 2036

Will and Melissa were the last to leave. Will was utterly exhausted. His physical state, in combination with the implications of the findings to which he had just been exposed, proved to be a burden with which he couldn't deal. When Melissa gently suggested that he lean on her as they slowly walked out of the astronomer's house, he took her up on her offer with no hesitation, first waiting, of course, for the last of the people walking before them to disappear beyond the fence.

The guests left quietly, with no parting words. Brief nods of acknowledgment were the only gestures exchanged. All of them appeared to be wrapped up in their own thoughts. Ramona, too, looked pensive. Apparently, the astronomer had concealed his findings from her as well.

Melissa tried to support him as they were entering the car, but he eluded her grasp and managed to twist himself into a seated position. They remained silent the entire way.

He knew a little about astronomy, had read quite a few articles on the subject, and was aware of the many asteroids that had struck and continued to strike every planet. However, he had never been exposed to such loaded, immediate information regarding a potential current strike that might have disastrous consequences for the human race. The Earth had been spared on this occasion, but for the first time, he found himself dealing with the inconceivable fragility of life on the planet.

Melissa observed from the sidelines, allowing him to try and exit the vehicle on his own. Only after two failed attempts did she grasp him firmly until he managed to straighten. The scent of her hair and its caressing touch brought back forgotten memories. For a moment, he felt like his old self, his fatigue and exhaustion evaporating, making him feel as if he was in peak form. He would have been so happy to maintain this position, to feel her arms around him with his face buried in her neck and his lips, as if they had a will of their own, yearning to kiss her. It was so hard to refrain from doing so, to allow her to disengage from him and return to reality. Had she noticed what he was going through? Did she feel something similar? He truly hoped so.

He managed to traverse the way from the parking garage to the elevator on his own, and then collapsed into the armchair in his apartment. Had she avoided supporting him once more? Perhaps she was experiencing similar sensations as well. Why had she stayed away from him? Would she now depart, leaving him alone in his apartment?

Apparently, she still felt at home. She disappeared in the

kitchen, from which the clatter of dishes emerged. Several minutes later, she appeared holding a tray bearing a coffeepot and sandwiches for both of them, then sat down across from him.

Wow, she's staying, he thought. *Who knows, perhaps she's feeling something for me after all.*

"Way to go! I was very skeptical about the odds of finding a link between the two accidents. What made you think they were connected? And what's your opinion on the whole story?" she asked, abruptly interrupting his train of thought, which had headed to a mythical land full of fairy godmothers in which every wish and dream came true.

In fact, since the accident and until she had asked the question, he had not thought about the subject as a whole. He was preoccupied with his condition, with thoughts of Melissa, and of the connection between the two accidents. He had not anticipated, even for a moment, being exposed to such unusual research findings with no scientific explanation.

Her question returned him to the hunt. What did he actually think of the entire story? And what had made him think that the two accidents were related? He was good at finding connections between seemingly unrelated events. That was how he made his living. His success had given him nearly absolute freedom in his work at the paper, always accompanied by his sense of responsibility and desire to succeed. However, he often acted based on gut feelings rather than intellectual analysis. Was that the case here? No matter how much he delved into the facts known to him, he could not find a reason for his desire to meet the astronomer; apparently, his perceptive gut had done its job again.

Melissa continued. "I can't find any rational explanation for the connection between the two accidents. Maybe the very fact that

I was involved in one of them made me feel empathy toward other people who'd been through accidents. And as for the entire story, I'm still having a hard time processing what we heard and saw. It all seems strange, and to tell you the truth, even frightening. What's happening in the space above our heads? For millions of years now, we've been living here on Earth, evolving, fighting and killing each other. Most of us are immersed in our day-to-day lives and don't even bother to look up, into the depths of the vast universe. If it weren't for a handful of curious scientists and enlightened governments willing to fund them, we'd be convinced that the sky above us is as far as we could go, and that the stars shining at night are little flashlights hanging from the dome of the sky. And as critical as it might sound, plenty of people are still certain that's how things are, while the majority of others are quite satisfied with such an explanation.

"In general, I can understand an ancient sect that has taken upon itself to prevent people from investigating and playing with God's building blocks, the DNA of the pinnacle of creation—humanity. But why were they interested in an astronomer researching asteroids, or more precisely, an astronomer researching asteroids that have been diverted from potentially striking Earth?"

"Hold on a minute," Will exclaimed. "You told me you analyzed some research by Dr. Thomas Lester for Jack. Can you tell me exactly what it was about?"

Melissa squirmed in her chair. His question had clearly made her uncomfortable. On the one hand, she had surely signed a strict confidentiality agreement, with violations triggering significant fines. But on the other hand, they used to be a couple, and were now working on the same side.

To some extent, he enjoyed watching her deliberate. He

wondered what would end up gaining the upper hand, her business obligations or their shared romantic history. Perhaps her reply would provide him with an answer regarding the chances of resuming their relationship.

Melissa wasn't the type to debate at length; she was decisive and clear-minded, even in awkward situations. Even when she had decided to end their relationship, she had stated this fact bluntly and with painful clarity that left no room for ambiguity.

Just as he'd hoped, she straightened in her chair and said, "Dr. Lester is working on two studies. One deals with human longevity extension and involves multiple research institutes all over the world. The other is an investigation of resilience to change and mutations in the human genome—quite an esoteric topic, if you ask me."

"Does extending longevity involve genetic alteration in humans? Are they really playing with God's building blocks here?" he asked.

"I don't think so," she replied. "The longevity-enhancement study has been subcontracted to them by a private company that divided the research among several labs. Tom's lab is responsible for one portion out of several. I'm sure they don't know what the other labs are doing, or how their research fits into the big picture. The research focuses on the existing genome, rather than examining other alternatives."

"Then what the hell is the sect's problem?" he interjected. "Why did they break into the lab, taking on a significant risk, and ultimately proceeding to murder an innocent person? Does something in the lab's research involve genetic experimentation?"

"I have no idea," she replied. "In the material I've seen about the lab's work, there's no reference to anything like that."

Will leaned back in the armchair, closing his eyes. His thoughts grew hazy. As if in a dream, he saw asteroids floating in space, a giant telescope observing the stars, and scientists staring at giant screens showing the asteroid belt, in which various objects were moving strangely. Slowly, these motions subsided, and he drifted off.

***

He was awakened by the assistant. Dr. Apexton was on the line. Apparently, Will had been sleeping quite deeply. For a moment, he didn't know where he was or who Dr. Apexton was, but his thoughts cleared quickly.

"Melissa and I want to truly thank you again for the amazing lecture, and especially for the weighty questions it evoked. Of course, we'd be happy to be updated on any progress you make in answering them."

"Naturally, I'll be happy to keep you posted when we know more. But I'm actually calling for a different reason. After you left, I surfed a few astronomy websites, and discovered a strange anomaly that was posted yesterday. I discussed it with Dr. Almog, who suggested updating everyone else who was present at the lecture as well. I'm sending you the link now. I suggest you peruse it, and later, I can explain what it involves, as it's quite technical. I'm sure you'll be calling me soon."

To his delight, Will discovered that Melissa hadn't left while he was asleep. She was staring at him now, a clear question mark reflected on her pretty face. She didn't need to ask her question; he knew exactly what she wanted.

"Dr. Apexton sent us a link to an astronomy article posted

yesterday, regarding another astronomic anomaly. He suggested we read it and then call him."

Neither of them understood much of the article's technical details, but they did comprehend that the authors had discovered stars that should have exploded but had not done so in this instance. The authors couldn't explain the phenomenon, but expressed great confidence in the observations and calculations that had led to a conclusion violating a scientific theory that had been proven through numerous documented explosions.

Both of them perceived the article as a debate between the acolytes of a reigning theory and those seeking an alternate one.

"I don't know how the Chandrasekhar limit was determined," Melissa said. "Apparently, the current technology, which is significantly more accurate, has revealed that there are some exceptions. It seems to me like one more theory that worked well at the time when it was developed, such as Newton's motion equations, which didn't take the theory of relativity into account and were later revised by Einstein. Or quantum theory, which explained odd phenomena in the behavior of nuclear particles. Or string theory, which attempts to integrate the theory of relativity with quantum mechanics, to create order in the quantum zoo, and, who knows, might even end up providing an explanation for dark matter and dark energy. Anyway, I don't see a connection between Dr. Apexton's discovery and this article."

Will observed her without reacting. *Melissa is pragmatic*, he thought. *She operates well within parameters that are familiar to her, but she doesn't think outside the box*. This required a different sort of thinking, one in which he had often proved himself capable of excelling. It would have been great if Melissa were also capable of this kind of thinking. However, she was still an excellent partner for a brainstorming session, thanks to her knowledge, her quick perception, and her agility of thought.

He suggested, "Why don't we talk to Dr. Apexton? I'm sure we can learn something new from him."

The image of Dr. Apexton, seated in his recliner, floated into the room. All the coordination and the fine-tuning were carried out in an instant by the assistants and their support network. There was no longer a need for awkward, muddled conference calls. The astronomer simply joined them at the touch of a button, with his voice emanating from his virtual mouth.

"Hi, Dr. Colette and Will. You're not astronomers or physicists and you still won't be when I'm done talking, either. Let me start with a brief clarification about the article authored by Professor Lia Rosen from the University in California, Berkeley, and Professor Benjamin Sheffy from Tel Aviv University in Israel, whom I know well. The fact that Professor Sheffy signed off on this article confirms its veracity for me, one hundred percent. The discovery this article documents will shake up the astrophysics world, where scientists are certainly scrambling for an explanation now."

Melissa said, "This isn't the first time in the annals of physics that tested and proven theories that endured for many years begin to show small cracks and discrepancies from reality, later explained by a new, more comprehensive theory. Could that be the case here, too?"

"That might very well turn out to be true. Or perhaps we'll find a new limit, with a new explanation. Anything could happen. If you don't have any further questions, I'll end here. And please, don't hesitate to call if any questions come up."

Will and Melissa looked at one another. Talking to the astronomer had not contributed to their understanding in any way.

"I suggest we take inventory of all the information we have," Will suggested.

"I see you've come back to life. It reminds me of Will from two years ago, with the sharp mind and the amazing deductive ability," she said, producing a giant white page from the top drawer of the desk housing the computer.

Wow, Will thought. *She still remembers the giant sheets of paper I keep in that drawer*. Melissa's teasing smile confirmed she was thinking the exact same thing.

"I'll take notes," she said, producing a dark blue pen from the box.

"Clean break-ins into biology research labs. Nothing stolen or damaged," he said while she wrote down his words. "A break-in at the University of Chicago's biology lab goes wrong. The intruder would rather kill a security guard than get caught. The investigation is assigned to Rick. The burglar–murderer badly injures an astronomer who is about to publish an unusual discovery that poses questions about what's going on in our solar system. Another astronomic discovery published around the same time contradicts a theory that's been established for decades. We don't know if there was an attempt to hurt the scientists in this case.

"The killer injures me, perhaps because he knows what I do and is afraid I'll publish the things you'll tell me about him. The killer belongs to an ancient sect trying to suppress studies dealing with genetic engineering in general, and human DNA in particular, as much as possible, guided by the divine commandment that humanity should not alter the human race. Do we know anything else?" he asked, focusing his gaze on her.

Melissa considered the question briefly and shook her head. "I think you've covered all the main points."

"You know what? I'd like to know more, precisely about the activity in the lab in which the murder took place, as well as in the other labs where the break-ins occurred. That might give us a direction to go in."

Melissa's breathing seemed to pause abruptly. She looked down, disengaging from him, and her face grew suddenly flushed.

What the hell is going on here? he thought. *Why did she react so strongly to my question? Well, obviously, she's hiding pertinent information from me. She knows a lot more about the intruder, and maybe about the whole story, than what she's told me. What should I do? How do I get her to tell me what she knows?*

She was obviously aware of the fact that she'd blushed, and that he had noticed. She would talk to him. All he had to do was give her time, and not allow the conversation to veer in a different direction. She would also not try to avoid the topic. She knew he was keeping quiet because he was waiting for her to speak. She might not tell him everything she knew; she might elaborate on a specific aspect, inflating it in order to try and satisfy his curiosity. He would have to be on guard and try to obtain as much information as possible from her. Her reaction definitely indicated that she had been caught red-handed. She knew a lot more than she was saying, and had avoided telling him about it intentionally, rather than by chance.

He felt sad. He had trusted her and shared information with her, even hoping to return her to his arms. At least now he knew her attitude toward him.

The minutes ticked by. Silence was on his side. All he had to do was wait and say nothing. Not lose his momentum. The passing of time and the silence were exerting more pressure on her than anything he could have done. He simply had to wait.

"I have to make a personal confession," she began, now looking directly into his eyes.

That's it. She's back to her usual self, he thought. *Back to utter self-control.* She would say what she wanted to say, and not an iota more. She had gotten over her embarrassment and would now tell him the minimum required in order to justify what had happened.

"Dr. Lester and I are having a secret affair."

It was the second punch he had absorbed in the space of a few minutes. He had already realized she was hiding something from him, but this was not what he had expected. He was stunned. For a moment, he forgot about the accident and the entire investigation, totally focused on her shattering announcement.

"I'm sorry," she said softly. The situation had been overturned in an instant. Only a few minutes ago, he had been in control while she was pinned down on the floor. Now he was humiliated, and she was the one consoling him. He felt as if he were trying to pick up the countless fragments of a shattered glass vase, a vase that had grown much larger during the three days since they had met again.

He had weaved so many dreams. He had already been hoping that this time, she would not slip away from him. That this time, they could make their relationship official. He had ignored the subtle signs that she did not see things the way he did. But there had also been moments that reinforced his hopes. Moments in which he had won her over. Perhaps, if he didn't give up, he might manage to conquer her heart. There was no doubt she hadn't forgotten him, that she felt something for him, at least. Perhaps if he did the right thing, refused to give up, and courted her, he might still get her back. Yes, this time he wouldn't give up. He would do everything he could, going above and beyond.

The adrenaline was pumping in his veins again. His mood shifted abruptly. In a pragmatic tone, he asked, "What exactly is the connection between genetic engineering and astronomy? Why is Jack interested in astronomy, anyway? Why would a sect that opposes genetic engineering for fear that it might change the human race also persecute an astronomer? Could it be a mistake?"

"I don't think so," she began, in a matter-of-fact voice.

Great, he thought. *We're back to business as usual. Maybe from here we can make gradual progress on the personal front, as well. Just don't rock the boat, and let time do its thing.*

She continued, "The man is sophisticated, focused, and motivated. He doesn't waste resources on anything unnecessary. As far as he's concerned, there must be an essential connection between these things."

"Interesting," he mumbled quietly, delving into his own thoughts.

***

She must have fallen asleep briefly, and was awakened by her assistant. "That's a work call I have to take. I'm stepping out for a bit," she said casually, and walked out to the cool, quiet street.

It took several rings of the doorbell to extract him from the cobwebs of his mind, from which he was attempting to weave a web linking an ancient, mysterious sect with plenty of resources that was attempting to prevent the genetic alteration of plants, animals, and especially humans, to an odd astronomic discovery that probably interested merely a handful of scientists.

Still wrapped up in his thoughts, he walked slowly toward the door. It was only when he saw Melissa in the doorway that he came to his senses, staring at her in confusion.

"Where have you been? I didn't even notice that you'd left the apartment."

"Yes, I still remember how deeply you can submerge into your thoughts and disengage from your environment. I've often envied you for that ability. I got a business call and preferred to take it outside. Anyway, I have to get going. I'll talk to you later. Another odd mystery might be developing, and it might complicate things even more. I'll call if I have anything new. If you come up with any ideas, don't hesitate to call."

She picked up her purse, gave him a light kiss on the cheek, and left.

The slamming of the door woke him up completely. *Where exactly did she take off for so hastily?* he wondered. *And what was the business call she couldn't take in my presence? Also, what's the complicated mystery she mentioned? What the hell is going on here?*

There were too many fragments of information that didn't fit together. Too many missing puzzle pieces. But in fact, this was his specialty, the one that provided him the greatest pleasure as well as a respectable living. He loved those moments in which there was no big picture at all, not even a direction, and knew how to toil and use his creative mind to supplement the missing information and form a cohesive whole. But this time, the missing pieces seemed too numerous to create any kind of structure. More pieces must still be found.

He was exhausted. The early discharge from the hospital, the long, tiring day, the mystery veering off in unclear directions, the lack of a resolution, and finally, the possibility that he had lost Melissa made him want to retreat into a deep sleep. But then hunger started gnawing at his stomach. *Great, I'm getting back to normal,* he thought happily.

***

Once she drew closer, Melissa peered up at the windows of her apartment on the eighth floor, as was her habit. The light shining there made her smile. True, they had agreed to meet in her apartment, but she hadn't imagined Tom would arrive so quickly. In their brief conversation, he had told her in an emotional voice that Eddie the linguist had given him a possible explanation for the strange structures, and that he had to see her soon, asking that she drop everything and come home as quickly as possible. He hadn't even been willing to hint at what Eddie had said. He had definitely sounded upset and frightened. She had never encountered this side of him before. He was always reasoned, in full control, pragmatic. It was odd how stressful he'd found Eddie's explanation regarding the structures.

Her expectant smile was instantly replaced by an expression of horror. Jack or Aaron, or whatever his name was, was waiting for her in her apartment.

Aaron didn't know to what extent the detective had involved her in his investigation. Her reaction when she found him in her apartment would reveal how much information he had shared with her, and to what extent she feared him. True, his very presence in the apartment might cause her apprehension, but he trusted his ability to distinguish between such apprehension and true fear.

He had already thought out the calming words he would direct at her once she came in. He had left the apartment lights on in order to let her know someone was waiting for her. And indeed, finding the lights turned on had not surprised her. Apparently, she had seen them even before she went up to the apartment. The smile on her face as she opened the door indicated that she was expecting to see someone else, someone dear to her, someone she knew would be waiting for her and whom she was anticipating seeing.

Her face darkened the moment she saw him, and for a moment, she lingered in the doorway.

She might run off, he thought. He had to act immediately.

"Melissa," he began. "You have no reason to be afraid of me. I'm not a bad person. I need your help. I've decided to turn myself in to the police, but I prefer to do it through you, so you can turn me over to the detective you've been in touch with." The words tumbled rapidly from his lips. He had to finish speaking before she ran away. Now everything depended on how persuasive she had found his statement, and even more importantly, on how frightened she was of him.

He had wanted to turn himself in from the first moment, but the Guardians' bylaws prevented him from doing so. Only now, after the Leading Gentleman's speech, once his connections with the Guardians had been severed so that they could no longer be found through him, did he feel free to obey his conscience.

The seconds went by. She didn't budge from her position in the doorway. He knew he should not move either; he mustn't frighten her. With an inviting gesture, he indicated the armchair across from him, using both hands. Every passing second calmed her down, increasing the chances that she would be appeased and listen to what he had to say. He didn't know her well. He knew she was hardworking and strong, but it was hard for him to anticipate her reaction.

He had reached the decision to turn himself in at the sect's meeting, just a few hours earlier. There was almost no hesitation on his part. He knew he would pay dearly, that he would serve years in prison. He could still run away, change his identity, and live a life of leisure until his last day.

But his conscience tormented him. He could not live with the stain of murder. He felt that he must bear the punishment, even if he had acted on behalf of a goal in which he believed with every fiber of his being. It was true, there were more direct ways of turning himself in, but for some reason, he felt that he preferred to have her mediate the proceedings. He also felt that he owed her a debt.

When she finally entered, he noticed that she did not lock the door. She was still uncertain, still wary of him, and had left herself the option of a quick escape. She asked him to keep his chair as far from the door as possible, then pushed the armchair he had indicated until it was adjacent to the entrance. She leaned back in the chair, her hand on the door handle, ready and poised to run for her life, nodding to indicate that she was listening. His speech was well-organized in his mind. He knew exactly what he was about to say.

"I'll start at the end. I shot the security guard in Dr. Lester's biology lab, and I'm willing and eager to bear the punishment. I could have run away and changed my identity, but my conscience wouldn't let me. I want you to call the detective and ask him to come here. You can tell him about my intentions, so he can be properly equipped when he comes."

"Dr. Lester is supposed to be here at any minute. I have to stop him."

"Let him come. I think he deserves to be present when I turn myself in. After all, the security guard was killed while protecting his lab. And no, don't worry; I have no intention of harming him. I have no intention of harming anyone else."

"Okay," she replied. "Until the detective arrives, you have to stay right where you are. Don't move."

Before he set out to see her, he had deleted his computer's memory, and then physically destroyed it. As he did before every meeting, he made sure to disconnect all the cameras in the streets around his apartment. They would be unable to link the other sect members to him. He knew that this was it; he would be unable to return to his previous life. Not that he had found that life particularly pleasant, but at least he had been a free man.

Rick answered her call immediately. Aaron assessed that he would be there within several minutes. Indeed, he showed up in the doorway with his gun drawn, demanding that Aaron stand up and turn around so that he was standing with his back to him. As he brought the barrel of the gun against the nape of Aaron's neck, he restrained him so that both Aaron's hands were cuffed behind his back in a strange pair of handcuffs. Then he walked several steps back, produced a small remote control from his pocket, and ordered Aaron to turn around and sit down, despite the uncomfortable pose in which he found himself.

"These are electronic handcuffs. Any unexpected movement from you will immediately result in burning pain in your hands," he explained.

Rick summoned Dr. Lester, who had been waiting by the door, and closed the door after him. "More police officers will be here in a few minutes to take you away."

"I want to say a few things before they do," Aaron said quietly.

"Go ahead," Rick said, and the three of them sat down across from Aaron.

"I'm a descendant of Eli, the Jewish high priest in the land of Israel, who was killed by Nebuchadnezzar's soldiers when they conquered and destroyed the temple built by King Solomon, hundreds of years before the birth of Christ, according to the

Christian calendar. Eli was killed while protecting the Ark of the Covenant, which is holy to the people of Israel. My family was commanded to preserve the secrets of creation in general and man, in particular.

"For over two thousand years, we were hardly required to intervene. However, during the last hundred years or so, as scientific discovery developed, we've dealt primarily with monitoring research trends in the pertinent topics, areas that might affect the essence of the human race, and thus meddle with creation itself. We tried to impede scientific developments that had the potential for influence of this kind. Lately, in light of the rate of progress of numerous studies, we've decided to terminate our activity. From this day on, we will not monitor scientists, and we will no longer interfere."

"Who are you people exactly? How many active members do you have? Who's responsible for your funding?" Rick barked out a barrage of questions.

"And what's the connection between the Jews' Ark of the Covenant and guarding the secrets of creation? What do you know about the secrets of creation? What's the source of your information about creation?" Tom asked slowly.

Everyone's eyes were on Aaron. For a moment, he appeared to be considering how to organize his answer, but then surprised them by saying, "That's it. I'm done. I've told you everything I know. Unlike you, I've never asked questions or interrogated anyone. I was just doing my duty, as it's been passed down from generation to generation in our family."

CHAPTER 34

Will's Mental Leap

Chicago, Friday, July 25, 2036

Will was sleep-muddled and confused, and could not understand what had woken him. Slowly, his focus returned, and he realized it was Melissa's voice emanating from the assistant that had roused him. He glanced at the clock at his bedside. It was after midnight. He wondered what had happened that was urgent enough to necessitate waking him. He recalled eating a sandwich and immediately dropping into bed after she'd left. He thought he'd been asleep for only a few minutes, when in fact, several hours had passed. He answered the assistant.

"I'm with Dr. Lester. We have to see you at once," she said. "We're on our way to you," she concluded, without waiting for his assent.

Will had a hard time dragging himself to the bathroom to

freshen up.

Dr. Lester was a handsome, well-preserved man, older than him by at least five years. He was indeed facing stiff competition.

"I'm sorry about the late hour. I know how tiring all of today has been for you, but after you see what Dr. Lester wants to present to you, you can go back to bed. I'm just not sure you'll be able to fall asleep," Melissa said with a mysterious smile.

The biologist laid out two large prints displaying rows of precise, appealing geometrical structures, photographed from two different angles. Will stared at the images, turning them around and looking at them again before laying them down on the table once more.

"I don't get it. What is in these images that's so urgent?"

Melissa and the biologist exchanged glances.

"Can you guess what any of these lines express?" she asked.

Will focused on the prints again. They were organized and symmetrical to some extent, and did seem to possess some logic. The structures repeated themselves in various arrangements. However, once again, he had to put them down and shake his head. The two watched him for a long while until the biologist spoke up.

"Each line represents a Boolean equation, the kind computer programmers use."

"That's really nice. And you woke me up for that?" he asked, snapping at them.

Another long silence stretched out, until finally, the biologist said, "These images were produced in a biological process, originating in human DNA, where they have been concealed for millions of years." He then gathered the prints and tucked them back into his bag.

"Don't talk about this to anyone but me. Call me whenever you have something to say," Melissa said. "Oh, I forgot. Jack or Aaron, the guy who injured you, turned himself in. You don't have to worry about him anymore." The two of them rose from their seats and departed.

Will was left open-mouthed, his glazed look directed at the closed door. He should have been too fatigued and exhausted to think clearly, but surprisingly, felt highly alert.

These images were produced in a biological process, originating in human DNA. These images were produced in a biological process, originating in human DNA. The sentence echoed in his head again and again; he couldn't break free of it. What did it mean? Mathematical equations in human DNA? What was the connection between the two, anyway?

Human DNA, like that of every life form on Earth, had evolved gradually, over billions of years, starting with the first primitive bacteria and perhaps even preceding it. What was the link between DNA and computer systems, which hadn't existed even a hundred years ago? And when had biological systems ever constructed such symmetrical structures? It was all so strange. His momentary alertness faded away, briefly replaced by an opaque veil of fatigue. All he wanted was to jump into bed. But no, first there was an urgent call he had to make.

The exhaustion that had suddenly assaulted him got the better of him. With his last remaining energy, he crawled into bed. His sleep was restless, consisting of a swirl of DNA sequences spinning and tangling with one another, occasionally producing the figures of prehistoric man, Neanderthals, primates, and contemporary people of various races. Occasionally, he floated in space, pulling stones and rocks toward him before throwing them at glittering stars, which occasionally exploded in colorful, breathtaking fireworks. He woke up and fell asleep again several times until he found himself completely awake.

Some elusive thought appeared and vanished. He didn't have time to perceive it fully. It contained a faint lead, an interesting direction that might provide an explanation. He tried to chase it, but couldn't focus on it. A short sentence he had heard, a handful of words uttered distractedly, perhaps jokingly—stars, people, but no whole sentence. And then, like a thunderclap, illumination hit him. He straightened in his bed, coiled and alert.

The late hour didn't bother him in the slightest. His assistant call was answered almost immediately. His interlocutor was also awake and alert. An instant agreement and the call was terminated. He waited quite a while for a response to his second call. The person on the other end of the line had been asleep, but agreed instantly once they finally spoke. Everything would be carried out on time.

CHAPTER 35

The Meeting at NASA

Chicago, Friday, July 25, 2036

Despite the early morning hour, everyone was present. Dr. Almog commandeered one of the less central conference rooms at NASA, hoping to avoid attention. Will recognized nearly everyone: Rick and Melissa; Dr. Lester, accompanied by a young woman who was probably the PhD student working with him; Dr. Apexton and his wife Ramona; and, of course, Dr. Almog, who locked the door once the last of the attendees arrived.

Tom examined the participants, some of whom he did not know. He hadn't wanted to take part in the meeting and could not understand what sorts of insights the journalist might provide; however, Melissa had insisted. She didn't know exactly what Will was about to tell them, but she had faith in him. She said he excelled at surmising the big picture out of an amazingly small array of seemingly unrelated details. She also said an astronomer and someone working for NASA would be present as well. Tom couldn't understand what sort of connection might exist between such distant branches of science. He had deliberated somewhat in regard to Lise, but had decided to bring her along to compensate for the stress she had been under since the structures had been discovered.

The attendees did not converse among themselves. All of them waited tensely, a sentiment clearly written on their faces.

"First, I want to ask everyone present to introduce themselves, on behalf of those here who don't know everyone," Will began, and thus learned that Dr. Lester's companion was indeed the PhD student working at the lab where the security guard had been murdered. "As for me, I'm an investigative reporter for the *Chicago Chronicle*, a job that's taught me to put together seemingly unrelated items of information and create a meaningful whole, and I've been doing that fairly successfully for quite a few years. I'll start by presenting three discoveries, two of which were made by people sitting in this room today.

"The first discovery: Dr. Gerald Apexton from NASA discovered that an asteroid moving into the solar system, which had the potential to strike the Earth, causing significant destruction, was diverted from its path while it was crossing the asteroid belt between Mars and Jupiter."

His statements appeared as an orderly block of text on the left part of the large presentation board at the end of the room. "Dr. Apexton has no idea what caused the asteroid to divert from its path. Dr. Apexton, is there anything you want to add?"

"No, I think at this stage of the meeting, your description is quite accurate."

"The second discovery was made by Professor Lia Rosen from the University of California, Berkeley, and Professor Benjamin Sheffy from Tel Aviv University in Israel. They discovered four stars that, according to the reigning theory, proved in dozens of cases, should have exploded into supernovas, and due to their proximity to the Earth, might have caused the destruction of all life on the planet. However, for a reason that remains unclear to us, they did not explode. Dr. Apexton, anything you want to add?"

"Not at this stage."

The description appeared in an orderly array on the board, under its predecessor.

"As for the third discovery, I must ask Dr. Lester to describe it in his own words."

Tom felt uncomfortable. Up to this point, he had only shared the discovery of the structures with a handful of people. He feared its implications and, to a large extent, was afraid for his life and the life of his family. It was true that Aaron, who had killed Oleg the security guard, had turned himself in and promised there would be no further investigations and interference. On the other hand, there was still Gaya (or Erie or whatever her name was) to contend with, and of course, the omnipotent Professor Goldon. What exactly was their connection to all this? Were they even connected to Aaron? Melissa had said that Aaron told her he worked alone with his family.

He had believed he was only coming to listen to Will, as she'd said; he hadn't thought he would be required to discuss his discovery within such an extended forum of people he didn't know. He considered asking Will to describe the discovery in his own words, or perhaps asking Lise, who seemed frightened, to do so.

He felt everyone's eyes staring at him, eager for whatever he had to say. *Actually, why not?* Will would know how to present the essence of the discovery in a way befitting the level of knowledge of those present.

"I'd be happy if you described it in your own words," Tom said.

"As you wish," Will replied, sounding pleased. That had been his preference, as well. "Dr. Lester and PhD candidate Lise Oliver, from the University of Chicago, carried out a biological process on human DNA, and to their astonishment, ended up with a series of symmetrical geometric structures matching basic computing equations. Was that accurate enough?" he asked. "Is there anything you want to add or clarify?"

Tom shook his head. He couldn't have summed it up better. Will was indeed a sharp and talented man.

Another paragraph of text appeared on the board after the previous one. All eyes were focused on the board, which now contained a description of the three discoveries as they'd been presented by Will, listed one after the other.

Will's gaze roamed between the board and the attendees. No one spoke up, each of them retreating into their own thoughts. "The riddle is right here in front of you," Will said. "Does anyone have any ideas?"

The minutes went by. People shifted uncomfortably in their seats, but no one said a word.

"Last night," Will began, "I talked to Professor Benjamin Sheffy, who's currently attending a conference in Berkeley, about his and Professor Rosen's discovery. The professor expanded on the anomaly observed in four stars, which has no current scientific explanation. It was a fascinating, challenging conversation. He explained to me that the masses of the stars they'd discovered were significantly larger than the maximum limit indicated by the known laws of physics. This phenomenon depicts white dwarfs that accumulate mass from an adjacent star, and then explode once they reach a fixed mass, calculated decades ago by a physicist named Chandrasekhar. Since the explosion takes place at a fixed mass, its intensity is fixed as well, as is its luminosity.

"This fact provided cosmologists with the 'standard candle' they'd been seeking for many years, creating an accurate means of measurement to gauge large distances in the universe. The distance calculated based on the explosion has been verified through other means on several occasions, and found to match.

"The discovery made by professors Rosen and Sheffy is the only exception found in this field, hence its oddity. Professor Sheffy didn't forget to emphasize that the irregular stars discovered were in our galaxy, and at such a proximity to us that one of them exploding would have resulted in the annihilation of all life on Earth. When I asked what might have caused this, he replied, perhaps jokingly, that it might be God, protecting us here on Earth from extinction. Just to remind you, Dr. Apexton said something similar at the end of his presentation."

His gaze slowly surveyed the faces of the attendees. He was expecting illumination, a significant response from any of them. It was true that only he and Melissa had first assembled all the items of information; they were the only ones who held the important details of all three discoveries. However, a bird's eye view of any two of the discoveries was enough to enable a leap to an unequivocal conclusion, especially since the discovery made by Dr. Lester and his PhD student was enough in and of itself to reach the conclusion he was aiming for. Perhaps they understood this, but were afraid to speak out, allowing him to be the messenger at the gate.

However, no one took the leap. All of them seemed wrapped

up in their own thoughts. It was obvious to Will that Dr. Almog still didn't understand the urgency and sense of exigency that Will had exhibited when convening the emergency meeting. Many theories in physics had changed over the last few decades, and apparently, he found groundbreaking revelations a routine matter. Other than Dr. Lester's strange discovery, he didn't seem to consider the findings presented to him as sufficient justification for an urgent meeting promising dramatic insights. Was there an expression of disappointment on his face? Will wasn't sure.

The minutes continued to tick by. No one said a thing. Some of them still seemed immersed in their thoughts, while others appeared to have given up and were exchanging smiles, as if implying, *Did they summon us to a meeting so early in the morning for this?*

"Okay," Will said. "At moments like this, when I have a collection of disparate details that aren't coming together, I try to observe them from a high altitude, an altitude at which minute details lose their sharpness and identity, and increasingly, what's revealed is a single image, blurry yet unified. On the right side of the board, opposite the description of each discovery, you'll see a statement defining the prominent common denominator between all the discoveries.

"The first..." With these words, the sentence "A higher power preventing the destruction of humanity" appeared to the right of the description of Dr. Apexton's discovery.

"The second..." Will continued, as the statement "An unexplained process preventing the destruction of humanity" appeared opposite the description of professors Rosen and Sheffy's discoveries.

People squirmed uncomfortably in their chairs. Here and there, a momentary expression of disdain appeared as well. Only then did he notice Lise's gaze, frightened to the point of sheer terror. Apparently, she had guessed what was coming next. He felt that he had to hurry before some of them sealed themselves off, losing interest in the next stage.

"And now for the summarizing statement," he blurted out quickly.

At the bottom right corner of the board, opposite the description of Dr. Lester's discovery, the final statement appeared: "An unexplained imprint upon the human race."

For a long moment, everyone's eyes remained fixed on the board.

An asteroid moving into the solar system, which had the potential to strike the Earth, causing significant destruction, was diverted from its path so that it would not strike us.	A higher power preventing the destruction of humanity
Stars that, according to the reigning theory, proved in dozens of cases, should have exploded into supernovas, and due to their proximity to the Earth, might have caused the destruction of all life on the planet, did not explode.	An unexplained process preventing the destruction of humanity
A biological process in human DNA resulted in a series of symmetrical geometric structures matching basic computing equations.	An unexplained imprint upon the human race

CHAPTER 36

Will

Chicago, Thursday, September 11, 2036

Will was frustrated. More than a month had gone by since the meeting at NASA, which had undoubtedly been the peak of his career thus far, a meeting that had given expression to his extraordinary ability to create a clear picture out of a collection of seemingly unrelated details. Since it had taken place, he still hadn't found a new subject to investigate.

It had been a long month. His injuries had healed almost completely, and in fact he had nearly forgotten about the accident that had almost caused his death. He had talked to Melissa many times, and she had even consented to meet him once. She was undecided about resuming their relationship.

Her current relationship with Tom was convenient, leaving her time for her various occupations without tying her down to a formal commitment. She had gotten accustomed to the freedom allowing her to do as she liked, and enjoyed it. It was true, in her youth, while living with her parents, she had dreamed of a family and children, a distant dream that was no longer even tinted in rose-colored nostalgia.

He was willing to have a loose framework, Will told her, with no rigid commitments, a sort of "couplehood lite," going with the flow of life and changing definitions and arrangements as suited them both. He went on to say that he was sure they were compatible, that they had matured, and could keep going from the point where they had broken it off.

She promised to think about it, telling him that Tom was leaving the university in favor of a major private company. He'd gotten an offer he couldn't refuse. She could not tell him any more than that.

Every day, he roamed the paper's offices, talking to his colleagues, often bothering them and distracting them from their work. He tried to check out various possible directions, but every subject into which he once would have delved with enthusiasm now seemed worthless to him. Several ideas proposed by his editor also did not ignite his interest.

He felt as if he was waiting for something big, perhaps a continuation of that same meeting. But what sort of continuation could it have? Everyone who had attended agreed to maintain strict secrecy in regard to its contents. He often reached this impasse in his thoughts when he tried to discover what, exactly, he was waiting for. In a password-protected folder, he kept his detailed research regarding the occurrences that had led to the NASA meeting. He wouldn't break his commitment to maintain confidentiality. He would not be the first to do so.

He had enjoyed dropping that bomb and the ensuing chaos in the conference room, but mostly the lively discussion that had followed, and the way three distinct camps had formed. Ramona, devout in her faith and lacking any doubts, had joyfully embraced all the revelations. They provided further proof of her belief system, and this time, it was even scientific proof, the kind no scientist could refute. She passionately defended the existence of God, and could not understand how it could be denied. The fact that she'd been married for decades now to an astronomer who, based on the expression on his face, did not share her opinion had no effect whatsoever on her.

At the other extreme were the two astronomers. They believed there was no place for a god in the universe. The universe didn't need such an entity; it got along just fine without one. No, they had no proof of this assumption. True, the discoveries were troubling and could not be explained at present, but they were certain that over time, an explanation would be found, just as it had for many phenomena attributed to the divine until science managed to explain them.

Melissa and Rick joined them, both using a similar line of reasoning: there was too much evil and randomness to assume the existence of God.

That left Dr. Lester, who hesitated and deliberated, and Lise, the frightened PhD candidate, who was too shaken up to even debate the question.

Only once the attendees' eyes turned back to him was he required to state his position. Oddly, although he had been the one to pose the question, he had never paused to think about his own stance on the matter.

Will recalled his conversation with Professor Sheffy and the professor's unrestrained laughter when Will asked him whether he thought that God was the reason the stars were not exploding. Obviously, the Jewish professor did not believe that a deity of any kind was performing miracles and protecting the denizens of Earth. No, he had no idea what Professor Rosen's beliefs were, and he hadn't bothered to find out. People's various ideas regarding faith did not trouble him.

Briefly, Will wondered whether he should have told Professor Sheffy about the planned meeting at NASA, about the other two discoveries and about the way his own findings fit in with the others. No, it was better not to tell him; he did not want anyone else to break the news. He couldn't compel Professor Sheffy to maintain confidentiality, and definitely couldn't ask this of Professor Rosen, when they had published their discovery with no hesitation. However, nothing would have made him happier than doing what they had done and making the entire story public.

The eyes staring at him were relentless. Everyone wanted to know his stance on the matter at hand. He still clearly remembered his own words. "I grew up in a free-thinking home," he said. "The topic of God never came up. I've never dedicated much thought to His existence or lack thereof. This is the first time I've confronted this subject, and since I'm not a theologian or a scientist, I have no choice but to join Dr. Lester and Lise, who are on the fence."

CHAPTER 37

San Francisco, Orlando

Friday, November 28, 2036

Excited and holding a bouquet of white orchids, Will stood at the gate of an American Airlines flight arriving at the renovated terminal at San Francisco International Airport early on Friday morning. For a week now, he had been totally immersed in an investigative story. He and Melissa had decided to extend the weekend in order to spend some time together. Her flight had landed and, in a few minutes, he would be able to embrace her. Life had never been better.

After a long, stubborn courtship, Melissa had succumbed to his pursuit. Her condition was a fully committed relationship, rather than an open one. "You can't swim in the ocean without getting wet," she had said, and they dove headlong into a wonderful romantic relationship.

He was looking ahead expectantly to the four joyful days awaiting them when he noticed her among the people streaming through the gate. Melissa hadn't been to San Francisco for many years, and was happy to spend some time in the charming city.

Both their assistants beeped nearly simultaneously.

"Dr. Almog from NASA asks when's the earliest time I can attend a very urgent meeting with him," she said.

"I'll check what my message was," he responded, asking the assistant to read it out loud. "Hey, he asked me the same thing. Reply on behalf of both of us that you just arrived in San Francisco for a long weekend with me."

"The message from Dr. Almog says, 'Don't leave the airport. First-class tickets for the first available flights to Orlando, Florida, will be waiting for you,'" she told him. "What should we do? I wonder what happened. What's so urgent?"

"Check in with Detective Rick and maybe with Dr. Lester too, to see if they've also been summoned. Maybe they know what's happening."

Their replies arrived within minutes. Yes, they had been called to the meeting as well, and had no idea what was going on.

The two senior military officers waiting for them at the exit gate at Orlando International Airport asked them courteously yet firmly to join them, and didn't bother to answer Melissa when she asked where they were heading. In fact, they didn't say a word during the ride, not even among themselves.

Melissa and Will had often been to NASA facilities as visitors, surrounded by numerous guests striding from attraction to attraction. This time, everything looked different. They did not see a living soul until they arrived at a nondescript office building and were led to a small conference room. Apparently, the attendees had been waiting only for them, since as soon as they sat in their assigned seats, a man in uniform showing no visible rank stood up. Will had time to recognize everyone who had been present at the last meeting in NASA's offices in Chicago. He knew everyone around him other than the man about to open the meeting.

"My name is Robert Fulton, and I'm the administrator heading NASA. I thank you all for showing up immediately under such short notice. I'm sure you all had plans for the weekend that had to be canceled, but I'm certain you'll understand the necessity once you hear what I have to say," he said, dimming the lights in the room.

"About two years ago, the Chinese first sent a spacecraft to the asteroid belt, just as we and the Europeans had done years earlier. Of course, it was reported with a note of emphatic cheering and pride, typical of the Chinese. This didn't evoke much interest in the scientific community, which was busy tracking the final stage in the installation of the STA. However, a short time after the vessel reached the asteroid belt, the Chinese sent two more robotic spacecraft to the asteroid that the first vessel had reached. This time, the spacecraft utilized plasma engines, which significantly shorten flight times.

"This immediately aroused our suspicion, especially in light of the fact that the Chinese hadn't announced the launches the way they usually did. In addition, intelligence sources reported unusual scientific activity among the higher echelons in the hierarchy of the Chinese regime. Senior academics were often seen entering and exiting government buildings. As if that weren't enough, several days ago, the Chinese launched their heaviest spacecraft, originally intended to host piloted flights to Mars, also equipped with a plasma engine, but didn't publicize that launch, either. This vessel left the Earth's orbit on the way to its unknown destination, probably the same asteroid. We have every reason to believe it's piloted, although it has never been tested in such an extended flight bearing human passengers. Something is definitely brewing there. The Chinese are under pressure and rushing full speed ahead.

"A persistent rumor also hints at a groundbreaking scientific discovery that the Chinese intend to reveal as proof of their technological and scientific superiority. To remind you, they're currently the only nation capable of launching spacecraft utilizing efficient plasma engines.

"And here's where politics comes into it. Emily White was elected as president largely due to the fact that she was the first African–American woman candidate. However now, as she's facing re-election, her popularity rates are quite dismal.

"A major Chinese accomplishment would cause China to supplant the United States' status as the scientific frontrunner in space research, for the first time since the space race commenced. Naturally, such an international defeat is inconceivable, and would further erode President White's status internally, as well. Therefore, as part of her attempts to seek any possible means of promoting her image with the public, Emily was presented with a summary of your findings, as well as their implied conclusion. She was very taken with the whole idea, and has therefore decided to address a speech to all residents of Earth in which she will present the topic in the clearest, most unequivocal way.

"We have all the material on the two astronomic discoveries. We need the material on the biological discovery from Dr. Lester as soon as possible."

"Luckily, we have everything," Tom replied. "It was blind luck that brought us to this discovery, and Lise, my graduate student, had to invest a lot of effort in fully recreating it. She'll send you everything immediately after the meeting. I understand that everything should be laid out so that any scientist can recreate the process in their lab?"

"That's exactly right," Robert replied. "We thought it would be appropriate to let you know about the president's speech, scheduled for tomorrow morning, and the publication of the results. Naturally, Mr. Thorne and his newspaper will receive exclusive rights to interview the president after her speech."

"Wow." Will exhaled softly.

CHAPTER 38

The President's Speech

Washington, DC, Saturday, November 29, 2036

A conservative estimate reported that over a billion people had watched or at least listened to the speech made by the president of the United States, which was broadcast live and simultaneously translated into every language on a variety of global media. The teasers for the speech had promised a dramatic announcement for humanity, and the utter secrecy maintained by everyone involved only ignited media speculation. Various experts delved eagerly into the dramatic promise, and in the absence of sources or leaks, developed a plethora of wild theories—from scientific conspiracies proving that the universe was actually virtual, and everything that appeared to take place in it wasn't real but was rather a software illusion on a global-wide scale, to a documented encounter with aliens who had landed in the White House and were about to relay their message to the human race.

The speech commenced on Saturday, at precisely ten a.m. Eastern Time, and was broadcast on all television networks and radio stations. The day and time had been carefully chosen to coincide with waking hours for most of the residents of North and South America, Europe, Africa, and Asia.

"My fellow residents of Earth, this is the first time an American president has addressed a unifying message to all people on the planet, wherever they may be. This planet has always been our home. All of us have grown and emerged into an endless, ongoing struggle between nations and groups clinging to different religions and faiths.

"Throughout the history of human culture, we have experienced battles, wars, lives lost, indescribable devastation, and immense resources dedicated to wars and destruction instead of to human well-being. All this was largely caused by differences of opinion between the acolytes of different religions. Brainwashed believers have tortured members of other religions to death in the name of God, crushing the skulls of women and children and destroying everything in their path while singing hymns of glory to this or that deity.

"Blind faith has propelled mothers to send their sons on suicide missions, in which thousands of innocents were murdered, so long as along the way, they elevated the name of the current god, a god of war and destruction, bloodthirsty and hungry for death, constantly insatiable. And in return, this god would reward the believers who sacrifice themselves on his behalf with an eternal life of luxury in some abstract site, also known as "paradise in the world to come," the world to which they would ascend and in which they would enjoy every sort of pleasure.

"The need to believe in a higher power is apparently rooted in human DNA. Every group of people, throughout the thousands of years of our development, and even in the most isolated, desolate places, has developed faith in some sort of supreme power. This began with a belief in inanimate objects and holy animals, progressing to demons and ghosts, and culminating in abstract gods who ruled the entire world, and their emissaries on Earth, the prophets and angels, as well as their contemporary representatives—rabbis in Judaism, imams in Islam, and priests in Christianity.

"The existence of a higher power has provided answers for every inexplicable phenomenon. God moves the sun that rises in the east and sinks in the west every day. God's will directs the rainfall. The hunter succeeds at his task, and the field yields crops based on His instructions. Therefore, He must be appeased with offerings, and the greater the value of the offering and the sacrifice it entails, the more God will be appeased, distributing his bounty to his children. The ultimate offering: human sacrifices, even babies.

"In contrast, advances in science have provided more grounded explanations for many natural phenomena. Scientists who act relentlessly to discover the mysteries of the universe and the laws of physics according to which it operates have often incurred the wrath of the believers. During the Middle Ages, scientists and research pioneers were burned at the stake. Even today, in certain places, many people of faith scoff at science. They prefer to believe that God is the one setting natural phenomena in motion, thus further glorifying His power, instead of accepting more down-to-earth explanations.

"The believers have an especially hard time accepting the diminutive nature of our world compared to the size of the universe as portrayed by scientists, as well as, on the other end of the spectrum, the theory of evolution, which indicates that human superiority over beasts comes down to merely a few genes, and that humans and chimpanzees share over 98 percent of their DNA.

"Up to this point, every scientific discovery has diminished God's realm of control. Well, dear listeners, recently there's been an upset, one that will enhance the believers' faith and change the worldview of many of the skeptics. And, amazingly, this upset was the work of scientists. I won't bore you with the scientific details; those who are interested will be able to see them online shortly. Scientists have recently discovered two occurrences in space, one in our own solar system and the other significantly further away, but still within our Milky Way galaxy.

"In the occurrence closer to us, a senior astronomer discovered a giant asteroid, of the kind that occasionally passes by in space around us, and which, according to all the calculations, was supposed to hit Earth with such a powerful impact that humanity would have regressed back to the Stone Age, and might have been entirely destroyed. The astronomer discovered that the asteroid was diverted from its path by an unknown element, to join thousands of objects orbiting around the sun between Mars and Jupiter. As stated, no scientific explanation has been found for this occurrence.

"Meanwhile, two astronomers from the United States and Israel have discovered four stars hundreds of light-years from Earth that should have exploded a long time ago, with an intensity that would have destroyed all life on Earth. Many similar stars at a great distance have been observed by scientists exploding precisely according to the existing theory's predictions, thus confirming it and the expected timing of the explosions that are indicated. Scientists have no explanation for the fact that the nearby stars with the potential to destroy humanity did not explode, although they've long since surpassed the explosion threshold. Something, or someone, is preventing them from doing so. Something, or someone, is watching over us, the people of Earth.

"A few more words in conclusion. At the beginning of my speech, I mentioned three discoveries. Well, the third is arriving from somewhere completely different, from the place nearest to us, practically inside us. In a lab researching human DNA, scientists discovered a DNA segment that, after a specific process is activated, displays symmetrical three-dimensional structures that depict mathematical equations from the world of computers. To state it simply, many years ago, something or someone hid a message to humanity in our human DNA, a message that has been waiting for us all this time, until the scientific development that led to its discovery. It's important to note that this DNA segment is present in all the human races, in members of all religions.

"People, residents of Earth. God is proving to us in an unequivocal way how much He takes care of us and watches over us humans, of all religions equally, in order to put an end to the deliberation. He has even allowed us to glimpse His signature, which He left in each and every one of us. Leaders and scientists of all religions are invited to receive instructions to examine the DNA and present the proof to their people.

"In conclusion:

"WE ALL HAVE ONE GOD. WE MUST NOT FIGHT ONE ANOTHER!

"GOD, PROTECT ALL HUMAN BEINGS."

***

After recuperating from his shock, the producer for CBS turned the broadcast over to his reporter at the giant Manhattan Plaza Health Club building in New York City, where a large audience had convened that morning to watch the speech. The attendees' applause and expressions of joy and excitement spread to viewers and listeners throughout the United States, further fanning their enthusiasm. Following CBS's lead, television networks throughout the world began to broadcast from the sites where excited people were beginning to converge in clubs and public squares, hugging and applauding.

This was not what they had expected. Their surprise was absolute. The common assessment had been that the president was about to announce an extraordinary scientific discovery, one that would have implications for all of humanity. The heads of the major media networks had already summoned expert scientists from various fields who were at the ready, prepared to explain the president's speech. However, none of the scientists agreed to go on the air. They were being cautious, or perhaps more accurately, were stunned by the declarations that had just been made.

Italian television reporter Alfredo Botteliani was the first to reach Vatican City in Rome, with reporters from other networks streaming in his wake. They were greeted by Archbishop Francisco Salvietti the Third.

"Yes, His Holiness watched the speech, and his immediate reaction was 'Well, what's new here? It has been clear to us for thousands of years that God watches over his children and protects them.' No one at the Vatican was surprised," the archbishop continued. "No practicing Christian needed any particular sort of proof. Despite this fact, the scientific proof caused much satisfaction to the Pope and those close to him. This is a major, blessed step for science, which had gradually been drifting away from religion, but has now changed course. From now on, religion and science are one, and as the prophet Jeremiah said in regard to the end times, 'And thy sons shall return to their borders.' Science, which had alienated itself, is returning to the arms of religion."

"Is this the god of the Christians, the Jews, the Muslims, or some new and unfamiliar deity?" a foreign reporter blurted out in broken Italian.

The archbishop leveled a long, penetrating look at the reporter, and then turned away, mumbling, "And once again, it all begins anew."

Less than twenty minutes after the speech ended, teasers began to air for a special report by MMB News, which would be broadcast at eight p.m. Eastern Time, and would include a broad-ranging panel discussion regarding the significance of the president's speech, with the participation of representatives from various religions as well as scientists.

A quick survey indicated that more than a billion viewers were eagerly anticipating the studio discussion. The world was abuzz. Anyone who was awake anywhere on Earth was discussing the president's speech. The fact that it had taken place on Saturday gave the world's residents free time to engage in such a discussion. In homes, on the streets, in stores, and in entertainment venues, everyone was arguing with everyone else. In nearly every group, even the smallest among them, there were people with different views: believers in the existence of God, those who were less devout in their faith, and complete atheists.

The social networks didn't need any experts; they were storming and raging. The faithful of the various religions were happy to be interviewed, their eyes glowing ecstatically. All of them were reciting the same mantra. No, they didn't need any sort of scientific proof; faith had guided them in the past, and continued to guide them today. As far as they were concerned, nothing had changed. The scientific proof was intended for the nonbelievers; they were the ones who needed it, and now, they were the ones who had to change and join the believers in order to worship the almighty Lord, a God who had bent the laws of physics that He had created in order to protect the lives of his creations. What higher and more solid proof could they ask for?

Apparently, the current consensus between the representatives of the various religions had caused them to forget their previous conflicts and the bloody wars they had waged against one another, wars that grew even more intense between various denominations of the same religion, such as the Sunnis and the Shiites in Islam, or the Catholics and Protestants in Christianity.

Surprisingly, among the more extreme of the believers, certain leaders emerged to reject the material "proof," which they found to be simplistic. Their God was purely spiritual. He did not leave behind tangible signs of His presence, certainly not ones discovered by humans, using scientific means. He had no need to leave His "signature" in humans, who were commanded to believe in Him blindly, with no need for any sort of corporeal proof.

Oddly, this blind faith transcended religious barriers. Devoted believers of various religions found themselves on the same side for the first time, united in refusing to accept the new "proof" of God's existence with which the entire world was obsessed. In an even greater instance of absurdity, they found themselves agreeing with atheists over the utter rejection of the "tangible scientific proof."

Ratings for MMB's evening broadcast neared 100 percent in homes, in the few restaurants that opened their doors to a handful of diners, and in workplaces. Anyone who could find the time to do so watched or at least listened to the newscast, offered on all stationary and mobile media. Even in the half of the planet still in darkness, many tuned in.

The discussion was hosted by Bob Hill, who had plenty of experience in moderating loaded debates. He had determined that two of the major religions would have two representatives each, one for each of its major denominations, with one representative sufficing for Judaism. Therefore, the panel featured a Sunni representative and a Shiite one for the Muslims, and a Catholic and a Protestant for the Christians. Judaism was represented by a single Orthodox delegate.

Due to time constraints, the representatives had arrived from various communities all over the United States, and were not familiar to the general public outside those communities. The panel sitting opposite the moderator included several people, two of whom were wearing what appeared to be official ceremonial garb, while the others wore suits or less formal attire. The chosen venue was a small auditorium, seating fewer than a hundred spectators.

The discussion opened with a rebroadcast of the president's speech. Bob was prepared for the general onslaught from all directions once the speech ended. With his familiar assertiveness and his booming voice, he immediately hushed everyone present.

"I'm here with representatives of humanity's three major religions. Each of them has its own traditions, customs, and belief system. Each of them worships its deity uniquely, and from an outside secular perspective, each of the religions appears to have its own god, one that belongs exclusively to it.

"This brings me to my first question to each of you: Who is the god whose existence was proved today by scientific findings presented to the majority of the residents of Earth by our president? And which religion or denomination represents him?

"As a delegate of the largest community of believers, let's start with the Christian Catholic representative, Cardinal Pietro Modoliense, who, luckily for us, happened to be visiting the States and agreed to come to our studio, despite the short notice."

The cardinal was revealed to be a cheerful man wearing jeans, a pink, button-down shirt, a red tie, and a short, casual jacket.

"Good evening, everyone," he began, speaking in English with a prominent Italian accent. "I'm sorry for my casual appearance. I'm visiting the United States for personal reasons, and was not planning on any sort of official occasion. I'd like to start by addressing the main points made by the president. As far as we practicing Christians are concerned, there was nothing new in what she said. Our faith is based on the existence of the Lord, and we have no need of any sort of proof; the words of scripture are quite enough for us. However, we're overjoyed that at long last the world of science, which has generally veered away from belief in God, has been confronted with His existence through the means in which scientists believe—scientific proof that exhibits His actions on behalf of humanity.

"And now, to answer your question, all Christians believe in one sole God and his emissary on Earth, and all denominations of Christianity agree on this point. The differences between the various Christian denominations are merely superficial, and are secondary to the faith that unites them."

"I understand—" Bob's voice rang out, subsumed by a chorus of shouts from the audience.

"That's wrong!"

"We disagree!"

"Hold on a minute," Bob roared. "I want one of you to tell me what's wrong. What do you disagree with?"

"Only God can determine everything. Man doesn't get to determine anything," a loud voice rose above the general ruckus.

"You must be a Protestant," the moderator retorted. "I suggest all of you continue your long-standing argument outside. Otherwise, we'll have to throw you out."

The threat had its desired effect, and the voices died down.

"I understand," Bob resumed, "but is the god that the president was talking about your God? And if that's the case, who are the gods of the Jews and the Muslims?"

"The gods of the three monotheistic religions—Christianity, Islam, and Judaism—are the same God. The source for some of the differences between the three religions is their origins, while other differences developed over the years. At the root of Christianity is the belief that Jesus Christ is God's representative on Earth."

"If that's the case, why did the Christians condemn the Jews and burn them at the stake, although they both believe in the same god?" the moderator challenged.

The cardinal shifted uncomfortably in his chair. "We're not proud of that aspect of history, or of Jewish persecution by Christians. The rift between the religions is a result of an unfortunate lack of understanding that was a part of a zealous past which took place two thousand years ago, and which has had terrible implications over the years. Today, these disputes are behind us, and we congratulate and embrace our Jewish brothers, with whom we share one God."

Apparently, none of the participants anticipated the applause with which this statement was received. Some members of the audience rose from their seats and clapped enthusiastically, while quite a few others continued to sit in protest. The cardinal, whose jovial face still bore an expression of surprise, bowed deeply and sat down.

"I don't believe my ears. If I'm not mistaken, such a clear public statement regarding Christian-Jewish relations has never been made. I have to confirm this. Is that what Your Eminence said?"

"That's right, I confirm my statement," the cardinal replied. "We are sorry and apologize for persecuting our Jewish brethren throughout history and embrace them. And yes, this is the Pope's opinion as well."

"Does the Protestant Bishop Henry de Sully share this opinion?" Bob asked.

The Protestant bishop straightened slowly in his seat. He was wearing ceremonial vestments, and with a British accent, replied, "Despite the significant differences between the Catholics and ourselves, and in spite of our violent history, when it comes to faith in the Lord, I agree with every word that the Catholic cardinal has said, and I have nothing to add."

In contrast to his usual vocal and confrontational nature, Bob did not say a word, but merely gazed slowly from one priest to the other and back, maintaining his silence until the Protestant bishop sat down once more.

"Such a blissful idyll, such brotherhood of man," the moderator said, slowly continuing in his booming voice. "What about the millions killed in the wars between Catholics and Protestants, the Thirty Years' War, Catholic persecution of Protestants, the enlightened Inquisition and the persecution of the Jews, the ongoing terror attacks in Northern Ireland? Indeed, one God for all, with millions murdered in His name. I have nothing to add now that you've heard this spirit of peace and brotherhood overtaking the Christians, blatantly ignoring the ugly reality.

"The next person from whom I'd like to hear regarding the identity of the god whose existence was proven today via scientific means presented to most of the residents of Earth, and the religion that represents him, is the Sunni Imam Ibn al Khattab."

The imam's black cape and large turban formed a contrasting framework to his cultivated white beard. He rose from his seat slowly, nodded at the interpreter sitting at his side, and began to speak in Arabic. Within seconds, the translator's eloquent voice rang out. "All Muslims everywhere, regardless of the sect or denomination to which they belong, believe in Allah and in his prophet Muhammad, the representative of the God of Abraham."

"For thousands of years now, you've been fighting and killing members of other religions," Bob interrupted, apparently unable to quell his raging emotions in response to the imam's mock-innocent reply. "And if that weren't enough, you've also killed millions of Muslims from other denominations. I wonder what your explanation is for this killing, which continues to this very day, as the news tells us." He paused briefly, and then continued. "I'm sorry to have interrupted you. Please go on."

The moderator's outburst had clearly disrupted the imam's train of thought. He could not continue with his relaxed, calm statements in light of what he had just heard.

"I cannot ignore what you've said," he resumed. "Evil, envy, narrow-mindedness, greed, and a desire for power have always tainted any human society, regardless of religion. There will always be those who exploit the ignorance of others for their own dark purposes. However, there is plenty of common ground among the various branches of Islam.

"Different interpretations of the Quran, the sacred text of Muslim believers, as well as battling egos and political forces, have led to the divergence of the different denominations. Over the years, the gaps between them have widened, leading to terrible bloodshed. Essentially, Islam is not an extreme religion, but an inclusive one, as indicated by hundreds of years in which a tremendous area, from the eastern end of Asia throughout all of North Africa and up to modern-day France, was under Islamic rule, an area that included many non-Muslim nations and tribes who lived peacefully with the Muslim regime."

"According to the Quran, the sacred text of Islam, aren't all you believers obligated to kill all infidels who don't believe in Allah, as we often hear from Arab leaders?" Bob asked.

"The world was a different place when Muhammad received the Quran from the mouth of God. Human culture was essentially different. Initially, Islam had to fight in order to forge a path in a world ruled by myriad Arab tribes, Jewish tribes, and Christianity, which was establishing itself. The value of human life was significantly lower than it is in our time. The heads of tribes and rulers of cities, controlling their subjects solely by brute force, executed many people based on momentary whims. The killing of infidels was appropriate during that time, but is certainly no longer appropriate today. Unfortunately, many ignorant Muslims interpret the words of the Quran literally, without taking into account the period and the conditions under which it was written, and we can all witness the results."

"In summary, is your Allah also the god of the Christians and the Jews?"

The imam cleared his throat and replied, "God chose the Jews to worship him, but they diverted from His path, and therefore, He punished them, and they have been persecuted and exterminated throughout history. Christianity, founded by the prophet Jesus, also did not follow the path of God, until finally the prophet Muhammad, who received the Quran from the Angel Gabriel, appeared, and we Muslims follow the path of God and do not divert from it."

Bob's distant expression conveyed his contempt for what he was hearing. "I want to thank Imam Ibn al Khattab. I only hope our viewers understood him better than I did. And now for Islam's Shiite representative, Dr. Imam or Imam Dr. Ali Abbas."

Abbas was a clear contrast to the expected image of a devout Shiite religious personage. He was wearing an elegant business suit that complimented his athletic form. The only characteristic indicating his faith was a well-groomed beard adorning his cheeks and chin.

"The Sunni imam described the situation well," Abbas began in fluent English. "We cannot change the past. As my predecessor stated, the seeds of dissension between the various branches of Islam sprouted during the religion's early days. It stemmed largely from a strong faith in the righteousness of each branch's way, naturally leading to a condemnation of the other, which then resulted in unnecessary bloodshed that has accompanied us ever since.

"Over the years, two main denominations developed and grew further and further apart until the circumstances we find ourselves in today, where every Islamic country is either Shiite or Sunni. Muslim communities outside the Arab countries zealously maintain this segregation as well. Each community has its own mosques and schools. As a general rule, most Muslims are devout in regard to their religion, and maintain its rules, preserve its original traditions, and do not mingle with members of the other branches.

"Naturally, rejecting and condemning the other are even more intense in regard to members of other religions, primarily

Jews and Christians.

"I, too, don't like many people, and even despise some of them. We don't share similar traditions, and I don't want much to do with them in general. But I've never acted violently toward them, and would certainly never think of killing them."

"Which happens pretty routinely in Islam," Bob burst out.

"I don't dispute your statement, and I don't intend to and cannot justify the violent acts typical of Islam," the imam replied. "Unfortunately, the ancient traditions still reign in quite a few Muslim communities. Occasionally, a radical, charismatic leader rises up and manages to recruit many people to participate in cruel killing sprees. Look, I've been living in the United States for many years, working full-time as a doctor in a hospital in which I faithfully treat hundreds of patients a year. I've spent most of my adult life here. In my everyday life, I'm no different than any of the audience members, other than my beard. Beyond that, in my free time, I act as a Muslim, make sure that my food is *halal*, pray in a mosque and lead my Shiite community in a peaceful manner."

"It's interesting," Bob murmured. "I've never been religiously inclined, and I don't remember ever having much interest in the subject, but for someone on the sidelines watching these conflicts and wars, and destruction that has taken place and continues to take place, all in the name of religion, it's hard to buy the theory that Christians and Muslims worship the same god and carry out their atrocities in his name. It's inconceivable that millions of believers have been murdered in the name of the same god, as we heard here today; it's simply impossible.

"And finally, we have Rabbi Nachman Shposelovich as a representative of Judaism, the most ancient of the three religions. I wonder if we'll ever get a clear answer to the question of what could cause people who believe in God to brutally murder other people who believe in the same deity. Considering their faith, aren't they afraid of God's vengeance? Or does the call of 'Allahu Akbar,' heard whenever Muslims kill members of their own people or others, actually denote a duty to murder others prescribed to them by God Himself?"

The elderly rabbi stood up slowly. He was clearly surprised and pleased by the respectful tone of the moderator's introduction.

"I assume there's no need to repeat our main question again. Go ahead, sir," the moderator addressed him.

"In the beginning, God created the heavens and the Earth," the rabbi began. His loud, powerful baritone was a startling contrast to his age and appearance. It seemed to emanate from some other entity, rather than the man himself. For a moment, even the rabbi seemed surprised by his own voice. All whispering in the studio ceased abruptly as everyone turned their attention to him.

"In the beginning, God created the heavens and the Earth," his voice boomed out again into the ensuing silence. "You've heard four representatives from the two largest religions, which together command millions of believers. All four have testified that they worship the god who gave his scriptures to my people, the people of Israel, after first freeing them from their enslavement to the Egyptian Pharaoh, giving them the Ten Commandments, leading them through the desert for forty years, defeating the nations of Canaan on their behalf, and settling them in the promised land. That was the only period in which Jews destroyed other nations in order to inherit their country as commanded by God, sometime thousands of years ago.

"We're not proud of it, even if it was done under the Lord's command and with His tangible, prominent help. To this day, 3,300 years after the events took place, we still regret them. But all that notwithstanding, throughout thousands of years of Jewish history, we've never embarked on a war of destruction against others. On the contrary, for thousands of years, we've lived among members of other religions throughout the world who have conquered our country, exiled us, enslaved us, and tried to exterminate us in sophisticated 'factories' and with nuclear bombs.

"Everywhere we've lived, my people have excelled, and our percentage among Nobel Prize winners exceeds the global average by a factor of one hundred. However, Jews have never collectively murdered people belonging to other religions or other nations.

"As for the first part of your question—who is the god whose deeds, even if just a tiny fragment of them, have recently been revealed by scientists—you've received your answer from the representatives of the two largest religions. Both of them confirm that it is the God of our forefathers, Abraham, Isaac, and Jacob, the God of Israel.

"As for the second part of your question, religions do not represent any god. God does not need any representation. The various religions provide a framework and support to believers, and so long as the believer behaves respectfully to his environment, including all its components, as long as he does no harm, the name of the religion and the manner of worship are completely meaningless. It can be Christianity, Islam, or Hottentot.

"That's also the reason Judaism doesn't try to convert believers from other religions, but treats all of them with respect. And as the president said, we are all—all of us—humans... Children of one God. Every single one of us contains a divine spark that should be expressed in our every deed. Only when we all internalize this and act accordingly will we experience the glory of God," the elderly rabbi concluded, sitting down once more.

For a long time, the studio was silent, as if everyone had ceased breathing. Then, at the corner of the hall, someone stood up and clapped a single time. Next was someone else at the other end of the studio who started clapping as well. They were joined by another, and another, until the entire studio audience was applauding wildly, all of them rising to their feet and clapping. Bob himself stood up and joined the applause, which gradually grew rhythmic, as if demanding an encore. For several minutes, he did not even attempt to calm down the enthusiastic audience.

Finally, he walked over to the rabbi, shook his hand warmly, then pulled him up until he was standing and facing the audience. The rabbi seemed uncomfortable with the prevailing atmosphere. He had never experienced such avid applause. Bob encouraged the imams and the priests to join them on both sides, and the six of them faced the audience, bowing their heads in gratitude.

"Such euphoria," the moderator continued after things had calmed down and everyone returned to their seats. "Such brotherly love between Muslims and Christians, Catholics and Protestants, Sunnis and Shiites, and especially between the various Islamic and Christian denominations and the Jews.

"It seems as if the end times have truly arrived. The millions sacrificed to the false idol of religion did not, apparently, die in vain. From now on, all of us, regardless of religion, are brothers," he declared in a slow, quiet voice. "Perhaps the scientific discoveries, the president's speech and the current panel really do signal a turning point for humanity. Future historians might define these days as the beginning of a new era in human history. An era characterized by a realization that the differences between the various religions and denominations justify a theological debate or a satirical TV show at most, but certainly not the slaughter of millions."

Mumbling quietly, he added, "Sounds great if you actually believe it..."

CHAPTER 39

God, Protect All Human Beings

Monday, December 15, 2036

The *Chicago Chronicle*'s editorial meeting was volatile as always. Will had recently been promoted to a senior position, as head of the Investigative Department. There was no doubt in anyone's mind that this rapid promotion was a direct result of the exclusive interview the president had granted him, in which she had complimented Will for his brilliant insight in finding the divine common denominator, so obvious in retrospect, between three such different discoveries.

Emily White, the first African–American woman president in the history of the United States, was re-elected by an immense majority to her second term as president. Almost all the editorials attributed this fact to her speech to humanity, and primarily to her closing statement, "God, protect all human beings." Religious America had become even more religious, and had thus crowned the president as God's representative on Earth.

Will was very pleased with the promotion and its accompanying benefits, but felt uncomfortable with the fact that the media treated him as a twenty-first century prophet who had uncovered God's tracks. He had never thought of himself as a believer. His inbox was flooded with requests for interviews and lectures all over the world, including offers for highly generous financial compensation. It was enough to keep him busy for many years as well as make him very rich.

The arguments in the paper's conference room resembled those in the global media at large. The believers had received scientific reinforcement for their faith. Finally, no one could assail them with the argument that there was no proof of God's existence. It had actually been the scientists, most of whom doubted the existence of a higher power, who had conclusively proved it.

And if it weren't enough that God existed and was watching over His flock, He had even bent the laws of physics to do so. This was more than mere proof. It was a knockout victory for religion over science—scientific proof, along with the collapse of formerly proven scientific theories. The sages of the various religions had not anticipated such a victory. Naturally, each religion declared that it was the only one to correctly worship God, in the way in which He intended, and each was entirely unwilling to accept any other path.

The senior councils in the major religious centers in Mecca, Teheran, Germany, and Vatican City conducted endless debates over the meaning of the recent discoveries and the proper way to address them. No details leaked from these discussions, and despite numerous attempts on the part of reporters, they could not discern even an iota of information regarding their contents. In contrast, chaos reigned in Jerusalem, and many conflicting details leaked from the representatives of the various denominations.

The majority of the scientific establishment distanced itself from debates on the subject, which were frequently featured in the media. Here and there, fame-seeking minor orthodox scientists consented to be interviewed and expressed their sweeping support for the discovery of divine powers. In contrast, Professor Eugene Leitner of Princeton University, considered a leading astrophysicist, claimed in a very brief article that although physicists still couldn't explain why the four stars discovered by professors Rosen and Sheffy had not exploded, he was certain that an explanation would indeed be found. He noted that many astrophysicists viewed the discovery of such a scientific explanation as a truly worthy challenge. He also did not hesitate to add that the divine explanation might be enhanced by the fact that other than the four stars cited, no additional stars with similar characteristics had been found.

Various surreal explanations were also suggested for the diverted course of the asteroid that had been forecasted to strike Earth. One of them suggested that the asteroid had entered into a state of resonance with the gravitational pull of other asteroids in the asteroid belt, which had collectively caused the change in its trajectory. However, no scientist tried to explain the three-dimensional structures discovered by Dr. Lester, although several labs published accurate and relatively simple instructions on how to recreate the experiment in order to produce the structures.

Professor Abe Alperovich, also a Jewish rabbi by education, had an easier task. In a sophisticated article, he portrayed the discovery of the structures as conclusive proof of the existence of the Jewish deity, as Judaism had been the first monotheistic religion. The article depicted the granting of reason and intelligence to an ancient primate and, steering it into a separate evolutionary track, as the creation of man by God as portrayed in the Bible, while the recently discovered structures were depicted as a divine signature of sorts, a claim of ownership.

The everyday life of the residents of Earth returned to normal, the religious revival they had experienced subsided fairly quickly, and only the various religious sages continued to intently discuss the scientific discoveries and their meaning.

Then, when it seemed as if the religious maelstrom had passed and routine had truly been re-established, the Council of Sunni Sages published its response.

“The unequivocal scientific proof of the existence of Allah reinforces the faith of Islamic believers that they are Allah’s final and successful choice among people. And as proof, after the first failed attempt with the Jews, He tried again with the Christians, and once this attempt failed, He continued with the Muslims. Had this attempt failed as well, Allah would not have hesitated to continue trying other nations. This indicates conclusively that Islam is God’s final, successful choice.”

These words were included in the comprehensive summary of a book written by the Sunni sages.

The next day brought the publication of the Shiite response. It was not a detailed book indicating thorough preparation, or a polished, precise manifesto. It was merely a press release. The Shiites did not need scientific proof, and in fact chose to ignore it. Apparently, they did not acknowledge the proof and did not discuss it. The only god who ruled their world was Allah, who had created man and had done everything necessary to protect and take care of only his Shiite believers.

It was a simple, straightforward response which, of course, ignored the entire controversy. Moreover, it claimed that Allah did not actually take anyone else into consideration, and that the blood of these people could be spilled with no consequences. The only deity in existence was Allah, the Shiite God. End of story.

As if it had been waiting for the first reaction to be made, the Vatican responded immediately. The press release was phrased with the full cooperation of Protestant religious authorities.

"There are no differences of opinion between us and the Protestants on this central topic," it declared. "With all due respect to scientists, as far as believers like us are concerned, nothing has happened. Our absolute faith requires no scientific proof. We feel God inside us at every moment, and carry Him with us wherever we go. Our God loves all people, both those who have faith in Him and those who deny Him.

"God created the entire world and determined its rules, which are investigated by scientists, who occasionally discover new ones. At His will, these rules persist, and at His will, he may change them. God created the world and everything upon it. He created both the believers and the heretics. God loves all people and does not discriminate between them.

"The Muslims' Allah commands them to murder those who deny Him. It is impossible that a God who created the entire world and controls every aspect of it would order some of his creations, the products of his will, to murder others, also created by Him. Therefore, there is no doubt that the God who created the world chose us to walk the righteous path, rather than the Muslims."

The euphoria and sense of unity among the different religions that had pervaded much of the public in the days and weeks after the president's speech, as well as the conciliatory panel in which the religious representatives had taken part, had been entirely blown to bits. Apparently, the quiet prevailing in the interval was covering up a process in which the opposing forces grew increasingly strained, gathering ammunition, biting their nails, and waiting eagerly for the eruption.

The Vatican's response broke down the dam that had been holding back the forces of evil. From that moment on, all the volcanoes erupted, and the sort of scenes that had been part and parcel of humanity since religions were first created resumed at full force. Every religion and every denomination appropriated the correct way to worship God solely for itself. In a newly initiated race, the sages of Christianity and Islam turned night into day in their search for verses in their scriptures proving this fact. Not a day went by without one of them providing "conclusive proof."

The public media debates also made their way into the churches, the mosques, and the streets. Riots broke out in most European cities with a significant Muslim population. Tensions between the various religions and sects, which had seemingly eased for many years, reawakened with new vigor. Police and military action, required to quell the riots in several cities in France, resulted in many injuries, including some casualties among the protesters.

A strident speech by the Muslim prime minister further fueled the flames, intensifying the riots, which often involved firearms. The results were many casualties, neighborhoods under siege, and streets that became unsafe to walk through. For lack of any other options, an emergency military regime was declared in Paris and Marseilles, the two French cities with a Muslim majority.

Sweden, in which there was also a Muslim majority, followed France in declaring a state of emergency. In Brussels, an extreme speech by the Muslim mayor inciting against Christians and Jews triggered violent riots throughout the city, forcing the Belgian government to also declare a state of emergency and send military reinforcements to its capital.

The riots in Europe paled in significance compared to the situation in the Arab countries. In Teheran, the goaded masses burst into the American and Russian embassies, killing everyone present and setting the buildings on fire. The images of horror distributed throughout the world also ignited the streets of Kabul, the capital of Afghanistan, and Islamabad, the Pakistani capital, in which buildings associated with the West were set on fire along with their residents.

Militant European movements that had flourished throughout the continent as Islam spread, acquiring a variety of armaments, took to the streets. They confronted Islamic movements, equipped with weapons of their own, while military and police forces tried to separate the warring factions and calm the streets once more, with only partial success.

The giant mosques in Paris and London were torched, followed by mosques in additional cities. The civil war pitting Muslims against Christians spread like wildfire throughout Europe, leaving many injured and dead, as well as many mosques, churches, synagogues, public institutions, and residences burned to the ground. The news channels reported massive deployment of American and Russian military forces to the Middle East.

CHAPTER 40

The Emergency Meeting

The United Nations, Wednesday, December 31, 2036

The emergency meeting convened by the secretary-general of the United Nations on the last day of 2036 devolved into a scene of fist-fighting, hair-pulling, and tearing of clothes among the representatives of the Muslim countries, as well as between them and the Western delegates.

The news channels began to report that the major Muslim countries, including Iran, Saudi Arabia, and Pakistan, had their armies at the ready and had prepared their nuclear weapons for launching, declaring they would not hesitate to use them if they felt threatened. The rising tension required the United States, China, and Russia to raise their levels of military alert as well, preparing their armies for action. All vacations were canceled, and the level of alert was raised to DEFCON 1, the final alert level preceding global war.

CHAPTER 41

Activation

Wednesday, December 31, 2036

Professor Andrew Goldon was perturbed, apparently significantly more so than most residents of Earth. The Guardians sect, which he headed, had been founded with the emergence of the monotheistic religions, more than three thousand years ago. Its one and only goal was to postpone, for as long as possible, the moment in which the human race would have to deal with the circumstances of its unusual past, which elevated it above the other animals on Earth.

The sect's method of operation ever since those first days had been to portray the countless celestial events that people perceived as supernatural as the work of God or His emissaries. This seemed like a logical path to take and yielded good results. The supernatural phenomena that the sect attributed to the deity glorified and exalted the name and powers of Almighty God. Belief in a single deity began to spread widely.

In a world awash with ghosts and spirits, in which might was right, a monotheistic religion with a socialist orientation and a set of rules protecting the weak won over many converts. During countless events in which people watched with wonder as the heavenly chariots traveled over their heads, there was always someone there to whisper the obvious explanation, which then spread by word of mouth, an explanation that matched the beliefs of the crowd and left no unanswered questions.

The first issues emerged later. Animals in nature are content with the elements most essential to their lives: food, protection from predators, and the ability to reproduce. Humans have many additional needs and urges, with the most prominent among them being the ego, the need to control others and obtain more than they had. And so, new monotheistic religions cropped up, gradually developing and later, due to that same ego, splitting into sects and denominations, each of which felt a need to assert its superiority over the others.

The belief in a single deity was supposed to unite the myriad tribes, providing them with a vital common denominator that might have resulted in peace and coexistence among the various human groups. The differences between the various religions, branches, and sects were for the most part minor ones; however, the human ego exacerbated and heightened them. Charismatic, power-hungry leaders goaded and enflamed their ignorant believers until they were willing to fight to kill those who denied their religion, or even willing to be killed while fighting them.

Human life continued in this manner for thousands of years, with one unnecessary war replacing the previous one. And so, millions of people of every religion and sect soaked the soil with their blood. Only during the twentieth century did the religious wars abate, and then only briefly. Alliances and partnerships between the different sects in the divided ranks of Islam often shifted, with today's allies turning into tomorrow's enemies and vice versa. Differences of opinion contributed to accelerated radicalism. Brutal murder of infidels and indiscriminate acts of terror turned life in many areas of the world into an unrelenting nightmare in which the value of life gradually diminished, until the major war in the Middle East. Local and foreign armies that had been fortifying themselves with armaments for years threw themselves headfirst into unrestrained battle. The most destructive weapons were deployed, cities were erased from the map, and millions of lives were sacrificed. The luckier among them simply evaporated in a split second in nuclear explosions.

The war was brutal and horrifying, but brief. After nine days of fighting, a ceasefire was declared with the consent of all countries participating in the warfare. The world experienced about ten quiet years in which terrorism nearly disappeared. An immense fortune was invested in the still-ongoing rehabilitation. The economy bounced back, and human lives were nearly back on track until, unbelievably, the president's speech. The amazing discoveries that had led to the speech were supposed to bring people together and unite them, but had an opposite, terrible effect. The tensions that had seemingly subsided reawakened once more, triggered yet again by the familiar combination of ego and religion. Once again, everyone was ready for an all-inclusive war.

The sect had never interfered in humanity's wars and deeds, even when horrific atrocities were committed, many of them in the name of some god or other. The potential for fatal harm to humanity as a whole was negligible. But this was not currently the case.

Reports were streaming to Goldon in real time, directly from the most confidential debates in the primary governmental centers. Surveillance abilities developed over many years with massive investment of funds proved justified in these moments. Only the ongoing coordination between the major superpowers and their influence over the more radical countries had thus far prevented all hell from breaking loose. Reports from government centers in the extreme Muslim states conveyed harsh conflicts between the pragmatists and the radical elements, who were looking forward to the great religious war, the War of Armageddon or Gog and Magog described in many holy texts, in which the believers would battle the infidels and the powers of the demonic. The radical religious sages had been yearning for this war for many years, anticipating seeing the raised sword of their god smiting down the infidels and their emissaries.

The information streaming Goldon's way left no room for doubt. The sages, who had accumulated power and status in the radical countries, had decided to proceed with no holds barred, once and for all. They were scheming to create provocations that would force the major superpowers to deploy military intervention in order to create global-wide warfare.

None of the previous leaders of the Guardians, over a hundred in number, had ever faced such dire circumstances. Never had such crucial decisions in regard to humanity been required. All previous events had been handled on a local level, and then forgotten. The weight of responsibility was unbearably heavy.

The activation instructions were whispered from leader to leader and had never been used. In every generation, they were familiar solely to the Leading Gentleman and one of his assistants. They had never been written down. The whisper of one Leading

Gentleman to his replacement seared the instructions into the new leader's consciousness, and so it had gone for thousands of years. He didn't need to make an effort to remember these instructions; they were frequent visitors in his dreams, and floated readily into his mind at a moment's notice. They were accompanied by unequivocal instructions permitting activation only when an event with extreme implications for the human race as a whole was imminent, an event that would retrieve the apple from humanity and return it to the Tree of Knowledge, or worse.

Somewhere, deep within the rock on which Jerusalem was built, in a nook illuminated with a soft, pale blue gleam, surrounded with human bones, a spark ignited.

RED BUTTONS

Wednesday, December 31, 2036

The missile appearing on screens in various control centers throughout the world left no room for doubt. The Iranians, either unintentionally or meaning to take advantage of the worldwide chaos, had launched a missile at Saudi Arabia, their longtime enemy. The Saudis' sophisticated defense system reacted quickly with a barrage of anti-ballistic missiles.

The Iranian missile turned out to have been launched intentionally rather than in error, as immediately after the first one was shot down, the Iranians launched a barrage of four additional missiles at Saudi Arabia. And then, the worst eventuality: two ballistic nuclear missiles were launched from the territory of the radical Islamic entity ISIS, one aimed at an unknown destination in Europe, the other heading for Israel.

In military control centers all over the world, shaky fingers fumbled toward red buttons with no safety function.

GOD, PROTECT ALL HUMAN BEINGS.

List of Participants, Institutions, and Locations

A

Aaron Gorong: member of the Guardians sect

Abe Alperovich: a rabbi and professor, author of an article on the scientific discoveries

Aerobion: a BL product

Ahiav, son of Elisha: team head within the Guardians sect

Alfredo Botteliani: an Italian TV reporter

Ali Abbas: the Shiite imam

Amy: an assistant in Tom Lester's lab

Andrew Goldon: CEO of the BL Corporation

Avi Tsur: an expert on star development from the Weizmann Institute of Science

Aviram: a soldier in the Guardians sect

B

Ben Apexton: Gerry's son

Benjamin Sheffy: an expert on exploding stars from Tel Aviv University

BL Corporation: the largest manufacturer of human genome-based products

Bob Hill: moderator of the first TV panel
Brad: Detective Rick Heller's deputy

C

CardioBoost: a BL product
Chinatsu: a member of the Guardians sect

D

Dan Auster: a NASA employee who assisted Will
Ditka's: a restaurant

E

Eddie: Oleg's brother
Elaine Apexton: Gerry Apexton's daughter
Eli: the High Priest
Emily White: the first female African-American president of the United States
Ethan Almog: the scientific supervisor in charge of the Space Telescope Array at NASA
Eugene Leitner: a leading astrophysicist

F

Francisco Salvietti the Third: an archbishop at the Vatican

G

Gaya/Erie: Andrew Goldon's representative for the meeting with Tom

Gerald (Gerry) Apexton: an astronomer studying asteroids at NASA
Glenhill: a company developing lifespan-enhancement treatment
Guardians sect: established during the Israelites' exodus from Egypt

H

Hannibal: the asteroid discovered by Gerry Apexton
Henry de Sully: the bishop representing the Protestants at the first panel

I

Ibn al Khattab: the Sunni imam at the first panel

J

James: a member of the Guardians sect
Jennifer Lester: Tom Lester's younger daughter
Jim: a longtime maintenance engineer at NASA
Johns Hopkins: the hospital to which Gerry Apexton is admitted

K

Karen: Andrew Goldon's secretary
Kazuki: a member of the Guardians sect
Kate Lester: Tom Lester's wife
Koro: a member of the Guardians sect

Kyra: Mike Easter's new girlfriend

L

Larry: a longtime maintenance engineer at NASA
Larry: a member of Johns Hopkins' security team
Larry: Rick Heller's cousin
Leanna: a police officer
Lia Rosen: an astronomer
Lily: Detective Rick Heller's secretary
Lise Oliver: a PhD student at Tom Lester's lab
Loyola University: place of employment of Eddie, the murdered Oleg's brother
LungBoost: a BL product
Lynn: an assistant at Tom Lester's lab
Lynn Lester: Tom Lester's older daughter

M

Martin Patterson: head of the *Chicago Chronicle*'s investigative department
Meirav: Aaron Gorong's younger sister
Melissa Colette: a biologist and expert in genetic engineering
Mike Easter: a PhD student at Tom Lester's lab
Mike Robertson: commander of the police precinct
MMB: the TV network that aired the first panel discussing the president's speech
Momo: Tom Lester's nickname for his personal assistant device

N

Nachman Shposelovich: a rabbi who is the Jewish representative at the first panel

O

Oak Woods: the cemetery where Oleg was buried
Oleg: the murdered security guard

P

Paul Longstrom: dean of the University of Chicago
Pietro Modoliense: a cardinal and the Catholic representative at the first panel
PlaqueDissolve: a BL product

R

Ramona Apexton: Gerry's wife
Reo: a member of the Guardians sect
Rick Heller: a homicide detective
Robert: a new maintenance engineer at NASA
Robert Collins: the *Chicago Tribune*'s science reporter
Robert Fulton: Administrator of NASA
Robert Shepard: head of NASA's Extraterrestrial Life Study Division
Rokoro: a member of the Guardians sect
Ron Colin: director of the University of Chicago
Ronnie: the ancient humanoid

S

STA264987B: a planet in the Cygnus constellation whose atmosphere contains oxygen

STA331047B, STA333654B: white dwarf stars discovered by Lia Rosen that do not explode as expected

Steve: head of the University of Chicago's security team

T

Takumi: a member of the Guardians sect

Thomas (Tom) Lester: a biologist

U

Uri: a member of the Guardians sect

W

Will Thorne: an investigative reporter for the *Chicago Chronicle*

Y

Yoni: a detective sent to protect Melissa

96022267R00250

Made in the USA
Columbia, SC
19 May 2018